The First Time
I Said Goodbye

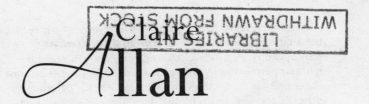

Claire
Allan

POOLBEG

Published 2013
by Poolbeg Press Ltd
123 Grange Hill, Baldoyle
Dublin 13, Ireland
E-mail: poolbeg@poolbeg.com
www.poolbeg.com

1

A catalogue record for this book is available from the British Library.

ISBN 978-1-84223-559-1

Typeset by Poolbeg Press Ltd in Sabon 11.5/16
Printed by CPI, Mackays, UK

www.poolbeg.com

About the author

Claire Allan is from Derry, where she has worked as reporter and columnist with the *Derry Journal* since 1999.

She shares a home with a long-suffering husband, two children who are growing up much too fast, and two cats – one of whom is officially (according to a vet) neurotic.

When not writing or working, Claire enjoys reading, baking, spending time with friends, trying to keep up at circuit classes and avoiding soft play areas.

The First Time I Said Goodbye is Claire's seventh novel. You can follow Claire on Facebook or on Twitter @claireallan.

For Avril and Bob, who inspired this story

And for daddy's girls everywhere

Chapter 1

It wasn't that I didn't want to go. I did. I wanted to go with all my heart but I suppose in many ways I was a coward in the end. It was too much. There isn't a day that has passed where I haven't missed you.

* * *

Meadow Falls, Florida, USA, May 2010

It seemed only right that it was raining. It would have been wrong if it had been anything but. You can't bury someone on a sunny day. I couldn't have buried him on a day when the sun was splitting the stones and the sprinklers were dancing around the lawns and when the Southern Belles were out in force, fanning themselves and thinking about getting back to the wake for an iced tea on the porch. Black on a sunny day wouldn't have been at all comfortable. Not that the shift dress I wore was comfortable anyway. It was starchy, stiff, far removed from the comfortable clothes I usually slouched around in. "It suits you," my mother said when I walked into the church. She was already sitting in the front pew, her hands crossed, her gaze fixed firmly ahead, her eyes hidden behind her sunglasses. She glanced at me only briefly as she told me I looked nice, and I sat beside her and reached for her hand. Now was not the time to brush off her compliment – to tell her I was afraid the dress might choke me or split at the seams. She had enough worries without me adding to them. I stared ahead too, trying to fix my gaze on whatever she was looking at, and squeezed her hand. She didn't squeeze back, but she didn't shrug me off either.

We sat there, together, awaiting the big arrival. Waiting for my father to make his final journey into the church – neither of us being able to face walking in behind him, having people gawp at us in our grief, nudge each other at our tears, give us that pitying 'poor them' look. No, we had walked in separately, ahead of the congregation, and fixed our eyes forward, barely touching, and I tried not to breathe out. I heard the door of the church open, the footsteps of our fellow mourners, and I felt my mother breathe in – and as she exhaled there was a small shudder which revealed to me just how she was feeling. I squeezed her hand a little again as the music started to play – wanting to make it better for her – and wanting to make it better for myself, and I thanked God it was raining, because it would have been wrong to bury him on a sunny day.

It would have felt all out of sorts, as if the world was spinning off its axis, to have had the sun smiling on us when inside there was a small part of me screaming as if I was still six years old and the only person who could make it better was my daddy – the daddy who was never coming back.

* * *

Craig's arm slipped around my waist. I instinctively breathed in, away from him, and I tensed as I felt his hand take mine. He cuddled up closer to me, asking softly if I was awake. Yes. I was awake. I didn't answer. I didn't want to talk. I don't think I had actually slept. Maybe I had. I vaguely recalled Liam Neeson walking into our room at three in the morning, so probably it was fair to say I had drifted off. The rest of the time, however, I had just lain there, looking at the red light on the clock, watching the numbers slowly changing. My father had been gone four days. I wondered when I would stop thinking of it in terms of days, in terms of weeks, in terms of time passing, and just think of him as gone. Maybe I never would. Maybe now I just had another day to mark – another day to count from. It was one day since his funeral. One day since I had stood at his graveside and willed my heart not to shatter as they lowered him into the ground. I was a grown woman. I was thirty-seven. Now was not the time to scream for "Daddy". My mother had stood stoically. I'm not sure if she cried – she didn't sniff. I didn't notice a dabbing of eyes but I noticed her squeeze my hand a little tighter as we were invited forward to toss some soil into the grave on top of his casket. I hated that part. Even though I could feel the almost overpowering, claustrophobic warmth of Craig behind me, I had shuddered there in the clammy warmth of the graveyard. My mother had been led away by her friend Louisa, while I stood there and stared, entranced by the hole in the ground.

"We should go," Craig had said and I'd glanced up to see we were all but alone in the cemetery, the majority of mourners having clambered into their cars and the waiting limos to be ferried back to the golf club for lunch.

I was shivering in the rain – my neck cold as the drops slid down my back. They weren't cold. I knew they could not be and yet they felt like ice. I felt like ice.

"I don't want to leave him," I muttered.

"Then stay here as long as you need," he said softly and he let me stand there until I was shivering so hard that my teeth were chattering. I felt . . . I felt confused. Broken. Torn.

"We'll get you warm, we'll get you changed and then we'll go on to Green Acres," he said softly, leading me away, and in a haze of pain and grief I'm almost ashamed to admit that my only thought was that I didn't own a single other thing in black and I would look like an insensitive heel at my own father's wake.

I found the next most suitable thing I owned – a soft grey cashmere dress – and I quickly showered, put on some fresh make-up and tousled my short blonde hair, grateful I didn't have a look that required more work, before breathing deeply and telling Craig we were good to go again.

"You're doing well," he said. "You're getting through this."

I smiled – a weak, watery smile – gratefully clinging on to whatever hint of reassurance I could find, regardless of where it came from.

"No choice but to keep on going," I said. "Time to go and mingle with the mourners, I suppose. To listen to them all tell me how he has gone to a better place, and isn't in pain any more and how he was a good man."

"He *was* a good man."

"I know. And I know folks mean well . . . but . . . you know . . ." I said, drifting off. Platitudes wouldn't make it better – no matter how well intentioned.

* * *

My mother had taken off her sunglasses by the time I arrived at Green Acres. She was sitting in a circle of friends, smiling and nodding. I was sure she was listening to the platitudes and being my mother – ever polite and afraid to offend – she was smiling at them. Part of me wanted to run over and tell her she didn't have to do that – but she would have killed me stone dead if I had made a scene. She would have glared at me, her lilting Irish accent which remained despite her many years away from home ringing in my ears: 'Don't you make a holy show of me or yourself, Annabel.' So I nodded in her general direction and set about fixing my own weak smile on and promising myself that I would not make a show of myself – not one bit. And I didn't. I behaved myself right until the very moment when the last guest went home and then I drank three glasses of wine straight, cried all over my mother who ended up soothing me as if she herself wasn't hurting, and had to have Craig tuck me into bed where I spent the following ten hours watching the clock flicker and change.

"We could go for a drive today," he said, in the half light.

"Get out of here – clear our heads."

"I need to go and help my mom," I said. "I was pathetic yesterday. I need to be there for her."

"You've been at her side for weeks, Annabel. You need a break. You will burn out – if you haven't already." His tone had veered from concerned to snippy.

My own mood changed just as quickly. "I've been at her side for weeks, so I can't just leave her now," I said, turning to face him. "He's gone. I can't just leave her in limbo now and clear off because the nasty business of the funeral is done with. She's spent her last few months caring for him. What in hell is she supposed to do now that she doesn't have that any more?"

Of course, I knew as I spoke that it was me that I was worried about – that without having to run to the hospital, pace the wards, feed my father softened food gently, hold his hand and read to him that I might be the one to fall apart. That I would have to finally accept this loss – and deal with everything else I had put on the back burner while I devoted my life to caring for the wonderful man who had always made me feel important.

My mother? Of course I worried about her too. She seemed calm – too calm – and that unnerved me. Then again everything unnerved me at the moment.

"She might want some space?" Craig offered and I shrugged his arm, which suddenly felt too heavy, away from me. "*We* might need some space from all this?"

"Not now, Craig," I said, sitting up and grabbing my robe from where I had thrown it on the floor.

He rolled back away from me. I knew without looking at him that he would be crestfallen – just as I knew I was pushing him away. But grief does funny things and I kind of wished it was socially acceptable to walk around wearing a T-shirt that said "*I'm grieving. Allow me to be a bit mad*" on it, because then I wouldn't have to try and make people understand. Surely they should know just how raw and horrible this felt? Surely they had all been there?

* * *

My mother sat on her bed, folding clothes and putting them into bin bags. T-shirts he barely wore, chinos that had become baggy and loose on him over the last few months.

"I'm packing them up," she said as I walked in, pushing her hair off her face and curling it behind her left ear.

"You don't have to do that now," I said.

"I know. But it has to be done sometime."

"But not now, Mom," I said. "You don't have to do it now."

"Annabel, pet, I know this is awful but I've been living with it for a long time. I knew this day would come. I was ready for it – sort of."

I didn't understand that, how she could be ready for it. Sure we had all known this wasn't going to end well but that didn't mean I didn't feel every shred of breath leave my body in the moment the breath had left his.

"I was there for him, Annabel. I was there and loyal and I loved him, right to the end. I always will love him but he's gone and, sweetheart, he's not coming back. So I need to move on."

She spoke so calmly that I felt the room swim a little. It was almost as if she were talking about paying the bills, or doing the grocery shopping. Something which might as well be done now. Not something that had ripped our lives apart. I rested my hand on the chair by her dressing table and looked at her again.

"I want to go home to Ireland," she said, folding his shirt – his checked shirt, the one he had worn when we went to the coast and walked along the beach. I had teased him for ogling the young, surgically modified women in their bikinis and he had told me he only had eyes for my mother. I looked at it: empty, folded, slipped into a bag. "And I'd love you to come with me."

I looked at her as if she were mad. She *was* mad. Maybe she needed the "*Grief makes you do funny things*" T as well?

"Don't look at me like that, Annabel," she said, lifting another shirt, folding it and placing it in the box marked for Goodwill.

Feeling churlish, I reached in past her and took it back out again, holding it tight in my arms, trying to get some hint of him back. All I could smell was her detergent and fabric softener – not a hint of coffee or musky aftershave. Not a hint of my dad.

"You want to go back to Ireland? And you want me to go with you?"

"It's not that hard to take in, is it?" my mother said, her face set in a way that let me know she was very much determined to go ahead with her plans – with or without me.

"But, Mom, you have a life here. I have a life here. I have the bakery. I have Craig. We have this house – your friends, your colleagues, your life." I was clutching at straws, of course. Straws of what I had, before. What I had before he was sick. When everything changed. What I really wanted to say of course was that I could not even begin to imagine how *she* could want to walk away from our home and our life, even though there was a part of me which wanted to walk away from my own life. I knew she was grieving but . . . I felt something constrict in my throat.

"Who said anything about walking away? I just want to visit. It's been a long time. I need to get away, don't you understand that? Everything has been on hold for so long . . . Everything has been so hard. Illness and death. Even this damn house – it doesn't smell like home any more. It smells of antiseptic and illness and the perfume of strangers come to pay their last respects. I just want to go home again. I'd love you to come with me – to see Ireland. Didn't we always talk about going? When you were small? Wouldn't it give us both a lift?"

Chapter 2

I never imagined we wouldn't be together. From the moment I met you I knew I had to be with you. I can't breathe without you, but I can't think of another way. Not without breaking hearts all around me. Do you understand? It's easier to break mine than theirs. I'm just so sorry, my darling, that you are caught in the crossfire.

* * *

I had never been to Ireland before. It was one of those trips we always talked about but never quite got round to taking. My Irish family members were people I knew from birthday cards, phone calls and, latterly, Facebook. Ireland was somewhere my mother spoke of wistfully – regaling tales of Irish dancing, dew-dappled mornings, the *craic* and the singing. I grew up on a diet of Maeve Binchy books and an annual family viewing of *The Quiet Man*. I am pretty sure my mother had hoped that one day I would enter the Rose of Tralee, but as my teens turned into my twenties and my twenties into my thirties and I showed no sign nor interest in reciting a poem or dancing a jig on Irish national television she let the dream slide. Dad, well, to him I was his all-American girl born on the fourth of July – my mother had a battle with him not to call me Sam.

"Sure, there's already a Sam in our family," she argued, my Aunt Dolores having delivered a boy by that very name a year before.

"Yes, but he's a he and lives thousands of miles away," my father had argued.

My mother had fixed him with a steely glare – not too unlike the one Maureen O'Hara gives John Wayne in *The Quiet Man* – and told him there would be no such name. So he had retaliated and vetoed her choice of Aoibheann ("Who on earth could pronounce that?" he had asked) and they had settled for the non-controversial name of Annabel.

Part of me couldn't believe that in just a few short hours I would be there – on that famous Irish soil.

I pressed the last of my sweaters into the case and zipped it closed while Craig watched from the other side of the room, his arms crossed. His body language screamed that he was not even a little bit happy with my trip – and he hadn't even pretended to be since I had come back from my mom's and told him that she wanted me to visit Ireland with her.

"You can't be serious?" he'd said as I'd flopped onto the sofa beside him and put my feet up on the coffee table opposite.

I was exhausted. The toll of the last few days, not to mention the last few months, was heavy. I didn't have the energy to fight so I said nothing, figuring my silence would be proof enough that I was serious.

"What about your business?" he said.

"Elise will take care of it. She's been doing a fine job while I've been nursing Dad. I'm sure she can continue to do a fine job while I'm away."

"But you have said all along how you couldn't wait to get back. How you were missing Bake My Day?"

"I am missing it," I said, which was of course just partially true. I missed what it had meant – to me, to Mom, to Dad. But I didn't much want to face what it meant now. But as I said, I was tired and Craig was not the person I wanted to have this discussion with. "I didn't expect it to feel so . . . final. So horrible!" I spat out, feeling tears prick my eyes. When we had first found out Dad was sick – terminally sick with no hope of recovery – I had reeled with shock. Then as I'd watched him suffer I'd started to tell myself that, although it would be hard, it would be a relief to see him out of pain. That comfort of knowing he wouldn't be in pain any more got me through many long nights, but the moment he was gone that had shattered into a million pieces around me. Now I just felt lost. I felt like I needed to try and find my way but I didn't quite know how. When my mother had suggested going to Ireland with her a part of me had, in spite of those initial reservations, felt a little glimmer of something . . . a glimmer that I could get through this.

"Going to Ireland is just running away," he said, gruffly, unable to hide his irritation.

"Perhaps I need to run away for a bit!" I bit back, my tone sharper than I intended.

In hindsight, although this was true, this was absolutely the worst thing I could have said to Craig.

He stood up, ran his fingers through his dark wavy hair and took a deep breath as if trying to steady himself.

"I don't mean run away from you," I offered quickly, trying not to think about whether or not I really meant what I was saying. "I just mean from here and now and how I'm feeling." The tears started. "And my mom needs me now."

"And what about me?"

I thought of everything we had been through – how we had weakened and broken along with my father. My father was beyond help now but, maybe . . . maybe Craig did need me more. But it wasn't him who was most broken now – it was my mother. And me, I suppose. I was broken too.

"She needs me more," I said softly and he turned and walked out of the porch into the summer rain, slamming the door behind him.

Of course he had come back and told me he was sorry, saying that he missed me already and that while he understood my need to take a trip I couldn't escape real life forever. I was painfully aware of that, I told him, but I needed to escape a little bit now. When I saw my mother's face light up as I booked the return tickets, I knew I had done the right thing and I could blank out all images of a gruff and grumpy Craig.

He offered to drive us to the airport, but I said I preferred to take a cab. If there was to be a scene at my departure, I much preferred that it would be on our own front porch rather than in his car. "It's not for very long," I said, as I threw my Kindle into my carry-on case. I'll be back before you know it." I zipped my case closed in time to hear a taxi beep outside. Craig sighed as if I had just told him I was leaving forever. I looked at him – his sorrowful face staring back at me – and I wanted to push away every negative feeling I had towards him. I walked over and kissed him gently on the lips, bristling slightly as my lips met with stone cold indifference from him. He was not making this easy.

"Goodbye," I muttered, pulling my cases behind me to the porch. He followed me but he didn't offer to help so I adopted an eyes-forward-do-it-myself approach.

Climbing in beside my mother, a little part of me breathed out.

"Is he still sore about you going away?" my mother asked, shifting in her seat and adjusting her seat belt.

"Not at all," I lied, looking out the window and watching Craig walk dejectedly back to the house as if I were walking all over his dreams and not just helping my grieving mother heal her broken heart. "He just, well, he worries about me."

"Ireland's very modern these days," my mother said. "And the North, well, it's not like it used to be. It's safer than most places here. Hardly anyone gets shot these days. He has nothing to be worried about."

I think we both knew that wasn't what Craig was worried about.

She took my hand and squeezed it tight. "The friendliness of the Irish – it's not just a thing of legend. It's real, you know. And the people of the North, we get a bad rap sometimes but, you know, hearts of gold. They've been through so much. I was lucky, I suppose – I left before the worst of the troubles started . . ."

"Is that why you never went back, Mom? Until now? Because of what was happening?" I thought of my mother and how she seemed to think wistfully of home from time to time but never mentioned going back. I had offered once, to pay for both her and Dad to make the journey back but she had shaken her head. "I've spent more of my life here than I ever did there," she said. "Sure it seems strange to even consider it home now. I'm happy with my memories." But she hadn't looked me in the eyes and I knew there was a part of her that wanted more than just memories.

She shook her head now, giving my hand one last tight squeeze before letting it go. "Oh no, darling. It wasn't that . . . it just didn't feel right." She leant back and closed her eyes, signalling that she wanted to snooze and that the topic of conversation was closed for now.

I looked at her, head tilted to one side, grey hair in a stylish bun, her fingers fine and delicate, soft as satin. She looked well, I realised, with a bit of start, and I'm not sure if it made me feel sad that she looked a little freer since Dad had passed or it made me happy that it wasn't only his pain that had ended. It had almost killed me to watch him suffer – Lord alone knows what it did to her. I looked out the car window – the fields passing by in a dull blur of green and I wondered if Ireland really was green and lush and if things really had changed.

I thought of Craig and his sullen face and pushed that aside. And I thought of Elise and her excitement at getting to hang onto the reins of Bake My Day for another while yet, and I pushed that away as well.

This trip, whatever it was, was my escape from what had happened – and my journey towards what would be and, whatever would come, I would make the very most of it.

* * *

"There's no hotel?" I was having to hold my tongue very firmly in place not to swear at my mother. I had never sworn at her before and I was not about to in the departure lounge of Miami Dade airport.

"Family don't do hotels, pet," she said, adopting a strange lilt to her accent which I hadn't heard in a while. It was as if she was transforming into an Irish cailín before my very ears. "It would be madness."

"Mom, I said I would pay – so if it's money . . ."

"It's not money, love," she said. "It's family. When you go home, you stay with family." Family who you have never met, I thought to myself and sighed. I thought it would be me and Mom in a hotel room, not crammed in someone's spare room like the invading Yanks.

"And you are not to be worrying, because I know you won't want me cramping your style so I'll be staying with Auntie Dolores and you will be staying with Cousin Sam."

The swear word nestled there on the very tip of my tongue, dying to burst forth, but I bit the side of my cheek instead. Sam – the name-stealer – who I had never met. Who I was "friends" with on Facebook but who I was pretty sure had me on a limited profile because all I could see were the occasional life-affirming quotes he posted and none of the good stuff.

"But I don't know Sam," I muttered, stepping forward in the queue towards check-in. "Surely Derry has hotels. I don't mind paying," I repeated.

My mother shook her head and smiled at me. "You may not mind paying but I mind making a show of myself and refusing to stay with family. I've heard Sam is a good boy. His mammy loves the bones of him – said all he needs is a good woman to sort him out. And he lives on his own – swimming in space, he is, so it would do neither of you harm to spend some time together. Sure he must know what all the young ones get up to."

Sam – who needed a good woman – who was older than me. Oh, sweet Lord above. I had images of being foisted on some late 30s Lothario who knew what the young ones got up to. Worst case, he was a creep. Best case, he was a momma's boy. Either way I could feel my skin creep and my desire grow for a simple hotel room with a power shower and Egyptian-cotton starched sheets, black-out curtains and lattes on tap with a simple call to room service. The thought of the spare room in the pad of a man with a penchant for life-affirming quotes was almost too much to bear.

I looked at my mother. Her Irish eyes were smiling as she fished in her bag for her passport and travel documents and the silent swear word in the back of my throat became a silent scream as I wondered what I had let myself in for. The thought of turning back home, facing life, reality and Craig, suddenly seemed a lot more appealing.

"I can't believe it," I heard my mother's voice break softly through my reverie. "I'm going home, Annabel. I'm going to see it all again – to breathe that air again. Is it so wrong of me to just want to take my shoes off and dance through the grass again?"

I looked at her and could imagine her, long blonde hair – now grey – dancing through the grass as a young woman, smiling, carefree – and the scream became a smile. I would do this, creepy Sam and all, if it made my mother happy.

* * *

I'm not sure if I was expecting some sort of emotional meltdown as we landed in Dublin. My mother slept through it and I decided to leave her to it – it had been a long day and her giddiness at the airport had given way to a plethora of tears as our plane had taken off out of Florida and headed eastwards over the Atlantic.

"I've never flown this way before," she said softly. "Your dad and I, we travelled – but only in the States. You know he never once left America? He was so proud of that, Belle." She smiled and I nodded.

Yes, a real Yankee Doodle Dandy – not quite as much as me, obviously, what with my birthday and everything. But he always had a flag flying off the front porch and he smiled every time he came home at the *God Bless America* sign that hung over our front door.

"He just liked his . . ."

". . . comfort zone," I finished and we laughed.

Dad certainly liked his creature comforts. We used to joke that we were pretty sure the father character in the sitcom *Frasier* was based on him – down to the ratty old chair he liked to lay back on each evening and the badge of honour he kept in his top drawer from his days on the force. Comfort and routine. Routine and comfort. You could do no wrong with either, in his book.

"Do you think he would have liked Ireland? Do you think he ever really wanted to go?"

My mother shrugged her shoulders as the plane levelled out and we started to cruise at a comfortable 35,000 feet. "He always said he had enough of Ireland in me – that nothing about Ireland could be better than what he had. Why did he need to see more of it when he had the best all to himself?"

I smiled and squeezed her hand but there was something in her voice that was a little bit too wistful. She took a deep breath with just the slightest of judders which made me realise she was trying to compose herself and she let go of my hand.

"Right, my dear," she said, "is it okay to drink on the plane? Because I would really like a shot of brandy."

"I think we have to wait until the lights go off. It shouldn't be long."

"Grand so," she said. "I can do that. I'm very good at waiting."

15

* * *

Ireland was as lush as the Maeve Binchy books had promised. Looking down over it, there was a patchwork quilt of greens unfolding below me. I wondered were there actually any cities in this country as field followed field followed mountain followed lake. Of course, as we began our descent little dots of houses appeared out of the greenness, and then more houses, and an industrial estate and lots of cars scurrying like ants along the network of narrow roads. The sky was grey and rained pattered against the side of the plane, trickling horizontally from one side of the window to the other. I guessed it would probably be cold and I was grateful for the sweatshirt I had packed and the sneakers I was wearing. No, they weren't very glamorous and they no doubt screamed "tourist" but they were comfy and my mother had warned me we had quite a bus-ride from Dublin before we reached the North. I wondered how long it would take and, as my mother slept, I asked the tired-looking cabin assistant who shrugged and said it would only take maybe three or four hours depending on traffic. I felt my heart sink. I was bone tired and desperately in need of a power shower, some decent non-airline food and a warm bed to sleep in.

"The roads aren't too bad," the crew member assured me. "Bit bumpy in places but you'll be grand."

I nodded my thanks, glanced out the window to where we were coming in faster and faster to the ground and had a momentary fantasy about the whole thing crashing and me getting a decent rest at least before the day was out.

Never mind, I laughed into myself as we bumped onto the tarmac, at least I would have Sam the Singleton's chintzy house to stay in once we got there.

Chapter 3

They say we have choices – and you may think I made my choices – but I didn't. It was beyond my control. It's beyond what I can do. This is not what I would have chosen, my love. It is not what I would have chosen at all.

* * *

Ireland, June 2010

The bus journey was exhausting. Not even the allure of the lush green hills and overgrown hedgerows and the quaintness of the villages we whizzed past could take away from the exhaustion that had crept up on me, sitting on my shoulder, jabbing me square in the neck every three seconds.

"You should sleep," Mom said. "Did you even close your eyes on the plane?"

I shook my head. I didn't sleep in public places – not even when I was tired right down to my very bones. I wasn't a great sleeper anyway – only ever truly drifting into a deep sleep in the calm darkness of my own room, all sounds silenced for the night, all glints of light hidden by an eye mask over my eyes – no one near me, not even Craig. My best nights' sleep were nights when he was working. I felt guilty for feeling that way, but that was how it was.

"I'll sleep when we get to Derry," I offered. "When I can lie down on a proper bed."

Again the thought of no hotel filled me with dread.

"I'm sure your cousin has a very nice room waiting for you – Auntie Dolores tells me he keeps a nice house," Mom said and I cringed. "He's a nice boy, she says."

I tried to block out my growing sense of unease as we wound through the roads. My iPod pumped tunes into my ears, the quiet melancholy songs of Adam Duritz soothing me.

Any emotions my mother had been keeping in check disappeared as we neared Derry. I saw her sit a little more rigidly as the signs directing us to her native town revealed smaller and smaller numbers. By the time we reached a village – which looked more like a street to me – called Newbuildings, she had her hands tightly clasped and was muttering some sort of prayer under her breath. As we swept through a set of traffic lights and caught a glimpse of the River Foyle weaving its way towards the city ahead her prayer had become a sob. A "Jesus, Mary and Saint Joseph" of emotion accompanied by gentle rocking. I reached for her clasped hands, feeling a tear fall to my hand before she shrugged me away.

"It's home, Belle," she said softly before losing herself again to her sobs. "It's home."

Sitting back, leaving her to her reverie, I tried to take in the sights around me. This was where my mother grew up – a place she hadn't seen in a lifetime – a place she had always said she was happy enough to leave behind. I was surprised to find a flurry of emotion rise up in me as we turned and swept onto a blue steel bridge and across a river which seemed to cut the city in two. There was a part of me here – right in this air, in these rain-soaked pavements, in the dull greyness of the sky and in the gentle sobs from my mother.

"It's so different," she whispered as we came to a halt at the redbrick bus station, where weather-battered hanging baskets swayed in the breeze. "It's just the same."

I nodded, pretending to know what she meant but I knew there was no point in talking to her further. Her eyes were darting around the platform, trying to find the familiar, as I helped her from her seat and lifted her bag from the overhead rack.

I think I saw Dolores before she did – a short stocky woman, whose grey hair was cut short and fixed in a curl but whose facial expressions mirrored my mother's. Once again my mother called to the Baby Jesus before alighting from the bus with not a care to her age, her slightly arthritic hips or the exhaustion from the long journey. Within seconds she was wrapped in her sister's arms, the pair crying as I pulled the weekend cases down the stairs of the bus and collected the rest of our luggage from the rear compartment. It didn't seem like one of those moments where I could just butt in and introduce myself, so I stood there awkwardly, lifting my weight from foot to foot, trying to bring some life back into my limbs after the long journey. Auntie Dolores seemed reluctant to let my mother go – her warm voice, a slightly harsher, deeper version of my mother's, muttered over and over that it had been a lifetime and that she couldn't believe it had been so long. She hugged my mother close. "Poor Bob!" she said, or at least I think that is what she said as her thick accent was muffled in my mother's hair. I could not hear my mother answer back but I was aware she was crying. A man, in flat cap and slacks with a heavy grey cardigan and obviously with Auntie Dolores, watched us from a distance, looking slightly embarrassed at the show of emotion before him. I nodded in his direction and he tipped his head at me briefly before staring off into the middle distance. I figured there was no point right now in trying to engage him in conversation – I would just have to wait for the reunion to cry itself out – which of course sounds harsher than I meant it to. But I had been travelling for the best part of twenty hours. I needed the bathroom and I could no longer feel my right butt-cheek. I was pretty sure that the slightly dodgy smell which had been lingering in my nostrils for the last hour might have actually been coming from me.

"Poor Bob," Auntie Dolores said again, stepping back this

time and taking my mother in from head to foot before turning her gaze on me, just at the time I was trying to stretch out a kink in my neck.

"You must be so tired," she said, reaching for me and pulling me into a group hug with my mother. "Dear God, it is just brilliant to see you. Brilliant! Of course so sad . . . poor Bob . . . may he rest in peace." She shook her head and made the sign of the cross on her ample bosom. "We should get you home." She looked towards the flat-capped man. "Shouldn't we get them home, Hugh? Sure won't they be wrecked?"

I was foolish to think that home actually meant the place where I would be staying. Although I dreaded being shown to my cousin's bachelor pad, I had started to crave going anywhere that provided a bed. I didn't even care if it was a comfortable bed. No, when Auntie Dolores said "home" she of course meant her actual home: a small redbrick house on a terraced street which looked like it would have fitted, in its entirety, into our back yard at home. It was the same redbrick house my own mother had grown up in along with her family, eight of them in total, squeezed in like sardines.

We, the four of us, pushed our way into an impossibly small room where at least eight other people stood, shoulder to shoulder, some of them looking vaguely like my mother. A door to an impossibly small kitchen was open, which at least provided a fresh supply of oxygen to the room. It wasn't warm outside but the room had a cloying feel as my mother was gathered into a tearful group hug by her long-lost relatives. Occasionally one of the group would look at me and back to my mother and ask if I was "little Annabel" and my mother would nod and I would feel about five years old. I stood, awkwardly once more, hoping they wouldn't grab me into their scrum. Feeling a little overwhelmed and more than a little overheated I made for the impossibly small kitchen where aluminium foil-covered platters of food sat on every available surface and the biggest kettle I had ever seen bubbled on the stove.

I pushed my way through the open back door into a small concrete yard dotted with plastic planters overgrown with flowers. Seating myself on a plastic garden chair, I put my head in my hands, and tried to take deep breaths to stem the slightly dizzy, overly exhausted feeling that was threatening to overpower me. How my mom was still on her feet, I just didn't know. I imagine she was fuelled with adrenalin and raw emotion at seeing her long-lost relatives again, and while I was happy for her – and I really was – they were strangers to me. This felt alien and claustrophobic and if one more person said "Poor Bob!" I would scream out loud.

I breathed slowly in and out, trying to find my centre in this claustrophobic concrete space at the back of a terraced house.

"They're not that bad," a deep voice said.

I looked up. A man – bald, late thirties, wearing low-slung jeans, a polo shirt and Converse – eyed me quizzically. I suddenly felt embarrassed. It was pretty obvious this man was one of my relatives: he might even be the name-stealer himself. And here was I, flustered and nauseous five minutes after meeting his family.

"I didn't . . . I'm not . . ." I felt my face blaze.

"I'm only teasing you," he said, breaking into a broad smile. "Why on earth do you think I've escaped out here too? I was just shocked to find someone else in my usual spot – and adopting my usual head-in-hands pose as well."

I felt myself relax and made to stand up.

"No, keep sitting. I'm thinking you've been travelling a while. You are probably wrecked and didn't expect the welcoming party."

I nodded my head weakly. "I don't want to appear ungracious . . ."

He sat down on the back-door step, his gangly legs stretching out in front of him. "I'm Sam," he said, reaching his hand out to shake mine. "You must be Annabel."

If I had been less tired I would have made a snarky remark

about his powers of deduction but, given that exhaustion was seeping from every pore of my body, I decided not to. It would have sounded all wrong and made me out to be a bitch – and I'm really, really not a bitch.

"Hi, Sam," I smiled, deciding now would also not be the best time to tell him he stole my name.

"They will calm down, you know. They're just so excited. It's like the return of the prodigal son. My mum said she never expected to see her sister again."

"Oh I know, and it's such a lift for Mom as well. It has been tough."

"I heard. That's too bad about your dad," Sam said, shifting his legs, trying to get comfortable. "Shit when people die, isn't it?"

I was taken aback by his bluntness. But he was right. And it sounded better in a Derry accent. It really was shit when people die.

We chatted for a while. I agreed to drink a cup of tea. Sam said I would be banished from the family before I'd even been properly welcomed if I refused. I nibbled at a sandwich and watched my mother come to life before my eyes – her eyes dancing with tears and joy as she reacquainted herself with people she had last hugged forty-eight years before, her eyes darting around the room trying, I imagine, to remember when it was her home. It was clear from very early on that this party was not going to end any time soon, so when Sam offered to take me back to his place I almost threw myself into his arms with gratitude.

Chapter 4

I think if you were here it would be easier – but you feel so far away. It feels like so long since I have held you and have felt you with me. What if it has all changed?

* * *

His house at least was not what I had feared. In fact, I actually did cry a little when I saw the whitewashed house with a beautifully manicured garden. The painted red door opened to reveal a modern, not at all chintzy, interior – light and airy with bucket-loads of natural light which did hurt my tired eyes a little but definitely did my heart good.

Walking down the long hall, Sam gestured to a shiny white kitchen before pointing towards a lounge which screamed minimalist elegance. My heart dared to hope that the spare room might not be the hellhole I had imagined. But what I hadn't counted on was the room being like something out of my dreams. A bed dominated the room – a very large wrought-iron bed. It sat under a bay window draped with light muslin curtains, but equipped with the best black-out blinds money could buy. And on the bed the plump eiderdown was covered in crisp white linen which Sam kindly informed was indeed Egyptian cotton (3000 count) and I had to fight the urge to lie down there and then. He pointed to a door that led to an admittedly small walk-in closet and another that led to a beautifully appointed en suite bathroom. The power shower called to me and I couldn't keep the smile from my face.

"A shower is not a shower unless you feel there is a real possibility the force of the water will take off a layer of skin as well," Sam said and, not for the first time, I fought the urge to hug him.

"Why not rest up? Take your time. I've a friend calling over later – you are more than welcome to join us, or you can just rest here until you feel recovered from the journey."

Still smiling like a woman delirious from hours and hours of travel, I said I would see how I felt after I washed off the grime of two continents from my skin and had a little lie-down.

He switched on the small antique lamp beside the bed and pulled down the black-out blinds for me. "Sleep well," he said. "Anything you need just holler."

As he left the room, I sat down on the edge of the bed, allowing the softness of the sheets underneath me to soothe my tiredness. Thinking I would just lie down, just for a moment, I put my head on the pillow and drifted off.

When I woke the house was silent. A glass of water had appeared on my bedside table with a note saying to help myself to anything in the kitchen. Lifting my cell from my bag I saw that it was gone 3 a.m. – my brain was too tired to figure out what that meant in US time.

I had a series of messages from Craig.

Through my still-exhausted fug I tried to make some sort of sense of them.

Are you there?

Are you safe?

Where are you?

Do you even care?

You leave the country and I cease to exist any more, huh?

Oh, shit. He was annoyed and I would have to try and appease him. I should have called, or sent a text or something, but it had all been so full on that, I was ashamed to admit, he had simply slipped my mind. But I couldn't tell him that: that he had simply slipped my mind. That would not go down well at all. Not one bit. I felt something sink in the bottom of my stomach – which given the fact I thought my stomach was already at an all-time-low-sunk place was an achievement. I tried to message something back, through my fuzzy-headed exhaustion and fat-fingered typing, but nothing made sense and, as a wave of jetlagged exhaustion washed over me again, I felt myself start to drift off. Given that I had barely slept in the last few months, I surrendered, blissfully, to it. Okay, it might well have been fuelled by a mammoth journey and a time difference, but I would take my sleep where I could get it.

When I woke again, despite the black-out blinds I could tell it was morning. There was a buzz about the place, the muffled sounds of cars outside passing up and down the street – the occasional call in a foreign accent which reminded me that I was somewhere new and different.

As I sat up in bed, I heard a knock on the door and Sam's voice carried through. "I've put some coffee on. I assume you drink coffee which is probably very presumptuous of me. My mother called earlier – she is bringing your mother over in an hour. You may need a dose of something strong to keep you going."

I called back a quick thank-you and stood and stretched. I'd just have a quick shower first, slip into some fresh clothes and then join Sam in his kitchen. I pushed all thoughts of Craig and his text messages behind me, feeling guilty that he hadn't been my first thought on arriving safely. Of course he would have been worried, of course I should have let him know. I would call him later and let him know that I was sorry, that I had been overwhelmed by arriving in Ireland and had been dealing with the welcome of countless relatives and that I would make it up to him when I got home. We would put our lives together again when I got home, I decided, as the hot water gushed over me. It's not that I would forget my father, but this seemed to be the final piece in the process of losing him. Once that was done I would move on. My return to the States would herald my return to Bake My Day and I would, I vowed as I washed my hair, make it all up to Craig. It would work out, I told myself as I towelled off, dried my hair, dressed in jeans and a sweat top, and swept some moisturiser across my face. I would do for now – until I'd had some caffeine anyway. Slipping some sneakers on my feet, I headed towards the kitchen where Sam called out that breakfast was ready if I wanted it. The smell of freshly cooked bacon hit my nostrils and I realised I was starving.

"This is a lovely welcome," I said, taking a seat at the kitchen island and reaching for the mug of coffee he poured me.

"We're a hospitable race," he said. "Famed for it."

He put a key on the table along with my coffee. "I have to go to work – no rest for the wicked. But feel free to use this house as your own. No rifling through my underwear drawers or anything – but, you know, make yourself comfy."

I realised then I knew relatively little about this man who had allowed me to stay in his house except that he had exceptional taste in bed linen and lived alone – and perhaps sometimes entertained friends in the wee small hours.

"Work? It's a shop, isn't it?"

He nodded. "Vintage clothing – all the rage, especially in these times when everyone is looking for a bargain. But not just any tat. People tend to think when you say vintage you mean stuff you rifled from your mum's attic. We're very particular – designer labels mostly and genuinely vintage – 50s, 60s and 70s, occasional 80s. None of this 'it was fashionable in 1994 therefore is retro-chic' carry-on."

"So your shop doesn't smell like mothballs?" I felt I could try a joke – he seemed up for it – but as I spoke I only hoped I didn't offend him. After all, I didn't know him from Adam – he was just a cousin who had saved me from death by Victoria sponge the day before.

He laughed, his blue eyes twinkling and creasing. "Perish the very thought," he said, sipping from his coffee cup. "We do get the odd old doll come in looking for something in a nice tweed or offering to sell her old Sunday best, complete with gravy stains circa 1976, but we are quite discerning. You should call in while you're here. I could set you to work. My lovely mammy tells me you run your own shop back home."

"A bakery," I said, although it had been at least eight weeks since I had done a day's work there and, if the truth be told, I felt a little removed from it. Bake My Day – it seemed like such a quirky, funny name back then but now it seemed stupid, childish even. The last eight weeks had changed me – still this was not the kind of conversation you had with an almost-stranger not even twenty-four hours after you met. You didn't launch into the horrors of grief and the fact that if you have to ice another cupcake ever again in your life you may do yourself · in with a spatula. "It does okay. My assistant is keeping it ticking over for me at the moment."

"I must get you to bake me something while you're here," Sam said. "Although I'm trying to watch my figure," he added, patting his almost-flat stomach. "Can't see any hot young thing falling for me with some extra padding around my middle."

He smiled and I was grateful he didn't push me further about work. Actually, as he picked up his car keys and wished me well, I was grateful he hadn't pushed me much about anything. Whether it was the jetlag or something darker I definitely felt a little raw that morning. I sipped my coffee, walked into his den and sat down punching buttons on his remote control until his TV sprang to life. Scrolling through the channels I clicked on an old episode of *Frasier* and started watching, until I found myself welling up at the scenes with Martin. Pull yourself together, I told myself, brushing my sleeve against my eyes. Positive mental attitude – back in Ireland with your mom – there is no need to cry every time anyone even thinks about their father.

Thankfully my slump into self-pity was disturbed by the arrival of my mother and Dolores – who were clearly in better spirits than I was. I heard them before I saw them, laughing as they came through the door – Sam's mother obviously having a key to her son's house. "Annabel?" my mother called, her accent now quite a bit more Derry than it had been.

"I'm in the den!" I called.

"'The den' – I love it!" Dolores said. "Sounds like something off the TV. I love Americanisms!"

"We have a unique turn of phrase here too," my mother said. "Remember the 'good room'?"

"I loved that room," Dolores said as they came in, still lost in their own conversation. "I've many happy memories of courting young men in that room, not that we got away with much. Not with Mammy and Daddy in the next room. Do you think they really put a glass up to the wall to listen to what we were getting up to – making sure we were behaving ourselves?"

My mother giggled – again a childish lilting laugh I hadn't heard in a long time. "Well, I wasn't prepared to take a chance. Were you?"

Dolores laughed heartily, "Ah no, that was what the Bollies were for! Sneaking up those lanes to the woods after dark – it felt so rebellious."

My mother wiped a tear of mirth from her eyes and looked at me. I must have looked a sorry sight in comparison, curled on the sofa, scraping tears of another kind from my eyes.

"Ah, pet," she said, sitting down beside me, "did you not sleep well? Are you feeling okay?"

I stared at her blankly, wondering how, in just a week, she seemed to have forgotten what we had been through and was no longer acknowledging that I might have a legitimate reason to be crying over *Frasier* at eight-thirty in the morning.

"I'm fine," I lied, because I didn't want to embarrass her in front of Auntie Dolores by shouting at the top of my lungs that it might just be the dead dad in my recent past which had put me in, as she would put it, 'bad form'. "Just tired . . . must be jetlag."

"Look, if you want to just shoot the breeze here today, that's fine. Dolores and I were going to go for a drive around Inishowen anyway. You should see the coastline – stunning. Well, I mean, you should see it, but if you are still feeling tired you can see it another day. Go back to bed, get a good rest. Get yourself well mended for tomorrow."

"I'll get Sam to look in on you at lunchtime if you like," Dolores offered. "And I'm sure he has a hot-water bottle somewhere if that would help – or did he give you one last night?"

I looked at them blankly, fussing like mother hens around me, my mother's usual stoicism lost in a haze of childhood remembering.

"I'm fine," I said. "Honest. I'd love to come with you. Just give me a chance to get properly ready."

"Ah grand so," my mother said and I looked at her strangely. She didn't even sound like herself any more.

Walking out of the room I heard Dolores whisper, "I see what you mean about a 'bit intense'," and I bit back the urge to adopt the best Irish accent I could and tell them both to shag off.

Chapter 5

I will always remember the blueness of your eyes. Even in the dark I could see them. And I see them now, every time I close my own.

* * *

My aunt's car was small. I didn't want to be all-American but this car was *small*. I don't consider myself to be overly tall but I felt cramped in the back seat while my mother and Dolores sat up front. Beside me was a cool box, which my mother told me was filled with leftover sandwiches from the day before's celebrations. I tried not to think of how long they had sat out in that too-warm room and plastered a fake smile on my face.

"That's lovely," I said and my mother beamed.

"It is, isn't it? Just lovely. A proper picnic."

Dolores launched into the chorus of some god-awful song about going on her summer holidays, even though it was raining and, in my opinion, very cold indeed. Dolores didn't seem to feel the cold though – she was wearing a T-shirt and a light rain jacket and said she was "melted". Compared to the Florida sunshine, nothing felt very "melted" at all about this.

"Let's get this show on the road," I said, and my mother turned to smile at me.

Let's see if Ireland and all it had to offer really was worth travelling all this distance for. I would call Craig later when I had something to tell him – something positive perhaps that made me sound a bit more like my old self. He was always telling me how I didn't sound like my old self any more and I had been doing a merry dance on and off over the last few months – making great big efforts to be all old-self-y to try and make him happy. Maybe this would actually make me genuinely happy, or if not happy then at least generally less miserable.

We drove for an hour, up back roads which dipped and rose like rollercoasters. I'm pretty sure I suffered a mild concussion as my head battered off the back window on one unexpectedly mammoth dip.

"I bet you don't get roads like this in Florida," Dolores chimed.

No, we have roads generally without potholes and with enough room for two cars to pass safely side by side whenever they so desired. "We sure don't," I said with a smile and she laughed wildly.

"I love that," she cheered, nudging my mother before putting on her best faux-American accent and laughing. "'We sure don't' – brilliant, just brilliant!"

There was a comfort in listening to them chat as we drove. They didn't exclude me from their conversation but I was more than happy to sit back and enjoy the easy way they spoke with each other, occasionally clasping hands and exclaiming it had been much too long since they had parted and apologising to each other for not making the effort to get in touch more often.

When we stopped, at a sandy bay down a very steep hill, we all stepped out of the car. Okay, this was not Malibu Beach. There wasn't a hope of getting a suntan and the wind as it came off the coast would have cut straight through anyone not suitably layered up, but there was a calmness and a stillness there that made me breathe out and relax just a little.

My mother, Dolores holding her hand, was staring out to sea.

After a while I noticed her brush a tear from her eyes and as the waves crashed into the shore, one after the other, the tears fell from her eyes one after the other too. I stood and watched as

Dolores wrapped her arms around my mother's hunched shoulders and I wanted to wander over and stand there beside her, my own arms wrapped around her, but it felt in that moment as if they were having their own private moment so I walked on through the sand, letting my feet sink into the soft grains and walking so close to the water's edge that when the waves crashed in I had to dash from them. Was it daft that I felt momentarily free – even though I was jetlagged half to distraction and concerned about my mother who was sobbing? I pulled my cellphone out of my bag to phone Craig and tell him of this little moment of freedom – and cursed at finding I had no signal. Wondering if it was simply down to my cell being American, I turned and walked back towards my mum and Dolores, and a whisper of their conversation caught me on the wind.

"There is no point in having regrets, Stella," I heard Dolores say, clearly unaware I was making my return up the beach. "So much has happened since then – good things. You've been happy, haven't you? That's real life – not some fairytale."

I probably should have alerted them to the fact that I could hear their conversation carry on the wind but I was intrigued. My mother was wiping at her eyes as Dolores held her. Perhaps I should have walked right up and asked what exactly wasn't a fairytale – approached the whole situation casually as if I hadn't been excluded from any part of the conversation even though I had wandered down the beach and away from them. After all, this was a family day out and this was my trip to Ireland with my mother; surely I was entitled to ask what exactly they were talking about? But there was something about my mother's demeanour and the way Dolores shook her head, her short curls blown almost straight in the breeze off the sea, that made me realise this conversation was definitely not for my ears. So I stopped and turned to stare out to sea, trying to catch every second or third word as they spoke. Occasionally whole sentences came to me. "You can't go back in time," I heard

Dolores say as my mother muttered something to her, her voice too low to be carried on the breeze. And then a few moments later: "You would be best to leave the past in the past."

I turned to watch as my mother turned on her heel and walked back towards the car on her own, leaving Dolores standing there running her fingers through her hair. I'm pretty sure I heard a swear word as well before she too turned and followed my mother, calling her name. I went back to staring at the sea, and then at the phone in my hand, wondering if I would ever get round to calling Craig . . . but more than that, wondering what on earth that had been all about.

* * *

"Tell me you take a drink?" Sam said as he pulled a delicious-smelling lasagne out of the oven.

"I take a drink," I answered with a smile. In fact, after the day I'd had with my mother I was tempted to take a very big drink indeed.

"Well, what's your poison, cousin of mine?" he said, as he fished about his drinks cabinet. "I have Coors, I have wine – both red and white. I have vodka. I have a rather suspect-looking tail end of a bottle of Drambuie and I'm sure there's some god-awful kind of a schnapps knocking about in the back of this cupboard somewhere."

"Red wine would be perfect," I said, already dreaming of the smoothness of the liquid as it slid down my throat.

"Grand job," he said. "I have a Rioja that is just out of this world." He opened the bottle with ease and poured two rather large glasses.

We had worked quite well together. I hadn't wanted to come across as a bossy American, nor did I want him to think that he had to wait on me hand and foot. To be honest, having felt like a spare wheel for most of the day, I was delighted to do something practical. When my mother had said that the jetlag was finally catching up with her and she was going to have a quiet night in, I had been glad of it. I had been even more glad of it when Sam came in from work, announcing he was going to make me a decent welcome-home dinner with not one hint of an egg-and-onion sandwich or slightly stale cupcake.

The car journey around the rest of Inishowen had been fraught with tense moments. When I arrived back at the car my mother had adopted the same stoic stance as she had at Dad's funeral. Her arms were crossed, her eyes straight forward.

Dolores had plastered on a forced smile as I approached the car. "Salt fair gets in your eyes," she said, glancing quickly at my mother and back.

I decided just to pretend I knew nothing of their conversation even though I was dying to ask them what it was all about. What part of my mother's past did she want to relive again? Why should she leave the past in the past? Surely Dolores had not been telling her she should be well over my father so soon after his passing? I had a feeling she was the kind of woman who would speak her mind but surely she wouldn't be that lacking in compassion?

My mother thawed a little as we drove. She even occasionally tried to include me in her reminiscences. She pointed out the beach they used to visit as children – the shorefront at Buncrana which seemed to them like the most exotic place in the world. But she would drift off into her memories and Dolores engaged in a game of births, deaths and marriages, listing off the fates of each of their acquaintances from their younger days – names that meant nothing to me but had clearly meant a lot to my mother in her time.

By the time we were back at Sam's – and Dolores had made us yet another cup of tea and filled us with yet another soggy scone – I found myself wilting. It wasn't as if I didn't want to be there – Ireland certainly had its charms, but a day crammed in the back of a small car while tensions ebbed and flowed between my mother and aunt had not been the best of fun.

"We'll get some time, just me and you, tomorrow," my mother whispered as she left. "Maybe we could hire a car? See the place in comfort?"

I kissed her cheek and wanted to tell her it would all be okay, that we always had each other, but Dolores was already hauling her down the pathway, telling her she was going to make her a "good old Derry stew" for dinner.

After they left I allowed myself a thirty-minute lie-down on the bed – now dubbed 'the most comfortable bed in the world' – and attempted once again to call Craig. He didn't pick up at work, nor did he pick up his cell so I left a semi-garbled message about how sorry I was for not getting in touch sooner, that I was fine, that Ireland was strange but lovely – and I added a quick "I miss you" at the end even though, if I was honest, I didn't really. Not much anyway.

By the time Sam came back I felt a great deal brighter, my power-nap having done me a world of good, so while he browned the steak mince for the lasagne I chopped the onions and mushrooms. While he made his sauce, I prepared a salad. He was easy to chat to. I felt somehow safe in his company, which was nice. I hadn't felt safe for a long time – not with everything that had been going on at home.

As we worked he apologised several times for his mother. "I know she can be a bit full on. She has been so excited by your mum's visit – it's all she has talked about since she found out. I get the impression she and your mum were very close at one stage."

"They do seem close," I agreed. "The whole family seems close. I grew up pretty much on my own with Mom and Dad – no family around us at all. So it does feel strange."

"Your dad's family? Were they not close by?"

"He only had the one sister and she lives in California – they weren't close. She sent flowers of course, when he died, and a card – but she didn't fly out."

He could barely disguise the hint of horror on his face. "She didn't come to the funeral? That's a bad show."

I bit my tongue to stop myself from pointing out that none of my mother's family had made the trip either. Somehow that had seemed more acceptable as they had been on another continent. As I didn't know them it hadn't really hurt me, but I imagine my mother had felt it.

"Things are different in America," I said. "I think it's all done differently with us. He was gone anyway – the moment he passed he was gone. He didn't look like himself – I didn't much see the point of people coming and sobbing over something that bore no resemblance to the man I loved so much."

Sam stopped stirring his sauce and pulled me into a hug without warning. I hadn't been crying. I had spoken very calmly. It was how I felt – I didn't need a big turnout of a funeral to let me know my father had been loved. If me and Mom had been the only two mourners, I would have still been confident that he had known more love in his lifetime than many people do.

But the hug was nice. It came with no expectations. It came with no agenda – it was just a hug from one cousin to another – an expression of sympathy.

When he pulled away and wordlessly went back to his sauce as I continued preparing the salad, I smiled to myself. So when he offered me a drink and poured those two large glasses of wine I felt myself relax completely in his company. Sam was on my side.

Chapter 6

*Do you remember that first time we met? Maybe you aren't in
the mood for remembering. I still remember every detail. I was
wearing a blue dress – you told me it accentuated my eyes. I
wasn't sure what 'accentuated' meant – so I asked Dolores and
she laughed at me. She told me it was a nice thing. That you had
complimented me. And I blushed so hard I thought my face
might catch on fire.*

* * *

My cell rang just after midnight. I was lying in bed, chilled out
after a lovely dinner with Sam and the better half of a bottle of
wine.

Sam and I had established several things. First of all, he had never
been aware he had unwittingly stolen my name; he apologised
profusely for his crime, but said that Sam was a boy's name anyway.
"Samantha is a watered-down version and you don't look to me
like you could be a watered-down version of anything."

Second of all, we established that he had reacted in the same
way as I had when he had been told (not asked) that his cousin,
whom he didn't know, was going to stay in his house during her
stay in Ireland.

"I don't even know you," he said. "And I'm pretty sure you
have me on a limited profile on Facebook."

"Guilty as charged, but then you have me on a limited profile
too," I challenged him.

"Can't have randomers looking at my holiday snaps!" he laughed. "I'm very selective about who sees the Speedo shots."

I laughed so much that I'm sure wine shot through my nose and we vowed to ease our privacy settings the next time we were online.

He told me he was jealous of my life in the States. He had always wanted to visit Florida ("Disneyland and *CSI Miami*, what more could you want?") and I told him how travelling back to Ireland had never really been a topic of conversation in our house before now.

"It's not that my mother stepped away from her roots. She has pictures of Ireland all over the house. She made me do Irish dancing – I still have weak ankles from a bad sprain I suffered in the process. But Dad never seemed keen on coming here and she kept quiet."

"I can't imagine moving so far from home and never looking back," Sam said. "Well, actually I can. And there are times I do imagine it – moving away and starting a whole new life where no one knows your past, no one judges and no one has any expectations."

His face had turned darker then and I nodded in agreement. There was something appealing about that – just walking away from it all.

"Anyway," he said, adopting a bright tone, "you wouldn't want to have been named after a Muppet anyway."

"A Muppet?"

"Sam the American Eagle. You're way cooler than he is."

When my cell rang as I lay in bed, and I reached for it, the warm glow of the evening was still enveloping me. I smiled when I saw Craig's name and answered with a bright, if sleepy, "Hello, stranger!"

"So you're speaking to me now?" He had a tone of forced politeness about him – as if he was trying to keep things light when I could tell he was cross.

I felt my heart sink. "I'm sorry. I did try and call you earlier.

I had no signal and then you weren't answering."

"I was busy," he said, silence following. The pause was unsettling – *he* had phoned me after all – and yet he wasn't talking.

"Well, I'm sorry to have missed you. Things have been hectic here. I don't even think the jetlag has caught up with me yet. I was just drifting off to sleep."

"Well, if it's too much trouble for you to talk me," he said.

I sat up, ran my fingers through my hair and took a deep breath. "I didn't say that, Craig. Please don't be like this. I know things haven't been easy lately –"

"Well, that's an understatement," he bit back.

Unexpectedly, tears welled in my eyes. "Please, Craig. I'm tired. I'm a million miles away. I've had a long day and a glass of wine and I wanted to call you earlier because I went to the most beautiful beach and I wanted to share that with you. I'm sorry." I felt the tears start to fall and although I tried to keep the sniffle from my voice I knew he would know I was crying.

"Don't cry, baby," he said softly. "I just miss you. I'm sorry for being a jerk. I just miss you and us. I miss what we used to be."

I let his soothing words wash over me, trying not to think too much about the mess we were in. It seemed he was feeling the same.

"I just feel like I'm losing you," he said. "And I couldn't bear it if I did. God knows what I would do."

"You're not losing me," I said. "I love you."

We ended the call on a happy note, both agreeing we loved each other and that we were staying together. So I couldn't quite explain why I felt a terrible tightness in my chest when I went to lie down.

* * *

My mother took me to the top of Austins, which laid claim to be Ireland's oldest department store, for tea and scones, the following morning. Scones, it seemed, were de rigueur in Ireland. No morning was complete without one.

As we sat in the top-floor café and looked out at the skyline of Derry, I thought of Bake My Day and the wide range of pastries, cupcakes and speciality baked goods that would be stocking the shelves that morning. I momentarily wondered how Elise was getting on. I had every faith in her but it felt strange to be so far away from my business. Even in the last few months when I had abdicated almost all responsibility to my second-in-command I had still been able to call in. The control freak in me had liked the ability to do those little spot checks even if I didn't care half as much about the business as I had done.

Watching my mother devour the scone in front of her, I wondered should we add some more traditional bakes to our menu, remembering the scones and treats Mom and I had baked together when I was a child.

I could remember the softness of her hands on mine. My mom. My mommy. Although a daddy's girl through and through, Saturday mornings were our time. Mom and me. The heavy Mason Cash bowl would be taken from the kitchen cupboard and sat on the counter with reverence – the wooden spoons, the measuring jug, a whisk and measuring cups lined up beside it. I'd pull my stool up alongside the counter as my mother slipped my apron over my head – a match for her own.

"Well, Annabel, what shall we bake today? Something for supper? Something sweet? Or bread – will we bake bread?"

She emptied the cupboards of sacks of flour and in the hazy Florida sunshine a puff of dust would rise and be caught by the rays through the window. We felt, at times, we were standing in our own glorious little snow globe.

Mom always dabbed just a pinch of flour on the end of my nose and I can't remember a time I didn't laugh when she did it. And, when my giggling had passed, I would dab flour on her nose and side by side we would stand, laughing at this private, shared and often-repeated moment.

I don't know why she always asked what we would bake . . . because we baked the same thing each week: bread, fresh and tasty; treacle scones, which my mother said reminded her of home; an apple-pie for my all-American father; and, because I loved playing with frosting, cupcakes, which were mine and mine alone to decorate. By age six I was a dab hand at piping, no Saturday complete without one of my creations, which my father would devour on the porch with a cup of coffee as he told me about his working week.

My mother would join us, sitting beside him on the swing, while I sat, kicking my legs on the porch steps, watching the sprinklers dance, and hoping Mom would say I could run through them.

I remembered her then, her head on his shoulder.

"You smell of freshly baked bread," he would say.

"You smell of coffee," she would answer.

The same conversation each week – there was a comforting rhythm to it – a calm and loving intonation in their voices, and I would close my eyes and feel the drops from the sprinkler mist across my face.

"Go on," Mom would say and I would run, the warm grass tickling my toes, as I plunged into the sprinklers and danced in their rain.

Tea, after a soak in the tub, when Mom would lay fresh pyjamas out on my bed, was toasted chunks of the fresh-baked bread smothered in butter, as I sat on the couch and we watched television together.

Days like those were perfect. It wasn't hard to understand why, from such a young age, owning a bakery had become my ambition. When my friends at school said they wanted to become teachers or lawyers, doctors or vets, I remained steadfast. All I wanted, forever, was my piece of heaven: my bakery where my parents could come and sit at the counter and where I could make my mother laugh simply by dabbing some flour on my nose as I worked.

I closed my eyes there in the restaurant in a strange country and wished with all my might we could have one of those moments again – just the three of us.

I smiled at my mother, seeing her younger, stronger for just a moment before seeing her as she was now – frail, tired.

"So did you sleep well last night, Mom? You looked dog-tired when you left."

"I'm not used to international travel," she said. "I forgot how much jetlag can knock you off your feet – not to mention the fresh air at Inishowen. I always told you it was a beautiful place, didn't I? Isn't it just gorgeous?"

"It is, Mom."

"We will have to go again before we go home. I could go there every day and not tire of it."

"Whatever you want to do on this trip, Mom, you say. It's your trip – make the most of it."

"I will, you know," she said, spreading butter thickly on another half of scone. "But it's your holiday too. You've been through the mill as well, my dear. Think about what you want to do. Is there anywhere you want to go? Anything you want to see? Just say."

"I'll think about it, Mom," I promised, sipping from my strongly brewed tea and looking again out over the rooftops.

It all looked so different to Meadow Falls, darker and gloomier if the truth be told, but friendlier too. I had already noticed that: how people smiled at you, how people you had never met before in your life seemed genuinely pleased to see you – even those who were not obliged by genetics to do so.

I caught my mother's gaze and she smiled at me softly.

"It's amazing, sweetheart, how quickly the memories come back," she said. "I thought this part of my life was all boxed away somewhere, but so much is coming back."

I reached over and took her hand. "Tell me about it, Mom. Tell me about this city – all your memories. You know, I wish I had done that with Dad more – talked about things. Talked about his life more. We did at the end, but it was awful knowing that we were trying to cram all those memories into his last few weeks. I want to know more about you – about Auntie Dolores – and how you were together. I want to know all about your life."

Mom brushed at a few crumbs on her skirt and looked at me, her blue eyes glistening. "My darling girl, I so want to tell you. I'd love to share my whole life with you . . . but . . . I'm not sure . . ."

My mind went back to our walk on the beach and her emotional reaction to whatever it was Dolores had said to her.

"Don't hide anything from me, Mom. You're the only family I have left."

She smiled, polishing off her scone and remaining silent while I wanted to shake her and get her to talk to me. The frustration rose up through me, but I knew better than to try and make her talk to me. My mother was like that – the strong silent type. We were close as a family, the three of us – in a kind of Christmas-card way. We did things together – went bowling, or shopping. We ate Sunday lunch together. We went to Green Acres at least once a month for a family afternoon, even though I was now well grown and it wasn't necessarily cool. I went to my parents' house for Thanksgiving and Christmas – New Year's I had spent with Craig, for the three years we had been living together anyway. But Mom and I? We didn't really talk – not the deep stuff. We talked soaps and politics and recipes from time to time. She was my biggest cheerleader and my fiercest critic. But heart-to-hearts, we didn't do those.

Not even when Dad was given his diagnosis. Not even on those nights when we sat up into the small hours mopping his brow and watching him sleep. I'm not sure what I had expected – perhaps my mother to regale me with stories of how she loved him, how he was everything to her, how they met and fell in love, but for most of those nights she sat in silence, staring at him. I imagined she was having some sort of silent conversation with

43

him, that inwardly she was telling him all the things I hoped to be able to tell the love of my life someday. I even felt jealous on occasion and would go home, when morning came and the desire for sleep became too much, and curl up beside Craig as he slept off a nightshift and inwardly tell him I loved him and hoped that he loved me too – the way I deserved to be loved.

"Can we go for a walk?" my mother said, after she had finished her tea and visited the restroom.

"I thought that was the point of today," I said, perhaps a little sharply.

She gave me a look, the kind of look which would have withered me if I had been even mildly afraid of her – and still eight years old.

"Sorry," I smiled.

"You're not too old to avoid a clip around the ear," she laughed, linking her arm in mine. "Let's just go for a walk and I promise I will try and talk to you – but you have to let me take it slowly."

* * *

Slowly, as it happened, was no exaggeration. We walked the City Walls – a mile-long trail around the very centre of the city – steeped in history. My mother talked – of course she did – but it was of the famine graves, the workhouse, the history of the cathedrals, the Siege of Derry and the Burning of Lundy. I was almost tempted to ask her if she had eaten a tourist guide earlier in the day but I decided to say no more.

"You know a lot about this place," I commented as we climbed down the steep stairs of the walls and crossed to a pub called Badger's, where my mother ordered two glasses of wine and looked at the lunch menu even though I was still full from the scones an hour before.

Taking our seats in a quiet corner, my mother sat back and sipped from her glass. "You don't get a place like Derry out of your mind," she said. "It's changed so much, sweetheart. So much of it looks so different to the place I remember, but it feels the same. It feels so safe and sound – it feels like home."

"Meadow Falls is home, Mom," I said softly.

"A part of me will always consider this home," she said. "And I suppose a part of me will always wonder why I left."

"You left because you fell in love with Dad," I said. "Remember?"

She sipped from her glass again, just as she had sipped from her teacup earlier, as if she was thinking very carefully about what to say next.

"I'm not sure . . . I don't think . . . there was more to it than that."

Chapter 7

Of course I miss you. Of course I love you. I can't imagine ever not loving you.

* * *

By the time I got back to Sam's my head was spinning, and not just from the mid-afternoon glass of wine and the slight tinge of a hangover from the night before. I had two hours to get ready for that night's entertainment – and two hours to try and process what my mother had told me. I doubted, as I turned on the strong streams of the power shower, that even the most invigorating of showers would clear the weird thoughts from my head. But I knew it had taken a lot for my mom to start talking to me – and that I would be expected to be the belle of the ball at the family dinner Auntie Dolores had arranged for us.

Sam had called me earlier to warn me what was planned – and warn me of the family traditions I needed to be aware of – such as the after-dinner drinking, singing and storytelling. "Pick your party piece," he said.

"My party piece?"

"The song you will sing."

"I don't sing."

"Yes, you do," he said confidently.

"No. I really don't. I was the only girl in High School asked to mime during our graduation ceremony."

"You're a Hegarty," he said. "You sing. Whether you like it

or not. Inability to hit notes does not exclude you from the after-dinner joy that is performing your party piece. You will sing or you will be tortured until you do. Have you ever seen *Father Ted*? The character Mrs Doyle with her tea? Well, the Hegartys are all like that about the singing. It will be all 'ya will, go on' until you blast a wee something out. So believe me, cousin, you are best to just choose something – a short something – and get it over and done with. They will not allow you to rest until you get it out of the way."

I contemplated this as I stood under the shower, and thought of my mother and the day that had passed.

"I didn't know your father when I moved to the States," she had said.

"Of course you didn't, not really. You don't really know someone until you live with them. And I'm sure in those days you didn't live with someone before you were married."

"No, pet, you didn't. But when I say I didn't know your father, I mean that we met after I moved over. Some years after, if the truth be told."

I looked at her, struggling to process things. "You didn't meet him until then? You left Ireland, without anyone to go to? I thought it was because you were chasing your big romantic dream?"

She gulped her drink. I don't think I had ever seen my mother gulp an alcoholic drink in her life.

"I was chasing something," she said. "It was such a long time ago. It seems silly now, to be honest. But I was chasing a romance – a romance that didn't work out."

"But which you thought so much of at the time that you gave up everything you knew to move to the other side of the world for?" I struggled to keep the incredulity from my voice.

"I thought it was worth it at the time," she said. "But it didn't work out – and then I met your dad. And I don't regret that for a second. He gave me you . . . but . . ."

"But?" There were no buts. I didn't want to hear any buts. So before she could speak I silenced her with a quick "Never mind!" as I gathered my belongings into my purse, telling her there was a lovely little gift shop I had spotted from the walls that I really wanted to visit and perhaps we should make a move.

"Annabel, you wanted to know more."

"I thought I did," I said, plastering a too-bright smile on my face, "but I was wrong and I'm not ready – so if you don't mind, I'd love to visit that little gift shop and see if they have anything which I could take back home to the States with me. I want to get something extra special for Elise – she's done a lot keeping the business on track. That shop looks just the ticket." I was speaking fast and I know I was rambling but I didn't want any awkward silences, so I chatted on, nineteen to the dozen as my mother would say, until she realised that the conversation we had been having would go no further that day.

She followed me, meekly, into the shop, where I cooed over an Orla Kiely bag and started a conversation on what my party piece would be.

* * *

I must have packed while on drugs – even though the only drugs I took were some Advil – because as I sorted through the suitcase I had brought with me, the suitcase I thought was too heavy and contained way too much, I found that I had nothing which really suited an impromptu welcome-home party. I'd been told it was taking place in a local restaurant, in a special function room, and that the entire Hegarty clan would be there en masse. So I sorted through my clothes – pulling out jeans and sweatpants and T's and three crisp white shirts when I'd thought I owned only two of them. I had packed sneakers, Havaianas and a pair of boots. No sandals or strappy shoes. I did find the black dress I had worn to Dad's funeral but even looking at it made me feel sick, especially in light of my mother's comments earlier – so I rolled it into as small a ball as I could and shoved it to the bottom of the bin in Sam's kitchen.

This, however, did not solve my problems about what to wear. I feared I would look pathetically underdressed as I selected a pair of my best-looking jeans, a loose-fitting white blouse and a new pair of canvas sneakers. I pulled my hair back, clipping a flower on the side, and brushed on some bronzer and blush. I slipped a simple silver bangle on my wrist, one that Craig had bought me for my last birthday, and I spritzed some scent on my neck – perfume that Craig had also bought me. It felt a little cloying but I figured that was because I was still tired from the journey, even though it had been three days since I'd left home and landed on Irish soil.

I poured myself a glass of water and sipped it while I waited for Sam to transport us to the party, hoping that would bring me round just that little bit. I figured I would need all the strength I could muster to make it through the evening.

Sam had done little to calm my fears about the party piece. "Don't think you can get away with it because you're not from round these parts. It's not all Irish laments and rebel songs, if you think that is your get-out clause. My mammy does a mean 'Lipstick on Your Collar', and I guarantee you will hear at least two versions of 'Sweet Caroline' so you better start thinking and thinking fast. It's like the Rose of Tralee, only with alcohol. You'll be lucky not to be interviewed in front of the masses."

I pulled a face which expressed just how completely terrified I was and he laughed wickedly. "I'm only teasing, but just a little bit. Don't think me mean – I just like it when the focus is not on me for a change. You know, the only single in the village. They would have an arranged marriage in place for me if they could."

"I'm single," I muttered and he looked at me quizzically.

"Do you not have a man, back home in the US of A?"

I blushed. Of course I had a man. But we weren't married. Technically I was single but I didn't know why I had said it and I wasn't quite sure how to unsay it.

"Oh yes," I muttered, mortified. "But we're not married or anything. So . . ."

"On a technicality?" Sam finished my sentence. "Okay, fair enough."

But I knew he thought I was a bit odd. Christ alone knew I felt a bit odd myself – about to go to a big party dressed in jeans, sipping wine and telling my cousin I was single when I had been living with Craig for the last three years. I didn't even know why it had slipped out. So I took perhaps too large a gulp of wine, put my glass down on the granite counter and asked Sam if it was time we should be leaving.

* * *

My mother was wearing make-up. Her hair was curled and set and she was wearing a pale blue dress which showed off her slim figure. She was even wearing a pair of modest heels – two inches at most – but I did a double take when I saw her all the same. She looked younger – it seemed with every day she was back on home soil a year or two of worry melted away from her. I was almost envious of how well she looked when I was hopelessly underdressed and feeling a bit like a butch lesbian in my fairly utilitarian jeans and blouse, while my mother glided up the stairs into the function room like a woman half her age who was a perfect advertisement for ageing gracefully.

When we reached the room itself Sam whispered in my ear that I should brace myself, but even his warning could not have prepared me for the blast of noise, colour and cheering which greeted us. I was vaguely aware of 'Welcome Home' blasting over the sound system and a gaudy arrangement of balloons and banners marking both our American and Irish heritage. Several trestle tables in a corner were heaving with yet another Hegarty special buffet, I assumed.

Crowds of cheery-faced people waved at us, some with glasses sloshing overfilled drinks in our direction, and let out a chorus of cheers, shouts, exclamations of great joy and the odd stifled sob. Some of it I understood – some of it, well, I wasn't even sure it was being said in English.

My mother was enveloped into the crowd so that I could just about see her hair bobbing in and out of great big hugs every now and again. I half-expected them to lift her above their heads and encourage her in a bit of crowd-surfing.

A glass of wine was thrust into my hand by a gruff-looking man in a starched white shirt, which groaned at the buttons. His head was bowed and he was grimacing as if he was trying to force a smile on his face when, clearly, smiling was alien was to him. "Cheers!" he barked and turned to return to the mêlée.

"You should consider yourself honoured," Sam whispered in my ear. "That's Uncle Peter. Never known to have bought a drink for anyone in his entire life. This may go down in the family legend book." He was smiling and I couldn't help but smile back.

"Let's get a seat before this crowd are finished with their grand big welcome and there isn't a seat to be had."

I followed him across the room, largely ignored by the crowd around me – word clearly not having got out there beyond Peter that I was the prodigal daughter's daughter. I was glad of the vague anonymity and was only too happy to slip behind a table and sip at my drink while Sam sauntered off to the bar to buy his own.

Such a family gathering was, it has to be said, a little overwhelming. We never had anything like it back home. I'd been to parties of course, but nothing as raucous as this (well, there had been a few sorority parties when I was at college, but even those were wildly different in their own way and I'd known more than two or three people at them – and of course, everyone spoke with the same accent as me and used words I understood).

Sam returned with two glasses and a bottle of wine. "Saves us fighting through the masses to get to the bar every time we want a top-up," he said, pouring his own glass and topping up the glass Peter had given to me. "I'd say, dear cousin, if we have to be here then we get sloshed."

"I don't really drink that much," I said, knowing that I sounded like a party pooper. But then again I was on my holidays and Sam seemed as if he would be a decent enough partner in crime. I saw my mother walking towards us, a host of grinning women looking at me as if I was a newborn they were setting their eyes on for the first time, and slugged at my drink. "Then again," I said, "when in Rome and all that."

"Good woman yourself!" Sam said cheerfully, slugging from his own glass.

As it turned out Sam proved to be a very effective deflector-shield. He was able to manage the hordes of aunties and cousins and family friends effectively – telling them about my business at the bakery and steering them away from too many questions about Craig. I guess the single comment had stuck with him. He was also able to steer the conversation away from my father when it started to get a little maudlin, and all the while he managed to make sure my drink was well topped up, which I was grateful for. Soon I found myself relaxing in his company and that of the family around me, allowing their warmth and friendliness to wash over and comfort me. It felt nice to be part of something bigger – to think that we were all tied in some way together. I liked it. It made me feel fuzzy and warm. I felt comforted in a way I hadn't in a long time – comforted and cushioned by the warm way they welcomed me into the fold. They didn't have to. I knew that. I was just a distant relative – someone they had never met before. I was a name on Christmas cards. A profile on Facebook. An entry on the family tree – somewhere off at the side on a very small branch. I wasn't someone they had sat round the Christmas table with or whose First Communion they had attended en masse. And yet there they were, buying me drinks, offering me hugs and, in Sam's case, treating me like a little sister who needed gentle care.

After three glasses of wine it was enough to make me feel a little weepy – so I stepped outside into the cool night air to catch my breath. Digging in my bag I lifted out my cell – a need to speak to Craig to tell him how this felt so good had washed over me. I dialled his number, put the phone to my ear and smiled when I heard his voice.

"Hey, babe," I said softly.

"Hey, yourself," he said jovially.

I felt myself breathe out and relax at the free and easy way he spoke to me and tried to push away that little nagging voice in me that wondered when he had stopped speaking to me kindly every time we spoke.

"I'm having a lovely time, Craig. You should be here. Ireland, you know, it's true what they say about the people being so friendly. You wouldn't believe it. You wouldn't believe it at all. They are having a party – for Mom of course, but I'm being made to feel so special too. Oh Craig, it's something else! It really is."

"Have you been drinking?" he asked, his voice still jovial but still I bristled.

"A few, but that's not why I'm calling. I just wanted to hear your voice."

"That makes a change," he said – not harshly, I noted, but with a sad sort of resignation and I felt myself inhale again.

"I'm sorry," I whispered into the air as one of my cousins, or uncles, or friends stumbled out of the door, winking in my direction and lighting up a cigarette.

"Aw-right, pet?" he nodded and I forced a smile onto my face although something was constricting deep inside me.

"I'm sorry too," Craig said.

"I do love you," I muttered. "And I do wish you were here."

"Annabel . . ." Craig said, before he paused, and I steadied myself, wondering what he would say next. "I wish . . . I wish I was there too."

We hung up, the conversation ended, and I turned to where my cousin/uncle/family-friend was puffing on his cigarette. I looked at it enviously. I had quit when my dad took ill – a futile act of solidarity even though his cancer wasn't in his lungs and he had never smoked in his life.

"Can I bum one?" I asked.

"No bother," he responded, proffering his packet to me.

I took it and he lit it for me, and I breathed in the warm smoke, letting it fill my lungs. I held it there, relishing the sensation of it in my chest before breathing out.

"Fancy a drink?" I asked the man before me. "It's on me."

"Never say no to a drink," he said smiling. "I'm Paddy – pleased to meet you!"

"Well, Paddy, I can categorically say I'm pleased to meet you too – so on to the bar!"

Chapter 8

I know you will be angry and hurt. I know that and that hurts me too. If things were different. I wish things were different.

* * *

Moments of the night before flashed before my eyes – my poor, stingy, slightly swollen and definitely bloodshot eyes. I peeled my tongue from the roof of my mouth and tried to will my eyes to open, but the very noise of trying seemed unbearably loud. I was aware I was lying face down, almost suffocating in the pillow with its fancy Egyptian-cotton cases. My head felt as if it was swollen to three times its normal size but a quick feel reassured me that it was still very much ordinary size. I quickly – well, actually quite slowly – ascertained that I was still almost fully clothed. A shoe appeared to be missing. My left one. Something in my head registered some memory of a Christy Brown, *My Left Foot*, joke.

That memory was followed by a flash of me performing my party piece – a rather tuneless rendition of 'The Star-Spangled Banner' standing aloft on a chair. My mother's face flashed into my mind – sitting on her chair, her face a picture of pride. She was hugging Dolores and clapping for me and I, like some child coming top of the spelling bee, was grinning wildly back.

I rolled over on the bed, my head seeming to take forever to follow the rest of my body and, feeling that the room was still spinning, I decided to make the long roll back to where I had been.

Other memories came back, one at a time, as I slipped in and out of sleep. I believe Paddy – he who I had bummed a cigarette off – had bought me tequila. After my conversation with Craig, and despite the fact I never drank hard liquor, I downed a shot, or maybe three – I lost count somewhere between that cigarette, which made me feel light-headed, and 'The Star-Spangled Banner'.

I had danced. Sweet God, I had danced. That was one of those other things I hadn't done in a while – apart from a quick shuffle around the dance floor at weddings with Craig. I even attempted some sort of jig. I know I saw my mother do the same – and I'm pretty sure it was with more decorum than me. Decorum – it was a word I didn't think I would ever be able to use in connection with myself again.

A knock on my bedroom door was followed by a cheerful hello from Sam who walked in, looking fresh as a daisy, and sat down beside me.

"A good night?" he asked with a smirk.

"I don't really remember," I grimaced as he handed me a glass of water and two paracetamol.

"I have other treats for you too," he said, taking a few boxes from his pockets. "Here, take a Berocca – it's a vitamin – it will bring you round a bit. And some Milk Thistle, perfect for hangovers."

"I'm not sure this is a hangover," I said as I glugged at the cool glass of water. "I'm pretty sure this is what dying feels like."

"And you said you didn't really drink?" he laughed.

"Don't," I warned, the very thought of alcohol making my stomach start to turn.

"Did you know Uncle Peter even bought you a second drink? *The Derry Journal* was nearly called, and *Ripley's Believe it or Not*."

I couldn't help but laugh. "Did I make an ass of myself?"

"No, cousin, you didn't. You let your hair down. I have a feeling you haven't done that in a while."

I shook my head (gently, this was no time for rapid movements) and tried to remember the last time I had let myself go with such abandon, quickly coming to the conclusion that actually I had never let myself go with such abandon ever before. Ever.

Sam stood up and walked to the en suite where he switched the shower on full blast.

"I've slipped some aromatherapy goodies in there – stuff perfect for the morning after the night before. You may get yourself washed and dressed and I'll have some breakfast ready. Take your time – no rush!"

"Do you not have to go to work today?" I asked him, aware that time was marching on.

"Shop doesn't open on Sundays," he said. "Actually, we have something a lot more hellish to do than work today. It's Sunday roast in my mother's house, which is a treat all of its own. And by saying it's a treat I don't necessarily mean in a good way. But count yourself lucky, Annabel – we could have had to go to Mass with them. Lucky for you and me both, I told them we went last night at half seven. If anyone asks, it was Father Paul, the Gospel was according to Saint Luke and the homily was about the perils of drink." He raised an eyebrow as he left the room and I gingerly set about getting ready.

* * *

It seemed the healing powers of a shower, Sam's patented hangover cure and his breakfast of bacon and cream-cheese bagels were doing the trick.

As we sat and chatted at the kitchen table, his glass doors open to the balmy summer morning sunshine, it struck me that of all the people and all the random memories which were coming back to me from the night before I couldn't remember too much of Sam. Of course I remembered him sitting with me, and I'm sure there was a challenge or two involving a drink of undetermined provenance, and I know he had cheered as I reached the high notes in my party piece, but still . . .

"Sam," I asked, "did I miss your party piece or do you still owe me that honour?"

"Ah, my friend, I should have told you. I'm exempt from party pieces. In fact, my mother strictly forbids it."

"Surely you can't be that bad? You've heard me sing? Surely no one can be worse than that?" I blushed involuntarily once again at the memory of my crooning.

"It's not my singing she's afraid of," he said, lifting another bagel and liberally spreading cream cheese on it. "I've quite a good voice if I say so myself. She just doesn't really like me drawing attention to myself. Not in any kind of flamboyant manner."

I thought of Auntie Dolores and her 'Lipstick on Your Collar' routine which left little to the imagination and I felt confused.

As if it was written all over my face, Sam piped up: "Anna, I'm not just the only single in the village. I'm the only gay in the village too – and my mother, well, she hasn't really come to terms with that yet."

I looked at him, startled and not sure how to react – not because I was horrified at him being gay – I was, at worst, a little shocked by it – but mostly because I'd just assumed he . . . well, I hadn't really assumed anything. I'd just seen him as Sam.

"Everyone knows, of course," he went on. "It's not something I keep secret. I don't announce it on first meeting people – because, well, there is nothing to announce. It's just who I am – but I'm not in the closet. My mother, well, she pretends to get it. And she even pretends to be cool about it – but I very quickly learned that she doesn't really understand at all. She still thinks it's just a phase and when I get it all out of my system I'll settle down with a nice woman and furnish her with 2.4 grandchildren and a dog called Buster."

The great boy his mother was so keen to marry off. How must that feel? In that moment I felt my heart ache for him a little.

"She tolerates it," he said. "She tolerates me."

"I think she loves you very much," I said and I meant it. I was sure there was more than mere tolerating going on.

"Okay, to word it better, she tolerates my lifestyle – only just. As I said, she keeps thinking, for whatever reason, that it's a phase. I try to tell her that twenty years is a bit more than a phase, and that before I came out I was gay and always had known I was, but I think there is a part of her which will always think I'm nothing more than an attention-seeker. She wants me to modify my behaviour – you know, so that when the day comes when I finally admit I love women instead, I don't have too seedy a past to dig over."

He was upset as he spoke. He tried to keep an upbeat tone to his voice but I could tell this was hurting him.

"Surely she should just accept you as you are?"

"She should," he said. "And in a lot of ways she does. I mean, we don't talk about it all the time. It's not this gaping chasm between us, but it is there and when things happen like family get-togethers I can feel her watching me out of the corner of her eye, scared of her life I'm going to cop a feel of a hot waiter or launch into a rendition of 'I Am What I Am'."

"Is that your party piece then?" I asked, stupidly. I don't even know why I said it. It felt awkward and horrible but I didn't know how to have this conversation with him. It wasn't one of those ordinary run-of-the-mill things you talked about with someone you had only known a matter of days.

"Ah no. The thing is, my mother lives in absolute terror of me acting the flamboyant queer when, apart from the frock shop obviously, I've never shown an ounce of queendom in my life. My party piece, should I ever have been allowed to perform it, is actually 'Fire and Rain' by James Taylor, which is pretty much middle-of-the-road, chilled-out, middle-aged toot."

I thought of my standing, American flag flying over my head, singing 'The Star-Spangled Banner' while Auntie Dolores cheered on and I pondered on the ridiculousness of it all. I was allowed to be flamboyant but only because I fitted the mould.

"I'm sorry to hear all this," I offered pathetically. I knew there was little point in telling him that it would get better and that she would more than likely wake up one morning and realise that it was okay to have a gay son and that she had nothing to be embarrassed about. And then I realised how horrendous it must be for him to feel as if the very person he was was somehow embarrassing to the people who loved him most. Perhaps I was being all sappy American about it, or perhaps it was the horrors of the hangover knocking my emotions all out of kilter, but I felt tears well up in my eyes.

"It sucks," I offered as a tear slid down my cheek.

Sam reached across the table and squeezed my hand. "As I said, it's not there all the time. But some times are harder to deal with than others."

I knew even as he spoke that, while it was not there all the time, it clearly was always there at the back of his mind, no matter how hard he tried to push things back and ignore them. I knew that because I was the self-confessed queen of hiding things and pushing them to the back of my mind when I felt they were too uncomfortable to deal with. I knew why sometimes that was a necessary evil.

Drying my eyes and sipping from my coffee, I offered a wry smile. "I suppose sometimes you just learn to live with things."

* * *

The day my father was told his cancer was terminal was the worst day of my life. It was worse in many ways than the day he died because we had to face the great big unknown entity that was preparing to say goodbye to each other. How do you do that? How do they expect you to do that? How does anyone expect you to live with the knowledge that someone you love so very intensely is going to suffer and fade out in front of your very eyes? And I was expected to keep going – to keep grinning as people came in to place their cupcake or their celebration cakes order and all the while I wanted to scream at the top of my lungs to just stop, have some respect and start believing in the cruelty of life rather than the beauty of it.

When Elise kindly, and with a great deal of bravery, took me aside and told me my grief was not conducive to the cake-selling business and she would be only too happy to offer some support to me, I sagged with relief. I hung up my apron, probably not a minute too soon, and I stopped pretending. I gave in to the grief – at least in my private moments. And I would visit my father every day and bring him just one cupcake – whatever flavour he wanted. He would make his very best effort to eat it and to start with he managed well. As he grew weaker he left more and more but we kept up the pretence. We kept up my baking this cupcake every night and bringing it to him. He would smile and tell me I was the best baker in town. And I would smile and tell him he was the best daddy in the world and he would pick at a few crumbs and promise to eat more later. We never let on to each other that we knew he wouldn't, or couldn't eat it. That we knew it would go in the bin or my mother would have a small piece with her evening tea. We knew that, but we learned to live with the charade.

Craig had tried, gently and perhaps not so gently at times, to tell me that what I was doing was futile and maybe I should just forget about the cupcake tradition. But I couldn't do that. You can't do that. You have to keep living even when you feel as if every ounce inside of you is dying. You have to do something to keep up the pretence that it is just normal and that life isn't cruel. You have to find your ways of coping.

Sometimes, you just learn to live with things.

* * *

Sunday lunch involved an impossibly small table with eight chairs crammed around it. Elbows speared ribs, hands brushed together while reaching for the salt and pepper shakers and shoulders were hunched forward to make us as small as possible.

My mother, despite her late night, looked radiant at the top of the table. She sipped from a wineglass (I was on water – water was a decent enough drink for me after the night before) and revelled in the conversation. My head, still fuzzy, drifted in and out of the patter, occasionally glancing towards Sam to check that he was okay. He seemed fine. He dipped in and out of the conversation seamlessly while his mother smiled, almost beatific at the sight of her only son. He was talking old movies and doing manly Humphrey Bogart impressions while his mother laughed and jostled those beside her.

"He's a star," she muttered, over and over again. "My boy. Such a talent. Such a catch."

I glanced at Sam and he looked at me, eyebrows raised just a little as if to say 'I told you so'.

"You must have some lovely single friends, Annabel?" she asked.

And of course I did. I had Simon and William, either of whom would make a perfect partner for Sam, I would bet, but I figured that was not what she would want to hear.

"I do, but it would be a bit of a commute for a date," I offered, spearing a green bean with my fork and making great yummy noises so that hopefully she would change the topic of conversation.

"I suppose," Dolores huffed. "And one member of the family running off to America in search of the love of their life was tough enough to deal with."

My mother looked down at her plate.

"I still can't believe you did that," Uncle Hugh said to her. "My God, girl, it took some guts heading over the water on your own. Still, it all worked out in the end."

I looked at my mother again. Her head was still down, a slight blush on her cheeks. The conversation we'd had the day before played in my mind. The belief that I always had that she went to America because she was in love with my father had been rocked to its foundations. The version of events they had told me – or maybe they hadn't told me, maybe it was something I conjured up in my own mind – was that they had become pen pals through a mutual friend and had eventually fallen in love. My mother had moved from Ireland to be with him and the rest was history. And yesterday she had told me she hadn't even met him until "some years" after she reached the States.

"Yes," my mother said, interrupting my thoughts, "it all worked out in the end. Sure didn't I have all those happy years with Bob? Didn't we get our Annabel out of it?"

"Oh I know," Hugh said jovially, sipping from a glass of beer that Dolores had poured for him. By the redness in his cheeks I deduced it wasn't his first or perhaps he was still slightly drunk from the night before. "And besides, I never could warm to Ray anyway. Coming from the Base all that time – sitting at your mother's table and never so much as bringing a tin of Spam with him. Never could."

There was an audible intake of breath. I'm not sure if it was my mother, Dolores, Sam, myself or all of us. My mother put her knife and fork down; Dolores glared at Hugh. I tried to run through every Ray I ever knew in my life to see if the name meant anything. Sam looked at me – a look similar to the one I had given him when his mother had asked if I had any single friends. Hugh drank on oblivious.

"And you like a mad one, heading off out of the country. Fair play to you, Stella. Fair play."

"Hugh!" Dolores stage-whispered and I heard a thump as, I could only assume, her foot collided with his shin.

"For the love of God, woman!" he yelped as my mother lifted her plate, dinner still half eaten and walked to the kitchen.

"You eejit!" Dolores staged-whispered again before turning to me. "He's had a few, pet. Never you listen to him."

I nodded and then kind of shook my head, unsure of what my reaction should or could be at this stage.

Dolores stood up and, leaving her own dinner half eaten, followed my mother to the kitchen.

"I don't know what all the fuss is about," Hugh said, tucking in heartily to the meal in front of him. "It's not like it's any big deal. It's not any big secret."

I looked at him, not sure how to tell him it was a big deal and it was a big secret. I wasn't hungry any more, so I put my own knife and fork down and sat back in my chair.

"I didn't know any of this," I said softly. "I didn't know it at all."

"But there's no harm," Hugh said. "So your mammy was once in love with a marine? It was your dad she married. I just don't understand why anyone is getting so het up over a bit of ancient history."

"Dad," Sam said, gently, "maybe it's best we just change the subject."

"Women!" Uncle Hugh muttered and went back to his dinner. Over the sound of him clattering his knife and fork I could hear hints of Dolores' off-stage whisper to my mother. The house around me, with its whispers and my tipsy uncle and the whole pretending Sam was not gay thing suddenly got to me.

"I think I'll go for a short walk." I stood up, pushing my chair back.

Sam pushed his back too. "I'll go with you," he said.

"There's no need," I replied but I quickly realised there was a kind of need as I didn't know one street in Derry from the next and there was every chance I would get very lost and get myself into a whole panic.

"There might not be a need as such but I'd like to go with you anyway."

I nodded and slipped my jacket on, leaving the whisperers in the kitchen and Uncle Hugh polishing off what was left on Dolores' plate.

Stepping out in the sunshine, Sam steered me towards the bottom of the street. "There's a park down here. Not much of one, but it makes for a decent enough walk when you want to clear your head before you hit someone."

"I don't want to hit anyone," I said. "I-I j-just . . ." I stumbled over my words because the truth was that I didn't really know just what I wanted or how I felt. My relationship with Craig was all but in tatters. I was hung-over and in the horrors from the after-effects of the alcohol. I had just discovered the great love of my mother's life had not been my father as I had believed – or maybe it had been. Maybe this Ray, whoever he was, really was ancient history? But then as I thought of my mother on the beach – the snippets of her conversation with Dolores which I had overheard – I wondered if the past really was in the past.

"You just don't know your arse from your elbow, as we would say around these parts?"

"I think that sums it up perfectly," I said.

We walked on through the tall iron gates of the park, up a hill and through the dappled paths. Sitting on a bench, with Sam beside me, I breathed in and felt some of the tension release from my body.

"I always thought I would come to Ireland one day," I said. "That perhaps Craig and I would come here on honeymoon, or that I would bring Mom and Dad here for their golden wedding anniversary or the like. I had great dreams about it. I would plan a long trip, I figured. You know, see the *whole* country. Dublin, the Blarney stone, the sun go down on Galway Bay . . ."

"*On Galway Bay*!" Sam sang, making me smile.

"And we would come here, of course, and we would have the big family get-together, but it just didn't work out that way."

"Life can be a bitch like that," Sam said. "I know this is a strange holiday for you – not even a real holiday as such."

"I came here because my mother asked me to come with her. I couldn't say no. Not after what she had been through with Dad. And if I'm honest I was scared to leave her on her own, which was silly because of course she is with family. But in my mind we were her family, Dad and I. There was no one outside

65

of us. Such a contrast to the big extended family here . . . I'm just not used to it . . ."

"I can understand why you feel that way. This family of ours, we can be hard to take in one big dose. And you were thrown in at the deep end – dropped into enemy territory so to speak – not even the breathing space of a hotel room."

I blushed. "Your house is nice," I offered. "Really nice."

Sam laughed – a big, deep hearty laugh. "Oh, I know that. I may not have got the flamboyant-queen gene when they were handing out the gay points but I did get the interior-decorator genes."

"I'm glad to have you now. You've been very good to me."

"That's what family are for, kid," he said. "Now, let's walk around a little more until we can feel the sun warm our bones and then we will head back. We'll take this one day at a time. I'll leave the girls to run the shop for a few days – show you Northern Ireland and all it has to offer. Take your mother if she wants to go. Or leave her to deal with her own demons. When you're ready, we'll find out what we can about Ray – if you want to. And as for your man back in the States – maybe a little distance is just what the doctor ordered."

He put his arm around my waist as we walked on and I felt my head lean in towards his shoulder. The warmth of his body was comforting, but it was the warmth of his friendship which moved me to tears. I couldn't remember the last time I had hugged someone without over-thinking the very act of physical contact. With my father, every hug for the last few months had felt like a countdown. I hadn't wanted to let go and every time I did a part of me died because I knew we were on borrowed time. As I hugged my mother and felt her get frailer, her hugs a little colder, I felt her slip away from me too. In a different way of course. It was always my mother's way to put on her best practical face and get done what needed to be done. She didn't have time for hugs. Not because she was a bad person but because she didn't want to let even one chink of emotion in her armour. She had to stay strong.

With Craig, it had been almost worst of all. He hugged me and I wanted to hug him back but, well, I suppose I had a bit of my mother in me. I didn't want to let my emotions out. I probably was a cold fish to him, I admit it. As the weeks went on and every ounce of my emotional energy was focused on my father, I didn't have it to give elsewhere. The more I pushed Craig away the closer he wanted to be, until every hug felt like a precursor to some greater need of his that I couldn't meet.

When my father died, of course people hugged me, in that perfunctory, pat-on-the-back, sorry-for-your-loss kind of way. But not a real hug. Not one where I actually felt an ounce of warmth.

"You don't need to do that," I sniffed.

"What? Take time off work? Look, Annabel, I'd have offered before you even got here but I wasn't sure you weren't going to be a complete pain in the ass. I've sized you up a bit now and I think I could tolerate a little more of your company. Besides, I can't have you going back to the States remembering this as the worst holiday of your life, ever. I think there is a law against letting people leave this country with anything less than a good impression of it. You stick with me, kid. It'll all come good."

Chapter 9

You're going to think I'm mad, and I probably am. But I can't be apart from you one moment longer.

* * *

Hugh was snoring in an armchair when we got back. Dolores and my mother were back at the table, all dishes and traces of the dinner cleaned away. They were sipping from china cups and still talking in hushed tones when we arrived.

My mother looked at me, her faced filled with concern. "Anna, are you okay, pet? We weren't sure where you had gone."

"Sam here looked after me," I said. "I'm fine."

"I'm sorry about that – about you hearing about Ray like that."

"Mom," I said, "I didn't hear anything except that you once loved a man called Ray and he didn't bring Spam around to your house. As far as I'm concerned that's in the past." I really didn't need to hear the details – I didn't need to think of my mother as anything less than perfectly happy with my father.

She sighed and Dolores gave her a strange look – a look which made my heart sink to my boots. They weren't going to let it go.

"Annabel, why don't you have a seat?" Dolores said.

I felt a slight panic – the same slight panic that Sam had just helped me over – rise in me again as I sat down.

68

I looked at my mother, whose face was blazing, and back at Dolores who was staring at my mother with her eyebrows raised and face contorted into some sort of strange expression.

"The thing is," Dolores started when it was clear my mother was not going to say whatever it was Dolores wanted her to say, "it's not strictly entirely in the past. We've heard that there is a Naval Base reunion next week. Of course only a fraction of the men who served in Derry over the years will come to it . . . but he might well come."

I shrugged my shoulders. "That's no big deal. The fact he might be there doesn't affect us in any way."

My mother raised her head and looked at me. "I want to see him, Anna," she said softly. "I want to see him again."

* * *

Derry, September 1959

She wasn't meant to be there. She had never been before and hadn't been at all interested in the boys from the Base. She wasn't interested in men or looking for romance at all at that stage, having just broken up with her boyfriend of two years.

"Stella, please," said Dolores as she brushed her hair in the mirror. "Mammy won't let me go if you don't go with me and I really want to."

She looked back at Dolores, her younger sister by just eleven months, pleading with her, a pout so full on her lips that she looked as if she had been punched square in the face.

"You're only saying this because you want to see that Jimmy," Stella said, knowing full well her sister had been courted by a twenty-one-year-old from Maine and she was totally enamoured of him.

"I'll go with you and you'll leave me sitting on my own like an eejit all night while you make eyes at GI Jimmy."

"I won't, I promise," Dolores said. "And besides, other girls from the factory will be there too. Ivy and May are going."

"To see their own fellahs, no doubt." Stella continued brushing her hair, at least 100 strokes a night were required for it to retain its gloss. She'd read that in one of her magazines and she was on Day 8 of her new regime. It was time to pick herself up again, she thought, after her relationship with Larry hit the rocks. Everyone had been so convinced they would marry – she'd even been half convinced of it herself, even though, if she was honest, something about it never felt right. Or at least it never felt like it was meant to be – not how it looked in the pictures anyway. She was twenty and felt time was flying on. If she wanted to get married and settle down, she couldn't let her appearance slide.

"Sure Ivy doesn't have a fellah, but she's keen on one of the Yanks. Jimmy promised me that if you come out he'll have a date for you too. You won't be on your own."

Stella pulled a face as she dragged the brush through her hair for the 97th time.

"Please, Stella," Dolores pleaded. "Please!"

Rolling her eyes and lifting a bobby pin to start fixing her hair, Stella sighed. "Okay, Dolores, but no funny business. No late night. And don't even think about letting me sit on my own!"

* * *

Ray would later tell her he saw her that night. He saw her as soon as she walked into the Base Social Club, her hair done up in large pin curls, wearing a floral tea dress which hugged her curves and brushed against her legs.

She didn't know that, of course. She was just there to keep Dolores company and to make sure she didn't get into any trouble. When Jimmy's friend – a gangly, red-haired, loudmouth who called himself Dusty – insisted she had a drink, she ordered a Babycham, trying to look sophisticated even though she had never drunk before. She would have refused if she had known Dusty would see her accepting the drink as some sort of invitation to try and get fresh with her when all eyes were turned towards the band on the stage.

Stella spent most of the night trying to avoid talking to, or being groped by Dusty. She pulled Dolores and Ivy – who herself seemed to have taken quite a shine to Dusty – onto the dance floor in turn.

Ray would tell her later that when he saw her dance, her head thrown back, a peal of laughter ringing from her lips, he fell in love with her. That night, however, she didn't know he existed. She was just glad to get home and away from Dusty and his wandering hands. She swore she wouldn't go back to the Base again.

* * *

Derry, June 2010

"You're very cross with me," my mother said.

We were sitting in Auntie Dolores' good room. A gallery of family pictures stared down at us – watching us, judging us like they were an audience on some sort of Jerry Springer-esque chat show.

I shook my head even though I was very cross with my mother but she was always someone I was never able to express my anger to. Telling my mother that I was cross with her would be like kicking a puppy or punching a kitten. I'd only end up feeling worse for admitting my feelings.

"No, Mom, it's not that."

"You are, aren't you? I can't blame you, with me telling you I want to meet this man from my past."

A little shiver ran up my spine. I didn't like to think of my mother having a past – ever. I was happy enough to see her in the present. I still struggled to find the words to tell her how I felt and the pause was enough for her to jump in with another plea for me to tell her I was cross with her.

"You can tell me, Annabel. I know you are. I can see it written all over your face."

"Mom," I started, her pleading starting to really annoy me, "can we just leave it?"

She straightened up and had a quick glance at our forefathers on the walls around us.

"Actually, pet, I'm not sure we can. I don't know why you're so keen on burying things and moving on."

"Seems to me that's exactly what you did when it came to Dad," I snapped, not even realising what I had been about to say before it was out of my mouth to the imagined gasp of the gallery around us.

My mother swayed, just a little tiny bit, while she closed her eyes and opened them again, and I knew my words had hit hard. I felt a flush of heat rise from my neck to my face and I wanted to start apologising because being confrontational wasn't like me. But maybe this is what needed to be said. I *was* cross, if the truth be told.

"I deserved that," my mother said stoically. "And I don't blame you for your reaction. But it's not what you think and I've not forgotten your father."

"Well, that's good to know, after over forty years of marriage. Nice to know he still factors in there somewhere."

"That's not fair," my mother bit back at me. "I was never anything less than a loyal and loving wife to your father. I nursed him to the end. I did my duty by him." Her eyes were wide and her voice filled with emotion.

"You did your duty?" I spat the words at her. She "did her duty". She wasn't supposed to do her duty. She loved him. They loved each other. She couldn't be allowed to take that from me.

"Don't be like that, Anna," she said. "You know what I mean."

"No, Mom. I actually don't know what you mean at all. And

tell me this," I continued, a thought landing in my head, "did you know about the reunion before we booked this? Was this in the plan all along? Did you bring me here knowing this is what you would do?"

My mother looked at me. She didn't move her head and she didn't open her mouth but her silence gave me all the answer I needed. In that moment I didn't care if I looked like I was kicking a puppy dog or punching a kitten, my anger and hurt was rising in me so fast that it was all I could do to stand up and walk out of the room without taking the door off the hinges as I pulled it closed behind me.

"Sam!" I called. "Do you think we could go home now?"

* * *

"Do you think there is a limit to the number of times you can storm out of a room before it loses effect?"

"Technically you didn't storm the first time," Sam offered.

"It felt like a storm. And second time was a storm – all it was missing was a slamming of the door but I don't think your mom would have appreciated it."

He shrugged his shoulders and with a slight smile switched on the coffee machine. "She likes a bit of drama."

"Well, she got that with me. I feel a little mortified, to be honest. If there is a limit to storming out of a room I'm pretty sure I reached it. And the look on my mother's face! Jeez!"

I knew I was angry with her – and perhaps more than angry I was disappointed in her, but I had hated seeing her face as it dawned on her just how angry I was. I had hated seeing her face crumple just that little bit. She had regained her composure quickly, of course, but that crumple . . . God, it cut right into me.

I took the cup of coffee from Sam and sipped from it while my mind raced with a thousand different thoughts. If she had known about the reunion before she asked me to come back here, just a day after Dad's funeral, then how long had she known? How long had she been planning this? Had she spoken to Ray? Had she been thinking of him even as Dad took his last breath? The thought brought tears to my eyes, which I brushed away.

"Do you have anything stronger than coffee?" I asked Sam.

"I thought you didn't really drink?"

"Exceptional times, exceptional measures. And perhaps it will blot it all out a little bit?"

Sam sat down beside me. "Annabel, I do have drink, if you want some. I'll gladly open a bottle or a beer or whatever you want, but I'm worried about you blotting it all out a bit. Now I don't know you from Adam and you owe me nothing and you are well within your rights to tell me to frig off with myself, but do you really, really want to blot it out?"

"Yes," I nodded, thinking to myself he had just asked me the stupidest question since stupid questions began.

Of course I wanted to blot it out – why would I not want to blot it out? Life had been one big massive, unwelcome and relentless reality-check of late and there were certain things that I was more than happy to continue to blot out. Surely there were only so many crappy things any one person should have to deal with at any one time? Surely blotting things out was something I was absolutely entitled to. I'm sure some therapists would expressly say it was something I should do. Take whatever life was throwing at me in bite-size pieces.

"Blotting it out works for me," I said.

He looked unconvinced. "The problem with blotting it out, cousin of mine, is that it is still there. It doesn't go away because you cover it up. It just feels worse when you have a hangover afterwards."

"At the moment a hangover is preferable," I said. "I know you think I'm awfully cowardly. But I quite like the idea of a pause button now. If it will still be there after the hangover, there is no need to rush it. Still there is still there. We can't get away from it."

Chapter 10

Every second that I'm not with you, not hidden away together in our wee flat, is a minute when I feel emptier and lonelier than ever before.

* * *

Derry, September 1959

The second time Ray saw Stella Hegarty was a week later. He hadn't been able to get her out of his mind. He had been annoyed with himself. He had been determined to keep things professional during his station in Derry. He had seen his fellow marines fall for their share of Derry girls. He had seen how the girls had fawned over them as if they were some kind of movie stars with their exotic accents, a bit of money in their pockets and the promise of a new life in America. He wasn't interested in that. He just wanted to get through his time in Derry and get back to the States where he would demob and return to civilian life. His father already had a job lined up for him in an up-and-coming construction company. He had his eye on a girl back home. He was happy enough to wait for her.

At least he had been until he saw Stella Hegarty, her perfectly preened hair and her sparkling blue eyes and that nervous smile which told him she was out of her comfort zone. She had nursed the same drink for over an hour and when it was finished he noted she didn't order another. She had seemed bored, not

75

dazzled, or pretending to be dazzled by what was around her. She looked a little lost and Ray was always a sucker for a damsel in distress. And yet, he couldn't bring himself to go and talk to her. He had been so cross with himself. He had promised he would not fall for a local lady so had stayed back and not gone to speak to her, until the urge to say hello got too much for him. But of course she had gone by then. He saw it as some divine intervention and had consoled himself with the thought that it simply wasn't meant to be. And yet still he couldn't get her out of his mind.

So when he walked into The Diamond Bar and saw her immediately, her head thrown back in laughter, he felt his heartbeat quicken. She wasn't dressed up to the nines that day – he reckoned she must work in one of the local shirt factories and had not long come from work. She sat in a group of friends, laughing loudly at some story they were telling. Her laugh travelled across the smoky air of the bar and he found himself staring, until he was nudged in the ribs by his friend Mike who told him to put his tongue back in.

"Get a grip on yourself, man," Mike laughed, hauling him across the room to the bar and ordering him a pint of stout. "Is the Iceman melting? Which one is it has caught your eye?"

He felt protective of her – he didn't want to say which one. He didn't want his men ogling her. He didn't want her to become a topic of gossip or speculation. If he told them, Mike would no doubt make her the object of his own attention and he didn't want that. She seemed better than that.

"Shut up and drink your stout, Mike," he said, noting that his voice sounded a little strange and strangulated. God, he hadn't even spoken with her and she was already making him lose his senses. He couldn't show his men any sign of weakness. They would never let him forget it. But still he couldn't help but look across the room at the beautiful, mysterious girl and when he saw her get up from her seat and walk towards the bar, something in him shifted. He knew that he had to say something.

That he didn't really care what the men thought. That Mike might well make his life impossible for the next however-long, but it wouldn't be as tough as it would be if he let her get away.

"Can I buy you a drink?" he asked, his voice strangely croaky again.

She turned, looked at him suspiciously, and he thought she would tell him to get lost. But then she smiled, that smile which he already knew he would never tire of seeing.

"If you're offering," she said, her lilting accent making him smile too. Her cheeks were rosy. He imagined she was perhaps a little tipsy.

He bought her a drink, and one for each of her friends and helped her carry them back to her table. They didn't speak much. Just enough for her to tell him her name and that she worked in Tillies. While the work was hard, she said the "*craic*" was good. She didn't imagine she would be back at the Base, she told him, and his heart sank. It sounded cheesy, he knew that, but even in the dark surroundings of the bar with its smoky corners he felt a strange light inside of him and he could barely draw his eyes away from her face as she spoke, her voice quiet, her accent lilting.

He knew, just as he had known he had to speak to her in the first instance, that he had to persuade her to come to the Base again.

"Maybe I could change your mind?" he offered.

She blinked back at him. "I'm not sure," she said. "I'm not one of those girls who goes for GIs. I only went to the Base because my sister wanted me to – and it wasn't the nicest experience of my life." She blushed.

He watched the colour in her face rise, the gentle pink flush her cheeks and he felt his own flush in return.

"I can promise you a nicer experience," he said. "If you just trust me."

* * *

Claire Allan

Derry, June 2010

There were three missed calls from my mom on my cell. I say 'missed', but the truth was I hadn't missed them. I just chose to let them go to my answering service. I felt bad every time. I never refused my mother's calls – not even when I was sharing an intimate moment with Craig. If my cell rang and it was my mom then I would always answer it. But I, perhaps childishly, didn't want to just now. I reasoned with myself that it was because I didn't want to hurt her feelings even though I knew that she was being hurt by my not answering in the first place. It was a strange logic but it worked for me. I wanted to figure out how I felt, and what I would say. Perhaps more than that I wanted to work out what I wanted to know from now on in. I could ask her, I reasoned, to tell me no more. I'd happily wander the streets of Derry and drive the hills of Donegal. I'd accompany her on a day trip to Belfast and on that weekend she wanted in Dublin but I didn't need to know about Ray, about what had happened and, most especially about what she knew or didn't know about the big navy reunion before she booked her tickets.

I had called Craig the night before – probably inadvisably, considering I had consumed two glasses of wine and things were still quite strained between us. I had made a silly attempt to tell him what had happened – but I knew my words were jumbled, more through emotion than the influence of the wine.

"I don't know what to do," I had said, my voice tight, inwardly begging him to say the right thing and to come up with the right answer to how I was feeling even though I didn't know what it was myself. I had stood there, shivering in the garden of Sam's cottage, hauling the sleeves of Craig's oversized hoodie, which I had brought out with me, over my hands.

"Come home," he said, softly.

I couldn't bring myself to tell him that I didn't know where home was any more.

* * *

78

"This is it," Sam said, tapping a code into a panel in the wall and switching on the lights in Second Hand Rose.

I'll be honest, I was expecting a smell of moth balls despite what Sam had told me about the store being a little more vintage than thrift. I was expecting, despite his flawless interior design at home, a series of basement bargain tables, some roughly hung dresses and perhaps a basket or two of well-worn pairs of shoes tied together with twine or elastic.

Second Hand Rose was quite different. As Sam switched on the lights a series of exquisite white chandeliers dotted around a perfectly white ceiling lit up a beautiful space. The perfectly white ceiling matched the perfectly white walls, which were dotted with platinum-framed vintage mirrors and gorgeous art pieces I instantly coveted. Clothes were exquisitely displayed, open-fronted wardrobes styled to perfection holding a myriad of them, as did the distressed tables. Jewellery boxes spewed out cocktail rings and costume jewellery which glinted under the light of the chandeliers above. There was nothing tatty, nothing "old" about this place. As I walked through the store, touching the delicate fabrics, the soft laces and silky satins, I felt, dare I even say it, jealous of this place. That jealousy grew when I looked at Sam and saw that small smile of pride on his face. I recognised it. I had it myself the day Bake My Day opened – and indeed for the first few years. I'd loved work. I mean, I'd loved my work. I was sickeningly happy with all aspects of it, even the tax returns and the cleaning up after a major bake. Even when I was scraping crumbs of cupcakes off the floors after customers left for the day. The bakery was my safe place – my happy place. It was a very public sign of my success. I didn't have to work at creating a wonderful atmosphere because one just seemed to exist there. I had spent hours upon hours designing the place – choosing the colour schemes, the counter tops, designing the menu, choosing the cups and saucers, the plates and the napkins. I even took a stupid amount of pleasure in choosing the towels for the restrooms.

I could see looking around Second Hand Rose that Sam had that same passion for what he did – that we had that passion in common. Or at least we had had. Bake My Day was more of an afterthought to me these days and I wished it wasn't. I wanted that passion back.

"It's amazing," I told Sam and he laughed.

"It does the job," he replied. "We do well – and we run an online shop as well so we can source and sell items from around the world – all around the world." He switched on the Mac behind the counter and fired it up. "Let me show you what we have on order at the moment. This is pretty special. I'm putting together a display just for it. I may never sell it but I'm going to enjoy looking at it for sure."

He clicked on a few links and pulled up a picture of a stunning lace gown – which looked for all intents and purposes like a bridal gown. It had delicate lace ruffles and a softly structured bodice. Instinctively I wrapped my arms around my waist, imagining for just a second slipping into the gown and how it would make me feel. I glanced down at my jeans and my fitted T, my Converse boots and the belted cardigan I wore. My hands moved from my waist to my hair, roughly pulled a loose curl back behind my ear. The picture on the screen was just a dress – but I tried to remember the last time I wore a dress. Apart from my father's funeral, of course. When was the last time I had dressed up, fixed myself up, done my hair and my make-up, had the wow factor about myself?

"It's Dior," he said proudly, standing back. "Cost a fortune. Too much really. A little indulgence but I had to have it. I know I'm not one of those out-and-out screaming gay folk but I am partial to a bit of Dior and I just decided to treat myself."

"It's stunning," I muttered, embarrassed to find tears pricking my eyes.

"It is, isn't it?"

He smiled at me and I forced myself to breathe. I gazed at the screen and back at the shop around me. He shooed me away to have a look around while he attended to some paperwork.

"Don't worry!" he called from behind the desk. "I don't have much work to do and then we can head out for the day."

I was thinking this place reminded me of my mom's bedroom and dressing-up as a child. It felt nice. It felt safe. And it was pretty.

"Actually, can we stay here?" I said. "Remember when you said you'd set me to work here? I'll do it, you know. I like the pretty things. So many pretty things!"

"Well, if you're sure?" Sam seemed a little hesitant. "I don't want to take advantage."

"You're not," I said. "I know maybe I don't look the part for a glam chic boutique but this place is just amazing. I could easily while away a few hours."

"It's your holiday," he said, shrugging his shoulders. Then he decided to make my notion a little more bearable. "Choose something to wear," he said. "Make yourself more presentable. No offence or anything but I have a reputation to keep up and while jeans and Converse are perfectly acceptable attire to drive up to the Giant's Causeway in, they don't scream 'professional saleswoman'."

I nodded and absolutely didn't take offence. To be honest, having seen the interior of Second Hand Rose, I wanted to try on as much as would fit in my size so I had to hide a small smile of excitement from my face as Sam started working his way through the rails of clothing before lifting out a cotton sundress, with a delicate floral pattern, capped sleeves and a thin red belt around the waist.

He held it up to me. "Elfin," he said. "You could definitely get away with this and I'd guess it is near enough your size. This one is from the late 50s – a timeless wee number. I added the belt myself when it came into the shop. And you know I'm pretty sure I have some chunky beads that would go with it and maybe a pair of pumps."

Whirling around the shop he collected the other items and

directed me behind a curtain into a small changing room. I undressed, catching a glimpse of myself in the mirror. It wasn't a pretty sight. If the truth be told, and this wasn't something I was proud of, I had become quite skinny. My boobs had never been my strong point anyway, but they looked pathetic now – my bra a little too big. My face looked gaunt. I wasn't really used to gauntness – working around baked goods, tasting all those recipes, generally ensured a certain fullness to my features. The strong lights in the changing room showed the dark circles under my eyes and I pinched my cheeks to try and bring a little colour into them. Taking a deep breath I slipped into the dress, adding the red chunky beads and slipping my feet into a pair of cream pumps. I looked at myself again – it was an improvement. Tucking my hair behind my ears, I saw a hint of something I hadn't seen in a while and when I smiled at my reflection it didn't feel forced. It seemed bizarre that it was happening in the changing room of a small shop thousands of miles from home, but there it was – a spark of something, a recognition of the relatively carefree person I once was. Plus, the dress really did make my boobs look more impressive than they were. That was a start.

* * *

Derry, October 1959

"He seems lovely," Stella's mother had sniffed.

"He is," Stella said, trying to ignore the slight hesitation in her mother's voice.

It had been four weeks since Ray had persuaded Stella, against her better judgement, to let him take her out to the Base Social Club for a date. She had been a nervous wreck. It had been fair to say the date was the talk of her section in Tillies for a few days before. Her friends had told her that the Yanks were known for their generosity and for being gentlemen. She tried not to think of the one Yank who had become a little frisky with her. She knew, somehow, that Ray was different. She knew as soon as he spoke to her that he wasn't the kind who had a girl in every port and a different line for each of them. She knew that he was as much outside of his comfort zone as she was. He seemed shy, even though he was clearly a superior to some of the men around him.

"I can't have you with a bad impression of us Americans," he said. "I have our national pride to consider."

She knew by the way he smiled he hadn't only been thinking of national pride and a little part of her right there and then was smitten. In fact, she had told Dolores as much as they made their way home that evening, arms linked together.

"Ah, our wee Stella! Falling for a handsome Yank! I have to say he does have a look of Rock Hudson about him. He's one of the quiet ones, you know. The girls tell me he's not been out with one of us before. Keeps himself to himself. A few of the girls have made a play for him but he's always been distant. You have something special, Stella."

Stella had blushed. She had never considered herself to be anything anywhere near special, but as she walked home with Dolores she felt a little something light up in her. Maybe she wasn't as plain as she thought. Maybe she did have something to offer. She couldn't help but keep grinning as they arrived home and sat down for tea with her mother and father at the top of the table.

"You've a quare glow about you, our Stella," her daddy had said, taking her hand and squeezing it, but her mother had raised her eyebrow, looking between Stella and Dolores for a sign of what had her smiling so brightly.

Stella felt a giggle rise up inside of her and, even though her mother's expression was vaguely disapproving, she couldn't help but let it out.

"Be careful," her mother said before passing down the serving dish of peas. "Just be careful."

* * *

She had been careful. She had picked out her Sunday-best dress and a new pair of stockings. She had set her hair the night before and used some of the scent her granny had bought her the previous Christmas. She had persuaded Dolores to loan her a pair of sterling silver earrings and had allowed her to help her with her make-up. She wasn't really used to painting her face. She didn't have much cause to – maybe a bit of loose powder now and again, but that was that. When her transformation was complete, pan stick and blusher at the ready, she looked in the mirror and smiled. She didn't look half bad. The only fly in the ointment was the slightly threadbare coat she had to pull on over her dress. She was saving for a new one – a decent one she had seen in Austins' window, but it was beyond her means just then. So slightly threadbare would have to do and if Mr American Pride didn't like it then he could clear off with himself. Buttoning her coat tight, she lifted her bag and glanced again back at the mirror, or at least what she could see of it with Dolores in the way. Dolores, acting as chaperone and still after her very own Yank, was teasing a final curl on her head up with a hair slide. She looked pristine – well groomed and womanly. She had a figure straight out of a Hollywood movie. Stella brushed her hands down her coat, her small frame and flat chest only too obvious to her, and she took a deep breath. Sure Ray had asked her out – not the other way round. He had seen Dolores too, but he hadn't asked her. Or any of the other girls. Sure he was the Quiet Man, they said – the Base's answer to John Wayne. She looked away from Dolores and the mirror and urged her sister to get a move on. She never liked to be late – even though Dolores said there was no harm in keeping a man waiting. She had agreed to meet him at The Diamond and they would walk together to get a taxi to the Base – and she simply didn't like the thought of him standing there in the cold waiting for her and wondering if she would show up or not. He might be tempted to go on and she wouldn't like that.

"Dolores, you are beautiful. Can we go?"

Dolores laughed – a flirty laugh that Stella guessed she had been practising just for the night that lay head – and grabbed her own coat and put it on. "Come on then, what's keeping you?" she joked, heading towards the door and calling a quick goodbye to her mother and father as she led Stella out into the cool air and towards her first date with Ray.

* * *

"Stay close to me," he said, as they got out of their taxi and walked into the Base. She felt his hand reach for hers.

Normally Stella would have found this a little forward – but there was something about him that made her feel safe so she let him take it, the warmth of his hand on hers making her feel a little giddy.

She would have to keep her wits about her. She would have a soft drink – no Babycham. She felt giddy enough in his presence already and didn't trust herself.

She was happy to stay close to him, allowing him to lead her into the smoky room. All eyes were on them – most likely because this was the first time Ray had ever brought a girl back to the Base – and she felt her cheeks redden further. She would most definitely have to keep her wits about her.

They chatted amiably. She told him about her work in the shirt factory. She was sure her work as a folder wasn't nearly as exciting as a job that required you to travel the world as part of the US Marine corp but he listened anyway – seemingly fascinated by her daily activities: the early call, the flat-out work, the camaraderie among the workers – how they would sing through the day and share their gossip over their lunch. She held some stuff back – she didn't want him to think she was fishing for anything by telling him about the savings club or how she had bought her new dress on tick from the Chada brothers who had arrived in the street with their car full of beautiful clothes and had been set upon by every one of the neighbours' girls eager to have something nice to wear for the next big dance.

She sure as hell wasn't going to tell him that she had a hole patched up in the bottom of her shoe or that she slept with her threadbare coat over her in the winter to keep her warm. She didn't think he would understand. Sure wasn't he from America?

But when she talked to him, when they chatted and he told her about the town he lived in – which sounded like it came straight out of a Hollywood movie, she allowed herself to be transported away into a different world.

Ray had kissed her that night. Just on the cheek – but she had felt a pulse of warmth spread right through her body and, when she lay in bed later, unable to sleep as she watched the night sky through her bedroom window, she still felt the warmth of his lips on her face as if he was there kissing her still.

She knew then she was utterly, utterly smitten and by the way he had promised that he would be in touch with her again she knew he was smitten as well. She never doubted it. She never wondered would he be true to his word. When he said he would get a message to her through one of the other girls, or arrange a time to talk to her on the phone in Mrs McGinty's house, then he would do it. When the other girls tried to warn her about the Yanks – how they spoiled you but sometimes, perhaps, used you to stop them feeling lonely so far from home – she would smile and get on with her work because she knew Ray was different.

And in the four weeks that had followed he hadn't proved her wrong. He had swept her off her feet. Not with grand gestures or sweet talk – not that he couldn't sweet-talk. She would often replay the conversations they shared, walking along the quay, as she went to sleep at night. He had swept her away simply by listening – by being interested in everything she had to say, everything she felt. She could talk to him – in a way she couldn't talk to her mum or to Dolores or to any of the girls. And, if the truth be told, the twinkle in his blue eyes, and the soft lilt of his accent didn't hurt either. Ray never pushed her – he never expected anything more than she wanted to give. It was an innocent sort of a love affair – she would blush when some of the other girls would tell her what they got up to but that didn't mean hers wasn't as passionate an affair as any other.

Four weeks in, crossing the bridge hand in hand to the Waterside, the moon wild and bright in the sky casting rippling shadows over the Foyle, he told her he was falling for her. His words were carried off in the soft steam of the cold night and she almost reached out to grab them. She didn't want to reply – to tell him she wasn't falling for him at all – to tell him she had already fallen and didn't ever want to get back up. Or, more accurately, she didn't know how.

So when her mum sniffed over dinner and told her once again to be careful she had wanted to tell her that it was already much, much too late.

Chapter 11

How many ways are there to say sorry? I could say it from now until the day I die if that would make any difference.

* * *

Derry, June 2010

"You can come and work here every day," Sam said, handing me a cup of coffee and directing me to a chair in the corner of his small but perfectly formed staff room, leaving the store in the capable hands of one of his assistants. He was providing lunch, coffee and sandwiches from a nearby deli, and I had only then realised how hungry I was. The coffee smelled and tasted glorious and I sighed with pleasure as I took a long sip. They say the coffee just isn't as good outside of the States but this was a pretty damn good cup of Joe. The sandwich Sam had provided looked equally appealing. I almost fell on it, just about remembering my manners and the fact I was wearing a really lovely dress I didn't want to spill sandwich-filling down.

"Is it always this busy?" I asked. Mondays were traditionally a quiet day for Bake My Day. People seemed to start new weeks filled with good intentions to eat well, spend less money, be more restrained: this generally did not bode well for baked delicacies. We had our usual run of office orders, the lunch menus and birthday cakes, but no one splurged. Thursday and Friday, as the week hurtled towards its close would see us run off our feet.

"Not usually," he said, with a smile. "And definitely not on a Monday morning. I mean, we always have our share of browsers but they don't turn into hard sales all that often. I think it's you, cous, with your gift of the gab. Sell ice to the Eskimos, you could!"

I glowed with pride. It was more than nice to feel useful – to feel I was contributing positively in some way. And I liked how he called me 'cous'. It made me feel part of something bigger. I wanted to grab on to every notion of family I could find and hold it. Plus, I had loved every moment in the shop. I had loved mooching through the stock, chatting to customers, finding their weaknesses and aiming for them (in a nice way of course). I had smiled so many times in that one morning that I wondered if perhaps I was going through some sort of manic episode.

I had sent a message to Craig – even though I didn't know what was happening with us – just to say sorry and that I was happy and that I didn't know myself any more. Knowing Craig, he would, when he woke and saw the message, look at it with the same look of sad resignation he often did when looking at my messages. He tried to understand. He told me all the time that he really wanted to know what was going on in my head and so many times I had wanted to tell him he was wrong: he really, really didn't want to know. But instead I would smile. Was this wrong, I wondered as I gift-wrapped a glistening antique bracelet – destined to be a 40th birthday present for a dear friend of the purchaser – was it wrong that it felt easier to talk to him from thousands of miles away?

"It's easy to sell stock as beautiful as this," I said to Sam. "I feel as if I have stepped into my mother's old dressing-up box – she had some style."

"She still has style," he said with a smile. "I can see my mother giving her the evil eye with her smart suits and her coiffed hair."

"She does care about her appearance. Never likes to have a hair out of place. She would love this place – absolutely love it."

"We should invite her in," Sam said. "You know, when you aren't at each other's throats." He winked as he said it but he was right, of course. The fly in the ointment of an otherwise glorious morning had been the pangs of guilt about my mother and our last encounter.

Coffee and sandwich consumed, I could barely wait to get back on the shop floor.

"You have a strange idea of what a holiday is." Sam laughed and I smiled back.

"I suppose I have the luxury of not having worked in a while, not while Dad was sick anyway. And this isn't my everyday job. I don't have to worry about the overheads or the tax bills or keeping the place ticking over. I just get to come in and play shop. This is okay for me, honest."

"I don't understand it, but if you keep making sales like you did this morning I'll let you away with it."

He put our sandwich wrappers in the bin, wiped down the small table and we headed back to the store where several lunchtime shoppers were examining his latest stock.

It was clear he had repeat business, and it was clear that he was quite a draw himself. One female customer almost fell over herself to say hello to him as soon as he reappeared and I couldn't help but notice she was giving me a touch of the evil eye – as if I were a threat to her future happiness.

"Sam," she cooed, all batting eyelashes and coy smile, "I'm in need of something very special to get me through the weekend."

"And the weekend just over, Niamh. Tell me, was it a good one?" He winked and she giggled coquettishly.

I had to stifle my giggles. It was fun to see Sam in his element – at ease with his work and enjoying this casual flirtation even if he and I both knew it would never come to anything.

"A quiet weekend," she responded. "A few drinks with friends – nothing out of the ordinary. But I've a big night planned for Friday. There's a charity ball at the Belfray. You should come! Be part of our gang! It's for a good cause."

"Well, we'll see," Sam said. "I've visitors at the moment and he turned to nod towards me, which didn't seem to please this Niamh.

She straightened her back and forced on a smile which didn't stretch as far as her eyes.

"Visitors indeed. Aren't you the sly fox?"

I extended my hand and reluctantly she took it, her handshake soft and jelly-like as if she held me in the greatest disdain.

"Hi," I said. "I'm Annabel. Pleased to meet you."

"Annabel," she drawled my name. "That accent's not local."

"Nope," I smiled. "It's American. Florida, in fact. I'm just over for a short break and I offered to help Sam here out for a bit. Isn't this store just amazing?"

"Yes, amazing." She directed her answer to Sam and not me. Her eyes were searching for some sort of explanation from him and I wondered just how frequent a customer she was. She was dressed in a standard business suit – black fitted jacket and trousers, high boots, a flash of colour from a T-shirt under the jacket. On her fingers she wore an array of clunky cocktail rings, individual and flashy. The kind of rings I had spent the morning admiring in Sam's store.

"Annabel is my cousin," Sam offered. "Her first time back in Derry. She offered to help out today, mad article that she is."

I pulled a funny face – I suppose to show I was indeed a "mad article" even when I felt not one bit article-y and I wasn't even sure what he meant.

Niamh's shoulders relaxed and her expression changed, her smile seeming more genuine now. Without the hint of jealous bitch about her, it was even a nice smile.

"Ah, your first time in Derry! We should show you a great time – shouldn't we, Sam? A night out? Oh, let's! Let me pick something up here – come on, you always do help me pick the most fabulous pieces – and we can talk about it."

She linked her arm in Sam's and walked away, towing him

across the room to discuss making me feel welcome in Derry. Clearly she was more interested in making herself a feature in Sam's life, which was becoming more intriguing before my eyes.

I was folding and refolding some of Sam's stock when the little gold bell above the door tinkled again and I saw Auntie Dolores walk in, pausing just momentarily to look around her. She paused again when she saw me, clearly a little surprised at my new look.

"Hi, Auntie! Sam sorted my new look – something a little different. He's just with someone now . . ." I nodded my head towards the rear of the shop where Niamh was laughing uproariously, presumably at one of Sam's jokes. "He has quite the fan club."

I stopped myself just before I went on to make a comment about him playing for a different team or not being interested in that kind of thing. Auntie Dolores had a look on her face which told me that she wouldn't really appreciate wry attempts at humour.

"Is everything okay?" I asked. "You look a bit flustered."

She looked at me, her eyes travelling up and down my new look. "God, girl, you are the living image of your mother. I don't know how I didn't see it before, not so strongly anyway, but you couldn't look more like her if you tried." Her eyes were misty and I felt myself flush.

"Auntie, is everything okay?" I repeated.

"Darling girl," she said, "we really need to talk. Can Sam spare you?" She tugged at my arm, not waiting for my response, and called to Sam: "I'm stealing Annabel for a while, Sam!"

Despite now knowing that I was in fact only Sam's cousin, Niamh almost jumped the height of herself in glee at this news while Auntie Dolores grabbed my denim jacket – which looked a little at odds with my vintage ensemble – and hurried me out of the door.

"Let's go for a walk," she said, turning to walk up Pump Street towards the tall cathedral, which looked out over the city's walls. "I need to get to know you a little better, pet, and I think I'd like to fill you in on a few things too." She said the words softly but there was a part of me that still felt as though I was walking headlong into an interrogation. "The Walls are lovely, aren't they? You see almost all of Derry from here. I never get tired of walking them – except in winter. The ice doesn't make them very pleasant."

She laughed, a deep throaty giggle, and I couldn't help but smile. I'm not entirely sure, however, if I was smiling out of an awkward sense of responsibility. The undercurrent that Auntie Dolores was cross with me was bubbling under the surface.

"Mom and I walked here the other day. She was keen to show it off."

"Your mammy always loved going for walks," Dolores sniffed as we walked on. "I'd say that's why she has the legs she has. The envy of the factory floor, she was. Miss Lovely Legs 1959 if I remember correctly. We might be sisters but we weren't from the same gene pool when it came to our legs – I've them cankle things. Isn't that what you young ones call them? And my feet swell up in the heat, but I'm sure you don't need to know about that." She smiled. "No one needs to know about that. But yes, I suppose there wasn't much else to do but your mammy walked everywhere – and she and Ray, I'm sure they walked the length and breadth of this city."

I bristled at the mention of *his* name and I felt Dolores rest her hand on my arm.

"I know this must be very difficult for you, pet," she said softly.

"You've no idea," I said with more force than I intended. "I love my father." The words stuck in my throat, bringing a bubble of emotion I had been trying to bury to the fore. "I loved him. I am a daddy's girl and all this time I thought it was just us three and that we were solid. I thought it was just us. This feels like the biggest betrayal of him. He's only gone a few weeks . . . and we're here . . . doing this and she didn't even tell me."

A tear slid down my cheek and I brushed it away, annoyed that I was crying here in public, ruining the look of this lovely outfit, embarrassing myself, letting my daddy down by not being strong and keeping it together.

"Aw, pet," she said. "Look, I know. I know what it is like to be a daddy's girl. I was the biggest daddy's girl in Derry. Your granda – you would have loved him. In my eyes there was no man like him and when he went . . . I couldn't breathe. None of us could. It tore us apart for a long time. I know the pain, doll. I know what it is like – when your hero is gone."

I was beat then and the tears that had been sliding turned into a full-on waterfall which I was powerless to stop. In fact the weight of the grief I felt at that moment was so, so heavy that it threatened to push me directly to the floor and I felt my knees buckle.

Dolores took my arm and pulled me into a hug – right there in view of the tourists who walked by, their cameras clicking at the Bogside below us and no doubt probably in our direction too at the drama unfolding in front of them. I allowed her to hug me, allowed myself to feel the warmth of her arms around my body holding me up.

"Shush," she soothed. "It's okay, pet. It will be okay. We only miss them so much because we loved them so much and sure there is nothing wrong with loving someone that much."

Gently, slowly, she guided me to some stone steps where we sat down. Reaching into her pocket she handed me a tissue and allowed me to rest my head against her shoulder until I felt able to speak again without turning into a snot-filled, sob-racked mess.

"I just don't understand it," I said. "Her bringing me here. He's hardly gone and she had to have known about this before, so it means she had to have been thinking about this – about coming back to meet *him* – while my father was lying there, trying to hold on." I surprised myself by how calm I sounded because even as I said the words it felt, once again, as if I was being slapped across the face.

Dolores sighed, looked ahead, as if she were composing her thoughts into coherent sentences. "It's not as simple as it all seems – it's not as calculated as it seems. I'm not defending her – I can see how it seems as if I am – but I told her, I told her this was not the best way . . . But you see, pet, when you are our age you don't have the luxury of waiting for a suitable time. You can't wait till a suitable period of grieving has elapsed. And when she heard of the reunion – she couldn't resist. This could be the only chance, before Ray Dawson would disappear back into the ether and she would never see him again."

"But she hadn't seen him in years, had she?" I said, the thought crossing my mind that maybe she had – maybe they had stayed in touch. I felt myself sag momentarily with relief as she shook her head.

"No, pet. She hasn't. She hasn't seen him, God, it must be fifty years. It was well before she met your dad. I promise you."

"So why now? Why not let bygones be bygones? Did she not love my daddy? Was he not enough?"

Dolores breathed in again. It was clear she was a woman who never spoke before thinking – even if Sam had made me feel like she was living somewhere in the moral Dark Ages.

"She loved your daddy. You know that, in your heart you know that. Please don't doubt it. But the thing with Ray, it was just something . . . It was one of those big love affairs – you know the kind you read about in books, or see in movies. It was a different time – a different era and they were the talk of this town for long enough. I suppose even when that doesn't work out – when it falls apart, and we all had our part to play in it falling apart – you don't forget it. Your mammy moved on. She was in love with your daddy – and she was very happy with him and never regretted any moment of her marriage with him – but with Ray, it was . . ."

"Different?" I offered, tiring of the word. I'm sure there was a hint of scorn in my voice.

"Yes, different. Look, I can only tell you so much – your

mammy is the one who can tell you everything. You should let her tell you."

"I'm angry, Auntie Dolores," I said. "I hear what you are telling me. I know what you mean but, you know, sometimes you have to just let things go – you have to accept the timing is just rubbish and that things don't always work out the way you wanted or hoped."

"Your mammy knows that more than anyone, Annabel. You may not understand it all now but maybe you will. Don't you ever wonder about what could have been? Has everything all worked out exactly how you wanted in your life?"

It felt like a low blow, except of course I was smart enough to realise that Dolores knew relatively little about my life. She knew what my mother had told her – that proud boasting about the successful business I had set up, the fact that I was in a long-term relationship with a man I had heard my mother describe as "a decent sort".

Then again, asking a woman several weeks after the loss of her father had she ever wished things had turned out differently was slightly insensitive.

"Of course I wish some things could be different," I said. "But you don't get do-overs. This is not elementary school. We are not wandering about just out of kindergarten shouting 'No take backs!' – we have to move on."

"But if you could, Annabel, would you not like a do-over on something?" She let her words hang in the air before standing up and walking on. "Talk to her, doll. Just talk to her."

Chapter 12

So much of who I am is because of who you made me. Who we made each other. I can't just forget that – I never will.

* * *

Derry, November 1959

It was a bold move. One that Ray knew would have had the men at the Base talking – those who knew about him anyway. It was a move that, if Stella's parents had found out – would have seen him run out of town. He didn't even know how Stella would react to the proposition but he knew that she loved to spend time with him as much as he loved to spend time with her. He knew how their time together was precious to them both and how they longed to have more time together – a place to sit and talk, to hold hands, to kiss, to be lost in a moment, together.

Everything about their time together was strange – a mix of the wonderful experience of falling in love while trying to cram as much as they could into those stolen moments together. He knew his station in Derry wasn't permanent and the clock was already ticking until he was demobbed. He didn't know what would happen to them then. But as every day passed he started to realise more and more that he could not ever be without her.

Ray was keenly, painfully, aware that Stella's heart was in Derry – with her family and friends. He wasn't sure, even though he knew she felt as strongly for him as he did for her, if she would come with him if he asked. He would chide himself as he lay in bed at night in the Base. Here he was, a marine – the toughest of the tough – and he was being turned into a soft touch by a bloody woman. He was trained to face the fiercest warriors in the world but he was scared of asking the woman he had fallen head over heels in love with to marry him – terrified she would say no and his heart would be shattered. It was insane – that she had so much power over him. A smile and he was lost – more lost than he could ever have imagined being.

Sitting in Battisti's, a pot of tea in front of him with two cups, he felt nervous. He checked the time again and looked out the window to watch the people scurry along Ferryquay Street, going about their business. She would be here shortly and he knew that there was a chance she would slap him square across the face when he told her what he had in mind. Still, he thought with a sneaky smile, perhaps it was worth the risk. In the last two months they had spent as much time as they could together – going to the pictures and sharing a box of chocolates, walking the streets hand in hand, meeting for their cups of tea in Battisti's or Fiorentini's, sharing sneaky kisses and passionate embraces whenever they could – but he just wanted more. He couldn't believe it when Dusty had come to him with the proposition – that boy sure had a finger in every pie. Ray had to admire that kind of moxie. What Dusty wanted he got and, while Ray normally liked to keep his distance from someone who could let his mouth run off with him a little bit too much from time to time, he was glad to have been offered the chance to get in on the latest of Dusty's dodgy dealings.

The tinkle of the bell over the door alerted him to Stella's arrival. She was brushing the rain off her coat and removing her gloves while looking for him when his eyes met hers through the smoky, steamy air of the café. Even though the place was buzzing with chat, he could see only her smile and as he stood to greet her, kissing her softly on the cheek, he breathed in the scent of her perfume and grinned.

"You are a sight for sore eyes, Miss Stella Hegarty," he breathed, sitting down and reaching across the table to take her hand. Her skin was soft and the touch of his skin on hers sent shivers down his spine.

"You're a sight for sore eyes yourself," she smiled. "I've missed you."

"It's only been two days," he said with a smile, even though the two days had felt like a lifetime to him.

"Two days is a long time," she said, her voice soft and her eyes looking directly into his. "I've missed you."

"I've missed you too, sweetheart," he said, rubbing his thumb along the inside of her palm, revelling in this most innocent of contact. Her smile spoke a thousand words and he felt himself relax a little.

He poured their tea and they chatted. He told her of the last few days, she told him about work – how they had been singing their hearts out just that morning and gossiping before the supervisor had told them they needed to get on with their work and they had spent the rest of the day with their heads down, afraid to so much as talk about their weekend plans or discuss their work with each other. She was tired, she said, but glad to see him – but she couldn't stay too long. Her mother wanted her home to help with cleaning the house – they were having a family party that weekend and her mother wanted to make sure every inch of the house was gleaming.

"The good delph she keeps in the cabinet in the parlour, that needs to be cleaned and everything, even though no one will see it anyway." Stella laughed, rolling her eyes. "When mother gets a notion in her head, it's hard to shift."

"You shouldn't have to work like that, not after a long day in the factory," he said, feeling protective of her. She did look tired and she had to stifle a yawn as she sipped at her tea.

"Sure we all have to work hard – and it's the least my mother deserves. It's not easy, raising the six of us. A bit of hard work won't kill me."

He nodded and noticed her shift a little in her seat.

"Ray," she started, "look, I don't want to push you but Mother wants to know if you want to join us for the get-together. I know it's a lot to ask – meeting all the Hegarty clan together and they do like a good interrogation – but we've been walking out for a while and I suppose they want to know if your intentions are honourable."

He noted she had been talking to the table rather than to him and he blushed at the word 'honourable', especially given the proposition he had been planning to make to her. Feeling the blush rise from the back of his neck to his face, he forced a smile on his face. "If it means so much to you, of course I will go and meet your family. As long as they won't try and run me out of town with pitchforks for being an out-of-towner!"

"They may try and kill you with tea and kindness, but I'm assured they'll be leaving their pitchforks at the door."

She smiled again and he thought of how he always wanted to see her smile – how he couldn't imagine ever tiring of seeing how that smile crinkled her nose – how her head tilted a little to the side, how her blue eyes would flash at him beneath the longest eyelashes he had ever seen. He wanted to reach across the table and pull her into his arms there and then and kiss that smile, to feel those soft hands at the nape of his neck, to feel her body against his. It almost killed him not to do it and he knew he had to put his proposal to her, honourable or not.

"Stella," he said, thinking it was now or never, "I can't bear to be away from you. I need to see you more, while I am here. I need to see you more. Dusty, well, he and a few of the guys, are just renting a small flat – a bedsit really – and they want to know if we want a share. I'll cover the costs. Don't worry. It's just somewhere we can use to be together. Just somewhere warm, away from the world. No pressure . . ." He looked at her face for any sign of her reaction but she just blinked across the table at him. "Nothing dishonourable – just our own space away from the crowds. Just a place where no one else needs to know we are there."

He finished and looked at the table, his heart thumping against his chest. Mentally he prepared himself for a slap across the face. Would she think he was just like the other 'Yanks', only after one thing?

In a small voice she answered him, "I'd like that," and he felt her hand reach for his across the table. "I'd like that very much."

* * *

It wasn't much. Little more than a room really – a cold room, with a little damp in the corners when they first viewed it. It could do with a good clean so he and the boys had rolled up their sleeves. They couldn't bring the girls back to the place as it stood – so they had spent a precious afternoon's leave up to their elbows in soapy water, cleaning every surface.

"Are we going soft?" Dusty had asked, a soapy sponge in one hand, while Ray set about stocking the small kitchen area with teacups, plates and a brand new teapot.

The place was already looking spruced up and, once Ray had a fire burning, he could see how it could even be seen as quite cosy. Still he'd better hurry up and get changed if he was to get to the Hegartys' in time for the big family gathering. He couldn't believe how nervous it made him feel – then again the butterflies in the very pit of his stomach could have been down to his excitement at transforming this little flat into somewhere he could be well and truly alone with Stella.

She had warned him all about her family – how her father was a great big bear of a man who would either take to him or against him, with no grey areas. Her granny, she said, would quite possibly have a Babycham and perhaps start singing. Her mother would have an air of calm about her but would go into a flap when she was in the kitchen – if he wanted to get on her good side he should offer to help even though she would refuse his offer. There would be little in the way of drinking, but he should take a stout to be sociable even though he didn't really enjoy stout.

Normally Ray was quite a confident man. Not arrogant – he had never been accused of that – but he could hold himself in a room of people. But he knew that this was a very different room of people – people he needed to impress. He didn't want to make a show of himself in front of Stella – to embarrass her – and he knew he would have to work extra hard to try and take in the accents around him. Derry people, they sure spoke fast. And there was to be a whole room of them who apparently saw him as the guest of honour. He had gathered what he could at the Base – a tin of biscuits, some chocolate, even a bottle of whiskey for Stella's father – determined to make a good impression.

Stella was nervous too, she had confided. He supposed she knew that, if her family didn't take to him, his time with her would be even more limited than it already was set to be. That was not something he wanted to contemplate. If things went well – well, if the bottle of Scotch went down well with her father – he had started to contemplate chancing his arm and asking her the big question. The thought of it made his hands clammy and his heart beat a little faster – but, he realised with a bit of a smile, in a good way. Just as the thought of spending time with her in the flat made him feel almost delirious with happiness.

He brushed his hair, slicked on some Brylcreem and glanced in the mirror. That night, in Derry, there was everything to play for.

* * *

It was Dolores who answered the door. Ray sometimes wondered how they were sisters – they didn't resemble each other at all, apart from perhaps having the same wide blue eyes. Dolores was shorter, a little plumper, and definitely more confident than her sister. He had seen how she would spend her nights at the Corinthian dancing – the two sisters laughing together but Dolores leading the charge when it came to starting the obligatory sing-song as the lights went up.

She greeted him at the door with a huge smile before pulling him into a hug. "Good man yourself!" she cheered, eyeing the bottle of Scotch he had brought with him. "That will go down well with the relatives. You know how to get your feet under the table. Stella will be down in a minute – putting a few finishing touches to her make-up. She never bothered much before she met you."

Dolores winked, and turned to lead him into the front room, which Stella had informed him before was the 'good room'. Yes, she had given him a crash course in Derry etiquette – telling him the good room was reserved for special occasions such as the visit of the priest, a family gathering or indeed a wake. He had shuddered at the thought of a wake – that was an Irish tradition he couldn't quite understand, but Stella had assured him that a wake was actually quite healing. Still, as he walked into the room he couldn't get the notion out of his head that her grandmother had been laid out there just a few months before – a corpse among the good china and with a semi-gruesome picture of the Sacred Heart staring down at her.

There was a buzz in the room – the chatter of friends and family, laughing and joking, smoke thick in the air and the clatter of teacups and stout glasses. He wished Stella was by his side – it felt strange, alien even – to be led into this room when she was still upstairs. That's not to mention the fact that he longed to see her – to tell her, when he could, when no one else was listening – how the flat was ready. The clatter of noise quietened as he walked in – all eyes were on him and he felt horribly self-conscious. Conscious of his height, his uniform, his accent. Conscious of the fact that when he thought about it he didn't really fit in here at all and, if he had his way, he would take away one of their own – one who did fit in.

"Well, well, if it's not Yankee Doodle Dandy," a gruff man in a flat cap and a tweed suit said, standing up and straightening himself before he walked across the room. "Here, everyone, here is the man who has been courting our wee Stella. Well, sure

103

doesn't he look smart?" Without introducing himself the man thrust a large, meaty hand in Ray's direction, grabbing hold of his hand and shaking hard, his grip firm.

Ray smiled back, feeling his bones crush. "Pleased to meet you," he said, still unsure of who he was talking to.

"Daddy, leave him down!" Dolores laughed.

Ray realised he was face to face with Ernest Hegarty – the man who he most needed to impress in that room. Suddenly it was as if the cat had got his tongue and he could not find the right words to speak – so he stayed dumb, thinking it was better, perhaps, to have people think you an idiot than to open your mouth and confirm it.

"Ray here has brought you something, Daddy," Dolores smiled, while a small woman, in a floral dress with her hair just a little out of place, stepped forward to stand beside Ernest.

"Dolores, that's lovely of him," she said, "but would you ever go and tell your sister her gentleman friend is here. I'm sure he feels as if he has been dropped in the middle of a war zone with not a friendly face to look at." The woman smiled – and just like Stella that smile of hers crinkled her nose and extended to her eyes.

"You must be Kathleen?" he said, offering his hand and not sure at all if he should be calling her 'Kathleen' or 'Mrs Hegarty'. Immediately he cursed himself for being so informal. What a first impression he was making – standing gawping like some idiot and being over-familiar. His palms were sweating now more than they should and everyone in the room, although they were all pretending to have their own conversations in hushed tones, was clearly looking to see what faux pas he would make next.

"Yes, I am indeed Kathleen," the woman replied, putting her hand to her head to push back the loose curl which had fallen forward. "And it's lovely to have you in our home. Stella has spoken very highly of you – she's walking around with her head in the clouds these last few weeks. You've made your mark – she doesn't give away her affection easily."

Kathleen's words were warm and her tone soft. The smile remained on her face but he wasn't blind to the implications of what she was saying. Treat Stella nice – she's a gentle soul. He wished he could tell her there and then that the last thing he ever wanted to do, ever, was to hurt this girl who had stolen his heart. Instead, blushing and self-conscious, he replied simply that he knew and that Stella was a credit to both her and her husband.

It was then he felt the gentle touch of her hand on his elbow and he turned around to see her before him – looking equally nervous. Should he kiss her? Shake her hand? Say hello? The eyes of everyone in the room were boring into them and he didn't know what to do and breathed a sigh of relief when she stood on her tiptoes and kissed him softly on the cheek.

"You came," she said, as if she had doubted that he would.

He looked at her, confused. Did she really not know by now that he would be there for her? That she was so quickly becoming his everything?

"Of course," he responded. "And I've been made very welcome."

"Not that welcome," Stella smiled. "Sure you don't even have a drink in your hand." She turned and called to her brother, a tall man two years her senior in a heavy jumper who looked him up and down suspiciously. "Peter, would you ever get Ray here a stout?"

"Just the one," Ray said, as Peter gruffly made his way out of the good room towards the kitchen. Ray made a mental note to keep his distance from him.

"Now, take your coat off, pull up a seat and try not to look so terrified," Stella smiled, taking the coat off him to put upstairs and directing him to one of the rickety-looking wooden chairs which had obviously been brought in from the kitchen for the occasion.

He was introduced one by one to the remainder of her family – her eldest brother James and her two young siblings, Michael, just nine and the baby of the family, six-year-old Seán.

The evening was fairly reserved. Stella sat beside him, drinking tea while he slowly made his way down his one stout. The room was warm with chatter and song, the tin of biscuits passed around with great glee. He offered to help when he deemed it appropriate – another shovel of coal on the fire perhaps or to carry the tray of teacups out to the kitchen, but he was told time and time again he was a guest and he was to take it easy. He guessed from conversation he had with Stella before it was more likely to be a case that outside of the good room, the Hegarty family didn't have much to show off and didn't want the Yank seeing that.

"They think all Americans are really rich," she had said.

He had tried to reassure her that that was not the case – that he was an ordinary man from an ordinary family. His father worked for the post office, his mother was a homemaker. They lived relatively simple lives. But, she had pointed out, a relatively simple life in America was still likely to be more exotic than a life in Derry – where there were eight of them crammed into a tiny house with one phone to service the whole street, where voting was not necessarily a right and a coat constituted an eiderdown on a cold night. He had probably never woken to ice on the inside of his windows or put paper in the bottom of his shoes to keep out the damp.

She had said all this light-heartedly, without a hint of bitterness in her voice. She was happy – her family was happy. There was always someone to talk to. He had his mom, his dad, his sister and that was it. And he couldn't remember the last time their house had rung with laughter like the Hegarty house on that night. He had found himself vowing to learn the words to the songs they were singing – to brush up on his history to discuss what they were discussing, to think of ways to get his feet under the table a little further and, when he looked to his side, to see Stella there, laughing and joking, teasing her brothers and sister, he thought of how much he wanted to be a part of all this. Forever. How he wanted to create his own family with Stella. Christ, he loved her.

As their evening drew to a close, Stella walked him to the corner of the street, delighted to be alone in his company after the evening that had passed. She had noticed how he had looked at her, a smile always on his face, his eyes filled with love. She realised she had been smiling back at him and felt just as in love. She realised, she supposed, though she pushed the thought to the back of her mind, that they were perhaps playing at romance – playing at house. Neither of them, she imagined, were ready for the talk about where this was all going – not really. They just knew how they felt – how they were in love and if they didn't think about it too much – the miles that would separate them at some stage – they could imagine it would all work out.

"Do I have the seal of approval?" Ray asked as they stood under the lamplight in the street.

"I think so," Stella replied. "You have mine anyway." She reached out and touched his cheek, her breath catching at the warmth of his skin.

"We'll be happy," he said, reaching for her hand and holding it to his cheek. "I will make you happy like this. Like your family. We will have a home ringing with love and laughter," he said. "If you let me . . ."

She silenced him with a kiss, her heart thumping at how she could be happy. How he could be her happy ending.

Chapter 13

Am I sounding desperate? If I am, it is because I am desperate.
So very desperate. Please, please, let me know you understand.
Let me know you forgive me.

* * *

Derry, June 2010

Things I would have done differently if I could? Sure we all have
regrets. Perhaps I would have tried harder at school. Perhaps I
would have tried to persuade my father to stay in touch with his
family more – but it was just his way that we were happy in our
own unit. Perhaps I would have pushed him to come back to
Ireland for a visit with my mother – perhaps she wouldn't feel
whatever longing she felt if she had been here before with him.

Perhaps, I thought as I walked back to Second Hand Rose,
mulling over Dolores' words, I wouldn't have held on to things
so tightly that didn't work any more. I would have, maybe, told
Craig it wasn't working and that while I loved him I wasn't sure
I was in love with him. I wasn't sure I ever had been, if the truth
be told. Yes, I had moments of affection, of what I thought was
love. I had moments of obsession when it seemed like the lyrics
of 'Groovy Kind of Love' were meant just for us – and moments
of lust. But shouldn't love be more? Shouldn't it be, even though
it pained me to think it, what my mother had with Ray – the
need to chase him down after all these years – something which,

even though she found happiness elsewhere, always stayed at the back of her mind – was always in her thoughts? I felt a surge of inner guilt, as if I was betraying both Craig and my father by even thinking this way, but the truth was there.

Craig and I – we were trying to fit together. We were desperately trying to make it work, and only in the end making it seem more desperate than it needed to be. My daddy always said I was too loyal – and this was to my detriment in this case. My head, and my heart, hurt thinking about it – thinking of the messages I had sent to Craig telling him that I was happy here. Just thinking about it made me ache for him – but not in a physical way but more because I knew the hurt I was going to cause him.

I pushed open the glass door into the warm, beautiful atmosphere of a shop that already felt a little like home.

"Was she tough on you? Mum can be tough," Sam said, looking up from his iPad and scanning my face for any sign of trauma.

I imagined the running make-up would give it away, so I rubbed at my face as if that would make it better.

"Not tough so much as, well . . . tough . . . but not in a bad way . . . I don't think," I jabbered. "But I'll take a few minutes and fix my face if that is okay."

"Ah now, a lunch break and taking a few minutes to fix your face. You just can't get the free staff these days," he said with a wink as I made to walk past him to the small staff room.

"Sam," I said, turning back to face him, "do you ever think that you really have no idea what you are doing with your life?"

"All the time," he said softly. "I just plod on and hope one day it clicks. I figure if you do no evil then someday the Karma Fairy has to pay you back in a nice way."

"I hope you are right," I said, walking on.

"So do I," his voice carried to me.

I looked in the mirror – the calm collected 50s-siren look Sam had created for me had faded more than a little. I took a wet wipe from my handbag and roughly rubbed it over my face before smacking my cheeks to try and bring a little colour into them. I quickly applied some very basic and not at all glamorous make-up, lifted my cell and sent my mother a quick message inviting her for dinner that evening – giving her the option of choosing where since I didn't know a thing about my surroundings. I was pretty sure that Sam wouldn't mind a night off from baby-sitting me. My cell bleeped back at me almost as soon as the message was sent – as if my mother had been sitting on it, waiting for me to message her. Of course she would love to see me for dinner. She was sorry. So sorry. And she would explain and make it up to me. And she loved me.

I had to allow myself the time to think properly about how I felt, so I simply texted back that I loved her too and would see her at seven. Now I just had to tell Sam I wanted to leave work early to get home and fix my face properly.

* * *

"Look, you can get me on my mobile if you need me," Sam said, typing his number into my cell so that I would have easy access to it. "I'm just meeting a few friends for coffee but if it all goes a bit tits-up, I can be there soon."

I thanked him and assured him that it was only my mother that I was meeting, but we both knew it was more than just a simple breaking of bread with a relative. We had chatted that afternoon in the shop – the mid-afternoon providing a lull in browsers and shoppers which freed us up to drink more coffee and gossip more.

"She must have really loved him," Sam said. "That's not to imply she didn't love your dad – but, wow, to come back to try and see him again, after all these years . . ."

"Unfinished business," I said, wondering would I ever feel so strongly about someone that even after 50 years I still felt as if a part of me was missing without them.

"Either that or the grief for your dad has sent her completely doolally," he offered with a smile and I suddenly wasn't sure which version of events I would prefer to be true.

I had left the fancy dress from earlier aside, despite Sam's protests that it made me look amazing, and had slipped into something a little more comfortable instead – some jeans from my suitcase, a fitted white T and a scarf from the shop he insisted I wore to make me look a little glam. "Fake it till you make it," he said, adding, "I know that sounds very Gok Wan and probably makes me sound more of a raging homosexual than I really am, but I like to see you look a little more confident, cousin – and if you can't feel it right now then you can at least look a little more glam."

I'd fixed my hair, put on some fresh make-up, slipped my feet into a pair of pumps and grabbed my cardigan from the end of the bed.

Sam drove me to the restaurant my mother had been assured would meet our supposed exacting standards. We didn't feel that we had to correct anyone by telling them we had no exacting standards and, with the exception of my father's funeral, I couldn't remember the last time we had eaten out.

My mother was standing, fidgeting with her hands, at the door of Brown's Restaurant as we pulled up.

"You know you can get me any time," Sam reminded me as I kissed him on the cheek and stepped out of the car.

My mother looked more diminished than I remembered even though it had been barely twenty-four hours since I had last seen her. She looked tired – perhaps even more tired than on the nights she had sat up by my father's bed, mopping his brow and adjusting his morphine through the night. She looked, well, vaguely lost and I felt the tables turn between us and I knew it was time for me to be the mom and her to be the child who needed a little bit of reassurance.

"You should have told me," I said, stepping out and hugging her. "You should have been able to tell me."

111

"I didn't know how," she muttered, allowing me to hug her. "I know I've been very foolish, Annabel, I know I have hurt you. I just didn't think – I was so caught up in everything and I needed to be here and somehow I thought I would find the words but they never came and before I knew it we were on the plane and it seemed real and scary and I didn't know how."

"One word at a time, Mom," I said, trying to hold back the mixed bag of feelings which were coursing through me. "Let's get a seat, and then just one word at a time."

* * *

"Your father and I never had secrets," my mom said while we waited for our bottle of wine to be brought to the table. "I don't want you to think I ever betrayed him, Annabel. I never did."

I didn't speak. If the truth be told, I wasn't sure I could speak.

"I loved your father very much but, and I know this will be hard for you to hear, he was gone from me a long time before he died. We knew that, him and I. We knew as he got sicker that what we always had had changed irreparably."

I felt tears sting at my eyes but I pushed them back, aware that the waitress would arrive soon with our bottle of Sauvignon and I didn't want to make yet another public show of myself. I nodded, not trusting myself to speak.

"I know you probably think who am I to carry on like this – at my age? That I should have more sense about me, that when he died a part of me should have lain down and died with him. And it did, you know, and it won't ever come back. There isn't a night since he died that I haven't cried myself to sleep – but it won't bring him back. Your dad and I knew this. He told me, pet – he told me that when he was gone I was to look for Ray. I was to look for him and get the closure I never had all these years. That doesn't mean to run off with him into the sunset – it just means to close the book on what happened all those years ago."

"So what did happen all those years ago, Mom? You loved

him. Presumably he loved you too – and what, it just didn't work out? That happens, you know. What I don't understand is why you have held on to it all these years."

"There's a part of you, Annabel, that always holds on to the first time you said goodbye. Especially when you didn't realise you were saying it at the time. Yes, I loved him. I loved the very bones of him – he gave me a confidence I never thought I could find. We were, I thought, a perfect match and we were bound for our happy ending. You know how you just know it's meant to be? When you don't have to question it? When you don't have to force it? You don't even have to think about it all that much – it's just there. It's just who we were. It was never meant to end – not the way it did anyway, and perhaps I have been a silly old woman to hold on to it all these years. But I never got to say what I needed to say."

She fished in her bag and pulled out a small sheaf of letters – old, crinkled, yellowing. "I never got to tell him I'm sorry. That's all I ever wanted to do. I broke his heart, Annabel. I broke his heart and I never got the chance to explain – not properly." She handed me the letters. "I don't expect you to take it all in – not straight away. But it's there – these are the letters I wrote after he went back to America. They were sent back to me . . . return to sender . . . unopened. I just wanted him to know I was sorry."

I handled them – they were now open – she had obviously reread them over the years. I wanted to hand them back to her straight away – felt as if I was seeing something I shouldn't be. But she was insistent as my hand pushed them back towards her.

"It was never simple, Annabel. And this? It isn't about love – not really. Not love now. I'm not silly, I'm not some hopeless romantic. I know what real life is like, Annabel."

She spoke in hushed, rushed tones as if she was telling me off, as if embarrassed at the same time, and I supposed this was awkward for her – discussing her love life with me.

She took a deep breath. "Ray wanted me to go with him to America. We were to be married. He had organised my passport.

He had given me money for a dress – a beautiful lace dress which I never dreamed I could have owned. We had so little, Annabel – I don't think you will ever understand how little we had. And he promised me the world – and I believed him. I believed more than anything that he could deliver it. But it was me who backed out. And when I went to find him it was too late. I don't want it to be too late again. All this time – all these years – I've regretted not being able to tell him – not properly. I never explained and he must have felt so betrayed. I want to make that right, you know."

I sat with my hand on the letters, wondering what full story would unfold in the reading. If it wouldn't have been deemed rude, I imagine I would have opened them there and then and started reading.

My mother's expression had become closed again – she was back to staring at her menu intently and, while I knew she wasn't taking in any of the words swimming before her, I also knew she wasn't going to be drawn further. The answers were in the letters, she'd said.

So first I had to try and get through dinner, even though my appetite had disappeared and my mouth was dry. The conversation would no doubt be stilted – how can you talk about the niceties when there is a giant big letter-shaped elephant in the room? I glanced at the menu in front of me, resolving to choose something light, preferably something which could be eaten quickly – hopefully my mother would do the same and we could both leave the awkwardness of this situation behind. I allowed the waitress to pour my wine, relieved to have someone else break the ice with something alcoholic. I nodded politely to her but she left all too soon. There is only so much small talk you can make with someone who clearly has other tables to serve and is under pressure in a busy restaurant. She left and I looked at my mother who sipped gingerly from her glass – following the first sip of wine by taking a sip of water. You know, just to make absolutely sure she didn't get drunk.

"So," she said, "how are you finding Sam? He seems a nice boy – well, man, I suppose. Is he looking after you?" My mother spoke in a sing-song voice with an air of forced jollity as if we hadn't just discussed her almost-fifty-year-old heartbreak, my father's death or how poor she had been growing up.

"He is, Mom," I said, realising it was better now to just play her at her own game. "He's lovely, very welcoming. We've really hit it off."

"Auntie Dolores never stops talking about him – how he makes her so proud. She just wishes he would settle down. Too old to be living the bachelor life. It's time for him to get married."

I gulped from the large glass of wine which had been put down in front of me. I decided it was best not to bring up the whole Sam-being-gay thing – one awkward conversation was enough. I simply nodded as if I agreed.

"Then again, don't you think it's about time you did too?" She looked at me intently over the menus. "You and Craig. You've been together a long time. Isn't it time you . . . well . . ."

"Peed or got off the pot?" I offered.

"No need for crudeness, Annabel," she chided.

"Mom, I don't think I can have this conversation with you now. My head is too busy. Just too busy."

"Life has taught me a lot of things, pet, and it's taught me regrets are hard to live with. That's all I'm saying." She put her menu down, gestured to the waitress that she was ready to order and adopted her sing-song voice again. "So, tell me about the shop!"

Chapter 14

I have nowhere else to write to but to here. I know you won't read this but still I hope, Ray, still I hope.

* * *

Derry, November 1959

Today was the day he was going to show her the flat. She had kept it secret from everyone – even Dolores. If there had been talk of a sailor's love nest she had feigned interest as if it was all news to her. Although her sister was always one to encourage her to live a little and push the boundaries, Stella wasn't quite sure if Dolores would see this as one boundary too far. They would be the talk of the town if anyone found out – and yet to her it was all innocent. She and Ray had spent so much time walking the streets, sneaking kisses in the movies when the lights were down and being under the watchful eye of all around them. This would just allow them the chance to be a little closer – to have time together, somewhere warm, somewhere cosy, somewhere private.

* * *

Ray had warned her it wasn't much. "Not more than a room really but it's dry and, when the fire is going, it's warm too." He had blushed as he spoke. "You know, one day, Stella, I hope to

116

give you more. What do you want? The porch swing? The picket fence? How many bedrooms? Name it – I'll get it for you. A big garden? A pool in the yard? Somewhere for the kids to play?"

She had held his hand as he talked, walking through the smoky streets, the late autumn rain beating off the ground and bouncing up, making her feet wet – and she could see it all now. Like something she could only imagine – something she had seen in the movies. She wasn't quite thinking of Tara from *Gone with the Wind* but perhaps the Bailey house from *It's a Wonderful Life*. She imagined living in a town just like Bedford Falls, close enough to the big city of Boston but quaint enough, with a strong community. Somewhere like home. Somewhere with a front gate and a neat lawn and maybe two bathrooms. Somewhere where there was no damp in the corners of the room and where it was warm enough to leave your coat downstairs even on a winter's night. Somewhere where every room was the good room. Ray made her believe she could have that and more than that – he made her believe she deserved it.

This flat, she thought, as he turned the key in the door and held it open for her, was just the first step towards that. It was just a stepping stone.

He hadn't been wrong when he said it was basic. It was little more than a box – and a cold box at that. She shivered as he went straight to light the fire which had already been set in the hearth. One stark, bare light bulb attempted to light the room. Two sash windows covered with heavy brown curtains faced out onto the street. A rickety table with two mismatching chairs sat by the wall while a single bed stood opposite, dressed with some thin blankets and a couple of cushions. A kitchen area, if you could even call it that, was against one wall: a small sink, a gas stove and a single cupboard providing the sum total of the provisions. A small sofa, which had seen much better days, sagged in front of the fire, the imprints from the seemingly considerable backsides of the previous owners quite obvious. The flames from the kindling licked around the coal, begging it to come to life.

It was as stark as it came but yet there were touches of homeliness too – signs that Ray and his men had tried to make it a little cosier for their girlfriends. There was a small wireless on a small table beside the decrepit sofa. On the table by the window a small vase contained a few flowers. The kettle on the stove was clearly new and beside the sink sat several new cups and a box of unopened tea. The place, while far from glamorous, was at least clean, Stella noted with relief.

"I know. I know. It's not much. It's not what you deserve," Ray said. "And it's a shared bathroom, down the hall. But we cleaned it – bleached the life out of it and there is no one else on this floor right now."

Stella took off her coat and walked to the kitchenette where she filled the kettle with water, lit the gas ring and started to make tea. Turning to face Ray – a thought that this could be her life crossed her mind, standing in a kitchen making a cup of tea for the man she loved and seeing him so eager to make her happy. She felt a warmth creep through to her very bones that was most certainly not caused by the small fire in the room.

"It's perfect, Ray," she said, walking towards him and taking his face in her hands.

She looked into his eyes. Okay, this wasn't Bedford Falls. Not yet anyway. This wasn't the porch swing and there was certainly no pool in the yard. There wasn't even a yard. But he had the Hollywood looks of a leading man and a twinkle in his eyes that let her know he loved her.

She kissed him then, a soft passionate embrace free from the watchful gaze of others. She felt his hand on the small of her back and felt the longing in the quickening of his breath. She pulled back, stroking his cheek and was surprised to feel that there were tears forming in her eyes. Stella Hegarty had never believed she could fall so completely and utterly in love. But more than that she had never thought anyone would ever love her back and certainly not in the way Ray did. She looked deep into his eyes and kissed him again, this time a little deeper, and she felt him pull her a little closer. It was only the whistle of the kettle letting them know that tea was ready that jolted them apart.

As she poured the two cups, her hands shaking a little and her breath still caught in her throat, she thought to herself that nothing that could happen in her entire lifetime could ever make her any less his.

* * *

They managed to escape to the flat once or twice a week and each time it became a little harder to leave. Stella knew it was play-acting – really. Yes, they had their plans and they talked of the future but she knew every time she entered that room and lit the fire, or made the tea or cuddled on the sofa, they were acting at something that wasn't quite theirs yet. There was something unspoken in each meeting even though she could talk to Ray in a way that she could never talk to anyone else.

Each kiss became a little more dangerous. Each touch became a little bit more charged. Each moment together made her fall deeper and deeper in love with him. She started to fear their meetings almost as much as she longed for them, knowing that all their good intentions could easily be thrown to the wind at the wrong moment. It would hurt her mother enough if she found out Stella was sneaking off to the flat at all – but if they made one wrong move, if God forbid she found herself pregnant – it would finish her mother off altogether.

Ray never pushed her. He never overstepped the mark but she knew it was what he wanted. If she was completely honest with herself it was what she wanted too. Each time she was with him it was harder to resist.

* * *

Molly Davidson wasn't the first of the factory girls to marry a marine. But somehow her wedding imprinted on Stella's mind like no other. Molly was eighteen – a natural beauty with an infectious laugh. She always arrived at work perfectly groomed and somehow managed, even after a long day over the smoother, to leave with her hair still completely in place. She had glossy dark hair which Stella secretly coveted. Her own hair was more of the flyaway kind and while she could tease it into submission it never quite had the Irish-beauty sheen of Molly's. She would make a beautiful bride and excitement was almost fever pitch as she waited for her papers to come through so that she could marry her beau before he returned to the States.

There was talk of little else in the factory and the week before her wedding she invited her girlfriends to her house where her mother was to throw a going-away party of sorts. As Stella arrived, Dolores by her side, Molly was almost giddy with excitement.

"Girls, you have to see all the bits and pieces I have for going away. David says I won't need all of it but my mammy and daddy and my aunts and uncles have been so kind. Come and see."

She led the Hegarty girls upstairs to the room she shared with three other sisters, where a large battered suitcase was sitting open on top of her bed. She started to pull out dresses, shoes, skirts and blouses. Then came the towels and the tea towels and the bed sheets for her marital home. Her own little dowry. Stella noted that even when all the items were back in the case, there was still room for more.

"Mammy has told me off for packing everything already," Molly said. "Says I'm jumping the gun and I'll have nothing to wear for the next week but sure I can just wring out my clothes at night and hang them out beside the fire. I like to see it all packed, makes it seem real, you know? This time next week I'll be a married woman and on my way to Boston, USA. I can barely believe it!"

She closed the suitcase over and hurried the girls to a tall mahogany wardrobe in the corner of the room and opened it. A simple white lace gown was hanging, with a short veil beside it, in a wardrobe that was otherwise almost empty.

"I know they say it is bad luck to show off your dress."

"Only to the groom," Dolores interjected.

"Well," Molly said, shaking her hair from her shoulders, "that's a good thing because I've been showing this to everyone in shouting distance. Trying to create a bit of excitement, you know?"

"You really know what you're doing, don't you?" Stella asked, sitting down on the edge of Molly's bed and rubbing her hand over the bobbly blanket. "You and David seem really happy. You've had a smile on your face since you met him."

"I have, haven't I?" Molly said with a smile. "But my mammy . . . well, she says she's happy for me but she's walking around this last few days like she's at a wake. Says she doesn't know how she is going to cope when I'm gone. I told her I'm only going to America – not dying or anything – but she said I might as well be dead for her." The smile wavered briefly on Molly's face as she ran the lace of her veil through her fingers.

Stella couldn't help but think, even though Molly was only a couple of years younger than she was, that she looked almost childlike there in the shadow of the wardrobe, running her hands over the veil as if she was playing dress-up.

"Well, I'll hardly be dead. Sure I'll be with David and his mammy will look after me. I will write and David said we can even come back on holiday. I don't understand why she's getting so upset."

Stella sat still on the bed, wondering if Molly wanted some words of reassurance. She was sure David did love her, but she did feel a pang of emotion for Molly's mother who she had noticed when she arrived, trying a little too hard to smile.

"I'm sure she'll be fine," Dolores said. "Sure you were bound to leave home sometime. And David is a good man. Better than some of the men from around here anyway. Sure why wouldn't she want you to have the very best of everything? I know what

121

I would choose if I could! A life in America – the land of opportunity? Or another few years standing behind the smoothers before getting married to some eejit and raising a load of wains? God forbid!"

She said it with a laugh and Molly joined in before the two of them looked at Stella, seeking some sort of reassurance from her, she imagined.

"Sure you'll be off yourself if you continue doing such a strong line with Ray," Molly said. "I can loan you this dress – well, technically, it's not mine. It's Marie Moore's but she said people might as well get the wear out of it now that her day is done. She'll not wear it again. And Ray is from somewhere near Boston, isn't he? We could meet up! It would be great."

* * *

Despite her bluff or blunder Molly cried the day she left the factory. Stella and Dolores, and a few of the other girls, went to the chapel on the morning of her wedding to see her off. It was not long gone nine when Molly arrived, looking pale in her beautiful lace gown. She smiled – grinning at the girls as she hooked arms with her father and carried the bouquet, which seemed almost as big as she was, into the church while her mother, face fixed in a stare, followed behind.

"Her mammy looks disgusted," one of the factory girls whispered.

"I imagine she'll miss her," another said. "It's not like she's only moving up to the Creggan or somewhere. It's across a bloody ocean!"

"But she's in love. She'll be happy. I tell you this, if someone gave me the chance to go to the States instead of staying here, I'd be off like a shot."

Stella stood and listened. Even though it wasn't she who was marching up the aisle, there seemed a sort of finality about it. "I'm sure it will all work out," she said, finding her voice, before wrapping her coat around her and turning to walk back down Bishop Street with Dolores and on to Battisti's for a cup of tea. She was to meet Ray later – and she was sure that the nagging feeling in the pit of her stomach would disappear the minute she laid eyes on him. When she was with him everything seemed simple.

"Molly seems very happy," Dolores said as they walked. "She seems on cloud nine."

"She does," Stella conceded, thinking how Ray made her feel on cloud nine when she was with him. They existed in a bubble together and, well, being with him, if they stayed together – and she so desperately wanted them to stay together – was never going to be easy. She had always known that.

Chapter 15

I thought I had lost you once before – now I know I have and I don't know how I will pick myself up again.

* * *

Derry, December 1959

Christmas was coming. There was a hint of something special in the air as November nudged into December. He vowed to get some holly to hang on the door of the flat and she vowed to get some mistletoe.

The talk by and large, though, was of the Christmas ball in the City Hotel. All the marines at the Base would be going and, by the sound of it, most of them would be bringing a local girl on their arm. Stella was almost dizzy with excitement. She had never been inside the City Hotel – but she had heard of its grandness, the plush carpets, the polished silverware, the sparkling chandeliers. She would walk past it sometimes – peeking in the windows at how the other half lived, wondering if she would ever walk under the awning and in through the doors. She didn't have to stay there. She'd settle for afternoon tea, or, if she was feeling daring, a glass of champagne in the bar. She imagined herself dressed in the best finery Austins had to offer with her good coat on (imagine having more than one coat!) and her best leather shoes, inhaling deeply through a cigarette-holder as she threw her head back and laughed.

When Ray had told her of the ball – and told her that just like Cinderella she would be going – she almost jumped to her feet with excitement.

"Really? Me? In the City Hotel? Will it be terribly posh? Will there be dancing? Will you dance with me? Oh, I should set my hair beforehand – I might go to the hairdresser's and not just let Dolores loose with the curlers!" She had felt as if her heart would burst with excitement.

Looking at Ray she saw him smile softly back at her. She felt suddenly embarrassed – what kind of yokel was she showing herself to be? Getting all excited at the thought of a dinner dance in a hotel! She settled herself and straightened up on the chair. "Thank you for asking, Ray," she said calmly. "I'm sure it will be very nice."

He started to laugh, a deep throaty laugh.

It disconcerted her and she felt herself flush. "Why are you laughing?" she asked, crossing her arms across her chest – just as she had seen her own mother do a hundred times when cross.

"I'm just laughing because, Stella Hegarty, you make my heart sing! It's okay to be excited about going to the hotel. It will make a great change of scenery from the Base, and from here even," he said, gesturing around him. "I'm going to take you out in front of all the men and all the women and show you off. You think you're the only one excited? Aren't I going with the most beautiful girl in Derry?"

She felt her embarrassment fade, her anger dissipate as quickly as it had risen. She should have known by now she could be herself with Ray – over-excitement at the prospect of a big night out and all – and he wouldn't mind one bit.

"You say the nicest things," she said, kissing him softly on the forehead.

"I've one more nice thing to say," he replied, reaching behind him and handing her an envelope.

Confused, she looked at him and back at the brown manila in her hand. "What's this?"

"Open it and see," he said, pulling back from her and sitting up straighter.

Gingerly she tore at the paper and opened it to see a fifty-dollar note fall out.

"That should be enough to get you something special to wear," he said. "And to get you a fancy hair appointment – but, Stella, you could show up in a potato sack and you would still be my Stella. And I'd still be proud to show you off."

She looked at the money – more than she could have imagined without selling all her worldly goods, or saving up for months and months in the clothes club at the factory. Her mind drifted to the gowns she had seen in the window of Moore's and her heart thudded. She would feel like a princess and look like a princess.

"I can't," she stuttered, pushing the envelope back to him. "I can't afford to match a present like this. Sure I'll borrow a dress from one of my girlfriends . . . I'll be fine."

"Stella, it's almost Christmas. I don't know how much longer I'll be stationed here. I don't know how long they will see the need to have a base in Ireland. Let's just make it a perfect Christmas."

"You'll come to Christmas dinner?" she stuttered. "You won't be alone at the Base?"

"If they let me have leave," he said, closing her hands around the envelope. "Stella, I just want to make it special – selfishly, for me as well as you, if that makes it any easier to take the money. I just want to give you something. Lord knows, this place isn't up to much. I've long told you I want to give you the world. This is just me giving you a tiny piece of it to be getting on with."

* * *

Lying in bed that night, huddled close to Dolores for warmth, Stella thought of how magical Christmas would be. She couldn't sleep thinking of it, and thinking of the money in her bag. She could have her pick of the gowns from Moore's and maybe even a pair of good dancing shoes as well. If she was lucky there would be something left to hand into the house, although her mother had told her she would do no such thing.

"It's yours fair and square, pet," Kathleen Hegarty had said when her daughter walked through the door that night and showed her the present Ray had pressed into her hand. "If that young man of yours wants to treat you right, then who am I to stop him?" She was stoking the fire as Stella made them both a cup of tea.

"I think I might love him, Mammy," Stella said, even though she knew there was no 'might' about it. She did love him and she had told him so many times. Sometimes, she thought, when she was with him it was the only thought that seemed to clarify in her head. She would blurt it out when they were doing the silliest things – just walking, just talking about work, just sharing a cup of tea.

"Has he told you he loves you too?" her mother asked.

"Yes, Mammy, he has. He says he wants to give me the world."

She had noticed a short pause in her mother's raking of the fire before she resumed her task, trying to eek out the last hint of warmth from the fading embers.

"My darling Stella, you so deserve it – and more. Let him give you the world, but be careful that world isn't too much to handle."

Stella wasn't quite sure what her mother meant but she saw a certain sadness in her eyes, the same sadness she had seen in Molly's mother's eyes on the morning of her wedding.

"Mammy, do you think I'm being terribly foolish?" she took the poker from her mammy and continued with the work on the fire.

"Love is never foolish," her mother said. "He seems like a decent sort, and you don't walk away from decent sorts. You cherish them. I'm always going to have mixed feelings, pet. You are my girl. I love you with every breath in my body and it's not always easy for a mammy to see her children grow and move on in the world. But if he makes you happy then hang on to it with both hands."

Her mother's voice was gentle – soft and lilting. There was a melancholy to her tone that made Stella want to cry.

She placed the poker back by the hearth and sat down beside her mother, resting her head on her lap in the way she had done so many times as a child. She felt her mother instinctively start to stroke her hair.

"I love you, Mammy," she said. "I don't say that enough but I really do."

"I love you too, pet," her mammy replied and they sat there in companionable silence until the last ember had turned black and the room had cooled.

"Bedtime," her mother said softly, and Stella nodded before taking herself upstairs, changing and climbing into bed, dreaming of shopping for dresses and of being the belle of the ball.

* * *

Derry, June 2010

The evening with my mother was mostly made up of awkward silences, idle snippets of chit-chat which ended almost as soon as they started. I was almost dizzy with relief when the waiter offered us our bill, and I paid up and swallowed my complimentary after-dinner mint in record time. We waited for a taxi – me with the little bundle of letters in my hand, my mother staring out across the Peace Bridge, which now joined both sides of the city together.

"I have so many memories," she said as the taxi pulled up. "Not all of them are good, you know. I didn't always get things right. I may well still be getting things wrong now, but I don't want to hurt anyone."

She didn't look at me as she spoke. For a moment or two I wondered if she was talking to herself. I opened the door of the taxi for her and kissed her on the cheek before climbing into the front seat myself and listing off both Dolores' and Sam's addresses.

"Ah, Yanks," the taxi driver chirped. "We've a lot of Yanks about at the moment. Most of them come in those tours though – you know, roll in on a big coach and leave a couple of days later after trailing round the Walls. You're not that kind? Or are you here for the big Base Reunion? Lots of marines and their families about these days. I'm not knocking it – sure it's keeping me busy."

"No, we're visiting family," I offered, blushing, and I could feel my mother tense a little bit.

"I'm from here," my mother said, her accent softer with those stronger strains of Derry coming through. "Haven't been back in years . . . a lifetime really."

"A marine take you away from here?" the taxi driver, who I reckoned to be in his late fifties, asked. "You one of those GI brides I've been reading about in the *Derry Journal*?"

I glanced at my mother who had her eyes fixed straight ahead. "Something like that," she offered. "Something like that."

Sam wasn't home when I got back. So I walked into his kitchen and did exactly what he had told me to do when I first arrived – I set about making myself feel at home. I kicked off my shoes and opened his fridge to find a bottle of Pinot Grigio cooling. I had barely managed to force down a glass of wine at the restaurant and now I was feeling a little thirsty. I searched through his cupboards until I found the wineglasses and took one out, pouring a generous glass. I picked it up, and my bag, and walked through to my room where I sat on the bed and looked at the letters in front of me.

I always admired my mother's handwriting and here it was before me on the front of ten letters. Each with his name and address neatly written and her own return address, with her maiden name clearly printed, on the back. The paper was yellowed and thin. I was almost afraid to open them and read what they contained. I wished Sam was here – but then I couldn't expect him, the man I hadn't even known a few nights ago, to baby-sit me. That was ridiculous. I was a grown woman and the letters, while they might fill me in on the back story, were unlikely to tell me anything I didn't already know. Not the big stuff – like how my mother loved a man before she loved my father and how she had never really gotten over him. I sipped from my glass. If Craig were to disappear off the face of the planet that very second would I spend the next fifty years longing for closure? Pushing that thought away, because I didn't want to consider what the answer might be, I took another sip of wine and opened the first envelope, pulling out two sheets of crisp paper – my mother's neat handwriting filling them both.

Lying back on the pillows I started to read, started to try and see this from her perspective. Tried not to think too much about my father. Tried to understand what had brought her, me in tow, back here.

The words – neat loops and lines, gently slanting letters – were filled with love and raw emotion.

"You promised me the world. And I took yours from you . . ."

Chapter 16

I'm starting to understand now. I get that you want nothing more to do with me – but still there is a part of me which hopes that someday, in some way, I can make it better.

* * *

Derry, December 1959

When Stella put the dress on she felt as if she was living someone else's life. Someone infinitely more glamorous. Someone with decorum and deportment who belonged on the arm of a blue-eyed marine walking into a fancy hotel. It was cream organza – like nothing she had ever owned before. She imagined it was the sort of thing Doris Day would wear as she wooed Rock Hudson in one of their glossy movies. Her shoes were new, smart and satin-covered, pinching at her toes as she walked – not that she cared. A neighbour had loaned her a fur stole which she draped around her shoulders and her hair was coiffed with enough lacquer to make sure there was no chance of it shifting – not even if a hurricane were to blow the roof off the City Hotel and whirl them all off to Oz.

Ray came to pick her up at the house, bringing with him a box of chocolates for her mother, which made her blush like a schoolgirl.

"You're very good, Ray," her mother had swooned while her father had sat back on his chair laughing.

"Kathleen, a man walks in here in uniform and you lose the run of yourself. What are you like?"

"It's not just the uniform, Ernest, and well you know it. He brought chocolates too! And sure hasn't he our Stella looking like the belle of the ball?"

"He does indeed," Ernest said, smiling. "You look stunning, my dear."

Stella smiled warmly back at him before turning to Ray who was staring at her as if he had never seen her before.

"She looks more than stunning," Ray said softly. "I promise I'll look after her."

"You'd better," her mother laughed. "Or I'll send her brothers after you!"

"To be honest, ma'am," Ray said with a cheeky wink that made Stella's heart beat a little faster, "I'm more afraid of Dolores."

This of course prompted a howl of outrage from Dolores who thumped Ray playfully on the arm. "And so you should be, marine! I could beat any one of you in a fight."

"I don't doubt it for a moment," he had replied, rubbing his arm. "But I plan not to test that theory, if that's all right?"

"Don't hurt my sister and you won't have to," Dolores grinned, winking at Stella who couldn't help but smile back.

"I wouldn't," Ray said. "You have to believe that, all of you, because this girl is the best thing that has ever happened to me."

"God, man," Stella's daddy chirped, "you have it bad! These women are turning you soft!"

Stella couldn't help but smile more, as she wound her arm in Ray's and said her goodbyes to her parents. She had a feeling that night would be a special one.

"Be good!" her mother called after her as they headed out into the street to walk the short distance, over Ferryquay Street and down Shipquay Street, to the hotel.

The night was clear and crisp, the stars twinkling brightly above them.

"You really do look so beautiful," Ray said, stopping by a lamplight on Shipquay Street and pulling her close to him.

She felt the warmth of his body against hers and instinctively leaned into him, revelling in the feeling of him being so close to her. Feeling his hand on her neck, tipping her head towards his, she closed her eyes and allowed him to kiss her and she felt herself shiver with a longing she had been trying to push down for so long.

Breaking away from him she took a deep breath. "We need to go to the ball, Ray. This will never do," she said with a smile, stroking his cheek and the soft bristle where his beard was already starting to poke through again.

"No, I don't suppose it will," he said, brushing his lips softly against her forehead. "So as it is clear you're not going to let me whisk you away to the love nest instead, will we walk on?"

"Much as I would love to let you whisk me away to the love nest, it would be a sin before Holy God and His Mother not to show off this dress so I'm terribly sorry, but on we go!" She laughed as she spoke but felt secretly delighted that he had wanted to whisk her off in the first place.

"Let's go then, my lady," he said and on they walked.

The function room at the City Hotel did not disappoint, especially not with the Christmas decorations glinting in the light of the chandeliers. The room was buzzing with chat and laughter. Glasses clinked, smoke hung heavy in the air. She glanced around at her fellow guests – women dressed to the nines, scent liberally sprayed, not a hair of out of place – and she was glad of the effort she had made.

Ray guided her through the crowds, lifting two champagne flutes from a waiter as he went.

"Here," he said, handing her a glass, which she eyed suspiciously.

She had never tasted champagne – she wasn't sure it wouldn't make her giddy and lightheaded. She felt every inch the sophisticate and, she supposed, sophisticated ladies didn't turn down complimentary glasses of champagne.

"To us!" she said, raising her glass to Ray who raised his glass in return and, clinking it against hers, repeated "To us!" They both sipped and, as the bubbles tickled the back of her throat and her nose, she felt herself start to cough and splutter. As much as she tried to hold it in, she couldn't – the sharp taste of the champagne was clawing at her throat, making her eyes water. He would think she was such a hick, she thought as she, face blazing, looked at him to see that he too was spluttering and wiping his eyes with his free hand. He caught her gaze and laughed.

"Have you never had champagne before either?" he asked while trying to catch his breath.

"No," she replied. "It's not really a popular drink around these parts. We prefer a nice cup of tea."

"So do I," he laughed.

They sat their glasses on a nearby table and walked on to find their seats for the evening. "We make a good pair, Stella Hegarty," he said. "Let's just sit here and behave ourselves and try not to let anyone know we are not the kind of people who drink champagne with dinner every night."

He squeezed her hand and she relaxed again, the plush surroundings of the hotel not seeming so daunting any more. Sure she had Ray and he had her and it was going to be a wonderful night.

* * *

By half past eleven her feet throbbed so badly she longed to take her shoes off and rub at her soles. She had barely left the dance floor since the band had started playing – letting Ray whirl her around the floor and sharing a few dances with the girls from the factory who had accompanied their own boyfriends. The mood had been light and even though she had stayed with soft drinks since the champagne debacle, she felt slightly drunk and as if she were floating. In fact, it was only the dull ache in her feet that reminded her she was very much in the here and now. She sat down, leaning against Ray as he softly kissed her head.

"My feet ache," she mumbled. "You might have to carry me home at this rate."

"Your feet can't be sore – we've one last song to dance to. They promised me a slow one and I'm not leaving until I have led you around the floor one more time."

She winced at the thought but, then again, a few minutes in his arms, she reckoned, would be worth the pain.

Ray took her hand in his and led her to the dance floor as the strains of "I Only Have Eyes For You" started to ring out. Turning her to face him, he pulled her into an embrace and wordlessly they started moving in time with the music. She rested her head on his shoulder, allowing herself to relax into him and in that moment she thought she never wanted to be anywhere else, again, ever, but in his arms.

"Don't ever leave me," she whispered into his neck as they danced. "Please don't ever leave me."

"I won't," he answered, kissing her head softly. "Always and forever yours, Stella. Always."

She pulled away and looked up at him, saw that his eyes were moist, his face sincere, and she kissed him and they stood stock still amid the crowds moving around them. This was their perfect moment – sore feet and all – she would hold onto that moment over the years that followed.

* * *

It was Christmas Eve. Stella had been awake since gone seven. Kathleen Hegarty demanded certain standards of her house on Christmas morning so Christmas Eve was as hectic as it could be. By eleven, Stella had already run the bed linen through the mangle and had hung it on the clothes horse to dry. She had taken the rugs from the good room and out to the back garden and had beaten them to within an inch of their lives and now she was taking to the windows with vinegar and brown paper. Dolores was helping their younger brothers stick together paper chains to hang from the ceilings. Kathleen was busying herself plucking and preparing the turkey and peeling enough potatoes to feed a small army. There would be soup to be made, of course, and a ham to be boiled. And when the afternoon turned into evening Kathleen would set about baking her apple pies while Stella and Dolores made sure all the good clothes were dried and pressed for Mass in the morning. There wouldn't be a spoon unpolished or an ornament not dusted and by the time they all retired, after going to the McGlincheys' across the street for a small Christmas Eve drink and a mince pie, they would all near fall into their beds with exhaustion.

While it was a busy day, it was one Stella loved. She loved the routine, the tradition, the singing of carols. She loved nipping to the corner shop and greeting her neighbours with a 'Merry Christmas'. She loved the smell of the clothes drying around the fire, the smell of the furniture wax, the cooking smells and how the house came alive. And she especially loved it when her daddy would come home from working at the docks, after stopping off for a seasonal stout on the way home, and hand each of them a ten-bob note. Even though she was twenty – a grown woman – she still loved to see her daddy come home on Christmas Eve: it was then that Christmas really began.

That particular Christmas Eve was a little different, however. She was distracted and while she carried out the chores that she was assigned she couldn't help but feel her mind wander. Ray had told her he was to get a few hours off that afternoon from the Base and would be headed to their little love nest. She had told him, of course, that given the day that was in it, she was unlikely to be able to escape from the family but he had asked her to try. So now as she set about her chores and the usual Christmas Eve traditions, her mind was on her marine, alone in their flat, and she found it hard to find the same fervour for the preparations as she normally did.

When Kathleen asked her mid-afternoon to run to the shops for some yeast for the bread she nearly jumped with joy. If she was quick she could sneak to see him for even five minutes – a sneaky kiss – and be back home with no one being any the wiser. It was strange now – she seemed obsessed with him. When she wasn't with him, all she could think about was how he spoke, how he smelled, how he felt, and she felt bereft at every second of not being able to drink him in. She was almost euphoric at the thought of being able to sneak out to be with him and she ran full pelt to her bedroom where she took off her pinny, brushed her hair through and applied a little lipstick.

"Dear God, woman, you're only going to the shop – no need to tart yourself up!" Dolores had quipped as she walked into the room to see Stella spritz some perfume on her wrists and slip on her new coat.

"I don't see anything wrong with making an effort," Stella snapped, face blazing that Dolores had caught her.

"No, I suppose not," Dolores sniffed, aggrieved at the tone in her sister's voice. "It's just not really like you. Can it be our ugly duckling is turning into a swan after all these years? Sure you're always primping and preening yourself these days. It's a wonder any one of us can get near the mirror. But then again, it's usually when you are off to see Ray and you aren't seeing him till tomorrow . . ." Her voice trailed off.

Stella's blush rose again. Dolores could always see right through her and she was pretty sure her sister could see all that was going on in her mind right there and then.

"Will you promise not to tell?" she whispered as her sister moved closer. "I'm going to see him just for five minutes. I won't be long. I just need to see him. Can you cover for me if Mammy asks what's keeping me so long? I'll be as quick as I can. I promise."

"Stella Hegarty, you sly fox. Imagine you, nipping out for a wee rendezvous! My God, woman, this all so very romantic!"

"It sure is," Stella smiled back. "I'm in love, Dolores. I can't help it, and I don't care who knows."

"Apart from Mammy obviously, who would knock your pan in if she knew you were heading out to see your fancy man when there is still brass to be tackled and wains to be washed."

"I won't be long, I promise," Stella reassured her sister and, buttoning her coat, she slipped down the stairs and out of the front door with an extra spring in her step.

She ran towards Carlisle Road where she would see Ray. Her smile was as bright as the Christmas lights sparkling in the windows of her neighbours' houses.

Running up the stairs to the flat, her heart beat fast at the thought of spending just a few illicit moments with Ray. She smiled as she turned her key in the door and pushed it open.

But the flat was in darkness – not even a hint of an ember in the fire or a note to say he had been called away. Just a cold dark room, and her heart sank to her boots. There had to be a reason, she told herself. She never doubted him, not a minute, but she couldn't help but feel sorely disappointed. All day she had hoped for this moment and now he wasn't anywhere to be seen.

Despondently she left, heading to the shop to buy the yeast her mother would be waiting for and as she walked she decided to call the Base just to see what had happened. He would never let her down, there had to be an explanation. Something must have come up. She would settle herself if she could just speak to him and hear he was okay – and for him to tell her he would still come to Christmas dinner with the family.

She walked to the phone box, dropped a coin in the box and waited to be connected. When a friendly voice answered she asked to speak to Ray.

"Is that Stella?" the man on the other end asked.

"Yes, yes, it is."

"Hmm. I was sure he said he was going to be with you. Or, you know, at least to try and see you. He was quite keen."

Flustered, Stella wondered who she was talking to and asked the marine who he was.

"It's Dusty, ma'am," he said with his Southern drawl. "And as I've said, Ray's not here. He said he was going to, you know, the love shack."

Dusty laughed a full and filthy laugh which made Stella feel as if she was part of some dirty secret. This on top of the news that Ray wasn't even to be found at the Base made tears spring to her eyes.

"But he's not there," she said through her embarrassment.

"I don't know, ma'am. I know he was very flustered leaving. I probably shouldn't tell you this – I know he would have wanted to tell you himself – but we got our shipping-out orders. We leave in six weeks. He was in a state when he left. Said he had some business to sort out – but we kinda thought you were that business." The dirty laugh followed again.

Stella had to steady herself to avoid falling to the ground. Six weeks. Six weeks was no time – it wasn't enough. And where on earth was Ray? Where could he be? Why had he not come to her? She put the phone down without so much as saying goodbye and turned to walk home, her mind racing as fast as her heart was breaking. She was grateful for the evening closing in – that it hid her face and the tears that were sliding down her cheeks. Her feet were no longer light, her step no longer carefree. She felt as if she had the weight of the world on her shoulders and as if she might drop to the ground at any second and weep at the injustice of it all. He had come into her life, changed it in ways she could never have expected, and now he could be walking out of it again. Was it not too soon to make this work? Despite their love for each other. Was it not just too much – and if he wanted it – wanted her – where was he?

Her head hurting, she pushed open the front door to her house and slipped her coat off, the smells and sounds of Christmas Eve no longer comforting but now irritating her.

Her mother walked out of the kitchen, dusting her arms on her pinny. "Have you the yeast, love? I need to get this bread proving or I'll be at it all night."

Stella fell to the bottom step and shook her head. "I'm sorry, Mammy," she muttered through her tears. "I don't. I forgot. I'm sorry."

She sat there sobbing until she felt the soft hands of her mother around her shoulders. "Dear Lord, child. What's the matter? And it's only yeast, for goodness' sake. Sure I can probably borrow some from Mrs McGlinchey. What on earth has you in this state?"

"Oh Mammy!" she wailed, feeling a raw grief bubbling up from within her and making her very skin hurt. "I'm scared. I'm scared I'm going to lose him!"

Chapter 17

Perhaps there is nothing more to say, except always and forever. Always and forever will never change.

* * *

Derry, June 2010

I woke to light sneaking in through the blinds and to the sound of the street outside coming to life for the day. The traffic hummed along while the chatter of neighbours calling to each other reminded me that I was a long way from home. I lay there for a while with my eyes closed just trying to ground myself – remind myself where I was, why I was there and how it was turning out to be a very different vacation from the one I had envisaged.

I had slept pretty fitfully. My dreams were filled with a love story that until recently I hadn't even known of. I tried to piece together the notion of my mother with the woman who had written the letters. I don't think I had ever seen my mother write anything other than a note to my gym teacher to ask her to give me a pass from dodgeball for the day. And yet for an hour when I got home the previous night I had seen a different woman reveal herself to me – one who was so very deeply passionate. Who so wanted her love affair to work. Who had, by her own admission, made grave mistakes. I thought of the picture of my mother which hung in our den at home – a picture taken when she must have been no older than eighteen or nineteen. Her eyes were bright, her smile wide. She was a beauty. She still was a beauty, even at seventy. Elegant, assured if a little reserved, as if the world had broken her heart in some way and she never quite managed to piece it back together. Of course, now I knew that was the case. And I understood and my heart ached for her.

I prised my eyes open and stretched in the bed, my hand brushing against the letters I had been reading the night before. There were still five more to read but for now I supposed I needed a little break from the emotional intensity of what was before me. This tale of love, and him having to leave. And my poor mother heartbroken.

My head hurt and I wasn't sure if it was from the wine I had drunk or the crying I had done or just the internal game of volleyball I was playing in trying to make sense of it all and how I felt about it. As I had read my mother's words and become engrossed in her story I felt a nagging guilt that somehow I was betraying my father even though Mom had assured me time and time again that what she felt for Ray pre-dated how she felt for daddy. Was I to believe that really all she wanted was closure and a chance to explain? Could you feel that deeply for someone and ever really push it away?

I didn't know, I realised as I sat up and pulled the comforter back, because I didn't think I had ever felt that strongly in my life.

* * *

People often wondered why Craig and I had never married, or even got so far as to get engaged. When my father was diagnosed with cancer and especially when we knew it was terminal, people had started to get extra edgy around us. I had called into Bake My Day one afternoon – just to check over the books with Elise and make a few plans for cover. She had been working on a wedding cake – a three-tier affair, each layer a different flavour, and she had looked at it and then at me.

"Would you not consider it?" she asked as I sat down on the stool across the workbench from her.

"Consider what?"

She nodded towards the cake and perhaps I'm particularly dense or exceptionally stupid but I didn't catch on.

"Cake?" I offered. "I consider cake all the time. Sure cake is my business."

"Wedding cake," she offered again and still, because I am a dumb-ass, I didn't catch on.

I looked at her blankly.

"A wedding," she said, the frustration in her voice obvious. "You and Craig. Would now not be the perfect time?"

"While my father is fighting to stay alive just a little bit longer?" I asked, eyebrows raised a little, hackles raised even more. "I can think of better times."

"But don't you think that maybe he would like to see you settled? That it would give him a boost to see his only child marry? Do you not think he would get some joy out of it? He doesn't have long left."

She said 'he doesn't have long left' as if it were news to me. As if that hadn't been the only thought to cross my mind, over and over and over again, since his diagnosis. I had thought of all the things he wouldn't see. He would never get back to California or see the Grand Canyon again. He would never write the book he always wanted to write. He would never hold any of his grandchildren. And among those thoughts was also the fact that he would never be there to walk me down the aisle. It had never occurred to me to make that happen – to arrange a wedding just for him. Something, I guess, had been holding me back. Still and all, I walked away from the bakery that day with nothing but thoughts of a wedding in my mind. We could do it – something simple, in Mom and Dad's back yard with a pergola decked in flowers, a wooden dance floor hired in. White chairs lined together for our guests – a red carpet laid for me to walk on. I could get a dress, something simple. I wouldn't quite go down the whole 'hippy in the back yard in her bare feet' routine but there would be no fuss or flounce or excessive frills. I would have a champagne fountain with old-fashioned champagne glasses – no fancy flutes – and I would bake my own wedding cake – or better still, cupcakes, just like Daddy liked.

I ran the thoughts through my mind and back again all the way home, trying to convince myself that it would be a good idea. And sure Craig and I were as good as married anyway so we might as well take the next step.

I was sure it was a great idea as I padded up the stairs to our porch and pulled open the screen door. I was almost, almost convinced – until I saw him.

I didn't think anyone actually did it. I didn't think anyone actually, *actually*, ever came home unexpectedly in the day to find their partner in bed with someone else. I thought it was something you saw in movies but was such a huge, massive cliché that it didn't actually ever happen. And I suppose, to be fair to Craig, he wasn't in bed with her. And thankfully both were, almost, fully dressed but the way they were kissing each other, grabbing each other and the way in which he was pressing her against the wall left me with no doubts whatsoever as to what their intentions were.

It was strange. I stood there for a moment and the world seemed to freeze-frame. My immediate feeling was not of disgust, or horror, or anger. My immediate thought was, there is Craig, passionately kissing another woman. Imagine that? I looked at the scene and it was as if my brain was trying to process what I was seeing. My second thought was not disgust, or horror or anger either – it was, Was this my fault?, and my brain strained to find some sort of acceptable explanation for it all and in doing so tried, in the passing of mere seconds, to see if there was any immediate way to make this all okay.

My thought process then segued quickly and painfully into a searing, almost physical pain of betrayal. I couldn't speak in this time so I watched them – I watched him push her against the wall, watched his hand grope at her breast, heard him gasp and moan, saw him thrust his groin tight towards her showing her what he wanted. I saw her fingers entangle themselves in his hair, pulling him towards her, and I thought of all the times we had kissed like that – all the times I had thought those kisses were only, and would only ever be, for me. Something in the very pit of my stomach lurched and I felt myself stumble backwards, still unable to speak, still unable to tell them I could see them. Still unable to scream "Stop!"

I thought of the wedding I had been planning to spring on Craig – me walking through the yard in my simple dress, the simple bands we would buy – and I watched him move to unbutton her blouse and groan that he wanted her.

And still I couldn't find the words, so I turned and walked out – careful for some reason I've yet to understand not to make any noise and not to disturb them and what they were at. I climbed into my car and drove until I reached the lake – the lake where we picnicked each and every summer when I was a child – and I sat on the grass, watching the water ripple and listening to the sound of people around me – enjoying their lives, getting on with things, just being together. I don't think that I have ever before or ever since felt as utterly alone as I did in that moment and yet still I didn't cry. My head swam and I played the scene I had just witnessed over and over again in my head but I didn't cry. I had other things to cry about – bigger things. Was it numbness or indifference? That question, as it crossed my mind, shocked me more than seeing my boyfriend grinding against another woman. Did I have the strength to deal with this right now? And if I'm honest, did it provide me with some sort of get-out-of-jail-free card?

I sat, picking strands of grass and running them through my fingers, wondering when life would start to make sense again, and then, when it was a time when I figured Craig would actually expect me home, I walked calmly back to my car, drove home and walked through the door and, as if nothing had happened, made us dinner and sat down to eat. If he noticed I was quieter than normal that night, he said nothing. He just ate his dinner and talked about his day – leaving out the obvious details – and after we finished eating I told him I had a migraine and so that I wouldn't disturb him with my tossing and turning all night I was going to sleep in the spare room if that was okay.

He nodded, asked if I needed anything from the drug store and cleared the table for me. I told him I was fine, I just needed to sleep and then, without addressing any of what I had seen or any of the wedding plans that had seemed so important just hours before, I poured a glass of water, walked past our bedroom without even going in to get my pyjamas or my toothbrush or as much as looking through the door, and straight on to the spare room where I closed the shutters, pulled back the covers and lay down and wished a real migraine on myself to distract me from the multiple conversations going on in my head.

Thankfully I fell, quickly, into a deep sleep and when the morning came I went about my business as if nothing had ever happened. I visited my father and we sat together in his yard and I pushed aside all thoughts of him ever walking me down the aisle. I held his hand and vowed that for that afternoon we wouldn't talk about cancer. We wouldn't talk about the reality of what lay ahead. And, although he was my nearest, dearest and most beloved confidant, I wouldn't burden him with what was going on. I would paint on the happiest of faces, as much as possible, and we would just be.

So we talked about *Star Wars*, and *The Muppets* and memories of my childhood. I told him how the memory of him dressing as Santa for my First Grade class still made me laugh – how I had defiantly told my classmates my papa was the "very real Santa Claus". And I told him that, even though I was a woman with a life of my own, I would always remember the times when he thought I was sleeping, when he would come into my room to kiss me goodnight and call me princess as he switched off the nightlight.

"You always were the love of my life, Annabel," he said. "And you always will be."

My daddy, I realised, would never hurt me. Apart from dying on me, which was killing me slowly and piece by piece, but if he could have fought that I know he would have – I know he would fight as hard as was humanly possible and never stop. But some things you can't change. I held his hand and tried not to think of how it was becoming weak and frail, his skin taking on a papery-thin quality, and I rested my head on his shoulder.

"Look at the clouds, Annabel," he said and I glanced up, taking in the scene above us – soft wisps of cotton stretching across a blue sky. "The funny thing about living here is that, probably mid-afternoon, we'll have a god-awful thunder storm. The rain will pelt down, the lightning will strike across that sky and, for all intents and purposes, if you let your imagination take it all in, for those few minutes it will look like the world is about to come an end. But you know what?" he laughed. "An hour later the skies will clear again and that sun will be shining just as brightly and the clouds will be just like that – streaking across the skies." He squeezed my hand as he spoke and I knew he was talking about more than the clouds and the weather and the humidity of a Florida afternoon.

* * *

"You look like you've been dragged through a bush backwards," Sam greeted me as I walked into the kitchen and poured myself a glass of orange juice.

"Good morning to you too," I answered, pulling myself up onto one of the kitchen stools and draining my glass in record time.

"Tough night?" he asked, sitting down opposite me and placing a plate of croissants between us. "Tell me, your mum is still alive, isn't she? You didn't stab her over the starters or anything over-dramatic like that?"

His teasing was gentle. I knew he genuinely cared about whether or not I was upset.

"Mom is still very much alive and, yes, it was a bit awkward, but it wasn't hell on earth. I just . . . I'm just struggling to get my head around it all, that's all."

"More pieces of the puzzle?"

"Big fat pieces – but it's a very big puzzle or else I'm very stupid because I can't make them fit." I lifted a croissant and bit into it, realising just how very hungry I was. "But then I haven't read all the letters yet."

I explained to him about the letters, handing him those I had already read and going over the minutiae of what was contained on the pages until he dragged me back into the bedroom and sat down to read them himself. If a part of me felt guilty that I was perhaps breaking some sort of confidence, I pushed it back down. I needed someone who could help me see this rationally and, as I was thousands of miles away from anyone I considered a friend back home and only had family to rely on here, he was the obvious choice.

"Jesus," Sam said, looking up from the letters, "I wouldn't normally consider myself to be a raging romantic but my heart is breaking for her – well, the 'her' she was in 1960. Seems like a whole other world."

"I suppose it was," I said, sitting back on the bed and picking up one of the letters to read it over again.

"How have you not read them all?" he said incredulously. "I want to read them all!"

"Because, I suppose, even though it is all very romantic and dramatic it's still my mother – and this secret or guilt or other life she has carried around with her all these years. I just wanted a break from the intensity of it all before I read the rest."

"What I don't understand, unless these unread letters reveal something groundbreaking, is how she ended up in the States anyway? What took her there if the situation was as bleak as it was?"

148

I shook my head. I suppose it had all been hazy in my head – a story of my mother nannying in the States, marrying my father, having me in her thirties when she had all but given up hope of ever having a baby and where she was asked if she was my grandma on more than one occasion – but the finer points, we hadn't ever really discussed the finer points.

"I don't know," I replied. "I honestly don't know."

Chapter 18

Dolores says hello. She says we should both stop being silly. I've told her I'm not being silly any more. I never was. I was stupid but I was never silly.

* * *

Derry, Christmas Eve 1959

Ray was a marine. He had been a marine for six years. He had been trained to be fierce in the face of any foe and yet he was sitting in The Diamond and his hands were trembling and his head spinning. His head had in fact been in a spin since word had come that his posting at the naval base in Derry – a place he had come to regard as home – was to end and he would be going home. The message had been delivered with suitable aplomb. "Great news for you, boys! You can tell your moms you're coming home. What a Christmas present, eh?"

His mom would be delighted but yet he hadn't found himself in the queue of men eager to phone home or send telegrams to break the happy news. He had found there was only one thought in his mind – one name, over and over again – Stella. His Stella. How could he tell her? How could he tell her they would be parted and so soon? Sure they had only been courting for a few months but it felt like a lifetime and he had become used to – and entranced with – their small bubble: their afternoons walking the Bollies, the evenings in their flat, the necking at the cinema. The thought that it was going to end –

150

that they would be ripped apart – almost tore him to shreds.

He went back to his bunk, sat there and wondered how he could tell her. Tomorrow was Christmas – he had been invited to dine with the Hegartys and he had presents wrapped. He had bought Stella a brooch and he had been so looking forward to seeing her face when she opened it. Now it seemed pathetic, all of it seemed pathetic.

Having been told to stand down for the rest of the day and through to Boxing Day, he picked up his jacket, his wallet and his hat, and left the Base without so much as glancing back. He had been due to meet Stella anyway at the flat, if she could get away, but he had to hedge his bets. He had to assume that, as she had said, she would be unlikely to get away. It was already afternoon and the shops would no doubt be closing early – and the pubs too – and he had so much to do.

He was going to do this all wrong, he thought. It was just all wrong. Not how he imagined it at all. He glanced at his watch. Perhaps Ernest Hegarty would be in the pub now, sinking one last pint of stout before heading home to his happy family scene. If he was lucky he would catch him and if he caught him he could still perhaps salvage some of this day – of this whole year. If he could win Ernest Hegarty over, when the following day came he would ask Stella to marry him and set about making plans for her to journey with him to the States.

It was a lot to ask of her, he knew. He knew deep down that, no matter how she loved him, she adored her family and he would be taking her away from all that. But outside of the Marines, what was there for him here in Derry? Even the local men struggled to get jobs. He knew there was work waiting for him back in Boston and that they could have a good quality of life, away from the abject poverty he saw around him, all accepted as part of the Derry routine. He wanted more for Stella. He wanted to give her everything but he knew that when he spoke to Ernest Hegarty he would be asking this hardworking family man to give him his own everything: his daughter. He'd heard tales, of course – of marines chased from family homes, told they couldn't take the girls with them. He'd heard of women wailing and screaming as the reality hit that they were actually boarding that ship and leaving their families behind, probably forever. He took a deep breath and pushed open the door of the bar, letting the warmth of the chatter, smoke and banter wash over him. The punters were clearly in great form, the thought of a short break from work at Christmas filling them with cheer almost as much as the stout was.

Ray scanned the room, trying to spot Ernest, half hoping he wasn't there and half hoping to see him quickly and get this over and done with even faster – like pulling off a Band-Aid. He walked around the room until the sound of a loud peal of laughter caught his attention and he turned to see Ernest, pint in hand, listening to one of his docker friends relate a story which would make even a marine blush.

Ray was standing awkwardly, moving from one foot to the other and trying to build up the courage to try and get Ernest's attention, when the older man looked at him, furrowed his brow as if trying to fit this jigsaw piece into a puzzle and broke into a smile.

"Well, Ray, son, what brings you here? Come and join us for a pint! I'll have a second if you promise not to tell Stella and Kathleen."

"Thanks, Mr Hegarty. I'll get them – another pint of stout?"

"Ha, the boy's trying to keep you sweet! He's after something, I bet," Ernest's raucous friend shouted. "Hi, Yankee Doodle Dandy, what is it you're after?"

Ernest looked at Ray and Ray was almost sure he felt the blood leave his face and pool somewhere around his feet. He realised it was now or never. It was strange that one moment – that announcement at the Base – could change everything. Now he had to make decisions and he had to make them fast . . . before he broke the news to Stella that he was being shipped home.

"Can I have a word, sir?" he asked to raucous laughter from Ernest's friend.

"I bet no one has ever called you 'sir' before!" one of the dockers roared while Ernest held Ray's gaze.

"Nothing wrong with a bit of manners – you could be doing with some yourself," Ernest said, pushing past his friends and leading Ray to what may have been the only quiet corner of any pub in Derry that Christmas Eve.

He took a seat and invited Ray to do the same.

"What is it, son?" he asked. "Is it about Stella?"

Ray nodded, trying to find the words to ask the question he so needed to. He blurted his question awkwardly and without grace.

"I want to marry her," he said. "With your blessing."

Ernest stared, his expression unreadable.

"Well, son," he said at last, sitting back and taking in Ray from head to foot, "do you love her?"

Ray considered the question for a split second – considered how to convince Ernest that not only did he love her, he loved her with all his heart in a way that he'd never thought possible.

"Yes, sir," he said softly. "I love her very much. And I know what I'm asking is a lot – but if you would give me your blessing, sir, to make her my wife, you would make me the happiest man on earth. I've my orders, you see, to ship out. And I know she is your daughter, and you love her very much – and she speaks so highly of the love she has for you – but if there was any way you could see fit to let her be with me, then I would be forever in your debt."

He watched the older man inhale slowly before lifting the pipe from his pocket and lighting it, sucking on it as the tobacco ignited and filled his lungs with its sweet-smelling aroma.

"My daughter," he said softly, the affection obvious in his voice, "my daughter deserves to be happy and you make her happy. God knows I've not been able to give mine much in terms of material things. There have been days when they've been lucky to have food on the table – but I've been able to show them love and raise them in a happy home. If you can promise me to offer her a happy home, every day of her life, and to put food on the table even when times are tough, and a shoulder to cry on when she needs it, then you have my blessing and that of her mother."

Ray nodded, annoyed with himself that he could feel the prick of tears behind his eyes at the older man's words.

"I promise you," he said, "that I will make her happy, and keep her safe and I will never hurt her."

"She'll need you, you know. She'll be far away from home and her mammy – and that girl loves her mammy. She'll need you to look out for her, to take care of her. Not to go drinking your wages like some of the boys here. Not to run about town. Once you have a family, son, nothing else matters. You will be her family."

The older man's eyes grew misty and Ray felt his composure wobble further. But he knew he would do as Ernest asked – and more. He knew that his life's mission from that point onwards was to make Stella happy.

"I won't let her down, sir. I won't let you down."

Ernest wiped the cuff of his jacket sleeve roughly across his eyes before leading Ray back to the marauding crowds.

"One for the road, boys!" he cheered. "Seems this man here is going to take my wee Stella for his own!"

Ray gulped back the shot of amber liquid put in front of him, not sure what was it was but definitely sure that he couldn't refuse it. He felt it warm his throat and burn in his stomach as one of the men patted him roughly on the back.

"Fair play to you, son!" the docker roared, the strength of his enthusiastic patting momentarily winding Ray. "And good luck taking a Derry girl away from her mammy!"

* * *

Stella had taken to her bed. Her mother had shushed her and rubbed her back and assured her that it would be okay and not to worry until she spoke to Ray directly. Of course she couldn't tell her mother the whole story – telling her the whole story would give the game away about the secret flat and her mother wouldn't be fit for the shock. So instead she had simply told her a lie – that she had met with one of the other factory girls who had told her that Ray's unit had been given their notice to return to the United States and that he would be going.

She had cried until even Dolores had shown an ounce of sympathy which, for Dolores was a big deal.

"Why don't you go for a wee sleep?" she said, looking at her sister's swollen red eyes and her tear-stained face.

"It's Christmas Eve, there's stuff to be done."

"There will always be stuff to be done," Dolores said softly.

Kathleen nodded and added: "And, pet, you are use to neither man nor beast the state you have yourself in. Take a wee rest, settle yourself. I'm sure it will all work out and you'll be laughing at this before long."

Stella sniffed, trying but failing to see how she could ever find anything about this funny. She was sure Dusty wasn't lying – that this was really happening.

"Just go, pet, have a wee rest and you may well feel much better then and it will all come right," her mother said.

Stella nodded, unable to talk any more and traipsed up the stairs, vaguely aware, through her tears, that Dolores was following her.

"There's more to this than you're letting on, isn't there?" Dolores said. "It isn't just what you heard at the shops?"

Stella nodded.

Dolores sat on the end of the bed beside her sister and stroked her hair. "I know he loves you, Stella. I've seen the way he looks at you. I've seen that and I've seen a lot of men in this town look at girls and I know the look of true love. Sure isn't it how Daddy looks at Mammy? And you would never doubt them for a second."

"Then where is he, Dolores? He should have been there. He should have been there to tell me."

"Where?" Dolores, looked at her sister quizzically. "At the shop?"

Stella shook her head, unable to tell her sister more even though she loved her and trusted her. She didn't want to let anyone know just how far she had fallen for her blue-eyed Yank. She curled into a ball onto the bed and let the tears fall. Was he really going to leave her? She couldn't bear it – she couldn't even consider the thought of him not being there. Offering a silent prayer that this had all been some horrible misunderstanding, she questioned why any God would allow her to fall so far and so madly in love with someone and then take him away from her.

She felt her sister lie down beside and they lay there as the darkness fell deeper and stars started to glitter in the Christmas Eve sky and she wished she were a child again and that she could make a simple wish for just one Christmas present.

Just him.

All she wanted was him.

* * *

Dolores woke Stella just after eleven. "It's time to get ready for Midnight Mass. I told Mammy to let you sleep on. That you don't need to be going to chapel with your eyes standing out of your head from all that gurning but, compassionate and all as our mammy is, you know that nothing comes between her and Midnight Mass."

"Can you not tell her I'll stay and mind the wee ones and youse can all go on?" Stella said, sitting up and rubbing her eyes, feeling how her skin was rough and dry from her crying. "I don't want to face anyone."

"I tried that, but Mrs Murphy is going to sit with the wains. Sure you know what she's like – holds no court with Midnight Mass – wants to be up and at it, swanning about in her finery at twelve Mass tomorrow. No good going when it's dark and no one can see your new jewellery."

Stella sniffed. "So there's no way out?"

"You were lucky to escape bathing the boys. Seán was a whole handling – over-excited about Santa. Mammy was threatening to hit him over the head with the rubber hammer if he didn't quiet down."

Stella laughed, a forced giggle at the thought of her six-year-old brother full of beans. "I should have been up to put him to bed."

"He was grand," Dolores said, opening the wardrobe in the corner of the room and pulling out their two good dresses. "I told him you had a cold. He said he would ask Santa to make you better."

Stella stepped out of the bed and walked to the dressing table where she caught sight of her swollen eyes in the mirror. They looked even worse than they felt. She rubbed some day cream on her cheeks, feeling the sting as she did so.

"I take it Ray hasn't been by?" she asked, knowing the answer even as she spoke.

"I would have woken you, pet," Dolores said softly. "But no, he hasn't been. But sure isn't he meant to be here tomorrow? Didn't he say he would be here tomorrow for dinner?"

Stella nodded but she knew that if it was true and he was being shipped out, and if he cared about her feelings even one iota, he would have been there earlier. He would have assured her it was okay – it was going to be okay.

She pulled the brush through her hair, dabbed on some pan stick to hide the worst of her blemished face and dressed in her Sunday best. "I won't make a show of myself," she told Dolores as she fastened a clasp in her hair. "I won't show Mammy or Daddy up. I'll go to Mass and I'll not let anyone know my heart is breaking. How's that?"

She brushed some blusher on her already rosy cheeks and sprayed some scent at her neck before slipping on her gold cross and chain. Slipping her feet into her shoes, she made her way downstairs where her mother, father and her two older brothers were waiting, all in their finery.

Her mother was in her usual tizz trying to get everyone organised and out the door, even though it was still a full half hour before the bells would toll, calling them into the chapel. She liked a good seat. She liked to be in the perfect place to hear every Latin word the priest muttered and to sit in silence as the choir sang "Oh Holy Night", and she liked to be one of the first at the crib to welcome the Baby Jesus.

"She'd have been one of the shepherds back in the day," Ernest used to joke each year as Kathleen was first at the crib to bless herself and sneak a few strands of straw to put in her purse.

"It's lucky," she would say. "Ensures your purse is never empty."

Ernest would laugh. "That may be the case, pet, but it's only never empty because it's filled with straw."

Kathleen would thump him gently on the arm and on they would go.

But as Stella walked down the stairs on that night, her mother stopped and looked at her, her eyes a little misty. She willed her mother to say nothing. Ask her no questions, not even how she was feeling, because she was determined to hold her head high and holding her head high would require not thinking about it . . . at all.

"Let's go then," Stella said, putting on her coat and scarf. "Can't have Mammy late."

She led the family out the door into the cool night air and walked silently towards the chapel, her breath forming on the wind. As she walked she felt an arm loop in hers. For a moment she thought it would be him – that he was there. She closed her eyes and tried not to think about the fact he wouldn't be.

"It will be okay, you know," she heard her father whisper in her ear. "I know it will work out, my sweet girl. It will be okay."

Unable to speak for fear of choking out a sobbing response, she squeezed her father's arm and felt him squeeze back. And she laid her head on his shoulder as they walked on in silence.

* * *

When Mass was ended and the priest had sent them on their way, Stella did not wait with her family as she normally did to kiss her neighbours on the cheek and wish them well. Telling her mother she would hurry on home to let Mrs Murphy away, she sneaked out and walked into the frosty air, waving at her neighbours as she went – a quick hand gesture which let them know she would not be stopping for idle chit-chat no matter what the date or whether or not the Lord was born again. She wanted the peace and quiet of her home, somewhere she could let her face fall and show her true emotions, if only for a short while. Hugging her arms to her against the gentle flakes of snow that had begun to fall, she scurried down Abercorn Road and on to her family home where Mrs Murphy was nursing a whiskey and hugging the fire as the embers faded.

"It's a cold one, Mrs Murphy," Stella said. "You can head on now. I'll mind the boys and you get on to your bed. But be careful not to slip out there, there's snow falling now."

Mrs Murphy drained her glass of the whiskey, not caring about appearing genteel and refined, and wiped her mouth with the back of her hand before staggering to her feet. Stella wondered just how much of her daddy's whiskey their neighbour had treated herself to over the last hour and a half – by the way she staggered to the door it was clear it was more than just 'one for the road'.

"Merry Christmas, young Stella!" Mrs Murphy cheered as she made her way out into the street.

Stella closed the door after her, took off her coat and made a decision to throw a wee half shovel of coal on the fire. There would be no sleep for another while in the Hegarty household anyway and they might as well be warm as they sat and enjoyed their post-Mass glow.

She was just stoking the fire when she heard a knock at the

door. Cursing to herself, convinced it was Mrs Murphy having locked herself out or fallen over or having endured some other mishap, she brushed down her skirt and made for the door.

When she saw Ray standing there, for a moment she wondered if she were imagining things – simply because she wanted it to be true so badly. He was there, the snow softly falling on his shoulders, in his uniform, a bunch of cream carnations in his hand.

She had so much she wanted to say to him that she barely knew where to start. Did she tell him she loved him first? Or that she was angry he had not been at the flat? Did she ask him was it true he was leaving? Did she ask how he had come to be away from the Base? Would he not be in trouble? She didn't know whether to kiss him or hit him so instead she just stared at him, drinking him in, trying to capture the memory of his face to keep forever.

"I can't stay long," he said, gesturing to a pick-up in the street where two other marines sat smoking. "Are you alone? Where are your parents?"

"Mass, they're on their way back from Mass. Why are you here? What's going on, Ray? Is it true you're going?"

He shivered in the snow and she stood, unable to move, barely able to breathe in fact until she heard what he had to say.

"I couldn't wait," he said. "When Dusty told me you knew, that you called, that you knew we are leaving, I couldn't wait."

Her heart sank. It was true, without a shadow of a doubt. She had heard him utter the words himself and there was no going back.

"I came to find you," she said, as tears filled her eyes. "I went to the flat. You weren't there. You said you would be there."

"I had something to do. Please, Stella. Let me come in for just a moment."

She stood aside and he stepped through the door and took her hand in his. She realised she was shaking but not from the cold.

"I had to see your father," he said. "I had to ask him. I needed his permission."

Stella felt the breath tighten in her chest and the tears that formed started to fall.

"In all my life, I never hoped and never dreamed I would find someone who I could love so much and someone who would love me back too. I can't be without you, Stella. From the moment we met, you were and are my life. Please do me the honour of saying you will marry me. Please come with me and be my wife."

She felt herself fall into his arms, whispering yes again and again into his neck as her tears mingled with the melted snow on his jacket. "Yes, Ray. I will. I will."

She lifted her head to see her family walking down the street arm in arm and in that second she exchanged a glance with her father which said more than words ever could. He approved. He gave his blessing. And she was going to America.

* * *

Christmas Day dawned and Stella could still hardly believe what had happened. Seán and Michael had bounded into her and Dolores' room first thing, waking them and shouting that Santa had been, and even though she had barely slept because her mind had been running at a hundred miles an hour since Ray's proposal, she jumped out of bed and gave Seán a piggyback down the stairs to where the older boys and her mammy and daddy were waiting and the fire had already been lit and the lights on the Christmas tree were sparkling. Despite the early hour, Kathleen was already dressed in her Sunday best but with her pinny on and the smell of cooking was wafting from the kitchen.

"Santa's been and the turkey's in, and our Stella is getting married!" Kathleen declared, kissing her daughter on the cheek.

"It's a Christmas miracle," Peter teased. "Any man being mad enough to take on our Stella. Fair play to him. You have warned him, though, what she's like? Maybe I'll have a wee word with him myself later!"

Stella knew her brother was teasing and she playfully told him to get away on with himself.

"I will miss you, you know," he said later as he helped her set up the train set Santa had brought for the younger boys.

She felt herself choke up and tried not to think of all the goodbyes she would have to say. Peter had watched out for her for as long as she could remember – not having him on hand to fight her battles for her would be strange and tough.

"I will have that word with him too," he said. "Except I'll be warning him not to hurt you. If he hurts you he will have me to answer to – and there is nowhere I won't go to make sure my wee sister is safe and well."

She hugged him and when they broke apart she noticed Seán looking at her as if she had two heads. "Crying at Christmas!" he said with all the dramatics you would expect from a six-year-old. "When Santa has been? You're mad, Smella," he laughed. "Mad, mad, mad as a mad thing!" He laughed and she revelled in his wide smile – still so babyish with just one missing tooth to show signs that he was growing into a big boy and she couldn't help but pull him close to her and laugh as she smothered him in hugs. She reminded herself she needed to get as many hugs in now as possible.

* * *

Ray arrived in time for dinner, a smile on his face this time. He kissed her as he walked into the house, when they were out of the eye-line of the rest of the Hegartys, and she almost had to pinch herself to convince herself this was real. He was really there. They were really going to get married. Yesterday she had been so convinced it was all going so horribly, horribly wrong.

"I can't believe I'm so lucky," he whispered as he looked into her eyes. "We must get everything moving as soon as we can. All the paperwork. Your passport. Everything. I know it might be a little rushed and maybe not the day you dreamed of, but I will make it special."

"Ray, would you not be so silly? The only thing I ever really dreamed of is that the man I marry loves the very bones of me and I love the very bones of him back."

"Well, you have that, Stella Hegarty. And there was me, steadfast in my belief that I would not let a Derry girl win me over and you have won me over hook, line and sinker. Come here . . ." He pulled her into the good room. "I have something for you. It's not a ring, not yet. And I was going to give it to you anyway but for now, until I can get a ring, this can be our token, proof of our engagement . . ."

He handed her a small green leather box which she opened to reveal a gold brooch, set with emeralds.

"Emeralds for my Irish girl," he said.

She gasped at it. She had never owned anything so beautiful. She wasn't even sure her mother owned anything so pretty. Even Mrs Murphy would be stunned into silence by this. Ray took the brooch from the box and pinned it to her dress, gently brushing close to her breast as he did, and her breath hitched in her throat. When he was done, and he stood back to look at her and she felt him gaze deep into her eyes, she had the urge to kiss him more passionately than ever before, right there and then – right in her mother's good room while the Baby Jesus was lying innocent in the crib and she could hear the roars of laughter from children in the street playing in the snow. She blushed as the impure thoughts danced through her mind and she thought how she could barely wait until it was their wedding night and they truly belonged to each other.

Chapter 19

Don't you remember how it felt? That Christmas morning? Don't you remember how we kissed – how it felt so right? I'm pretty sure we could make it feel right again.

* * *

Derry, June 2010

Sam walked back into the bedroom where the letters, read and unread, were scattered over the bed. It seemed obvious to me that we were setting up some kind of council of war there for the day.

Sam had disappeared at one stage to phone Second Hand Rose and tell his staff he wouldn't be in. I felt a little disappointed, to be honest. There was something comforting about that place and I kind of liked the idea of escaping into that calming alternative reality again. But even I knew now, as we delved deeper and deeper into my mother's past, that this was crunch time.

I felt, in some ways, wracked with guilt. If it had been me who had handed these most personal of letters over to someone else and was waiting for their response, I would have driven myself sick with worry about it all. I would have been checking my cell every three minutes to see if they had sent me a message and fighting the urge to call. I didn't like the thought that my mother could be driving herself mad with worry like that. Then again, as I had to remind myself, my mother was not me. She was likely to have adopted a calmer approach altogether. I'd rarely, if ever, seen my mother get rattled about anything. I'd rarely, if ever, heard her utter a cross word (except, perhaps, when I refused to take Irish dancing lessons). I could count on one hand the times I had seen her cry – she wasn't one to get sappy over advertisements on the TV. It took big things – returning to Ireland after almost fifty years, holding my father's hand as she said her final goodbyes to him – to make her shed a tear.

That's not to say she was cold – not really cold. She was a good mom. We were happy. She kept me in line. But she wasn't the more affectionate of my parents. That was Daddy – always would be. As an adult I had come to realise she showed me her love by making sure I had clean, fresh clothes, that I had help with my homework, that there was food on the table, that she was there every day when I came in from school, that she would kiss me every night on the cheek before I went to bed. But with Daddy it was bear hugs, and 'love yous' and long chats into the small hours. He just loved me in a different way.

Now, reading my mother's letters, I found it hard to square this passionate, tactile, affectionate woman with the lady I knew. But then, wasn't this trip all about surprises?

Sam sat the coffee cups down on the dresser before climbing back beside me on the bed. We lay there for a bit, staring at the ceiling, listening to the world go about its morning outside while we lay, me in my pyjamas, Sam in his work suit minus his tie, thinking about what was unfolding. I started to wonder why he had made coffee. We sure as hell weren't going to drink it. That would require too much thought – and all our internal memory was being gobbled up by the skeletons tumbling out of the closet. We read on, gripped by what was unfolding.

"Have you ever been in love like that, Sam?" I asked, the letters read and cast aside.

He gestured around them. "I am fast approaching forty. I think if I had ever been in love like that there would be a fair chance I wouldn't be a single man, now isn't there?"

"It doesn't always work out," I said, gesturing to the letters. "And I would say from those they were pretty much madly in love."

Sam rolled onto his side to face me and rested his head on his hand. "Cousin dear. I wish I could say yes. Part of me wishes there was a 'big one that got away' story, but there isn't. Maybe I'm doing it wrong but I seem to have stumbled from one disaster of a fling to another. The longest I've been with someone was eight months and even then that only worked, I think, because we were long distance. In real terms we probably spent a fortnight together. I'm not sure I'm relationship material."

"Do you want to be? Do you think it's a matter of meeting the right person? If your 'Ray' was to walk in here now . . ."

"All dressed up like Richard Gere in *An Officer and a Gentleman*? I could go for that."

He laughed and rolled onto his back but I recognised that certain hollow echo in his voice.

"So what went wrong? Was it the distance? Was it too hard?"

"Something like that," he said, picking an imaginary piece of fluff off the immaculate eiderdown. "When it reaches a stage where your significant other really wants to meet your parents but you know that's not entirely possible, it doesn't always go down well." His voice was softer now, more serious.

I reached out and took his hand. "Would she not come round? I mean, if you were happy. Surely all she wants is for you to be happy?"

"She's not a bad person, Annabel," he said. "But she is stuck in her ways. And why wouldn't she be? It's just a shame."

It *was* a shame, I thought as he got up to sip from his coffee cup. And if I was being honest with myself I was shocked Dolores could act in such a manner. She who preached to me the very day before about accepting people for who they were.

I shook my head. "Do you ever talk about it?"

He shook his head then shrugged his shoulders. "Been there, done that. It doesn't end well. I mean, I'm sure once I find the man of my dreams I'll fight hard enough and my mother can go hang but . . ."

"But you haven't yet? Or this is putting you off?"

He laughed, a short bitter laugh. "You Americans and your crazy ways. Always trying to analyse everything. There is no need to come over all Dr Phil on me. It's not some big psychological block, you know. It just is what it is." He paused and we were both lost in our thoughts for a moment.

"Of course I'd love to find someone. I'd love to have a civil ceremony and settle down and become a living cliché of a middle-aged, settled, boring gay man but, as the song says, you can't always get what you want."

"But if you try . . ." I offered.

"Tell me this, cousin," he asked. "Do you believe in the big love affair? I mean, we're reading about it here but it went wrong, didn't it? And look around you? How many people do you know who are truly, madly, can't be without each other in love?"

"You're very cynical," I said, but even as I spoke I wondered if he had a point. Sure people loved each other but does being in love last forever? Do people settle? Had I settled?

"Are you happy then?" he asked. "With your man who you barely speak of? Is he the one? Does he love you like no other? Would he, like Ray, trudge through the snow to propose to you on Christmas Eve?"

I felt those blasted tears prick at my eyes again. "No," I muttered, shaking my head. "He wouldn't."

I felt disloyal talking about him, letting anyone have a hint that all was not well, but at the same time I had been holding all this in now for so long.

I never told anyone about Craig's infidelity. I never even let Craig know that I knew. Part of it was selfish, I know. I had enough on my plate and I just couldn't face another drama – instead allowing myself to stay part of a relationship where I could barely think about him touching me without thinking of him touching her. But I only had a finite amount of emotional energy and in those moments when I was trying to make sense of it all I realised there was only one man who deserved my tears in those weeks and months. And it wasn't Craig.

Perhaps it was then I started to close myself off from him – or perhaps I had already been closed off anyway. Maybe it was my fault – maybe all the doubts and niggling fears I'd had over the last few years had been felt by him too.

I spent even less time at home, initially working longer hours at the bakery and then, as my father's illness progressed, spending more time at home. There were many nights spent in my old bedroom, with all the vestiges of my teenage years staring down at me as I tossed and turned in a bed that no longer felt like my own.

Craig seemed not to notice for a while and I'm not sure if that made things better or worse, easier or harder. I would have liked to think that me cutting myself off from him would set alarm bells ringing loudly in his ears. But I think, perhaps, instead he revelled in his new-found freedom. On those nights alone in my bedroom in my parents' house, listening to my mother crying in the den after Daddy had gone to sleep, I tried not to think about what might or might not have been going on back home in my bed.

Not that it felt like my bed any more either.

He did catch on eventually, I suppose. On one of my less frequent stop-overs at home, as I gathered fresh laundry, took a long hot shower and made myself some soup, he prowled around as if trying to think of something to say. I didn't, again, have the emotional energy for small talk so I went about my business.

Eventually he spoke, his voice low, wounded even, as if it were he who was hurting. "What's going on, Bella?"

"What do you mean?" I asked him, knowing full well I was teetering on the edge of facetiousness.

"You seem distant? What's wrong?"

I turned the burner off under the pot of soup I had been heating and turned to face him. I realised it was probably the first time I had looked directly in his eyes in a month. "What's wrong? I'm assuming you're looking for an answer more complicated than my father is dying?"

He shook his head, ran his fingers through his hair and slumped back against the worktops. "I can't figure you out. I can't get inside your head. It's more than your dad. I know it. I feel it."

I noticed his fist had tightened, could see the whites of his knuckles. I could feel the vibes of frustration bounce off him but I knew if I spoke, if I started, that too much would be said. Too much would be done that couldn't be undone.

"I'm tired, Craig," I said. "I'm just tired."

I ladled my soup into a bowl and turned to walk through to the den when I felt him stand in front of me. Before I could blink, the bowl was out of my hands, the hot soup splashing on my wrists, forcing me to pull them back into myself.

"*You are always tired!*" he shouted, hurling the soup bowl at the tiled floor.

I watched it smash, as if in slow motion. I watched it splinter and shatter before the pieces settled into the hot, orange soup as it slowly slid and stretched across the floor.

I suppose he was expecting a reaction. He was probably even expecting a fight. But I turned, stepped over the soup and walked out of the house – even though I was in my pyjamas – and went for a drive until the gas-light was blinking on my car and I was getting too tired to see straight.

When I got home, the kitchen was clean – as if nothing had happened – and when I climbed into bed, wordlessly, I felt Craig, still asleep, slip his arm over me.

"I'm sorry," he whispered and I lay awake for the rest of the night, listening to him snoring gently while I wondered just when we would admit it was all, irrevocably, broken.

"He's not a bad person," I told Sam.

"But . . ."

"Well, I think, if I'm honest, coming here was running away from him a bit. Running away from us." I don't know how I expected to feel saying those words out loud. Relieved? Horrified? Instead I felt a certain numbness. As if the last few months, maybe even the last few years, had put an emotional barrier between me and Craig. I felt as if I was simply stating facts, not acknowledging publicly that my relationship was in tatters.

"So has running away helped? Do you want to run back?"

I shook my head. "I've tried," I said. "I've tried and tried to rationalise it and make it work but it doesn't. He was seeing someone else, Sam, and that should have horrified me but it didn't. It felt as if it was, in some way, expected. I always knew this would happen. Not because I don't feel worthy or anything but, maybe, because I know that we weren't ever really meant to be. We just fell into a rut that neither of us knew how to get out of."

"Do you know how to get out of it now?"

I shrugged my shoulders. Knowing the right thing to do and doing it were often two entirely different things. And I started to understand my mother a little more.

Chapter 20

If I could go back in time, I would undo the mistakes I've made. I would do anything for things to be different. But I can't – so I will carry this with me forever.

* * *

Derry, January 1960

The paperwork was underway. Stella had applied for her passport. Moves were in place to arrange her visa. There was talk of a wedding – a simple ceremony in a local church. She would borrow her friend's good suit and have a bouquet of silk flowers made. She still had the shoes she had worn to the night at the City Hotel, which she would wear again. And she would maybe splash out on a new haircut. Kathleen and Ernest said they would put on a small spread in the house – sandwiches and cake – and invite the neighbours round.

Sitting together in the flat, with Ray's arms around her, she felt blissfully happy. She felt so safe there, so sure of herself.

"I'll get you a proper ring when we're settled," he whispered. "And we'll do it again, you know, the wedding – some day – with a white lace gown and everything you have ever dreamed of – just for you."

He kissed the top of her head and revelled in the feeling of his lips brushing against her hair. She cuddled in closer to him, feeling his arms draw her closer still. If it could be like this forever she was sure she could never be happier.

"I know this is more rushed than you hoped, or you wanted," he said, "but if I could do it differently . . ."

"Stop apologising for things you can't change," she chastised him, looking into his eyes. "Things happen for a reason – life happens for a reason – and this is just the way it is going to be for us."

"I'll get you a good house. We'll be happy," he said.

"We already are."

* * *

January bit cold. Stella consoled herself as she walked to work through the snow that soon she would be in America. Ray promised her it would be different there. She wouldn't have to work. The spring and summers were warmer and by the time they reached the suburbs of Boston the worst of the winter would have gone.

She pulled her coat tight around her, wrapping her bright red scarf as high as she could around her face to keep off the biting wind. Her feet were already wet and frozen and she knew that she faced eight hours standing on the factory floor – although the heat of the irons would keep her warm – she was at least grateful for that.

In her highly emotional, newly engaged state, she even started to feel a certain fondness for the machines that left her so weary at the end of the day. She had started to count down her work in terms of weeks and days, and she started to try and cram as many memories in as she could.

"Once you're gone, you're gone," one of the supervisors on the factory floor had said. "You won't see Derry again. You young ones think you know it all and won't miss a bar of Derry – but when you are far from home you might think differently. Take it in, my girl – home will always be home."

Stella blew her hair from her face, wiped her hand across her forehead and smiled sweetly at her supervisor. "Home is where the heart is," she said, "And don't we all make tough decisions for love?"

The older woman sniffed, crossed her arms across her ample bosom and went about her work while Stella continued with pressing the shirts ready for folding. She wasn't the first girl to leave the factory to set off for a new life, and she was sure she wouldn't be the last. She wasn't aware of the others having been given a hard time. Then again the only girl she had been very close to was Molly Davidson and nothing could have burst her bubble. She had practically floated out of the factory on her leaving day, singing "From the Candy Store on the Corner to the Chapel on the Top of the Hill" as the girls joined in loudly, her laughter filling the factory floor.

She didn't imagine she would float out singing – it wasn't her style – but she would smile as she left, knowing that while she was sad that a chapter of her life was ending, a whole new chapter was beginning. Any doubts she had were gone when she was with Ray – and while she wasn't naïve and knew that it would feel like her heart was being ripped from her body when she left her family behind – she knew it was time she made a new family and she knew Ray would make her a perfect husband and that their life would be happy. She just felt it with every breath she took. They were meant to be together.

So as she watched her supervisor's back as she walked away she vowed to just get on with her work and count down the days until the factory would become a distant memory.

When it was clocking-off time, she grabbed her coat, wrapped her scarf tight around her again and made for the door before the girls could stop her. They would want her to go for a cup of tea and a gossip, but she couldn't – not tonight. Not that she would tell her mother and father that. She was due to meet Ray in the flat and hoped to sneak in an hour together before going home. She would, of course, tell her parents she had gone for tea with the girls, but she had better plans in mind.

Smiling, she ran through the door and up the hill where she let herself into the dark flat, switched on the lights and quickly set to work, keeping her coat on to try and keep warm. Setting a small fire in the hearth, she lit a few candles and made a pot of tea before nipping to the small bathroom with the very small mirror to try and make herself look presentable. She had brought the bare essentials with her: some pan stick, a small brush to smooth her hair and a bottle of scent. She washed her face in the icy water and shivered as she redid her make-up and brushed her hair. He would be here any minute and she was almost giddy at the thought of seeing him even though it had only been twenty-four hours since she had last felt his lips brush against her. She gently touched the brooch which she had pinned to her dress. It might have seemed a little ostentatious with her factory clothes but she didn't care: it symbolised all he meant to her and she had vowed she would wear it every day, no matter what the occasion.

This little hour they would have together now would be precious: a chance to get intimate. She felt a little guilty even to think this way but with every day they were together she wanted to be closer and closer to him. She longed to feel him touch her, to caress her. She felt a little dizzy at the thought. She could feel herself blush. She wasn't a bad girl, she knew that. She had friends who had slept with their boyfriends before they were married. Rumour was that Margaret from down the street had slept with her man before he had even asked her to marry him. Rumour was that Margaret had to get married – not that anyone in her family would ever admit it. But Stella was able to work the dates out and that baby was very big for one who was supposed to be born so early.

She didn't judge, not really. But now, well, she knew it was only a matter of weeks before she would be Ray's wife and, while she was nervous as hell about what to expect, she found herself longing to be intimate with him, to feel him kiss her skin. Sometimes when they were alone they would find it hard to control themselves. When he kissed the nape of her neck, she would almost lose the run of herself. She couldn't quite understand how something which felt so right, which was such a part of their love for each other, could ever be considered wrong.

She blushed again as she brushed down her dress and waited for the sound of his key turning in the door. The fire had caught and the candles were casting soft shadows on the wall. She planned to hold him close to her as soon as he walked in, to kiss him softly in the way she knew made him groan which in turn made her insides turn to jelly. As she heard the turn of the key and listened to his footsteps climb the stairs she thought of what her life would be – how she would wait for his returning from work each day. How he would always come home to her. She closed her eyes and imagined the life that awaited her and felt a slow smile spread across her face.

Standing up, she turned to watch him walk through the door, her breath catching as she saw him, and the sadness in his eyes, and she felt her world slip out from under her feet.

* * *

Ray was aware of the hissing of the kettle on the stove and the crackle of the fire. He tried to focus on them to escape, just for a moment, the sound of Stella crying. He had tried to reassure her but he knew that this was not what they had planned. When the announcement had been made at the Base he had felt his heart sink. He had gone directly to his superiors to plead his case but there was no leeway. The decision had been made. Ray and his men were to be shipped out in less than forty-eight hours. The increasing tensions with Russia meant that they were to be relocated back home as soon as possible to await further orders. There was no room for manoeuvre, even though some of the marines would remain stationed in Derry. There were no plans to close the NAVCOM Base but, as they were next to return to America anyway, the decision had simply been made to move their date forward.

"But you are demobbing anyway," Stella had said. "Can you not just demob now?"

"In June. And no, they won't let me. I've asked, Stella. I've asked every question I could think of. I've near enough begged."

"But there is no way the paperwork would be in place by then . . . my passport . . ."

Ray shook his head, his heart hurting at the pain in Stella's eyes. This was not a time of war. There would be no fast-tracking of their wedding. The reality was that he would travel on ahead of her and she would have to follow him and they would marry in Boston.

He knew he was asking a lot – he was asking her to give up having her father walk her down the aisle – to give up the small wedding which wasn't even half of what he wanted to give her anyway. And he was asking her to travel on her own – that horrible journey – Ireland to America – with not a friend to her name. All he had ever wanted to do was to protect her and now he was letting her down and there was nothing he could say which could make it any better.

If anything he was only going to make it worse. "I'm not sure I will get away from the Base tomorrow," he said, looking at the floor. "I was pushing my luck to get a pass tonight but I told them I needed to see you."

Stella looked up, her blue eyes red-rimmed from crying. Tears fell freely and as quickly as he could wipe them away more would fall. He didn't care that he was crying himself now – that his heart was breaking.

"This is goodbye?" she said, her voice stilted.

He nodded, simply because he could not bring himself to say the words.

"Oh God," she muttered, and he closed his eyes as he felt her hand on his cheek.

"You will come to me, Stella," he said, kissing her hand. "I'll have it all arranged and you will come to me and we will get married and I promise I will make it better."

"But you're leaving . . ." she said as if she were trying to make sense of what he was saying. "I won't see you, for . . . how long?"

"You'll come as quickly as we can get it organised. I promise, as quickly as we can get everything in order, you will come to me. I have money, Stella. Everything will be paid for – your transport, your paperwork. I'll be there to meet you as soon as you step off that boat. I promise. I'll be there and I'll never let you go. I promise."

He looked straight into her eyes, their tears mingling as he reached forward to kiss her. He tilted her head towards his – kissing the tears from her cheek before softly kissing her lips. He felt her respond, her hair move to his face, caressing his cheek and he reached to the small of her back and pulled her closer to him. As she grasped at his hair and pulled him closer, kissing him deeply, he felt himself gasp. He pulled back from her, searching her eyes for some sign it was okay.

"Are you sure?" he asked and she nodded, taking his hand and leading him to the small single bed in the corner of the room where nervously she lay down and pulled him closer to her.

As he kissed her and felt her body pressed against his, the softness of her skin against his body, he knew that while they were not legally married they could not be more a part of each other than there and then.

"It will be okay," he whispered as he kissed her neck and heard her gasp. "We will be together soon. I promise you. Nothing has changed. Nothing will change. I promise you."

* * *

Stella woke in darkness. She could feel the soft warmth of Ray's breath against her neck. She felt his arm wound around her waist and for a second, before the reality that this was goodbye kicked in, she revelled in the feeling of his skin on hers.

As she lay in the darkness a tear slid down her face and she quickly wiped it away. She would not have Ray's last memory of her to be one of a crying mess. This was not goodbye – this was a temporary glitch before they could be together for the rest of their lives. Reluctantly, she pulled herself up and started to dress in the dark. She didn't want to think of what time it might be, or that her parents might be going off their heads worrying about her and where she might be. She would deal with that later.

Ray didn't stir and she knew she should wake him – that he was probably expected back at the Base as much as she was expected back home – but she wanted to revel in this silence, this togetherness, just a little longer. This, she realised as she slipped her feet into her shoes, was the last time she would be in this flat. She would walk past it again, of course, and look up at the window but he would never be there waiting for her again.

"It shouldn't be long," he had assured her. "Before you can follow me. Please, Stella, promise me that you will follow me."

She had nodded as he caressed her, as they lay in the darkness, their bodies tight against each other. "I'll always follow you. I promise."

When she was dressed, when she had combed her hair back and put on her coat and her scarf, she sat down beside him again and gently kissed his cheek. She wanted to make this as painless as possible. If they were to see each other again in a matter of weeks there was no need for tears, she told herself even though her heart felt as if was shattering as she felt the softness of his skin against her lips.

"Ray, wake up. Ray, it's time to go. I need to be home. You need to be back at the Base. They'll be expecting you."

He blinked awake and she gazed into his blue eyes, dimly lit by the flickering candles in the room. He nodded as she bent forward to kiss him again.

"I'll follow you," she whispered, trying to stop her voice from breaking. "I promise. Wait for me, Ray, please. Don't give up on us."

He nodded wordlessly, taking her hand in his and kissing it.

"Now," she said, mustering all the strength she could, "I'm going to leave."

"Let me walk you home," he said.

"No," she replied, firmly this time. This was difficult enough. She had to leave now before she begged him not to leave even though it was beyond his control and she knew that there was nothing he could do. "You get back to the Base. They will be expecting you and I'd better get home and face the music myself. We'll be together soon." She brushed a stray tear away and cursed inwardly at herself for letting her emotions show when she had promised herself she wouldn't.

He nodded as she stood up and left the room. As the door closed behind her and she padded down the stairs and onto the cold street she vowed that she would be with him again – soon – come hell or high water. It was only as the rain started falling as she walked towards her house that she allowed her tears to fall. Dear God, she would miss him. She would miss him so very much.

Chapter 21

Ray, I'm not giving up. Please know I'm not giving up but this is the last letter I'll send you. If you still want me, then please, please give me some sign. Just anything, Ray. Please.

* * *

Derry, June 2010

Sam's phone beeped to life, cutting through the silence in the bedroom. After I had come to the realisation that, as Sam put it, I was "still with Craig because it was easier than not being with Craig", I had become lost in my own thoughts.

It wasn't that he had said anything I didn't know. I wasn't foolish. I had known for a long time that what Craig and I had was broken . . . but hearing it out loud, it made me feel . . . well, a mixture of emotions. Sadness, I suppose, because now it would be almost impossible to put it all back into a box and ignore it. A sense of failure too, maybe. I had clung on for a long time hoping against hope that something would change. I had made so many excuses. When his work settled down, things would be better. When my business was up and running and I had more time, things would be better. When my father's illness didn't take up every minute of my day, I would be able to devote more time to fixing my relationship with Craig, and things would be better. Except everything had come and gone and still it wasn't better, and sitting a few thousand miles away from the situation I could

180

see that it wasn't going to be. I had sent him those text messages since I had been here, trying to cling on to some semblance of something. I felt affectionate towards him – despite his cheating, despite his controlling ways. I could see that he was trying in some cack-handed manner to try and fix things himself – or make sense of them. Did I feel angry at him? I suppose no. I felt sad – that this is what we had become. All our hopes and dreams – all *my* hopes and dreams – had come to this – a realisation that we were never going to be together again. And I had to tell him. That in itself pushed aside the sliver of relief that was creeping in – the relief that these doubts were no longer a secret.

Sam had held my hand while I cried and laughed and had a minor freak-out.

"Things work out, cous," he said. "They do. And whatever is to come is not going to be any worse than losing your father, is it? Nor will it be any worse than living with someone you can't trust – who you don't feel close to, who you feel betrayed by."

He was right, of course, and now it was just a matter of trying to figure out how to move forward but at the moment my head hurt too much. This was all too much to take in – my mother's letters to Ray, my relationship with Craig. I felt overwhelmed, so after a while Sam and I had just lain there, on the bed, in silence, listening to the sound of the world outside.

The beeping of Sam's phone was a welcome distraction from it all and I watched as he sat up and read the message he had received.

"It's Niamh," he said.

I shrugged my shoulders, trying to place the name.

"From the shop," he offered. "One of my best customers."

"Ah, your biggest fan," I said.

"The very one," he said with a wink. "She's looking for that night out tonight. She doesn't waste any time."

I raised my hand and made a stabbing motion, and making an 'eek' noise mimicked the iconic scene from *Psycho*. "You do know she fancies you, don't you?"

Sam laughed, as if he couldn't believe anyone would ever fancy him. "Wise up. Anyway, I'll just message her back and let her know we're otherwise occupied."

"With what?" I said. "Sitting here discussing old love letters about someone else's life, worrying about the messes we have made of our lives? I'd say a night out could do us the world of good – as long as you do accept that she does, indeed, fancy you and that there is a fair chance that by the end of the night she will make some sort of a move on you."

"Annabel, you are too funny," he said. "Niamh's just a friend. A very eccentric friend – but nothing more than that. But if you want to go out, so be it! Glad rags on tonight and out we will go!"

"Good. Although you are aware that I have a serious dearth of glad rags?"

Sam shook his head. "I don't understand you, cousin of mine. A beautiful woman like you – with a lack of fancy things."

It was my turn to look on in disbelief. I wouldn't say I was ugly. I wasn't that self-effacing – but I would never say I was beautiful either. Average – that's how I would describe myself and I suppose I dressed accordingly.

"I promise before I go home to take myself shopping in Second Hand Rose and buy a whole shopful of fancy things – but for now you will have to settle for me, my jeans, some sneakers and a fitted T."

"You'll still be gorgeous, cous," he said, jumping to his feet. "With genetics like ours, we can't help it!" He laughed and I laughed back – so delighted to be looking forward to a night letting my hair down – not thinking about all the serious, grown-up nonsense running around my head.

* * *

On the day Daddy died, after he was gone my mother and I sat with him for an hour. I'm sure some would consider it wrong –

morbid even – but even though I knew that he was gone, I couldn't bear to be away from him. I held his hand, rubbing it – willing some warmth back into it while my mother – grief wracking through her body – lay with her head on his chest. It was as if she was waiting for his heart to start beating again – for him to admit it was one of those big jokes he so loved to play on us. Letting go – physically letting go of his hand – was one of the hardest things I have ever done. I imagine it was one of the hardest things I would ever have to do. I'd never lost anyone before – not there – not in front of my eyes. My grandfathers had both died before I was born and I never knew my grandmothers. I suppose that came with living away from family – just us three. I considered myself fairly lucky, if I'm honest. I saw friends lose their grandparents, their parents, their aunts or uncles and I felt as if I was somehow lucky that there I was – just us three. And nothing was going to come between us. I never had to say goodbye and this, this first time, was almost more than I could bear. You never truly understand grief until you feel it yourself – until it overwhelms you, hitting you in relentless waves as you try and convince yourself everything is going to be okay while every part of you screams that it won't be and that it can't ever be okay again.

Letting go of his hand – when there was no trace of warmth left and the hand that used to squeeze mine when I was a child now felt strange and waxy and wrong – I stumbled out of the room, past the doctor who was standing by and the undertakers who were waiting to take his body and prepare it for his final journey and I stumbled out into the yard gasping for air – trying to fill my lungs to still the screaming in my head.

Rocking back and forth, hugging my knees to me as I sat on the porch steps, I took my cell out and dialled Craig's number and waited for him to answer. His voice, when he did, seemed distorted. The world seemed distorted. "He's gone," I managed to whisper before silent, wracking sobs ripped through my body once again. I heard Craig say my name as I dropped my cell to the ground, realising that there was no comfort to be had in his voice.

* * *

Craig, the dutiful if not entirely faithful, boyfriend came over. He stood awkwardly in the doorway as I answered it, telling me he was sorry for my loss and making to hug me – but I couldn't, in that moment, hug him back. The feeling of my father's hands was still on me and I didn't want to touch anyone – to detract in any way from that feeling or that memory even though the cold stillness of him had felt so wrong. I leant towards him slightly, my hands still at my sides and felt his arms around me.

"He's at peace now," he said. "It's the best thing, no more pain."

And I nodded because that is what you do. You don't say, 'No, it's not the best thing. The best thing is never going to happen. The best thing is him being okay and not in pain and not bloody dead.' I didn't and couldn't get angry, because I wouldn't make a show of myself as the undertakers did their work, even though I was sure they were more than used to people making scenes.

So I just nodded and then stood straight and walked back to the living room where the doctor was soothing my mother and offering all kinds of pills to help her get over the pain. Stoically she refused.

"I have to feel the pain," she said. "Because if I don't it's like he didn't mean anything to me. And he did."

I was a coward then because, when the doctor went to get her a glass of water I wasted no time in asking for a few of those pills myself. He meant everything to me too – but maybe I just wasn't as strong as my mother.

* * *

We met in a small pub on Waterloo Street, where Niamh waved at us furiously as we walked in, indicating she had kept us a place on the wooden benches. It was still relatively quiet but Sam pointed out it wasn't even nine yet and by Derry standards this was still the middle of the afternoon. I blinked. By Florida standards this was almost stretching into the wee small hours of the morning.

Outside of her day-to-day self-imposed uniform of a business suit, Niamh was transformed into a colourful explosion of style and fashion. She still had the cocktail rings on her fingers, of course, but in addition she wore a bold patterned 60s minidress which she informed me she had bought at Second Hand Rose. She bought, she said, most of her clothes there . . . "Well, what I wear outside of work anyway. They expect a certain level of decorum in the courtroom!" she laughed. "You see, I'm a family law solicitor." Under the dress she wore a pair of purple opaque tights which covered her impossibly long and thin legs down to a pair of shoes that might not have looked out of place on a court jester. They were decorated with flowers, bells and ribbons. "Irregular Choice," she smiled and I nodded that they certainly were. Her hair and make-up matched her ensemble perfectly. Her eye make-up was a splash of sparkly blue with long false lashes accentuating the natural green of her pupils. Her hair was teased, backcombed and spiked. And yet she looked amazing. I knew if I had tried to get away with such an ensemble I would have looked as if a clown had thrown up on me, but she looked almost peacock-like in her magnificence. It was enough to make me glance down to my jeans and sneakers and cringe. I looked so stale – so absolutely all-American boring and plain – that I might as well have ironed a crease directly up the front of my jeans to complete the 'day release from Fashion Rehab 101' look.

Niamh oozed confidence and when they were together Sam oozed a certain extra confidence too. Not that I had ever necessarily seen him as lacking in it but with Niamh there was a boisterous side to him that I had never seen before.

"I took the liberty of ordering some drinks," Niamh said,

gesturing to the table in front of her and an array of glasses of varying sizes. "I figured if you were going to have the Irish experience you'd want to try a Guinness," she said, handing me a pint glass of the thick black stout.

I baulked, realising that part of my Irish heritage must be faulty. I never had the desire to try Guinness but, in the face of the glorious peacock-like Niamh, who was drinking from her pint glass already, and Sam who was grinning and shouting "*Sláinte!*", I knew that even at thirty-seven and a grown woman I was about to give in to peer pressure.

Sipping tentatively, I choked and slammed the pint glass down, wiping at my mouth with my sleeve as the tears hit my eyes.

"Sweet God," Sam laughed, patting my back until the choking fit subsided. "It's not that bad."

"It's not that good either," I spluttered.

"Well," said Niamh, handing me another glass with a short in it this time, "we'll just have to find you another drink you do like."

"I'm partial to a spritzer or just an ordinary glass of wine," I offered.

Niamh looked at me, amused. "When there is so much choice in the world?"

"I know what I like," I said softly. "I've never been much of a drinker."

She shrugged her shoulders as if in disbelief. "Well, a glass of wine it is then . . . and more of this for us, eh, Sam?" She laughed, gesturing to the table before lifting her (sparkly) bag and heading off towards the bar. For a moment I feared she would come back with one glass of every variety of wine on offer but she turned back and asked me what kind.

"She's a bit full on," I said to Sam when she left.

"There's no badness in her," he said. "She's a nice girl, Annabel. She just likes to let her hair down. Her job can be very intense. I'd say she was just trying to be generous."

He looked at her then back at me, and I realised I'd had my back up since before we came out. I suppose it had been a full-on day for us all and maybe I could do with letting my hair down too. Suddenly I wished I was wearing the dress from Second Hand Rose that I had worn the day before – that I was dressed a little less conventionally, that I was able to relax with a drink in my hand and wasn't so stuck in my ways.

Sam must have noticed my sudden introspection. "Cheer up, Annabel. We're here to relax. Let's try and put Ray and your mom, and Craig and my lack of a love life, and even, if you can, your daddy, out of your head for a just a little while."

"I stick out like a sore thumb," I said glumly.

Sam sat his pint down and rubbed my arm. "My darling cousin. We all stick out like sore thumbs – we all feel it. There's our beautiful peacock at the bar batting those eyelashes at the barman. Here am I, a gay man whose mammy can't accept what he is, and there you are in your jeans and perfectly ironed T-shirt wondering what the hell you are doing with your life. And look around the room, everyone here is wondering the same, and dealing with their own issues and feeling, at times, like they don't belong. All part of the human condition if you ask me." I glanced around while Sam sat in silence. Then he started laughing. "Dear God, I just realised how completely miserable that sounds! I'll have you leaping off the Peace Bridge in despair, talking like that. Look, pet, here's the deal. This is a snapshot. It's one night. And it's not forever. And you will feel like you fit again – I'm sure you did before. Life has just spun you around like a mad thing lately – is it any wonder you don't know which way is up? But we'll get there. I promise."

He hugged me as Niamh returned, a large glass of chilled white wine in her hand . . . with a cocktail umbrella stuck in the top.

"Thought I would jazz it up a bit," she said with a wink, sidling onto the bench beside Sam.

"I'm all for jazzing things up a bit," I laughed, lifting the glass and sticking the cocktail umbrella behind my ear. "Cheers to you and to sticking out like sore thumbs!"

Sam and Niamh raised their glasses, clearly more used to sticking out than I ever was or ever would be.

"To good times!" Niamh said.

* * *

Three hours later, things were considerably jazzed up. I now wore four cocktail umbrellas behind my ears and a selection of Niamh's chunkier rings on my fingers. A feather boa had been donated to my cause by a passing hen party. I had switched to a bottle of Budweiser which I was using as a makeshift microphone while Niamh and I did our best Commitments backing-singer routine to Sam's Andrew Strong impression (complete with facial contortions). Niamh was almost bent double with laughter as I tried to perfect a Dublin accent to mutter the immortal line "Ride, Sally, Ride" and the live band in the corner of the bar had more or less become our personal jukebox as we bombarded them with requests. We had already made it through 'Galway Girl' and 'Don't Stop Believing'.

I felt swept up in an atmosphere of goodwill and belonging. The bar was singing and I was too – and it may have been the drink talking or just the reality of the situation, but I felt as if I was home and I was being me and it was bloody great fun. I didn't have to pretend for anyone or be strong for anyone. The realisation was enough, mid-'Mustang Sally', to bring a tear to my eye which I hastily brushed away before completing our performance with aplomb. It was only when it was over, and Niamh and I were wrapped around Sam, our heads thrown back in a song that no one else was singing that I extricated myself from our huddle and went to the restroom where I could stare myself in the face properly.

This was me. This was who I was and who I was going to be. The power to be happy wasn't in anyone else's hands but mine.

Perhaps I had tried too hard to put that on Craig, or even on my father. Perhaps – no, there was no perhaps about it – I needed to put it on me. I splashed cold water on my face and the back of my neck and stood tall and looked at the thirty-seven-year-old woman looking back at me. If I wanted to be happy it was up to me to be happy. I breathed out, the strains of 'Like a Virgin' carrying in through the door as the band reached new levels of cheesy cool.

"You okay?" I heard a voice ask.

Niamh had walked in the door and stopped halfway to the stalls to look at me.

"I will be, thanks," I said with a half smile.

"You don't have to keep it all in, you know," she said and I looked at her quizzically.

"I'm not sure I know what you mean . . ."

"You. You're a closed book. I can see that, but you don't have to be."

I felt myself blush as I nervously pushed a curl behind my ear, dislodging one of the cocktail umbrellas and sending it tumbling into the sink.

"Look, you don't know me from Adam," she said, "and I'm just some ballsy Derry girl who wears clothes that are probably a bit too colourful and whose Dublin accent beats seven shades of crap out of yours – but I've seen stuff and know stuff and all I'm saying is, you don't have to hold it in."

A slightly worse-for-wear woman coming out of the other stall, still adjusting her skirt and looking almost cross-eyed in the mirror, chimed in. "She's right, love. Let it out. No good holding it in till it drives you mad."

I looked at Niamh and back to the woman who was now trying to fix her hair while focusing with one eye open and one closed and her tongue stuck out at a funny angle. "Don't worry about me. I'm going to be okay," I said.

"Good woman yourself," the drunken woman said, patting me on the back a little too fiercely.

Niamh took me by the hand and dragged me through to the smoking area.

"I don't smoke," I protested.

"Neither do I," she laughed, "but there are occasionally some hot men out here and I'm just checking out the talent. Oh, Annabel from Florida, you have much to learn! Sam's a good one," she said as she glanced around her. "He will keep you right. Such a shame he's into men, or I'd have him snapped up in a heartbeat."

"I thought you had the hots for him when we first met," I said.

"I did. I do as a matter of fact, but Sam and I figured out a long time ago we would just be friends – you know, given my lack of appropriate genitalia and all!" She laughed brightly and I couldn't help but laugh too.

"But you seemed suspicious of me?"

"I'll let you into a secret, pet. I'm suspicious of everyone – and protective of my friends. Sam, well, people see he does well for himself. He has a generous nature. They like to take advantage of that. I've seen a lot of people hurt him so I suppose I can't help but feel protective of him. He's a good guy."

"He is."

"But he didn't tell me he had a cousin coming to visit, so I didn't know who the hell you were. But you seem okay."

"If a little closed?"

"If a little closed. But stick around, kid – because, between Sam and me, we will knock that out of you."

By the end of the night we had made it to a little bar called Bennigans close to the river. In the corner a band was playing its own original songs. I'd removed the remaining cocktail umbrellas and the feather boa and was drinking water, while Niamh and Sam sat in deep conversation. I felt calm and rested and allowed the mellow music of the band to wash over me.

My thoughts were interrupted by the voice of one of the older locals who came to sit down beside me.

"Enjoying yourself?" he asked jovially.

"Yes, thanks," I replied, sipping from my glass.

"Ah, a Yank," he said as if it would be news to me and I nodded in response. "I remember the Yanks in Derry," he said. "Through the war and up the 60s. My sister married a Yank – left in '62. She came back last year for a visit, couldn't believe the change in the place. Did you know Derry had a marine base? Did you know the German U-boats surrendered here at the end of World War Two?" He spoke with great pride as if he had witnessed them waving the white flag himself.

I nodded. "I had heard, yes."

"Mad times," he said. "I was only a boy but I remember it well. I used to do the odd wee job at the Base. They would give me chocolate. Never tasted chocolate like it before or since. I still remember it even now. But some of the local boys weren't too happy – the Yanks coming and stealing our girls. The girls, they loved it though. Felt like they were dating real-life movie stars."

I smiled. "My mother was a Derry girl and she dated a Yank."

"Ah, did she marry him? Was your daddy stationed in Derry then?"

I shook my head. "It's a long story," I said. "No. She didn't marry him in the end. I suppose life got in the way."

"Life does that sometimes," the old man said, setting his pint down. "But sure she must have gone to the States anyway. Didn't she have you? So I'm sure it all worked out for the best."

I smiled. "You're very kind."

"Ach, it's easy to be to a lovely girl like yourself. Now, you make sure them two lovebirds beside you get you home safe and sound."

I smiled again and thanked him for his company while he moved on to the next table to have his bit of banter.

When the band had finished, and we got up to leave, Sam said he had something to show me. He took my hand and walked me to the top of the street where a large monument, two men reaching out to each other, stood. Niamh told me it was called *Hands Across the Divide* – a symbol of a healing city. Across the street was just the blackness of the night.

"That," he said, "behind that monument, was Tillie and Henderson. Where your mother worked. It stood here for years – until it burned down, ooh, ten or fifteen years ago. It was a great building in its day." He grabbed my hand and spun me around. "And that," he said, "is Carlisle Road. Somewhere there on that road is their love nest. Can you imagine it?"

I stood for a moment, trying to ground myself, my head still swimming slightly from the wine and beer. I tried to imagine my mother – just twenty – running down this street to her work. I tried to imagine her opening one of these doors and climbing the stairs to see Ray and I tried to imagine what it must have been like for her on that last night.

I couldn't speak. I could barely think. I just stood there and allowed myself to feel for a bit.

I was conscious of Sam on one side of me and Niamh on the other and, when I had stood for a while and started shivering, we left and went home.

The party was continuing in its own way in the living room but I climbed into bed and lifted my phone. It was a cowardly way to do things, I know. But I didn't want any drama – not any more. And, I supposed, I didn't want to hear him reply that it was okay, he didn't mind either.

I'm sorry, I punched in, **but it's over.**

Chapter 22

I have to let go. Not because I want to – but because I can't make you forgive me.

Derry, January 1960

If Ray had known that he would not see her again, that he would not kiss her again, that he would not feel her skin against his again, he would not have let her leave the flat. He would have begged her to stay. He would have risked the wrath of his superior officers and whatever they could throw at him to get just a few more minutes with the woman who had stolen his heart. But he believed, just as Stella believed, that they would be together again in a number of weeks. It was, he told himself, the only way he could bear to be parted from her. He was angry at himself, as they left Derry and began the long journey home, that he could find no joy whatsoever in returning to his native America. Not even the thought of his mother's home cooking could comfort him as they travelled away from Derry. He felt as lost as he had ever done and he started to count down until the moment he would see her again.

* * *

Derry, February 1960

The news of Molly Davidson's return from America came as

quite a shock. It wasn't more than months since she had left and, once word reached the factory floor that she was returning to her family, it quickly became the main topic of conversation. Stella, although curious about Molly's return, was also a little relieved. She herself had been the main fodder for the gossips since Ray had shipped out. There were those who chose to believe that she had been jilted – that there had never been a wedding planned in the first place. There were others who, while accepting her version of events, adopted the pose of the doom-monger, telling her that out of sight meant out of mind and sure wouldn't everything be different when he was back in America with the local women throwing themselves at him? "I don't mean to worry you," Meg, a stitcher, had said, "but I've heard it a hundred times. Sure their heads get turned as soon as they are back among their own." Stella had just shrugged, put her hand to the brooch she wore every day and willed them to be wrong. Ray was different, she was sure of that. Theirs was not some silly romance – it was true love. It rivalled anything she had seen in the movies and what would the girls from the factory floor know anyway?

"They're jealous and that's an end to it," Dolores said as they walked home from the factory. "There are people in this world who can't bear to see others happy when they themselves are not."

"You don't think they might be right? That he might forget me?"

Dolores laughed. "He couldn't if he tried. Sister, dear, you have to put these worries to one side. This is just a blip and sure you will have your big romantic reunion and this will be a story you tell your grandchildren in years to come."

Stella hoped her sister was right but, if she was honest with herself, with every day that passed and with every moment they were apart she wondered just a little if it had been real? Had her head been turned? She willed that her paperwork would sort itself out, that the call would come from the States and that she would be able to go.

But at the same time, she dreaded it as well. That big goodbye.

Linking arms, the sisters walked back to their house where they could hear their mother setting about making the dinner while the younger boys ran in and out the front door, leaving it wide to the world.

"They'll catch their deaths," Kathleen muttered as she popped another potato into the pot and dried her hands off on her apron.

Stella took her coat off and hung it up, kicked off her shoes and put on her slippers. She then put on her apron and set about helping her mother lay the table for dinner. It was a small table, and really they didn't all fit around it, especially now that the older boys were grown men, but nonetheless Kathleen Hegarty would insist they sat down together every night – all six children, herself and Ernest – and ate their evening meal together.

The Hegarty household worked well because it ran like clockwork. Then again it needed to. Ernest would have to be at the docks first thing to see if there was any work in for the day. The older boys had taken to joining him, but there wasn't much going, especially not for the boys who were not known to the port officials. More often than not Peter and James would slink back home where they would spend their days doing odd jobs for the neighbours or trying to get a lead on whatever job they could. There wasn't much labouring going then, either, and any decent jobs, it seemed, were sewn up. So more often than not Kathleen Hegarty would find herself with two, fed-up, grown men under her feet for the morning until the two youngest came back from school. Then she had four boys to keep in line. Despite whatever money Ernest could make at the docks, and whatever Dolores and Stella could put into the house, times were tough.

Stella noticed as she set the table how some of the crockery was looking past its best – a crack here and a chip there. She vowed to save up to buy a new set – and quickly remembered she wouldn't be here to save up. She would be a million miles away, worrying about a new set of her own. The thought almost winded her until Dolores nudged her firmly in the ribs.

"Get a wiggle on there, Dolly Daydream. There's work to be done. And I want to get out of here early tonight. The Corinthian waits for no woman. Why don't you come along? Shake that sad face right off."

Stella shook her head. "I don't think so. It wouldn't be right and besides I'm really not in form for it."

"You can't hide yourself under a rock until the call or letter comes from America, you know. You'll be away from us all soon enough. Get out and enjoy yourself."

Dolores was teasing. Stella knew that but still she felt herself bristle. What company would she be, out and about with a sour face on, watching courting couples on the dance floor while she nursed a cordial and missed Ray?

"Maybe you should go out, love," Kathleen said softly. "It might do you good."

"I'm grand, Mammy, honest. Actually I thought I might go and call on Molly later. See how she is? Must be terrible for her to have to come back from America. I wonder what happened?"

Stella watched the expression on her mother's face change and darken slightly. "I'd say she's tired from the journey, pet. Best give her a day or two to settle."

Stella nodded and continued pouring a pitcher of water. Any second now the front door would rattle and Ernest would come through it and the kitchen would fill with four hungry boys all ready for whatever Kathleen had prepared for them. Tonight it was spuds and cabbage, with some bacon cooked for Ernest who had been out working all day. The girls, though they had been working too, would eat the same as the rest. That was simply the way it was and while the smell of the bacon made her mouth water, Stella never thought to question it. She knew there were nights they were lucky to have a cooked dinner on the table at all.

"So you've no excuse not to go to the Corinthian then," Dolores said.

"Dolores, please! I'll just stay in with Mammy and Daddy. Leave me be." Stella knew she was snapping but she didn't want to go and her sister's pestering was starting to make her short-tempered.

"Okay," Dolores said, backing off. "But I would have thought you'd have liked the chance to let your hair down a little. You've been so miserable lately."

"You would be miserable too if you were me," Stella replied, her temper flaring.

"Girls! Now enough or I'll knock your heads together! Your father will be home any minute after a long, hard day and the last thing I want him coming home to is the pair of you bickering like children. Dolores, your sister says she doesn't want to go, so leave it and that's that. And Stella, your sister is only trying to get you to come out of yourself a little, so try to keep calm. Honest to goodness, as if I didn't have enough on my plate with the younger boys to have to step in between the pair of you – grown women and all!"

Stella blushed and felt embarrassed. It wasn't often she got a dressing-down from her mother and, feeling suitably chastised, she apologised immediately and offered to go and make sure the younger boys had washed up before dinner.

"You need to check on those older boys too!" Kathleen called as she left the kitchen. "They're likely to be muckier than the wains."

* * *

Dolores had skipped out of the house – a smile on her face, her hair curled and set and a new dress on her back. Stella had, she had to admit after all, felt a little jealous to see her run out – so carefree. But nonetheless, she had known the moment she had met Ray that things wouldn't be the same again and if that

197

meant, in this instance, sitting in with her parents instead of dancing the night away she was happy to do so. She put the two younger boys to bed. Michael shrunk from her grasp as she tried to hug him while Seán held on tightly and begged to sleep in her bed that night.

"Are you really going away, Smella?" he asked, his eyes bright.

"Yes, pet, I am."

"And I'll only have one sister then," he said sadly, his face dropping.

"You'll always have two sisters, Seán. You don't get rid of me just because you can't see me. I'm still your big sister and always will be."

He held on extra tight and she felt herself holding him a little tighter too.

Back downstairs, her mother stoked the fire while her father snoozed in his chair. It had been a backbreaking day at the docks, he had said when he got home and he was exhausted – but not too exhausted to polish off his bacon and cabbage. But now, after a bath, he was fit for nothing but sitting with his eyes half closed while Kathleen did her knitting in the corner. Stella imagined for many twenty-year-olds this would be their idea of hell but she took it all in and tried to capture the simple images before her in her memory.

As she made them all a cup of a tea, she started when she heard a rap on the door. It wasn't often they had visitors at this time of night and she had been planning to make for her bed as soon as she had drunk her tea. Opening the door she saw Mrs Murphy, almost fit to burst, on the doorstep.

"I had to come, pet," she said, pushing past Stella and into the hall – her coat already half off before Stella had the chance to say hello. "I had to tell you . . ."

"Mrs Murphy," Stella said, "do come in."

"Is your mammy here, doll? She should hear this too? And your daddy."

Stella turned to see Kathleen walk out of the scullery to see what the commotion was.

"Ah, Kathleen. Grand, so you are here. Is Ernest here too?"

"He's having a wee sleep. Eileen, what on earth is this about?"

Mrs Murphy took a deep breath and nodded towards the kitchen. "If you've a pot of tea on I could tell you over that. And some biscuits if you have them."

"Stella, would you put a cup out for Mrs Murphy?" Kathleen said, shooing the gossipy neighbour into the kitchen.

Stella dutifully did just as her mother asked, loading the cup with sugar just the way Mrs Murphy liked it.

"Well, you know me," Mrs Murphy started, "not one to gossip and all – but seeing as Stella here finds herself in a similar situation I thought it was my duty to tell you."

Stella felt her heart beat faster. Was there something wrong with Ray? No, she told herself, that couldn't be it. Sure what would Mrs Murphy know about Ray? She mustn't let her mind run on with itself. She sat down and lifted her own teacup, her hands shaking slightly, and sipped gingerly from her tea.

"That poor girl," Mrs Murphy continued, a glint of something – perhaps enjoyment at having some juicy gossip to share – in her eye. "Poor Molly."

Kathleen Hegarty bristled at the name – it was slight but enough for Stella to notice from across the table. "I don't think we need to be worrying about Molly Davidson," she said and Stella knew that whatever it was that Mrs Murphy was about to impart with such glee from across the table, her mother already knew.

"But of course we do," the older woman said. "You can't have your Stella here running off to the States not knowing what she might be landing herself into. It would be remiss of me not to tell you," she said, turning to look at Stella directly.

"Eileen, please," Kathleen said, but her protestations went unnoticed.

"Stella, you see these men – all stories about love and romance and how great it is going to be. Well, Molly Davidson would tell you different. There she was all the way over there and then . . ." At this Mrs Murphy blessed herself and looked up to heaven while all Stella could do was wish she would spit it out. "It was all lies. All lies."

"Eileen, you can't tar everyone with the same brush!" said Kathleen.

"But all the way over there? Jesus – the critter was over there and it was nothing like he said. No nice house, no lovely garden. She was in some tenement with him and his family and countless other families –"

"Sounds no different to life here, Eileen," Kathleen said.

"But it was worse – and him, he didn't know what to do with himself. First night there, by all accounts, he goes out on the drink and he comes home and beats seven shades out of her. And his family, sure they were as bad as each other – she was treated like no more than a slave. You'd get better treatment in the cotton fields. He never let her leave the house – and when she did, he'd lay into her again." Mrs Murphy blessed herself again, throwing her eyes once more heavenward. "It was only by the grace of God that the Davidsons had family in New York and they were able to get her out of there. And the poor critters have themselves pawned to within an inch of their lives to get her back. She's in an awful way, I hear. Awful."

Stella felt the bile rise in her stomach. She felt for Molly, so far from home – and how she had left so full of dreams, so convinced she was doing the right thing, and she felt as if she might burst into tears right there and then.

"Word is, they were lucky not to be getting her home in a box."

"Eileen," Kathleen said as softly as she could, "it's a terrible story, I know. Sure I saw Mrs Davidson this morning myself – but this is not how it ends for everyone. For goodness' sake, there are plenty local girls have gone over there and found themselves as happy as they could want to be. And there are plenty local men just as bad as yer man – there's no need to be scaremongering."

"Well, all I'm saying is that I wouldn't take the risk if it were my daughter," Mrs Murphy said, sniffing and reaching her hand into the biscuit barrel. "They were lucky they had family over there – but do you, Kathleen? If the same were to happen to our wee Stella here would you be able to get her home?"

"Eileen, it's not going to happen," Kathleen said, taking the biscuit barrel from her and placing it back on the shelf.

"Ray isn't like that," Stella blurted out. "He would never be like that. He's a good man. An honest man."

"You saw young Molly before her wedding, didn't you?" Mrs Murphy asked, a slight ominous tone to her voice. "Did she think her David was a good man and an honest man too? I bet she did."

Stella looked down at her cup. She knew that Mrs Murphy was stirring in the way that only Mrs Murphy could, and that nothing she could say would deter the old bat from the notion that she was right and everyone else was wrong. Her urge to defend Ray to the hilt was overwhelmed by the sense of futility which always came with getting into a discussion with Mrs Murphy.

"You wouldn't understand," she offered, hoping that would be enough to bring the conversation to a swift conclusion.

"Trust me, my girl," said Murphy as she drained her cup and stood up. "I know a lot more than you think I know. I'm a lot older than you – I've seen more. I've seen the world and you young ones, you think you know it all. But you know what, you know so little. It's not all fairytale endings."

"Eileen, I think it's high time you left. It's getting late and you've said enough."

"Oh, I'm going," Mrs Murphy sniffed. "I know where I'm not wanted. And there was me, only trying to help. Well, sure, maybe I won't help any more and she can just get on with things – but let me tell youse, if it all goes wrong, don't come running to me."

"Eileen, pet, when have we ever come running to you for anything anyway?" Kathleen said, shooing her neighbour out of the door before turning to look back at Stella, who felt numb from the exchange.

She was horrified at the thought of what had happened to her friend – and her stomach felt queasy. She felt fiercely defensive of Ray – even though none of this had anything to do with him and she knew that he loved and cherished her. But, perhaps more than all that, she felt scared. Kathleen pulled her into a hug and she let the embrace of her mother soothe her.

"My darling girl, you are to pay no heed to that woman. Do you hear me?" Kathleen said as she brushed Stella's hair back from her face and kissed the top of her head. "She just likes a gossip and the more salacious the better. She no more cares about Molly Davidson or you than she cares about the man in the moon. She is just one of those misfortunate creatures who like to be the bearer of bad news – and can't wait to see everyone else's reactions. You know your Ray, don't you, pet? You know you can trust him. And let me tell you this, my darling baby girl, should you ever need to come home, ever, we will do everything we can to get you back to us. You are never to be afraid to ask. You are never to question it. You just say you want to be home and we will sell everything belonging to us if we need to."

Stella nodded, her emotions divided. She was both comforted by her mother's words and unsettled as well. Would she ever need to come home? Could she, like Molly, have got it all wrong?

She went to bed wishing she could pick up the phone and call Ray – just to hear his voice, just to hear him reassure her that everything would be okay. Just to tell her she was being silly having any kind of doubts because they were stronger than that and to hear him tell her of the house in the suburbs, with the bathroom and the bedrooms, and soft eiderdown quilts and a roaring fire in a spacious den and a kitchen that was state of the art. And how he would always look after her as if she were the most precious thing in his world. But she couldn't talk to him so she sat by her bed instead and wrote a letter, pouring out her thoughts and feelings, her worries and her hopes, and then she changed, climbed under the blankets and looked out the window into the night sky. He was there somewhere, she knew it, and she was foolish to ever doubt him. Nonetheless as she slept her dreams were fitful and when she woke the next morning she found herself dressing and heading straight to visit Molly.

Chapter 23

I miss you. I can say no more.

* * *

Mrs Davidson looked surprised to see Stella at her front door. Stella herself was surprised to be there. She shifted awkwardly from foot to foot, proffering a bag of apples she had bought at the market that morning. "I brought these," she said. "I didn't know what else to bring."

"Come in, pet," Mrs Davidson said, leading her into the hall.

There was a silence about the house that seemed to match the seriousness of the situation. Stella was aware of a whispered conversation in the scullery as she walked past. Mrs Davidson led her upstairs to the bedroom she had been in, not that long ago, chatting excitedly to Molly about her wedding and the plans she had for her happy-ever-after.

"She had a decent night – well, compared to the night before. She's still quite sore – but it's her heart that is broken more than anything. She hasn't spoken much, doll – but maybe she would talk to you, for her father and I can't get through to her." Mrs Davidson's eyes were pleading – as if she were at the end of her tether. She didn't look as if she had slept much herself.

Stella said she would do her best but already she felt a little out of her depth and started to wonder had she been wise to visit in the first place.

Mrs Davidson opened the door. Molly's bedroom was in

complete darkness. Mrs Davidson walked across the room and pulled the curtains open.

"You have a visitor," she said to the lump in the bed. There was no movement. She opened the window slightly. "A bit of fresh air will do you good, pet," she said and again there was no response.

Stella took a seat on the wooden chair beside the bed and noticed the bottle of pills on the small wooden table and the glass of water.

"Molly, it's only me, Stella. I just called to see how you are."

"I told my mother I didn't want visitors," Molly muttered, her voice muffled by the blankets hauled up around her face.

"She thought it might do you good," Stella said. "She thought it might brighten you a bit. I just wanted to see how you were."

There was a snort of derision from under the blanket. "The talk of the town, am I?" Molly said, her voice breaking. "The silly wee girl who had to be rescued? Who made an eejit of herself running off for a new life and coming back battered and bruised?"

The grief was evident in her voice – the shame and the embarrassment.

"No one . . . no one thinks you're an eejit," said Stella. "You weren't to know. How could you have? Look, Molly, if anyone understands it's me. Here I am waiting to run off into the sunset myself."

"Well, I hope you'll fare better than me," Molly said, turning in the bed to show the fading bruises across her face and the fading cut from across her eyebrow.

Stella closed her eyes, so as to stop herself from gasping, and opened them again to see Molly looking at her square in the face, her eyes filled with tears.

"I've been such a fool," she said. "I believed it all. That he loved me. That we would be happy. That what we would have there was better than what I had here and that it would all work out. I was smug about it, I admit. I just didn't think."

Stella reached out to her friend and held her hand as she cried.

"I made my vows in good faith," Molly said. "I meant every word. The richer and poorer and the 'in sickness and in health' and even the better and worse. Was I wrong to run? Was this not the worse bit? Am I a sinner, Stella? Did I not take it seriously?"

The childish enthusiasm Stella had witnessed in this very room not more than a few months ago was gone – it was replaced by a pitiful sadness that made Stella's very heart ache.

"No one thinks you're a sinner, pet. Not even the Lord himself would expect you to stay there – not when he was hurting you like that."

Molly reached up to her face, revealing her bruised hands. "He told me he would kill me," she said softly. "That I was worth nothing to him and that he would kill me if I disobeyed him. I didn't, Stella. I didn't, I swear."

"I know," Stella said, forcing the words from her mouth as the shock seeped into her pores. "I know. You will get over this. I promise. You will be back on your feet before you know it – back at the dances and smiling like you were."

Molly rolled over in bed again, facing the wall and pulled the blanket gingerly back over her face as if every movement sent a shockwave of pain through her body. The conversation was over and Stella sat for a moment before walking back down the stairs to the hopeful face of Mrs Davidson, who seemed to be waiting for a miracle.

"I imagine it will take a bit of time," Stella said, feeling strangely out of place talking to the older woman in this way.

"Thanks, pet," Mrs Davidson replied and Stella made her way back out onto the street not sure how she felt or why she had come in the first place.

She walked along Carlisle Road and glanced up to where the flat was before pulling her coat more tightly around her against the cold and walking home.

Dolores was helping with the washing when she arrived. "And where were you off to on this cold morning? You couldn't have been sneaking off to see your fancy man since he is on the other side of the world."

"It doesn't matter," Stella said dejectedly, setting about helping with the work.

"You've a terrible sour face on you," Dolores teased. "But are you not going to ask me why I've such a smile on mine?"

Stella looked at her sister, who was beaming from ear to ear, and felt relieved that the focus of the conversation was being shifted from her.

"Well, why then?" she asked.

"I've met someone," Dolores said. "At the dance last night. Hugh Doherty his name is, and Stella, he's lovely."

Smiling back and getting on with her work, Stella enjoyed listening to her sister's tales if for no other reason than to distract her from her own thoughts. No good could come of them at all.

Chapter 24

Am I making it worse? All this time. I don't know what else to do, Ray. I feel helpless – and hopeless and I just hope you will forgive me.

* * *

Derry, June 2010

I woke to the shrill ring of my phone, although it took me a while to register what was going on. My head was still swimming just a little after the excesses of the night before even though I had been relatively sensible and had drunk the requisite pint of water before retiring for the night on Sam's instructions. I wasn't sure how long I had been asleep – I knew that it was light but as it was summer and the dawn started to crack shortly before five, that was no real indicator. My eyes and my brain still bleary, I reached for my cell and made several attempts to answer it, swiping my fingers – which appeared to be still asleep – across the screen and swearing under my breath. When it rang off, I slumped back on my pillow – focused on the screen and saw it was a missed call from Craig. A vague memory of the message I had sent him before I drifted off to sleep crept into my mind, but it didn't make my heart sink. Looking at the time, I saw it had gone six. I had sent the message at two. He had taken four hours to call. It either meant, I reckoned, that he was so devastated by the news it had taken him four hours to compose himself enough to call me, or that he cared so little he had let it slide for a while. My bets were on the latter. Or somewhere in between. I didn't regret sending the message – not one ounce. It had to be said and it had to be sent – and I felt, I dunno, even in my still semi-conscious state, relieved to have finally done it – to have pulled that Band-Aid off once and for all and exposed what had been so very rotten in the state of our relationship for so very long.

I'd have to call him, of course. I couldn't be that person who let it all just go after our years together with a text message, but in that moment there was a part of me which was enjoying believing that maybe, just maybe, he was suffering a little.

Suffering just a little the way I had suffered.

While I had never told him I knew about how he had cheated on me – how I had witnessed the cheating in front of my eyes – it had eaten away at me. At us. Each and every time he had tried to comfort me I had felt myself pull from his grasp, even if only mentally. The thought of him with her, in her – it made my stomach turn.

I saw her once – in Walmart, as I was grocery shopping. I was pushing my cart along the aisles when I saw a wave of blonde hair in front of me and she turned to take something from the shelves. She looked like a nice person – not a stereotypical bit on the side. No short skirt and big boobs and high heels. Just a young woman, jeans and a T-shirt, a bright smile and a polite nod of the head towards me as she reached up past me to lift down a tin of beans.

I wondered did she know who I was? Or did she care? God knows, we didn't live in a big place and Bake My Day was a popular bakery. My picture was in my house – the house she had been in at least once. Did Craig talk about me? Did he tell her I was a terrible partner and that I didn't understand him? Did he tell her we didn't have sex? Did he say he would leave me except that my father was dying and that he didn't want to come across as the bad guy? Did he make up some sad story to cover for his unfaithfulness or did he not care? You would think after ten years together you would know a person – you would know how they think, or how they feel, what way they act and what they say. But I didn't know him – not at all. I realised that now and I nodded back to the blonde woman with the shopping basket for one and went on my way.

My cell rang – Craig again. This time, more awake, I swiped my finger across the screen and answered the call.

"Craig," I said, simply.

"What are you playing at, Annabel?" His voice was calm, jokey. Dismissive even. 'Annabel goes off on one again' – I could almost see him rolling his eyes. Laughing, getting ready to tell me I was being overly dramatic.

"I'm not playing at anything, Craig," I said, trying to keep my tone soft. Trying not to show the anger that was threatening to bubble up and jump out.

"It's over?" he said, and laughed at the end. "What do you mean, it's over?"

His laughter, for some reason, brought tears to my eyes. Even in this – in breaking up – even now he could not understand where I was coming from. Or maybe he didn't want to. Everything is okay with Annabel and Craig as long as the sun is shining and life doesn't get in the way.

I took a deep breath. "I mean it's over, Craig. I'm sorry. And I'm sorrier still to do this over the phone but now it seems so clear and it's unfair on both of us to keep this hanging on for a minute longer than it needs to."

"Anna," his voice less mocking – more urgent this time, "you need to think about this. You need to calm down."

"I have thought about it, Craig," I started.

"What? Over a few glasses of Guinness with your cousin? Yes – perfect atmosphere to make life-altering decisions."

I shook my head even though I knew he wouldn't see the gesture and rubbed my temples. "No, Craig. Please listen – for once in your life, please listen. I've been thinking about this for a long time. It's just, away from it all, away from you, it has started to come into focus for the first time."

He laughed again. A mocking bark of a laugh which felt like a punch in the stomach. "Off chasing the pot of gold at the end of some goddamn rainbow with your leprechaun friends. You were fine before you left. We were fine."

"Were we? Really? That's why you stalked around the house the day I left like a spoiled child. Because we were fine?"

"I didn't want you to go. Was that so wrong of me?"

Whatever I had expected of Craig, I had not expected this – this lie upon lie about what he wanted. What he needed. That he thought we were okay.

"No," I said. "But what was wrong of you, Craig, was you having sex with someone else while my father was dying."

He was silent. I could hear him breathe softly down the phone line. I remembered all the times I had listened to his breathing softly: in the early days, when we had spent hours and hours together, I would lie awake and listen to him breathing, telling myself this was love. This is what it was. God, I was stupid. I had learned so much about love even in the last few days and it wasn't what we had. It was so completely removed from what we had.

"I only did that," he stuttered, "because you were lost to me. I didn't know how to get you back and I was lonely."

"I can't say I can tell you how you could have got me back, Craig, but I can tell you that having sex with someone else was not the way to go about it." The tears that had been threatening to fall started to slide down my face but I didn't want to give in to them so I hastily brushed them away. "I saw. I came home and I saw it. The two of you. And I don't know how many times and I don't know if she was the only one and, you know what, part of me doesn't need to know because what difference would it make anyway? It was one thing, Craig, but it wasn't everything. Don't you know we have been broken for a long time? And I'm just admitting it openly first."

"It didn't mean anything."

211

Claire Allan

"If it didn't, why did you risk us for it?"

"People make mistakes, Annabel. You're not perfect."

"I never said I was."

"You pushed me away. You had no time for me."

"My father was dying!" I almost roared – the words sounding as harsh as the experience was as I let them out.

"But you weren't. You gave up on life. You gave up on us the day he had his diagnosis and there was no getting you back."

He might have had a point. Perhaps. Perhaps I did give up on life. In the very moment I learned my father would die a part of me died too. And the part that was still living? That part didn't want to go on. She didn't want to wake up every day to the knowledge that death was coming. She didn't want to watch her hero fade before her eyes. She didn't want to face a world without her father. So perhaps I did give up. Perhaps I crawled into some far unreachable place where I tried, and failed, to shield myself from the pain that was to come. But he was my daddy; the man who had carried me on his shoulders when I was a little girl; who had put my hair in lopsided pigtails and beamed so proudly; who had been the person who taught me to ride my bicycle; who cheered the loudest when I graduated, and who was first through the door at Bake My Day when we opened. And the world was taking him from me and there was nothing I could do it about. Nothing. No amount of money would save him. No amount of prayer would make a difference. He was going. And I wanted to go too.

But maybe even more than that I wanted someone to hold me up – to listen to me cry. To take it on the chin when I shouted. To tell me they were just as angry as I was and damn right, it wasn't fair. It was rubbish. I wanted that person to be Craig – and it wasn't. It never was. I didn't give up on us. I just realised there wasn't really an 'us' there to begin with.

"I'm sorry," was all I could muster.

I could be angry, I realised. And I was – but more than that I was sad. And more than sad I was relieved.

"You're making a mistake," he said.

"I don't think so. We shouldn't hurt each other any more," I said, and ended the call before switching my phone off.

Then I lay back, in the soft light of the Derry morning on the bed that I had all to myself and I waited for the tears to start falling properly. I waited for the sobs and the heartbreak and the questions over whether or not I had done the right thing. I waited for the horrors to hit and the urge to call him back and say it was all a mistake to come. But none of that happened.

Instead, I fell back into a sleep where I dreamt I had one last day with my daddy – sitting in the garden, holding his hands – still warm, not cold as they had been the last time I held him – and he was telling me he loved me and that all would be okay.

I woke, gasping, half expecting him to be in the room with me but while he was, obviously, not there, I could feel his warmth around me, telling me it would be okay. And if Daddy said it would be okay, it would be.

* * *

Sitting in Dolores' front room, I tried to imagine the life I had read about so much in my mother's letters. I tried to think about my grandparents, whose faces stared down at me from the walls, and how they made this house a home, even in tough times. I imagined my Uncle Seán as the gap-toothed boy my mother had written about, even though he was now a grandfather. I imagined my mother laying the table in the impossibly small kitchen – which of course Dolores had remodelled numerous times since she had taken over ownership of the family home – and I imagined the night my mother and Ray stood in this room toasting their engagement. I closed my eyes and tried to feel the echoes of the world I had come to know so much about in the last few days – to try and understand them all better. Especially my mother.

I felt a peace towards her now. An understanding of why she

did what she did. An understanding that she loved my father very much but that before him there had been someone else – someone she had loved desperately, whom circumstance had kept her from.

I still had questions of course – pieces of the jigsaw puzzle that needed piecing together and now that I had read the letters I needed to know the rest.

Dolores had smiled at me when I turned up at her door, then looked over my shoulder expecting Sam to be there.

"He's gone to work," I explained and she nodded.

"He loves that job. Loves that shop. Works too hard sometimes too. I'm glad you're here making him take some time off for a change."

"I don't think he considers it work most of the time," I laughed as she poured me a cup of tea and directed me to the front room. "Says it's like playing dress-up for a reason."

Her shoulders stiffened at this remark. "Yes, well. He always was a little flamboyant," she sniffed.

"Auntie Dolores," I began but she turned to leave the room.

"I'll just go and get your mother so you can concentrate on matters concerning your own family."

With that she was gone and I tried to marry the impression of a young, flighty, carefree woman painted in my mother's letters with the woman in front of me who seemed to deny her son so much.

"You can't fix the world," I heard my father's voice somewhere in my head. But I knew I had to try. Okay, I would start with Mom. But Sam too. And Dolores. We could all do with some fixing.

Chapter 25

I was in shock. I have never felt shock, pain like it before. Not until now anyway Ray. Do you understand? I hadn't realised I would never get the chance to say goodbye.

* * *

Derry, February 1960

A moment can change the course of your life forever. All the plans – dreams and hopes you thought you had can suddenly disappear. Life can take a new direction. Things change. Decisions are made – decisions that you think are the best for everyone at the time but that have consequences so far-reaching you can't possibly understand what they will mean for you. Stella Hegarty learned that on February 16, 1960, when just as it seemed as if the paperwork would finally come through for her new life with Ray, her life turned on a hairpin and things would never be the same again.

* * *

By February Molly Davidson had started work again at the factory. She told Stella, who she had come to confide in, that she was terrified of walking through the doors again and of what everyone would think. Stella had told her to hold her head high – that she had done nothing wrong but still, bowed and broken by her experience, Molly had replied that she knew the girls would laugh.

"They carried me out of there singing before – and now I'm scuttling back in. A divorcee in the making."

"Your mammy will get that annulment sorted, pet," Stella had soothed her. "Sure hasn't she been up to the priest already?"

Molly had nodded but in her head she felt like spoiled goods and Stella knew that no matter what she could say to her it would make her feel no better. She was just going to have to work through it. As she had walked home from Molly's house that night she had wondered how her friend would cope when she, herself, went to America in the coming weeks. As much as Stella had made herself available to the young, devastated bride, others had stayed away. Molly was right to feel nervous about going back on the factory floor but she had little choice. Both Mr and Mrs Davidson had been up to see the supervisors to make a case for their daughter to be allowed back to work – and it was an income they sorely needed after borrowing a hefty sum to get Molly back in the first place.

Walking home from Molly's house where the pair had sat talking until she felt her eyes droop, Stella wrapped her coat around her and assured herself that it would be okay as long as she was there for the first few days and weeks to ease Molly in. The gossips might never forget the young girl who had left so full of hope and wonder but hopefully they would move on and, in time, treat her like one of their own again.

Letting herself in, Stella climbed the stairs to the room she shared with Dolores to find it empty. Dolores must be out with Hugh again, she thought. The pair had quickly become inseparable after that first night in the Corinthian and Dolores had been mooning about the house ever since. Should Stella have dared to have rolled her eyes at her sister's monologues of how Hugh was the most handsome man in all of Derry, she would have received a sharp comeback that she was jealous because Hugh was very much still in Derry while Stella's relationship was now held together by a weekly letter and the promise of a visa.

Dolores could be cruel when she wanted to be, Stella thought.

There wasn't a day that passed that Stella didn't long for a letter to arrive or didn't hope, even though she knew it impossible, that she would open the front door and find Ray there, that twinkle in his eyes and that smile she loved so well on his face and that he would tell her that it was okay and they were together again.

She undressed and climbed into bed to keep warm, taking the latest letter from him out from under her pillow. It had arrived that morning and she had been saving it for bedtime to read. She knew it would make her heart ache with longing and she didn't want to rush off to work with her face tearstained or missing him more than usual. Having something to look forward to had got her through the day. She found more and more she needed these little pick-me-ups. Just like she needed to look at the suitcase at the bottom of the bed, which she had started to fill with items from her bottom drawer – bits and pieces she had picked up along the way for when she started married life. Looking through it made it feel more real – like it was happening. Sometimes as the days passed she started to wonder if it ever would.

Snuggling down under the blankets, she took out the two pages with his scrawling handwriting and held them close to her. It was silly, she knew. No doubt some would feel she was a foolish young girl with her head in the clouds, but to think that his hands were the last thing on this paper, and then to feel that paper against her body, made her feel closer to him.

My darling Stella,

Has it really been five weeks since I saw you? I swear I look at your picture every day – the one your father gave me before I left – and I try to imagine you here with me.

The boys, they say I've gone soft, but I haven't, Stella. I just know a good thing when I find it.

I'm getting closer to having all our arrangements sorted this end – the marriage quarters won't be fancy but after our nest in Derry I know we will manage just fine.

When they let me out, I hope you don't mind if we live with my parents for a while – just until we have the deposit together for a nice place? Don't worry – they have a basement which they have converted for us. We have our own front door and everything. We won't even realise they are close by a lot of the time. They are so looking forward to meeting you, Stella – the woman who stole my heart away. My mom had high hopes for me settling down with the girl next door but I told her you knock the socks clean off any of the local girls – my Irish rose.

These days are so hard but I know that with every one that passes I am closer to seeing you again and when I see you I won't let you go. You mean the world to me – I could never have imagined meeting someone so caring, so loving and so selfless.

You make me want to be a better person. Does that sound corny? Does it sound like something the leading man would say in one of those movies you love so much?

I hope so, and I hope it made you smile because I want so much to see you smiling, my Stella. Seeing you crying on our last night just about broke my heart. Have faith, my darling.

Know that whatever happens now, we will be together again and just like in those movies we will have our happy ending.

Yours, always,

Ray

X

Kissing his name softly, Stella lay back in bed and wiped a tear from her eye, then forced herself to take a deep breath and not give in to the tears. He was right, of course he was. It was only a matter of time before they would be together again. She had to see every day as a countdown – as a step closer to their reunion. She folded the letter carefully and put it back in the envelope before slipping it under her pillow just as she heard a knock at the door.

"Stella?" her mother's voice called.

"Come in, Mammy!"

Kathleen Hegarty pushed open the door and carried in two cups of tea. "I thought I would bring you up a cup of tea before bed, pet. You didn't come in to say goodnight. I'm worried about you, pining over your young man."

Stella pulled herself up to sit and offered her mother a weak smile. "Thanks, Mammy. You're very good to me." She took the cup from her mother and began to sip the tea.

"Look, you have to take care of yourself," her mother said softly. "I know this is hard for you, especially with your sister gadding about with her new man, but you know it's only temporary."

Stella nodded. "Sometimes it feels like forever."

"Ah, the wise words of the young," Kathleen said with a sad smile. "Wait till you're my age – then the days go flying by."

"You're still young, Mammy. You and Daddy both."

"Almost fifty," Kathleen said. "With a family half reared. Just waiting on you all to settle down now and get out in the world to fend for yourselves. Maybe your daddy can take it a bit easier then."

Stella nodded. She knew Kathleen was worried about Ernest and how hard he worked. When he wasn't down at the docks he was looking for work wherever he could find it – trying to make sure the Hegarty family had food on the table.

"Will you manage when I'm gone, Mammy, without me paying into the house?"

"You're not to worry about such things. Sure I'm not going to keep you all under my roof for the sake of a few bob!"

She smiled but Stella wondered how forced it was. She also knew she was a born worrier and nothing her mother would say would change that. Still, it was another dose of guilt that she knew she would have to deal with if she left.

She finished her toast while she and her mother talked and then, when her teacup was drained, she pulled on a pair of socks and her old cardigan and followed her mother downstairs to sit and enjoy her company for a while longer.

Ernest and the older boys were listening to the football on the wireless in the back room. Every now and again Stella would close her eyes and soak in the sounds. What a position to be in, she thought to herself, to leave the family she loved so dearly to be with the man she couldn't be without.

When it was clear that the Hegartys' favoured football team had won, the boys made their way into the kitchen full of cheer and ready for some supper. While James and Peter tucked into their wheaten bread, and supped their tea, Stella watched her mother and father sit together, hands held, laughing at some shared joke. She was sure, if they had to, each of them would go to the ends of the earth for the other.

* * *

There was never any need for an alarm bell to sound in the Hegarty household to wake anyone up. The sound of Ernest Hegarty up and about, slipping his feet into his hobnailed boots and clumping around the house whistling as he readied himself for work was enough to have the whole house roused. Kathleen would generally follow her husband down the stairs – putting a pot of porridge on the stove which would see him off to work with a full stomach. The younger boys, light sleepers at the best of times, would follow, and the girls, getting ready for the eight o'clock factory horn would be shortly after. The older boys were the only ones who needed a shake to get out of their beds and out looking for work.

The morning routine was hectic but by gone half past eight the house was usually back to its calm self – the children off to work, school or the labour market, and Kathleen would set about her daily chores.

There were no lie-ins to be had at the Hegarty house – so when Stella woke to find the streets light and the house silent she felt uneasy. It must have been at least half past seven if not eight for there to be light coming through the curtains. She looked to her side where she could see Dolores still out for the count, her hair in rollers peeking over her blankets. Since meeting Hugh, Dolores never left the house looking anything less than a million dollars. Stella listened carefully – trying to pick up on the sound of her father's hobnailed boots, or his whistle or the sound of his porridge bowl clattering into the sink followed by Kathleen's voice gently scolding him for being so rough. There was no sound of the younger boys. Seán had yet to pop his head around the door or jump on her bed to wake her.

Stella lifted her watch from her bedside table and, squinting at it, saw that it was five to eight. She had just five minutes to make it to the factory floor or she would be reprimanded, her wages maybe docked. She hauled herself out of bed and called to Dolores to wake up, stepping over to shake her.

"We're late, Dolores! Come on! Get up! Mammy and Daddy must have slept in. We've all slept in. You go wake the boys for school and I'll go and wake Mammy and Daddy. Come on, we need to get there as soon as we can!" She threw her dressing gown over her nightdress and left the room, shouting once more to Dolores, who had just sat up and was still disorientated from her sleep, to wake the boys.

Why she decided she would be the one to wake their parents, Stella didn't know. She didn't think about it. She wished, in the days and weeks to come, that she had woken the boys instead – that she had turned in the landing and walked the other way. But instead, eager to get to work, worried that her daddy would miss a day at the docks and the family finances would be in dire straits, concerned about getting the younger boys to school, worried there was no porridge on the stove, she walked into her parents' room to wake them.

She stopped almost as soon as she opened the door. Her brain tried to process the sight in front of her. The room was barely lit – but yet she could see everything as if a light were shining, as if it were glaring at her.

Her father lay, motionless, pale, his lips a strange blue-ish tint, his face contorted into some strange expression she didn't recognise. Her mother, her shoulders shaking, lay with her head on his chest, holding his waxy-looking hand in hers. Stella stood, aghast, as she saw that hand flop to the bed as her mother rubbed her father's arm and raised her head to look at her daughter.

Stella felt the room sway, was aware of the sound of Dolores waking the boys. Was aware of the pleading in her mother's eyes as she looked at her and back to where Ernest lay. She was aware of the footsteps of Seán as he left his room. She felt the panic rise in her throat and she looked around for something to hold on to, grabbing at the door frame to steady herself.

"Smella, are we late?" Seán chirped. "Can you believe I slept an' slept an' slept?"

She turned to her brother and tried to find the right words, while she thought of how his life was about to be torn apart.

"Dolores!" she called, trying to keep a degree of control in her voice. "Can you take the boys downstairs and put the kettle on?"

"I need to get ready for work," Dolores huffed. "You know we'll be in trouble."

"Dolores, please," Stella said. "Please take the boys downstairs and I'll be down in a minute."

"Dear God, Stella Hegarty! Who died and made you boss?" Dolores squared up to her and Stella, momentarily stung by her sister's words, had to fight back the urge to tell her just who exactly had died and made her boss but she didn't. She couldn't and she wouldn't. She had to stay calm. She had to be the grown-up.

"Just do it, Dolores," she repeated firmly and her sister stomped down the stairs, the two younger boys hot on her heels.

"Where's Mammy and Daddy?" she heard Seán ask as they went into the kitchen and she closed her eyes to steady herself once again before turning back to the room where Kathleen was now stroking her beloved husband's face and raining a hundred kisses on him, trying to smooth the contorted lines.

"I'll get the doctor," Stella said.

"There's no point, love," Kathleen said, never for one moment taking her eyes off her husband. "He's gone, pet. I woke up and he was gone. He's cold," she sobbed, pulling the blanket up around him. "How could I not have known? How did I not feel him slip away right beside me? How did my own heart not stop beating too?"

Stella felt a lump rise in her throat which she forced down. She wanted to cross the room. She wanted to kiss her daddy too but she was scared. She didn't want to feel the coldness of his body. He didn't look like himself and the expression on his face frightened her. She felt horrified at her own reaction and yet, in that instant, frozen to the spot.

"There are formalities," she mumbled. "I'll get the older boys up, and get Mrs Murphy over and get the doctor."

Kathleen nodded, again her eyes not leaving Ernest, her head resting once more on his chest. Stella turned, glad to look away from the scene before her – but knowing she would never forget it for the rest of her days.

Her legs shaky beneath her, she walked to the boys' bedroom where she called to Peter and James to get up. "Boys, I need you up and no complaining."

They stirred, turning to look at her, their eyes still heavy with sleep.

"You look like you've seen a ghost, our Stella," Peter said.

"Boys, please," she said, her voice cracking. "It's Daddy. Daddy's gone. I need to get the doctor and you need to get up to help Mammy."

The boys – grown men older than she was – looked at her, wide-eyed, trying to take in her words.

"The wains, they don't know. Or Dolores. Mammy is with him and I need to get dressed, so you need to get up and get a fire lit and make sure the front room is sorted. They'll be putting him there. And make sure the younger boys are looked after. Help Dolores get them washed and dressed. You'll have to help me tell them." She tried to suck some air into her constricting lungs.

"Jesus," she heard Peter say as he stepped out of bed and buried his head in his hands. "My da."

She willed herself to stay calm. "We need to hold it together, boys. For now. We need to hold it together. Can you do that for me? Please. Can you? For Daddy. For Mammy."

She looked at her brothers, looking at each other like lost children, and she thought of how she had been scared to hold her daddy's hand and she felt something buckle inside her so that she slumped to the floor.

"Stella!" James called, leaping up to help her back on her feet.

No, she would be fine. No, she wouldn't be fine, but she wouldn't let her daddy down. She wouldn't show herself up, nor him.

"I'm grand," she said, pushing the boys away. "Now do as I say and I'll go and tell Mrs Murphy. She'll know what to do. She'll help."

Stella dressed quickly, pulling on the skirt and blouse she had left at the bottom of the bed the night before. She slipped her stockings on, followed by her shoes in an almost robotic fashion. She dragged the brush from the dresser through her hair, but only enough to make herself vaguely presentable. There would be time to fix herself properly later. Then she hurried down the stairs, grabbed her coat and walked out into the cold morning.

It was bright and fresh – the sun was shining, reflecting off the polished cobbles. A hint of frost made the ground slippery but Stella walked on, crossing the street, trying to ground herself in some way. Was she really on the way to tell Mrs Murphy to call the doctor and the undertakers? Was her daddy really dead? How could he be? He had been fine last night – tired-looking maybe, but who wouldn't be tired after a day at the docks lugging around whatever cargo had come in? But he had laughed and joked with them last night – drank tea, kissed her mother.

He couldn't be dead. People didn't just cease to exist for no reason, did they?

She pulled her coat around her, hugging her arms to herself before she knocked on Mrs Murphy's door and settled herself to say the words she didn't want to.

Mrs Murphy opened the door with her usual cheery nosiness. She looked at Stella quizzically – no doubt aware that the Hegarty girl should be at work and not standing at her front door at this time on a weekday morning.

"Whatever is it, Stella?" she asked.

"M-Mrs Murphy," Stella stammered. "C-could you be s-so good as to call the doctor for us? It's Daddy. He's gone, Mrs Murphy. He went in the night."

Mrs Murphy's eyes widened, her hand flew to her chest. "Sweet merciful Jesus, child! I'm so sorry."

Stella took a deep breath. She would hold herself together. She would not let herself go. Not when there were things to be done – the boys to be told, the house to be readied, the funeral to be arranged. No, she would do her daddy proud. It was the least she could do for him.

"I know," she replied solemnly to her neighbour. "And then, if you would be so good, could you mind the young ones here for me? Just for a bit? Just till we get the house sorted. I don't want them upset more than they need to be – and there'll be all that to-ing and fro-ing."

"Of course I will! I'll be over for them now. And I'll phone the chapel, child. Don't you worry."

"I should have thought of that. The priest. Can they still give the Sacrament of the Sick if he is gone? Oh, Daddy would have wanted that."

"I'm sure the priest will do what he can, pet. You head back. I'll make the phone calls and I'll be over as soon as I can. Anything you need, you ask. We'll sort it between us."

"I need to tell Daddy's family," Stella said, her mind filling with the things she needed to do – which she had no experience of before. She had seen death before, but not this close. Not on her own doorstep. Not her own family. She had always just been a mourner, calling by to pay her respects – to say a decade of the Rosary at an open coffin and tell the grieving family she was sorry for their troubles. She didn't know where to start. Daddy would know, she thought, before quickly realising that while her daddy would know he was no good to her now. The thought winded her momentarily.

"You look after your own family first, pet. News travels fast in Derry and the people who need to know will know soon enough. For now you have your sister and brothers to be worried about. And your poor mother. How is she?"

Stella shook her head. It was a simple enough gesture but one which conveyed what words could not. How could you adequately describe the hurt and heartache that was tearing through her mother at the moment? How could she ever tell anyone of the look of loss, of desperation, she had seen on her mother's face as she had cradled her dead husband and willed warmth back into his body?

Mrs Murphy started to cry, and blessed herself, muttering a prayer Stella could not hear as she turned and walked back to the house to break the news to her baby brothers and Dolores.

Walking in the door, she could hear the younger boys fighting and Peter letting a roar at them to calm down and have some respect while Dolores was demanding to know exactly what was going on and demanding to be let upstairs to her parents. "Something's wrong," she muttered, over and over. "Tell me, Peter, tell me."

Stella slipped off her coat and walked towards the kitchen, only to see her mother, who had taken on the appearance of a ghost, walking down the stairs in her cardigan and slippers.

"Did you phone the doctor?" she asked.

Stella nodded. "Mrs Murphy is doing it now. And she's going to phone the chapel to get the priest down and she said she will come to take Seán and Michael out from under our feet while the undertakers do what they need to."

Kathleen nodded. "You're a good girl, Stella. Now, could you do me one more favour?"

"I was just going to tell Dolores and the boys . . ."

"That's not a job for you, pet. You leave that to me. But I don't want your daddy up there on his own. Can you go and sit with him for me, pet? Don't leave him on his own. And keep the curtains drawn, would you?"

Stella nodded, the fear of seeing her father's lifeless body creeping in again, but she couldn't and wouldn't say no. No one had an easy task. Nothing about today would be easy. Or the next days and weeks and months. "I'll not leave him."

"And, pet, I know, it's silly. But don't let him get too cold. Keep the blanket round him."

"I promise, Mammy."

"You're a good girl," Kathleen said before taking a deep breath and walking towards the kitchen.

Slowly, her heart thudding, Stella made her way back up the stairs and into her parents' bedroom. The sight of him was not as shocking this time – he had more of a look of himself about him. Or maybe it was just that, in some way, she had started to process the fact he was gone. Still, as she saw him, she expected to hear him snore. Or sit up, open his eyes and wonder where his cup of tea was. She expected him to do anything rather than just lie there. Stella sat on the edge of the bed, still determined not to let her tears fall, and then she looked around her. The doctor would be here soon, and the priest. She stood up and started to tidy, fixing the blankets on the bed, pulling them tenderly up around her daddy and smoothing them down on the side where her mother had been lying. She gently arranged the items on the dresser – not that they were untidy or that there were that many of them – but it gave her something to do. Then she turned and lined her mother's shoes against the wall and folded the dress her mother had been wearing the previous day and slipped it into a drawer. She turned to see her daddy's work clothes hanging over the chair, ready for him to wear. And his boots, lying on the carpet where he had kicked them off. Kathleen always hated him bringing his work boots upstairs. She was forever telling him to kick them off at the door. Stella bent down to pick them up – boots that seemed so big, so heavy, so strong – and at that moment she heard a wail from downstairs as Dolores took in the news her mother had just delivered. She heard the thump of her sister's feet on the stairs, the sobs as she rounded onto the landing and pushed into the bedroom, throwing herself at her father and crying as if her heart had broken into a thousand pieces. The younger boys followed, clinging onto Kathleen's cardigan as if for dear life and Stella watched them walk gingerly in, their eyes wide with fear, sadness and curiosity. She watched them approach the bed, Seán asking was Daddy really never waking up and Michael begging him to play one more game of football with him.

And she sat there, with that work boot in her hand, and felt the life she had planned slip through her fingers.

Chapter 26

I feel better now – not all better though. I still miss you with every breath.

* * *

Derry, June 2010

"He was a great man. Hardworking. Funny. Loving. It's true what they say that a daddy is a girl's first true love," my mother said, her fingers tracing a picture of my grandfather in an old photo album she had taken down from a shelf in Dolores' good room.

I had seen pictures of my grandfather before. My mother said there hadn't been many around so she had brought just two with her when she came to America. One was a family shot – all eight of them smiling at the camera at a park. And the second was one of my grandfather looking quite stern in his work clothes and flat cap. If I'm being completely honest I always thought that picture was a little creepy – that he looked like he would shout at you quick as look at you – but looking at each of the pictures before me now, he seemed to be smiling in all of them. And the smile transformed his face. I was sad, in that moment, for the grandfather I never got to know, who died thirteen years before I was even born. It struck me that he never got to know any of his grandchildren – none of Dolores' six children was born before he died. She wasn't even married to Uncle Hugh then. He never got to walk his daughters down the aisle and give them away. It made me feel inexplicably sad and not only for him but for my mother. I knew the pain of losing a parent. I felt it every day and she, so much younger than I was, she had felt it too. Only losing her father had caused her to lose so much more. Then again, if Ernest had not died she would have gone to America and married Ray and, well, where would that have left me and my father?

"He really looked after us," my mother continued. "You wouldn't really understand it, nor should you, pet. But the life I lived growing up was a far cry from the life you led. Your father and I, well, it wasn't necessarily our choice, but when we had you we were in a much more secure position. There was work at home that your grandfather never could rely on here. That's not to say we were in want – not really – well, we never felt different from anyone else – maybe that was the difference. I had a happy childhood and that was down to him. And your granny. How I wish, pet, they could have met you. They would have been so proud. Your granny, you know, carried your baby picture in her handbag until she died. Dolores told me that – said the rest of them felt their noses were out of joint because there they were with as many babies as she could want to bounce on her knee and she talked of you as if you were sent down from heaven itself." Her face was wistful, her eyes watery.

"Do you regret going to America?" I asked and she shook her head, brushing away a tear.

"Oh no, pet. I had to try, you see. I had to try and make it work – to find him again. And your granny, well, she near put me on the boat herself. But I do regret not coming back before. I do regret not seeing her again. Letters weren't the same and phone calls, as occasional as they were, didn't allow you a hug."

She turned the page of the photo album to a picture of my grandparents, smiling together on their wedding day. My grandmother was wearing a simple gown – one which would no doubt be considered the very height of fashion these days, with a bouquet of trailing ivy falling to the ground. My grandfather, his hair sheared into a short back and sides, looked little over the age of eighteen or nineteen and grinned from his starched suit, his head bent towards my grandmother's as they smiled for the camera. There was an innocence in that picture – a purity. No messing about wondering if it was true love. No to-ing and fro-ing over the years deciding whether or not it was a good idea to get married. No silent dinners wondering what to say to each other. It was love. It was two people in it together – in it for everything. For better and worse. Raising a family filled with love, keeping food on the table and keeping things going. I don't imagine there was much time for navel-gazing when there were eight mouths to be fed. I felt jealous of them in a way – and I wondered, looking at the picture, would I ever find a love like that? One that was simple – that had that purity?

"Craig and I have broken up," I blurted out.

My mother raised her eyes from the picture and looked at me, her face giving nothing away.

"What happened?" she asked softly.

I looked her square in the eyes. "It wasn't right, was it, Mom?" She looked unsure of what to say so I continued. "I don't want to make do. We weren't making each other happy. Not for a long time. I didn't like the person I was when I was with him and I didn't like the person he had become either. I think we were just clinging on to each other out of habit, or boredom or, I don't know, a sense of it being the right thing to do – of not wanting to admit we had got it so wrong. But, Mom, these last few days, the letters, being away from home, having the space to think it made me realise some stuff . . . I deserve more, don't I? I deserve to be loved the way you and Daddy were loved. I deserve to be loved the way Ray loved you and you loved him. I was angry for a while, or confused, or something . . . I didn't get it. But I think I do now. You didn't and don't love Daddy any less because of Ray, do you?"

My mother shook her head. "Your daddy healed my broken

heart. But I broke my heart myself, Annabel, and I broke someone else's at the same time. Someone who never did anything wrong, who just loved me. And if this is my chance to make it better . . . then I have to take it."

She turned the page of the album and I saw her staring out at me – in her organza dress and her court shoes, and a handsome man in uniform by her side, his hair wavy and brushed to one side. Though it was a black-and-white picture I could swear I saw the twinkle in his eyes.

"He was so very handsome," she said, her hand resting on the page.

"You were beautiful too, Mom. You still are."

She squeezed my hand and sighed. "You say the nicest things. I must have raised you well."

She sat back and I sat and looked at her. "So, Mom, tell me what happened – what the letters don't tell. How you ended up going after him after all? And what happened? How did it not work out?"

Chapter 27

I suppose I fooled myself into thinking you were with me anyway. That you would understand once I told you. But I see now I left it much too late.

* * *

Derry, February 1960

On the second night of Ernest Hegarty's wake, Stella stood in the back yard trying to get a breath of air. Her feet ached from running back and forth with pots of tea and plates of sandwiches all day.

The mourning had taken on a strange atmosphere with the men of the family, Ernest's old work mates and neighbours sipping whiskey, smoking and regaling stories of some wild nights passed.

The days had been strange – a rollercoaster of emotion which knocked Stella for six and yet still she hadn't cried. She had been too busy, she told herself. There were things to be done. The room had to be prepared – the mirrors covered, the clocks stopped. Her father's best suit had to be pressed and laid out for the undertakers to dress him. The younger boys had been despatched to Mrs Murphy who had bought them a bag of sweets each from the corner shop to try, in some way, to soften the blow of their loss. It had distracted them, for a while, but there was no denying they looked lost as they sat, in their Sunday best, on Mrs Murphy's sofa with not a word of cheek from either of them.

The neighbours had rallied round and while Kathleen had helped the undertakers as best she could, Stella supervised the arrival and arrangements of kitchen chairs in the wake room and trays of good crockery and spare teapots. The milkman left extra milk and a box of tea and told her not to worry about paying. The bakers sent up a tray of buns and several loaves, while the butchers sent up several pounds of their finest ham. Neighbours arrived with pots of soup – "You must eat, keep your strength up" – and Stella had accepted them all gratefully while Dolores had sat staring at the wall, her grief having rendered her incapable of helping in any fashion. She only moved from her chair when Hugh Doherty arrived, and she threw herself into his arms sobbing while he shushed her and reassured her he would take care of her. The older boys were worse than useless. Consumed by his grief, Peter had gone and spent what little money he had in the pub and had returned home in a state. James had been not far behind and it had taken every ounce of strength Stella had not to beat them up the stairs with the wooden spoon. When they had sufficiently sobered up she had lectured them on respect as they snivelled like schoolchildren. They had promised to behave themselves but she knew that when it came to reliability it was down to herself and no one else.

Kathleen was doing her best but her grief was felt most keenly and though she tried to be strong, Stella knew that all her energy was being used to stay upright and not fall onto the floor and stay there.

So it was Stella who had fed the priest and thanked the undertakers kindly, telling where best to sit the floral arrangements and candles and where to burn the incense. She had prayed with the local priest and discussed the appropriate readings for the funeral Mass with her mother while arranging for a few of the factory girls, known for their singing, to sing the psalms at the graveside as her father was interred. She stopped occasionally to sit for a while, to drink a cup of tea her mother insisted she drink or to listen to a story from one of her father's friends when it seemed no one else was listening. She had made sure her mother had something suitable to wear and had borrowed a black coat from one of her friends.

And she had not slept.

She had not kissed her father either. Or touched him. While he no longer looked so strange, and looked more at peace laid out in his coffin, she could not bear to feel him cold. She did not want to kiss him – to say that goodbye – so while she did the dutiful daughter routine and sat by his side greeting mourners as they traipsed in and out, a part of her felt like a fraud – unable to let go herself.

Sitting on the step now, her shoes off and her feet against the cold ground to ease the ache in them, she realised just how tired she was. But she needed to stay strong. She needed to get through that night – awake by her father's side. And she needed to be there to hold her mother up the following day. She rested her head on the doorframe, closing her eyes, and despite the biting cold drifting off into a half-asleep state.

She was woken by Mrs Murphy settling beside her and handing her a cup of tea. "Stella, pet. I've been watching you and you've not stopped or rested. You'll not be any good to anyone if you don't take it easy and take some rest."

"I'll rest after tomorrow," she said.

"That's when your mammy will need you most, pet. It's one thing – all this fuss and carry-on with a wake – but it's not then you have to worry about. It's what happens afterwards when the house falls quiet again that she will need you most. There will be a lot to be done, Stella. And you're the reliable one. She'll need you."

Stella knew what Mrs Murphy was getting at. She didn't need her to spell it out any further. She knew because the thought had entered her mind the moment her father had exited her life. She was the reliable one. The sensible one. The one Seán had climbed into bed beside the night before and sobbed to, as she hushed him into sleep before spending a night staring at the ceiling thinking that no matter how it would break her heart there was no way on earth she could leave now.

And it wasn't just that her family relied on her for what she did around the house but also because she knew her mother would not recover from this easily. And with one wage now – the wage that put the roof over their heads in the first place – there was no way the family could manage without her own contribution. No, she would have to stay and she would have to direct more of her wages into the house to keep them afloat. Maybe if the older boys found work she could think again – but then again could she trust them not to drink their wages down the pub? She was sure their priority would not be making sure the wains had shoes on their feet and food in their tummies. She had mulled it over through the night and it seemed the only way forward.

So when the postman had dropped off her passport among the condolences the following morning it had seemed particularly cruel. She had hidden it in the bottom of her drawer and mentioned nothing to anyone – not even to Molly Davidson who had come to offer her sympathy and had told her life was too short not to take risks. She had just nodded and offered a sad smile while thinking that it was one thing to take a risk with your own life but not with that of the family that needed you.

"Mrs Murphy," she said, on the cold step, "thank you for your kindness. I know what my mother will need and I intend to be here to support her as much as she needs me. You have nothing to worry about on that score – please believe me."

"Good girl, Stella," Mrs Murphy said, understanding perfectly well what she was being told. "Your daddy would be very proud."

* * *

Mrs Murphy had been right, of course, about the quietness of the house after the funeral. With not even the clocks ticking the place seemed almost desolate. There was no music playing on the wireless. The younger boys had gone to play in the street and Stella watched them through the curtains kicking a football half-heartedly, as if they were doing it just to amuse her. Dolores had gone for a walk with Hugh and the older boys had gone to the bar with some of their neighbours for one last toast for Ernest.

Kathleen sat in the empty front room – just a few chairs left, the mirrors still covered, the rest of the furniture shipped out to neighbours to accommodate Ernest's coffin. She sat and she stared at the wall, her face sheet-white. She had maintained her decorum through the Requiem Mass, while all around were falling apart. Stella, yet to break down, had held her hand, hugging Seán into her on the other side. But as they walked to the cemetery to lay his remains to rest, she thought her mother might collapse. As they lowered Ernest into the ground Kathleen's sobs had echoed through the city cemetery and had cut through Stella like a knife. And yet, she found even then, as she gave herself permission to cry, no tears would come. She stood, angry at herself while mourners passed on their best and she walked away, dry-eyed, wondering what part of her was broken.

Looking at her mother now, in her chair, she wondered perhaps if her mother was broken enough for both of them.

"Mammy," she said softly. "Why don't you go to bed? You've not slept. You need a wee rest and I'll bring you some soup later."

Kathleen nodded and Stella helped her upstairs and slowly helped her change into her night clothes before tucking her into her bed, trying not to think about the fact her father had died there not two nights before.

She kissed her mother softly on her forehead. "Try not to worry, Mammy. Try just to rest. You must be exhausted. I'll take care of the children and get the house back in order. You take as long as you need."

Kathleen rolled onto her side and, with a soft sob which was almost as heartbreaking as her cries at the graveside, she fell into a deep sleep.

And she didn't get out of her bed for two more weeks.

* * *

Stella fell into a routine of sorts. She talked to her supervisors at the factory and they let her leave for home half an hour earlier to make sure to have dinner on for the family. She would get up half an hour earlier in the morning to put the porridge on and stay up later at night to make sure the school lunches were prepared and all the clothes washed and ironed for the morning. She would rake out the fireplace and set it before she left for work, instructing the older boys to light it in the late morning, and Dolores would help her peel the potatoes for dinner. Each night it felt like a slap in the face to set two places less at the table. She would set a tray for her mother and carry it upstairs and coax her into eating. Kathleen rarely spoke and if she did it was to tell Stella that she was a great girl and that she would be lost without her. There was no mention of Ray. No mention of the move to America. No one asked and Stella didn't mention it. Meanwhile a letter had arrived – from Ray, unaware of her great loss and wondering why she had not been in touch. Just like her passport, she stashed that letter in her bottom drawer and the suitcase that she had been filling at the bottom of her bed was now back on top of the wardrobe. She said nothing still and, the times she spent not caring for her family, she spent wondering just how she would break the news to Ray that she could no longer come. She knew, in her heart, that he would not let her go easily. But she could see no other way. She had tried to convince herself that it would be okay. That her family would be okay. But she knew in her heart of hearts that it was down to her. She had even considered asking Ray to move back to Ireland when he was demobbed – but to what? No jobs? No prospects? When he had it all waiting for him at home? A refurbished basement apartment. A job which no doubt paid better than anything that could be offered in Derry. And what kind of a wife would she be to him anyway? Overnight she had inherited a ready-made family – her own family admittedly – but one which she would have to take care of for a long time. The boys were young. Her mother – God love her – she didn't know when she would get out of bed and when and if she did how well she would be. She couldn't imagine Kathleen without Ernest. The pair had been completely and utterly inseparable – much like she had hoped she would be with Ray. She knew she had been with him only a few months – and she wouldn't dare in her mind compare her relationship with him to that of her parents, thirty years married, but she felt in a way she understood what her mother was feeling. But she was about to tear apart the great love of her life. She had wondered if she had been melodramatic to think that way – to imagine her and Ray's relationship to have been some great love affair in the grand scheme of things, but she felt it was. She felt he had taught her so much, that theirs was a unique connection. So because she knew he would pursue her, she knew she had to make the break as clean as possible and the only way to do that was to lie. Lie and tell him it was never true. That she never loved him.

In the darkness of the night, when the younger ones were in bed and she was alone by the fire she put pen to paper and wrote.

Dear Ray,

I hope this letter finds you well. I am sorry that I have not written but it has taken me time to find the right words. This is not an easy letter to write and it won't be an easy letter to read and for that I am sorry. I am more sorry than you could ever know. If there was any other way I would find it, but I'm sorry.

You should never have put your faith in me. I was never worthy of the love you gave me. I played along, because I was caught up in what we had. I was caught up in what you offered me – what you thought of me, what you made me believe. But it wasn't real. You must have known that? It was a fantasy and I'm afraid to say, Ray, I used you. I was going to go along with it but you are too decent a man for me to do that. You deserve better. You deserve a love affair with someone who loves you back – not just someone pathetic like me dreaming of a life in America.

The fact is, I was using you, and I'll understand if you hate me. But at least I am telling you now. Telling you before we make the mistake of getting married and being lumbered with each other. That girl next door is probably still available, Ray – and she will love you because you are truly loveable. But when push comes to shove, I just can't lie any more. I want to stay here – to find my true love. To be with someone who means something to me.

I'm sorry to have lied to you. You deserve better and with God's grace you will find it.

Forgive me. I never meant to hurt you.

Sincerely,

Stella

She sat back and read the words again – hoped they sounded as harsh as she had planned. Each one had hurt her as much as they would hurt Ray but she needed to let him know that it was done – that her place was in Derry – that they had no future together. She would post the letter without telling anyone. If her mother asked, she would say it was she who received a Dear John letter and that she was sad, but happy to stay. She would put the whole thing down, if anyone asked, to a moment of madness. Tell them she had been carried away by the romance the twinkly-eyed stranger from America had offered her.

Folding the letter and putting it in the envelope, she sealed it, wrote his address and slipped it into her coat pocket to post the following morning.

Then she raked the fire one last time for the night, knocking the fading ashes out of the grate and into the pan. She put up the fireguard, switched off the lights and climbed the stairs to bed. She peeked at her mother, lying unmoving in her bed – still on her own side with her hand reached over to where Ernest used to lie. In the darkness Stella could not tell if she was asleep or just lying there, awake and silent, as she did so often these days.

Stella pulled the door closed and went to the bathroom as she did every night and brushed her teeth. Then she went into her bedroom, closed the curtains and undressed before brushing her hair and climbing into bed and pulling the covers over her.

It was then, and only then, that she finally gave in to the tears which had eluded her for the last few weeks. Her pain was such she was sure it was physical – she wondered if her heart was about to give out and, though she was only twenty, she was destined to follow her father into the grave. She cried then until her throat was sore, her eyes dry and her pillow soaked and until she could do nothing but give in to sleep.

When she woke in the morning, she knew that finally things had changed – and they would never be the same. And she knew the pain she had felt the night before was the breaking of her own heart. Only she was still breathing, just – and there was porridge to be made and children to be got out to school and a house to be run. That was simply how it was meant to be.

Chapter 28

I should have trusted you to tell you the truth. But I thought I was doing the right thing. I was a fool, Ray. A silly fool and I will never forgive myself, nor should you. But still I hope you will.

* * *

Derry, June 2010

"I had to make him believe there was no chance. And more than that I had to make him hate me," my mother said, her eyes watering. "It was the only way. I know that sounds silly, but I knew he would have given everything up for me – but it wasn't the life we had planned. I couldn't ask him to do that for me. I couldn't ask him to move away from his family, from his prospects, from the life we had planned, to come here and take on responsibility for the Hegarty clan. There were no jobs. No prospects. I couldn't bring him back here to nothing."

"But Dolores? And Uncle Peter and Uncle James? Would they not, could they not have stepped in?"

My mother shrugged her shoulders. "I didn't feel they could at the time. With the benefit of a life of experience I've often wondered if I was too soft on the lot of them – but that's hindsight. I know that at the time I was being told I was the sensible one – that my mammy needed me. And she did. She cut a pathetic picture in those days, Stella. She was lost without him." A tear slid down her face. "She had it tough when you think of it, with a young family to mind and no money coming in. I was lucky to have your father as long as I did. I was lucky in a lot of ways. I'm not saying I'm any great hero because I've got out of my bed every day since your father died, but it was different for my mother. She was a strong woman – please don't think she was anything other than that – but in those early weeks and months I think her heart was just so clean broken she couldn't function at all. We didn't talk about depression or the like in those days – not really. Everyone had it tough and everyone just got on with it or hid it behind closed doors. She did try but it was hard on her. Very hard."

"But it was hard on you too," I said, as softly as I could.

She smiled weakly. "Yes. We were a great pair, two broken hearts under the one roof. Great *craic* we were in those days – I think we near drove each other mad."

"But did no one ask? Did no one press you to go to America? Did Ray not write back?"

She shook her head. "I never heard from him again. I couldn't blame him. What did I expect? I told him I had lied, that I didn't really love him and that I had been using him. There was no response to that, was there? All I heard, eventually, was formal notification my visa request had been turned down. I imagine that was down to him but he never approached me again.

And as for people asking? There were some whispers. The factory girls of course. That supervisor of mine had a laugh to herself. She enjoyed the old 'I told you so' for quite some time. With my mother, I just told her that it had ended. She either didn't have the strength to ask more or was afraid of what I might say. The older boys were delighted that someone else would continue to put food on the table for them, but to be fair to them they upped their game when it came to looking for work. And Dolores?" At this my mother dropped her voice to a whisper. "Well, she quickly became too concerned planning her wedding to Uncle Hugh to worry about me. I think she knew not to push me too far for a response. She might not have liked what she was going to hear. The only person who ever knew the truth was Molly Davidson – strange, isn't it? The pair of us became confidantes of sorts. A miserable pair we were too, for a while." My mother snorted. "Nursing our broken hearts together. She walked me into the factory every day in those early weeks. She said it was sad how things don't always work how you would have planned and I suppose she should have known. I've often wondered how she is now. How she got on. I must look her up while I'm here."

With that my mother closed the photo album and stood up.

"You know, I think it's time for a cup of tea. I'm parched. Have you noticed, Annabel, how the tea is so much nicer here? After I moved to the States I used to get your granny to send me little care packages – always a box of tea and some biscuits. The biscuits rarely arrived in one piece but I would stretch out that box of tea as long as I could – one cup of decent tea a day would make the box last for ages. And then I would get her to send me another box."

I followed her into the kitchen, trying to imagine how it used to be. She put the kettle on and stared out into the back yard. "God, it seems like a lifetime ago," she muttered as the kettle boiled and fizzed. "It was another world. Not the worst, but different."

I thought of how her life had turned on its head and wondered for a moment how she could think it was not the worst? And then once again I reminded myself just how lucky I was – bereavement and relationship breakdown aside. At least I had made the decision freely to walk away from Craig – even if I hadn't made it sooner. At least I had choices where my mother had felt she had none.

"Do you not feel bitter about it? Angry even?"

"I did," she said, dropping two tea bags in the teapot and pouring boiling water on top.

She moved around the kitchen effortlessly, taking cups from the cupboards, milk from the fridge. It may have been someone else's home now – it may have been far removed from what it was when she was younger, but she clearly still felt a sense of belonging here.

"I mean," she continued, "not at the time. Not when it was happening. I didn't feel angry or bitter. I just felt desperately sad for a long time. And then, I suppose when I went to America and it didn't work out, I felt angry for a while. I felt it had all been such a terrible, terrible waste and I felt angry then. It just felt unfair. I'd watched enough movies and read enough books to believe that people should get their happy endings and I really thought I would get mine. So when I eventually went to the States – when I went to find him – that was when I got angry and bitter. And I'm not proud, Annabel. I wasn't a very nice person for a while. I was horribly unhappy and I closed myself off from everyone. Those days were darker than the days after your grandfather died and it was only when I met your daddy that I came out of them."

She poured the tea and handed me a cup.

"He saved me, you know. Your daddy. He brought me back to life."

"Was he never worried about you and Ray?" I knew it was an awkward question to ask but still I had to ask it. If you loved someone so much, surely a part of your heart would always remain with them? Sure weren't we back in Derry now looking him up – planning to go to a Naval Base Reunion, trying to close some circles?

My mother shook her head. "There was nothing to be worried about. Of course I always felt like there was unfinished business between us – even though I knew I never deserved a reply. I always wanted to tell him the truth – that I had indeed loved him, that I had not lied and that he had not given his heart to someone who was just using him. I suppose I wanted to make my peace with him. I never dreamed this was how it would work out. That your father would be dead – that we would be here. I suppose I never really thought about how it would work out at all. Like so much in my life, I have just found myself here."

"So you went to America to find him? What happened?"

My mother sat at the kitchen table and poured milk for both of us.

"Well, it started with the letters. I suppose that was about a year and a half after your grandfather died."

Chapter 29

I have no right to get in touch after this time. No right at all.

* * *

Derry, July 1961

Dolores stood in their bedroom and turned around, trying to catch as best she could a glimpse of herself in the mirror on the dresser.

"Stand at peace," Stella urged, laughing.

"I'm just trying to see if I'm beautiful," Dolores said, her face flushed.

"Of course you are, but if you don't stand at peace I'll end up sticking one of these flowers in your eye or your ear – or your mouth to keep you quiet!" Stella teased.

Dolores stuck her tongue out then laughed, looking all of twelve years old, and Stella wondered for a moment how on earth they had reached their adult years when it seemed like only yesterday they were sharing secrets beneath their blankets and hoping that neither Ernest nor Kathleen would hear them talking when they were supposed to be asleep.

"You can't be mean to me today, sister dear. It's my wedding day – the one day in my whole life when you all have to be extra nice and treat me like a queen."

"Well, Queen Dolores, I'm pretty sure even Her Majesty herself sat still when they were putting the crown on her head so

247

she didn't get a jewel in her eye – so can you be at peace till we finish with these flowers and this veil? Mammy will be in to see you in a minute and don't you want to be as near as done by then?"

Dolores stood at peace, apart from the fidgeting of her hands, while Stella pinned the last carnation on her head and slipped on her veil.

Stella could not deny it – her sister made a beautiful bride and it was heart-warming to see some happiness brought back into their family at long last. It had been a long, tough eighteen months but the last week or so, with the arrival of some glorious sunshine and the promise of a grand day at Dolores and Hugh's wedding, had lifted everyone's spirits. Even Kathleen had come round to herself and, apart from a few quiet moments and a few tears shed for absent friends, she had thrown herself into the wedding preparations with an energy Stella had been delighted to see.

"You look grand, a real beauty," Stella said, standing back to take in her sister in all her glory. In a simple, knee-length dress with her short veil, she looked so very fashionable and chic. Her simple bouquet of carnations, roses and baby's breath sat waiting for her but the most beautiful thing of all about her was the almost beatific smile on her face.

"I'm a very lucky girl," she grinned.

"You are, pet," Stella smiled, as she slipped on the dress she had bought with her Christmas money from Ray to act the part of the bridesmaid. She felt strange putting it on – it was somehow tainted now – but she didn't want to show Dolores up by wearing just any old thing and it was the nicest thing she had in her wardrobe. She got her sister to help zip it up and stood back to try and look at herself in the mirror. She didn't want to look too closely though – not wanting to be reminded of that magical night in the City Hotel. The dress felt looser, she noted. She had definitely been eating less and she reminded herself she needed to make sure she kept well – she had a lot of responsibilities after all, although in recent weeks both older boys had found fairly regular work and she hadn't had to push them too hard to put money into the house. Dolores was set to move out after the wedding – having secured a small flat with Hugh – and while that would mean they were down her contribution, it also meant there would be one less mouth to feed. Kathleen had even taken on some light sewing work and, while Stella had told her she worked hard enough and didn't need to go to any extra effort, she had assured her daughter she actually enjoyed it and enjoyed getting out and about to meet more people.

There was an air of life about the Hegarty household again. Stella no longer felt she had to tell the younger boys to keep it down. They weren't afraid to laugh any more, or have the odd squabble. They no longer felt they had to speak in hushed tones or wander about in a state of enforced mourning. That's not to say they, any of them, missed Ernest any less. There were still nights when Stella would hear her mother cry herself to sleep and there were nights when she would creep in beside her and cry with her – pretending, she was ashamed to admit to herself, she was weeping for her father when she was in fact weeping for the love she had lost herself.

But for the most part, with the passing of that first awful year of horrible anniversaries and missed family moments, and the arrival of an untainted spring and then summer, laughter and hope was seeping into every corner of the Hegarty household.

Stella lacquered her hair and slipped on a pair of lace gloves. Then she called to her mother to come in and took hold of her sister's hand.

"Here we go, Dolores. No going back now, girl!"

Kathleen entered the room, her eyes bright with emotion.

"I have promised myself, and your father's memory, that I am not going to cry today," she said. "There have been too many tears in this house of late and today is a happy day. The first of our children to get married – I'm not sure I ever thought this day would really come. That I would see my children grown and round me." She faltered a little before taking her daughters' hands in her own. "My gorgeous girls, I am so utterly proud of you and proud of the women you have become. You are a credit to yourselves and to us. Your father and I could not have asked for better. My darling Dolores, you look so beautiful. I wish for you everything I had – a man who loves you, and I believe your lovely Hugh does, years of happiness and a family who will look after you when you need them."

She turned to look at Stella then and while both their eyes were filled with tears there was no need for words. What could be said? Stella didn't want to let the thought of how it should have been her who was married first cross her mind. She didn't want to think of how she'd had a man who loved her and could have offered her years of happiness and a family who could look after her, and she had thrown it away for the sake of this family who needed her so desperately.

"I love you, Mammy," Dolores said. "But we better get a move on if we're to get to the chapel on time. I want the whole street to see me looking as gorgeous as this. The girls will be so jealous of this dress. Imagine no one else in Derry having the same dress yet! Me, one of a kind?"

With that same characteristic childish giddiness, Dolores Hegarty led the way from the room to the wolf whistles of her brothers who were waiting in their Sunday best to walk their sister up the street to the Long Tower for her wedding.

"Behave yourselves, boys!" Stella and Kathleen chimed almost in unison before laughing and holding hands.

No, this would be a great day out for the Hegartys and nothing was going to take away from it.

The ceremony was simple and Dolores beamed throughout it, enjoying every moment. Stella smiled as best she could and Kathleen managed to keep composed as Peter and not Ernest walked her daughter up the aisle.

They retired afterwards to the backroom of a local bar where a spread of tea and sandwiches had been set out and where a piano in the corner would help lead the sing-song later in the day.

The sun was bright and it was warm and, as Stella sat and nursed her cup of tea in the corner, she tried to ignore any pitying looks which came her way. At various intervals she would be asked out for a quick dance by one of her uncles or urged to lead a sing-song but she never was one for singing and was happy to sit back and watch the day unfold around her.

When Mrs Murphy took a seat beside her she knew she was in for all the latest gossip and their neighbour's take on the day.

"She looks lovely, doesn't she?" the older woman began.

"Yes, Mrs Murphy. She does, a real beauty."

"I mean the dress, well, I might have gone for something a bit longer if it was me but I suppose you young ones have to have your style, don't you?"

Stella nodded.

"It's nice to enjoy a happy occasion for a change," her neighbour continued. "Always nice to put the past behind you and move onto a nice new future."

"Yes," Stella said absently. "It's been a bit of a blessing for us all to have something positive to focus on."

"Do you think it might be you one day?" Mrs Murphy asked over the top of her spectacles, her lips pursed in a perfect 'o' as she sipped from her teacup – pinky pointed outwards.

"I wouldn't be holding out any hopes for that," Stella replied, not particularly liking where her neighbour was taking this conversation.

"Never say never. You know, you coming out the other side of the grief for your father, maybe it is time you came out the other side of the grief for your young man as well."

Stella bit softly on her lip and took a deep breath. It had been a lovely day, although not without its sadness, and she wanted it to remain that way but the manner in which Mrs Murphy spoke made her bristle. If it were as simple as putting her grief for her young man behind her she would have done so. If he had, as everyone believed, been the one to break her heart she was sure she could perhaps see some sense in what her neighbour was saying but, being blind to the full facts, Mrs Murphy just managed to stir up feelings that Stella would rather stay buried.

"Mrs Murphy," she said, softly and quietly, looking directly ahead, "just because we are smiling and singing today, that does not mean we have got over the loss of my father or come out of the other side of our grief. Each day will be hard – and there will be hurdles to be crossed. We are just learning to manage. We are learning to make the most of a horrible situation in which we would not find ourselves able to move if we thought too much about our loss. Please understand – for me, my feelings are the same about my young man. No, I don't see this," she gestured to the bride and groom laughing with each other, "in my future and nor do I want to see it. I do not deserve this. I do not deserve the happiness they have. So, Mrs Murphy, as much as you have been an invaluable help and support to my family over the last number of years and more, when it comes to matters of my own heart – understand that you know nothing."

Mrs Murphy hunched her shoulders and sat her saucer and teacup on her lap.

"Stella, pet. I've been around long enough to know more than you give me credit for. Whatever it was happened with your young man – whatever sacrifices you made for the sake of your family and whatever stories you told to cover them up – you need to realise that this is your life and yours alone. Perhaps I was guilty of pushing you when your mother needed you – but I knew you were the one person she could rely on. The pain of losing your daddy will never leave her but, as you say, she is learning to manage and with each day she is managing more. God knows those men in your house even seem to be getting their act together. All I'm saying, it is time you put yourself first, just for a bit, to see what happens. Everyone, Stella, deserves to be happy. Even those of us who feel we don't."

She reached over and gave Stella's hand a gentle squeeze then lifted her saucer and teacup and moved on to the next table where she would hold court with someone else.

By evening, young Seán had tired himself out and was asleep on his sister's lap. She thought of how he had behaved so well that day, helping the grown-ups by fetching their drinks and offering sandwiches round. "Daddy would want me to be a big boy," he had said, his gappy smile now more filled in with teeth that looked that little bit too big for his head. He had even slept in his own bed the night before, leaving Stella alone for the first night in months. She held him in her arms as he slept and kissed his head, thinking about what Mrs Murphy had said. As she held him she watched Peter sing along with her mother, whose head was thrown back in laughter while Dolores kissed her new husband.

Maybe her neighbour was right – maybe it was time to start thinking about her own life. It wouldn't make her a bad person, would it? She was entitled to a happy ending. She closed her eyes and thought of Ray, imagined for a moment that he was here. That it was she in the wedding dress and him leading her around the dance floor, cheek to cheek. She could almost hear the drawl of his accent, smell his cigarette smoke. She could almost, if she concentrated really hard, remember what it was like to be with him – to be in the flat. God, that seemed like such a long time ago. It seemed so foolish – so unreal. Playing houses together – none of it real life, all of it a fantasy. But she wanted it, she wanted it so badly. She wanted so much to be with him. All she had to do was tell him the truth – tell him that although she had lied she had been trying to protect him. Tell him that her thoughts had been for him – and how she wanted him to be happy and to move on without her. She wondered should she dare ask him for a second chance. Sitting there, she wondered did she even deserve a second chance?

But it was worth trying.

So that night, when the house was quiet, thoughts of the great day they'd had dancing in their heads, she wrote the first letter. She told him she was sorry. She told him her father had died and she'd had to stay in Derry. She told him just how she had to break his heart and that she hoped it was not broken enough that he wouldn't even consider forgiving her. She told him she had been scared – scared of what would become of her family if she left them.

She poured everything out on her notepaper – her loss and longing and most of all her love. She relived every moment of their time together and told him no one had made her feel the way he had and that no one ever could.

"It wasn't that I didn't want to go. I did. I wanted to go with all my heart but I suppose in many ways I was a coward in the end. It was too much. There isn't a day that has passed where I haven't missed you," she wrote.

The letter was posted at the Post Office two weeks later, when she had stared at it, re-read it time and time again, discussed it until she could think no more about it with Molly and realised just how much her heart ached and always would ache for Ray. With it went her hopes and dreams. She took a deep breath and hoped that the Ray she loved would read it, understand and love her back. She hoped against hope that he would believe her. He had to.

"You have a quare spring in your step this morning," her mother said as she walked back into the house, slipped on her apron and set about helping with the chores.

"Do I?" she asked with a smile.

"You do indeed, pet, and if you don't mind me saying so, it's great to see. Not sure when I last saw you look contented."

Stella hugged her mother and kissed her on the cheek as she opened the sack of potatoes and started peeling them in preparation for their evening meal.

"I am contented, Mammy, or at least I think will be. Does that make sense?"

"It does, pet. I know things have been tough for you lately."

"They've been tough for us all."

"But you took on the biggest burden. Don't think I didn't notice. I know I wasn't much use to man nor beast in those early days but I know what you did for me, pet. I know how you kept things running until I was fit to do it myself."

"It was nothing," Stella fibbed, knowing full well it was everything and knowing just how much she had done.

"No, it wasn't nothing. It wasn't nothing at all. You had your heart broken too – that man of yours leaving you like that. You didn't lie down under it – you kept going and you kept us all going with you. Her mother dried her hands on her apron and pulled her daughter into a hug. "I love you, Stella Hegarty, and all I hope for you now is that you find the contentment you so deserve."

Stella allowed herself to sink into her mother's embrace. "Me too, Mammy."

The women worked amiably together through the day, Stella biting back the urge to tell her mother of her hopes and dreams and the truth of what had happened with Ray. She would tell her when the letter came back from him – when he wrote to tell her he still loved her and that he still had a home waiting for them in America. Telling her mother beforehand – letting her know how she had thrown away her love for the sake of her family would only make Kathleen feel wretched with guilt. No, when it was all sorted she would break the news and, if Kathleen was honest about wanting contentment for her daughter, she would understand why she needed to go to America and why she needed to be with the man she loved. Until then she could go on believing in her daughter's broken heart.

* * *

Derry, August 1961

Molly and Stella walked back from the factory together. It had been a long day and the summer sun was still warm, too warm.

Stella's hair was sticky with sweat and she was dreaming of changing into a light cotton dress and maybe having a wash to freshen up. Her feet ached and she wanted to kick off her shoes and wander around the house barefoot with the coolness of the oil cloth under foot easing the ache.

As they walked into Stella's street, Seán came running at her for a hug and she lifted him into her arms, enveloping him in a warm hug before he accompanied her towards the house, holding her hand and rattling on about the day he had just had.

"Mammy said there's a letter for you," he said solemnly. "She was cross about it – in bad form altogether."

Stella turned to grin at Molly. "He's written. It has to be him. No one else sends me letters. Oh Molly, I think I might faint from the excitement. Even if Mammy is cross I know I can talk her round and it will be fine. Oh Molly! It's him!" She felt tears prick at her eyes and she hugged her friend and then ran the rest of the way to the house, no longer caring about the ache in her feet or the pull in her back. She had waited for this letter for a month and it was here and she just was not able to wait for it for a single moment longer.

Bustling through the door, she threw her bag to the floor and ran to the kitchen where she knew she would find her mother. Kathleen looked up from where she was bent over the sink scrubbing some clothes and Stella could barely hear a thing around her, her heart was beating so fast.

"Seán says there's a letter," she gasped.

Kathleen dried her hands, her face drawn. Stella tried not to read too much into it. Even though her mother had told her she needed to find her own happy ending, she had known she would be wary about her hearing from Ray again.

"Yes," she said, reaching to the shelf. "Why don't you have a seat?"

"I don't want a seat, Mammy. I just want the letter. Is it from him? Is it from America?" Her nerves were rattling so much she could barely think. She just needed to see what he said – she needed to feel close to him again. She needed to know she was forgiven and that he understood and most of all that he still wanted her.

"Pet, please, have a seat. There's no rush."

Stella could see the letter in her mother's hand, she could see the crisp envelope and, unable to resist for a moment longer, she reached out and snatched it.

"Stella!" her mother said.

Stella looked down at the envelope and the familiar writing before her. Her heart sank. She didn't understand. There had to be some problem. She turned the letter over, trying to make sense of what she was seeing. It was her writing, her return address as she had penned it on the back. He would have known it was from her and yet, in a scrawl she didn't quite recognise someone had written *Return to Sender* and popped it back in the post. It wasn't even opened. He hadn't even read it. And who had sent it back? Her heart sank when she thought of how she had poured her heart and soul into every page. There must be some mistake. She looked at her mother – as if there was a chance Kathleen would have the answers and would be able to tell her it was all some mistake.

"I don't understand," she muttered, sinking to the kitchen chair, the ache in her feet and the pull in her back all the more acute. And this time they were accompanied by a dizzy, floating feeling right at the back of her neck. Kathleen poured her a glass of water from the sink and sat down beside her.

"I don't understand," she repeated. "I don't . . ."

"Maybe it's for the best, pet. The past is sometimes best left in the past," her mother said.

"But, Mammy, I was writing to tell him I was sorry. To explain that I didn't mean it. That I loved him."

"You didn't mean what? Oh, Stella, pet . . . what did you do?" She slumped to a seat and took her daughter's hands in hers.

"I told him I didn't love him. I couldn't leave you, Mammy . . . not when . . . not when things were how they were and I had to make sure he didn't come after me. I thought . . . I thought I would get over it." Stella shook her head, staring back again at the letter.

"You stayed for me? For us?" Her mother's voice broke.

"You needed me, Mammy."

"Oh, pet!" Kathleen said, pulling her daughter into a hug, "I love you with all my heart. You didn't have to do that."

Stella didn't respond. She knew that when Ernest had died she had done the only thing she could have done and stayed.

Taking a deep breath, she continued: "I broke his heart, Mammy, and he doesn't forgive me. That's the only explanation. I wrote telling him I loved him and I still wanted to be with him and he couldn't even bring himself to read the letter."

Kathleen sat wringing her hands. "Oh, pet. What have we done? What have I done to you?"

"You're not to blame yourself, Mammy," Stella said, guilt heaping on guilt that her mother was being hurt by this anyway. "I'm a big girl and I made my own decisions . . . I just . . ." She turned her face to the letter again. "Oh, Mammy," she said, tears falling, "where do I go from here? How do I make him understand?"

"You try again, pet," her mother said. "If he's worth it, you try and you keep trying. True love is, well, it's hard work but you don't give up on it. You don't get many chances in this world at it so you sure as hell don't give up on it when you think there is still a chance. You try, my pet, until you can't try any more. He was a good man – and if he is half the man your father was he will listen eventually."

Stella nodded and hugged her mother before picking up the letter and standing up to go upstairs.

"Dinner will be ready soon, pet!" Kathleen called after her.

"I'm not hungry," Stella replied as she made her way to her bedroom, took out her notepad and pen and started to try again.

"Try again," she whispered, "and try harder."

So for a second time she poured her heart out, imploring him to read the letters to try and understand. And in addition she wrote about her day – about the sunshine, about how the sun glinted on the Foyle and the river was calm. She wrote about the shiny cobbled streets and how Molly Davidson was doing really well, thank God. She wrote about the latest gossip from the Base and how she was sure some of the men were still using their little flat. And then she wrote of how she could never forget him, how she would be sorry for the rest of her days and she begged him, once more, to give her a second chance.

When she sealed the envelope and wrote his address on it – his home address in the suburbs of Boston where he had told her there was a basement apartment waiting for them – she kissed his name and offered a silent prayer up to anyone who was listening that this time the letter would find him and he would find it in his heart to forgive her.

And at the same time she vowed to pull that old suitcase down from the top of the wardrobe and start filling it again for the day when she would travel to America and she would see him again.

Even when the second, and the third, and the fourth letters were all returned to sender, she kept the suitcase resting on Dolores' old bed and filled it with bits and piece and stored some of her wages in a small savings jar in the left-hand corner.

And each time the letters came back, after she allowed herself a time to feel that crushing blow she would whisper to herself the words her mother had spoken to her that first day. "Try again. Try harder."

And when Christmas arrived, with still no sign of the man she loved loving her back – when Dolores was telling her to give up and move on – her mother gave her a simple card with a short inscription.

"*When Life says give up, Hope whispers 'Try it one more time'.*"

In that envelope her mother had placed a bundle of notes . . . almost enough, along with her own savings, to ensure a passage to America.

Stella looked at her – her eyes wide with disbelief. "We don't have this kind of money, Mammy. How did you?"

Kathleen smiled sweetly. "That's nothing for you to worry about. You just worry about finding a job, getting a visa. Getting sorted. I know you want to go, pet. I know you want to try and see him face to face, so this is your chance."

"But we can't afford this."

"Never you worry, pet," Kathleen said, kissing her daughter. "It's the least you deserve."

It was only later Stella realised her mother was no longer wearing her engagement ring or her wedding ring.

Chapter 30

I hope you understand why I couldn't give up. Why I can't give up. I have to be able to tell myself I did everything I could. That I tried everything I could. I couldn't live with myself if I didn't.

* * *

Derry, July 2010

"So my grandma sold her jewellery to pay for you to go to America?"

There was no two ways about it. I was gobsmacked. But also in awe. I could not believe my grandmother would have parted with the jewellery which was no doubt so precious to her.

"It was the only thing she had of any monetary value," my mother said. "But she said material things were unimportant to her. Sure she had all she could want with us, and after how I looked after her when Daddy died she was determined that I get something back."

"But to go to America? When he had been returning your letters?"

"It was madness," my mother laughed. "When I think of it now. If you had told me you would do something similar at twenty-two I would have given you a very stern talking-to but at the time it just seemed like the right thing to do. And, dare I say it, it felt hopelessly romantic. But you didn't go to the States for a holiday in those days – you moved, lock, stock and barrel – so

261

when we decided I was going I had to set up a life for myself before I even left. Thankfully Molly's family in America was able to set me up with a nannying job prospect in Boston, which would get me my visa, and cover my board and lodgings with a little bit left over, because Lord knows every penny was sunk into getting me there in the first place. You know in those days you couldn't leave with nothing either – you had to have a suitcase filled to bursting to prove to immigration you weren't destitute. Every neighbour in the street gave me their cast-offs to make up the weight." My mother was smiling, lost in a memory of a time gone by.

I wondered why I had never heard these stories before – perhaps it was because I had never asked. My mother had always seemed so much older than me – so distant in many ways. We never had the bond some mothers and daughters have – we never had the bond she clearly had with her own mother. Then again I was such a daddy's girl, I never gave her much of a look-in. It was my father I ran to when I was hurt or needed advice or wanted a hug. My mother – I suppose I had taken her for granted. Seen her as a square – someone who lived her quiet life in her quiet house in her quiet town. I hadn't realised the heartbreak she had lived through. I had never stopped to listen to the stories of her life back in Ireland, preferring my father's company. And now, the more I heard, the more she was developing into glorious Technicolor before my eyes and the more I wanted to know – about her, about Ray, about Dolores and Peter and Molly Davidson and the cast of characters who were coming to life for me.

God, I had been selfish. So wrapped up in my own life – my own misery – to pay much heed to anyone else. But that would change, I knew it.

"So the funny thing was I arrived at the O'Donnells – in their fancy brownstone which had two bathrooms and fluffy eiderdowns on the bed and a garden with a swing-seat. I thought I had arrived at Buckingham Palace! Mrs O'Donnell showed me

to my room – my very own room – in the attic and I swear there
was more furniture in it than there was in the good room at
home. A dressing table, and a wardrobe, a bed and a locker, a
chest of drawers too and a desk where I could write letters
home. The curtains . . . I'll always remember the curtains for as
long as I'll live. Red velvet they were. I was almost tempted to
haul them down and make myself a fancy dress like Miss
Scarlett in *Gone With the Wind*. Of course when I unpacked my
case – all the decent stuff, not the fillers from the neighbours –
I swear I only filled one drawer and not even half the wardrobe.
Probably not even a quarter of the wardrobe. I had two pairs of
shoes – my work shoes and the fancy ones I had worn to the
City Hotel with Ray. Well, Mrs O'Donnell, her face a perfect
picture, asked me when the rest of my stuff was arriving. How
could I tell her this was the rest of my stuff, and half the
neighbours' too?" She topped up my teacup and moved closer.
"Her children were terribly terribly spoiled, you know, and she
expected the sun, moon and stars for my board and lodgings. I
had thought life at the factory was tough! But the thing that
kept me going, which got me through the long days and the
longer nights missing my family back home, was knowing that,
as soon as I could I would travel to Ray and see him face to
face."

"But he still hadn't responded to your letters?"

She shook her head. "Not a one was opened. You have seen
it yourself. Each and every one of them marked with *Return to
Sender*. I knew he must have been very angry – so I suppose if
I'm honest I was scared and, ridiculous as it sounds, given that I
had travelled half the world, I put it off a little. It was one thing
to have a dream – but when I started to worry if that dream was
foolish, if he would reject me to my face . . . then the fear really
kicked in. I could take the letters, in a way, because I could tell
myself he was reacting to an inanimate object – and he could
pop a letter back in a post box. But once he saw me he would
have to listen to me. And if he didn't forgive me, he would have

263

to tell me, face to face, to leave. I wasn't sure I was strong enough for that."

I sat and looked at the woman across the table from me, her hair soft and white glinting in the sunlight streaming in through the kitchen window, her hands frail and thin. I thought of all I had read and heard. I thought of how she had nursed my father through his illness – never faltering, never leaving his side – making him feel loved and cherished. I thought of how stoically she had sat at his funeral, how she had held court at the wake afterwards when all I was capable of was lying in a heap until Craig persuaded me to at least try and be sociable with the mourners. I thought of how she held her family together after my grandfather's death and I wondered how anyone could ever doubt how strong this woman was.

"But you had to do it?"

"I did." She sat her teacup down and took a deep breath. "I never in a million years could have imagined what happened that day. In hindsight I was foolish, but it had just never crossed my mind."

Chapter 31

Autumn in New England was stunning. The leaves fell in a cavalcade of rustic colours, covering everything they could before being whipped by gentle breezes into gutters and gullies. The rain fell hard, but it still had a hint of warmth about it so that a walk in the rain remained something pleasurable, even with two unruly children who still thought it was fun to play tricks on the nanny. How Stella longed for home and the familiarity of Seán's smile! He could be a wee devil of course but when she told him to behave he would do as he was told – unlike Laura and George, who would stick their tongues out and go on with whatever devilment they had been up to. After a particularly trying week in which Laura had developed a dose of chicken pox and was, as a result, even more huffy than usual, Stella had been almost delirious to get off two days in a row. Her earlier fears about tracking down Ray had dissipated in a final flurry on the day Laura had thrown up on her three times and blamed Stella herself for standing in the way. Nothing in life could be as scary as life with a precocious eight-year-old.

Thankfully Mrs O'Donnell was all too well aware of how challenging her children could be – and had frequently thanked Stella for her efforts. "I know they're lively," she had said nervously over her cup of tea. "But with you it seems to be a little more contained."

Stella had nodded and tried not to think about what it was like before she was on the scene.

However, feeling a debt of gratitude to the young nanny, Mrs O'Donnell had granted her request for two days off together and had dropped her at the bus station that morning without asking too much about where she was going. Stella had simply said she was going to visit an old friend – one she had known in Derry – and allowed her boss to believe it must be a GI bride or similar.

For the two-hour bus journey all she could think of was how he would look, what she would say and if it would work out. She played out every imaginable – or so she thought – scenario in her head. She tried to be positive, to think of home. To be strong. She tried, though her hands were shaking, to tell herself that she had not made up the time they had together – that she was not looking at it through rose-tinted spectacles. That it was okay – that it would be okay. That no matter what life had thrown at them they had been so madly in love. She touched the brooch he had given her gently on her lapel and closed her eyes as the bus juddered along the city streets. She had come this far and she could not go back now.

* * *

The street was just how she had imagined it when he had spoken of it. Tree-lined. Large lawns, now covered with a carpet of orange, gold and brown leaves. An elderly man was raking the leaves and stopped to tip his cap to her and smile and she smiled back, wondering about the futility of his actions. Sure ten minutes from now his lawn would be covered again.

The houses were perfect little boxes, with steps and porches, swing doors and screens. Almost every porch nursed a swing-seat or deck-chairs – even now in the cooler weather. She imagined you could fit two or three of the houses in her street back home into every house on this street. A few lawns had American flags flying by the mail boxes. It was the picture of perfect suburbia and she wondered how her life would have been had she moved here and married Ray the previous year. Would she know the name of the man now raking his lawn? Would she know which kid on the street had left their bike at the end of the driveway? Would she be at home in their basement flat making Ray's lunch waiting for him to come home from work? Would she have been pregnant perhaps? She put her hand to her stomach. She could have had a baby just like Dolores, who had given birth in June to a downy-haired baby girl. Leaving her niece had been hard – but then the arrival of Baby Bernadette had seemed to give Kathleen a whole new lease of life. It had made her own parting a little easier to bear – although there had been one moment when she wondered if her mother would ever let her go.

There was little point, she thought, as she walked on looking for the number of the house where he lived. She hoped he would be in – or someone would be in. She hoped he was close by. Wouldn't it just be wonderful if he could sense that she were here – if he could feel it?

Legs trembling, her breath unsteady, she reached his house – painted a pale blue with white sash windows, a small picket fence running along outside. The garden was perfectly tended, a pick-up truck sat in the drive. A window, perhaps the living room, was open and she could hear music drifting through it. She steadied herself, walked up the path and knocked at the door, stepping back and waiting – hoping – to see who would answer.

A woman appeared at the door – tall, dark hair pulled back loosely off her face. She looked, perhaps, to be around the same age as Kathleen but better presented. Like her life hadn't been so tough. She wore make-up and neat court shoes although she was wearing her apron and her hands were dusted with flour.

"Mrs Cooper?" Stella hazarded a guess.

The woman eyed her suspiciously, looking up and down.

"My dear, thank you for your troubles but we are not buying today."

"No, sorry. You misunderstand me. Mrs Cooper? I'm looking for your son Ray. May I speak with him, please?"

The suspicious gaze grew even more intense. Stella imagined it was because her accent was no doubt giving her away.

"And who would you be to want to speak to my son?"

"Mrs Cooper, I'm a friend of his from Ireland – Stella Hegarty. Perhaps he spoke of me?" she offered, knowing full well that when they were courting Ray had spoken to his mother often about her. She wondered would her polite introduction entice Mrs Cooper to welcome her with open arms.

"You've come a long way, my dear," Mrs Cooper said, taking not one step back to invite Stella across her doorway.

"I've been working for a family in Beacon Hill, nannying. I just thought . . . well, I just wanted to see Ray. I've come out today . . ."

"Well, my dear, it seems you have it all planned out. But I'm afraid you've had quite the wasted journey. Ray isn't here. He's at work." Her tone was sharp – unwelcoming.

"Would you know when he might be back? I don't mind waiting."

"No, I'm sorry. I don't know when he might be back and I really don't think it would be appropriate for you to wait for him."

"But I just needed to talk to him – wanted to explain . . ."

"I think you explained enough," Mrs Cooper said sharply, stepping back as if to close the door. "As I've said, it would not be appropriate for you to wait. I don't know when he will be finished work but I do know that when he is finished he won't be coming back here. He'll be going to his own home. To his wife. I would ask you, if you care even one jot for him – and I doubt very much after how you treated him that you do – then you leave him, leave them, be. Ray is happy now – he does not need you walking back into his life, following him like some Little Girl Lost, using him for a permanent visa or whatever else you have in mind, destroying his life for a second time. Now, if you will excuse me, I have a cake in the oven and I wouldn't want it to get ruined."

With that, Mrs Cooper – the woman Ray had spoken so warmly of, who he had assured her would welcome her with open arms – closed the door and left her standing on the porch.

Standing there, trying to process the news that Ray was married. He had moved on – and she knew Mrs Cooper was right. She could not walk in and destroy his life again. So she turned on her heel and walked, back past the abandoned bike. Back past the man, still raking his lawn, and back to the bus station where she sat, staring silently, wondering what on earth she would do with her life from that point on.

Chapter 32

Derry, June 2010

"And that was it," she said. "I didn't see him again. I didn't hear from him again. When the internet came about I did one of those Google search efforts – but do you have any idea how many Ray Coopers there are in America? It seems quite a lot. And I suppose by then I was very much settled down, married, raising you – contented. It was curiosity, I suppose – I always wondered what if. I always wondered did he hate me or had he just moved on as his mother said? Did he just put what happened in Derry and those months afterwards down as a bad experience and think no more of it?"

"But you stayed in America? Why? Did you not just want to come home?"

She shrugged her shoulders. "I did. But it wasn't that easy. You didn't just hop on a budget flight – it took time. So I started saving and, I suppose, for a while I didn't want to go home with my tail between my legs. It was bad enough everyone thought he had rejected me once – how desperate would I have looked landing back home with two rejections from the same man under my belt? I had some dignity! Besides, the longer I stayed the more I felt at home. Believe it or not, Laura and George actually grew to like me – or at least respect me enough not to be horrible little terrors. Mrs O'Donnell and I grew to be friends of sorts, and I met other nanny friends. We would go out drinking, listening to music – there was freedom there you never had back here. I'm not saying I threw myself into the swinging 60s or anything, but I found another place to call home. I stayed in Beacon Hill for a few years, then moved on to a new family. Three years after that I met your father, we moved to Florida and the rest, as they say is history." She shrugged her shoulders. "Do you understand a little, Annabel? Do you understand why there is a part of me that needs, still, to see him and explain that I had actually loved him? I know it's terribly selfish of me when you think about it, expecting you to understand when you have just lost your father – most people struggle to find one big love in their lives and I had two."

"No, Mom. I don't think it's selfish of you. I think Grandma was wise: if something matters then you try again and try harder. Okay, she probably didn't think you would still be trying now," I said with a small laugh which came out as a sort of strangulated sob, "but I think it would be perfectly wonderful if you tried again and he understood. And I think Daddy would understand. All he ever wanted was for the pair of us to be happy."

My mother took my hand again and I revelled in the warmth of her skin on mine – the softness of her touch.

"I know your daddy isn't here any more and I know, because it frustrated the life out of me for as long as I can care to remember, that you are a true out-and-out daddy's girl, but I'm here for you too. I can listen and I might not always get it right – and I might not be able to advise you in the way your daddy would advise you – but I can try."

I nodded, tears sliding down my face – in little ways washing away my grief.

"How about we both try, Mom?" I said. "We've only got each other now."

"Well, that's true in a way," she said. "But you have more, pet. Look around you – you have a family who love you. I've been watching you since you came here – and I know I have given you a lot to think about and perhaps even brought you here under false pretences but I've seen you come out of yourself this last week in a way I hadn't seen for a long time. God, I don't remember the last time I saw you laugh so much as I've seen when you and Sam have been chatting. It's done my heart good."

"I do feel better," I admitted. "I can't believe it – since essentially I'm now homeless and have no boyfriend." I pulled a face as the realisation of what I was facing when I went home dawned. "But even with that I feel better. That probably makes me weird? That losing that has made me feel freer?"

"Not at all, pet," my mother said. "It doesn't make you weird. It makes you human."

We sat in silence for a minute or two, my head aching slightly – perhaps from all I had heard or perhaps from the alcohol the night before.

"So where do we go from here?" I asked.

My mother looked at me, her head a little bowed. "The reunion dinner is next week. I suppose I decide if we are going."

"Of course we're going! We haven't come this far to stop now. God, woman, you are infuriating! What would young Stella do? Would she fall at this final hurdle or would she march right in there and see if he was there?"

"I'm sure she would have marched right in, but older Stella is a bit wiser and maybe a bit more scared. He might be there. His wife might be there. He might tell me to get the hell out – and a rejection three times is beyond the pale."

"I think enough years have passed for him to offer you the time of day."

"But what if he doesn't remember me?"

"Not possible, Mother dear. You are unforgettable."

"But what if the seventy-year-old me doesn't live up the memories of the twenty-year-old me he had. I mean, of course they won't. I'm an old woman – but what if he's still angry with this old woman? Or worse – what if I'm a part of his dim and distant past he hasn't thought about in decades?"

"On the first point, I'm sure he's not in his mid-twenties any more either, Mom. As for the rest, I can't answer those questions for you. Only he can – but I can't imagine a man who came back to Ireland for the reunion hasn't thought of you at all. You're special, Mum. I'm sure he has thought of you, many times. How could he not?"

"And you don't mind?"

"It will be strange," I admitted. "But no, I don't mind. I'll be there with you. Hey, I'm young, free and single myself now. Maybe I could bag myself a rich old marine in his twilight years?"

My mother swiped at my hand, smacking it with an air of indignation. "Behave yourself!" she chided before bursting into a broad smile – one I couldn't help but share.

* * *

"That's just about the most romantic story I ever heard," Sam said as we strolled arm in arm along the quay.

"Well, it's not the greatest story ever told, is it? I mean, she married someone else – admittedly a wonderful, wonderful man – but didn't ever see Ray again."

"But she might – next week. How amazing would that be? You know, stop me if I'm being grossly insensitive, but imagine they got married? Oh, I love a good pensioner wedding – all that promise that it's never too late to get a happy ending! I'd like to think, you know, that one day I'll find mine. Maybe when my mother shuffles off this mortal coil and I won't wound her any more with my rampant homosexuality."

I squeezed my cousin's arm as we walked on. "What I don't get is the Auntie Dolores, the mad article who loved to party Mom wrote about in her letters – I can't reconcile that with how she is with you. How she judges you."

"I don't know if it's blatant homophobia as much as her just not wanting her baby to be gay. I was her surprise extra – her 'wee late one'. She doted on me – the sun shone out of my rear end as far as she was concerned. I was perfection. It really annoyed the living daylights out of my sisters and brothers – so they were delighted to see my crown slip. Mammy, on the other hand, she just liked to pretend it was still there. It's okay though. I can deal with it."

"You shouldn't have to deal with it though. You should be able to be who you are – and have the big gay flamboyant wedding if you want – no holds barred. Matching tuxes – designer of course. And I'd be only too happy to wear that Dior gown to be your bridesmaid."

Sam laughed, throwing his head back and squeezing my arm. "Oh, darling cousin of mine! You are amazing. And I'd have you as the best woman, don't you know? And for you, well, I might just let you wear the dress. It would be just divine! Which, you know, gives me an idea." He looked away and then back at me. "The reunion, next week – I have some amazing 50s-style dresses. I'm sure one of them would look outstanding on you. Why don't we have a bit of fun – dress up? Make a proper night of it?"

"That sounds like a plan," I smiled, wishing my hair was longer and could carry off a Victory roll or two.

"We should get our mums into the shop too – kit them out. Get them out of slacks and twin sets, into something super-sassy."

"When you say things like 'super-sassy'," I laughed, "do you really think there isn't a person alive who doesn't know you're gay?"

* * *

Sitting in his garden later, a glass of wine in hand, we planned out the perfect evening. I admit I was caught up in the story of my mother and Ray. I wanted so much to meet him – to see the man she had talked about. I doubted he would look much like the handsome young marine in the picture she showed me but still I wanted to see him – to see if that twinkle was still in his eye. And for the Stella I had read about and heard about, I wanted to see the story play its way out. It would, as Sam said, be nice to have hope that stories could be resolved in a positive way – that happiness could come no matter what sadness life throws at you.

"Any regrets?" Sam asked and I raised my eyebrow at him.

"About what?"

"Your man in the States? Breaking up with him?"

"Of course I have a few regrets," I said honestly. "I didn't imagine it would work out this way – and I'm sorry if I hurt him. I'm more sorry for me though. Sorry that I let him hurt me and didn't have the guts to stand up to him and tell him to stop."

"You did that when you were ready to. That's something in itself. Everyone thinks they know how they will react when faced with certain scenarios. That's not always the way it goes, though, is it? Emotions get in the way. Life gets in the way. And sometimes you just can't see the wood for the trees."

I snorted, thinking that not only had I seen the wood for the trees, I had seen my boyfriend having sex with someone else and it still hadn't been enough to bring the inadequacies in my relationship into full focus. "Oh, I saw the wood for the trees all right! I just had too much on my plate to deal with it and I suppose I was too afraid to admit it wasn't working. It was easier in a lot of ways just to go on as we were. I suppose coming here gave me the space to see it for what it was."

"And when you go home? Do you think you will still feel that way?"

"As regards Craig and me? Yes. That's done now. It won't change. I don't know exactly where I go from here – pick myself up and start again – sell up, split the proceeds, move back in with my mother, maybe, until I find a place. She could probably do with the company."

"Yes," he said, looking off into the distance, "I imagine maybe she would."

Yes, there was no way I could go back to the home I had shared with Craig. It didn't feel like home – it hadn't felt like home since the day I had found Craig having sex with someone else – and if I was honest with myself it would be a relief not to return there. Even if not returning there meant returning home to my mother at the age of thirty-seven – thinking about starting all over again.

* * *

Sam seemed to know everything there was to know about vintage-clothes buying. With a click of his mouse he could log into any number of websites and pull up any range of clothes for sale.

We had a good scout around Second Hand Rose the next morning and pulled together a few ideas for me, my mother, Dolores and even Niamh who had somehow managed to invite herself along to the reunion.

"Do you think they will mind us all gate-crashing like this?" I asked as I wandered around the shop, revelling in the stunning clothes hanging on the rails and in the antique wardrobes.

"Not at all. They'll be grateful to have such stunners as ourselves grace their soirée," Sam laughed. "In fairness, we're not gate-crashing as such. My mother had many friends in the Marines and your mother near enough married one. We're going as moral support for them – well, for your mum. I don't think my mother ever needed moral support for anything in her life. She just blunders on with things."

I smiled at him and nodded my head in agreement. He had a fair point.

"I'll just be delighted if I get my mother in here to move out of her comfort zone and try something new," I said.

"Seems to me she was more daring in her day than you give her credit for. Secret rendezvous in love nests. Travelling half the world on a whim to win the love of her life back. I'd say she could easily be persuaded."

"You underestimate the appeal of the twin set, my friend. I'd swear if she could have got away with wearing one in the heat of the Florida summer, she would have."

He smiled and set about his work on the computer while I set about continuing my mooch through the merchandise of Second Hand Rose.

"Do you love coming here every single day?" I asked him, once again falling under the spell of what was essentially a dressing-up box for grown-ups.

"Honestly? Most days, yes. Days when the tax returns are due or the like, I'm not a big fan, but apart from that it gives me great pleasure. I meet different people – see how women can be transformed by a dress, or a piece of jewellery. I see women come in and relive their glory days – memories flooding back of great nights out and the like just by seeing a dress, or a pair of shoes or some other trinket. Do you not feel the same about Bake My Day? I mean, you set it up from scratch – you must be proud of it."

I shrugged my shoulders. Now, there was a question. And I suppose, at one stage I had been exceptionally proud of it and all it had meant to me. I had, at one stage, loved seeing my regular customers come through the door and keeping up with their news and gossip. It had felt almost like an extended family of sorts. But then, I suppose, when Daddy had become ill I had first of all had to deal with customers treating me like it was me who was ill. People who didn't know what to say, or how to react so who would, for the most part, simply come in, order something without really making any sort of meaningful eye contact or who would look at me so sorrowfully that I had wanted to start crying.

Making cakes, while once therapeutic, started to feel twee. Meaningless. Helping people celebrate seemed wrong. And then as Elise took on more and more responsibility for the day-to-day running of it I started to feel far removed from it. If I was honest, it didn't feel like mine any more.

"I was once," I said. "Really proud of it. Maybe I will be

again, but it just doesn't feel like mine any more. I've been trying to fool myself that I'm dying to get back behind that counter when the truth is it's been a case of 'fake it till you make it'. If I'm being honest, lots of what was home and what was my life doesn't feel like my life any more. Not even my café, which was once everything to me."

"It's hard when you don't feel you fit in," Sam said, "but you have to take it easy on yourself. You've been through a lot – the loss of a parent and now the break-up of your relationship. You need to give yourself time to heal."

"Do you know, Sam, I think I'm starting to heal," I said, and I meant it. "More than that, I think I'm starting to remember who I was – or who I was meant to be. I think I've given up on me for much too long – forgot who I was – but I think I'm getting back there."

He smiled. "I'm happy to hear that, my gorgeous cousin. And if you are starting to feel a little more positive, maybe you could be persuaded to bake me some of those delicious cupcakes I have heard so much about?"

I took a deep breath. The last time I had baked had been for my father – for the cupcake he couldn't eat – but these were the cupcakes he loved so much. Maybe I could bake them again? It was, after all, the very least I could do for Sam even if I suspected he had some sort of ulterior motive for getting me back in the kitchen again.

"Name your poison," I said. "Vanilla, chocolate, red velvet?"

"Is it too much to choose one of each?" He winked. "Although I am trying to watch my figure! Look, why don't you go back to my place and get baking – not much of a holiday, I admit – and we can have our two mothers over for tea later? We can formulate a proper plan. I do love making plans!"

"Okay," I said. "If you can take me to the store to get ingredients I'll see what I can put together. Although I warn you I might be a bit rusty."

"A master baker like you, no chance!"

* * *

Sam's kitchen was remarkably well stocked with ingredients for a man who swore he never baked. He said he blamed his crush on Paul Hollywood from the *Great British Bake Off* for his collection of tins and bowls, and I made him Google the same to see what the attraction was. I had to admit he had a point.

We had gone to the supermarket and stocked up as best we could with the remaining ingredients needed, and now I was standing in the kitchen, Sam having gone back to the shop, looking at what were the tools of my trade. I took a deep breath – tried to remember the good memories. Tried to remember when my father had eaten three cupcakes in a row and complained of a tummy ache – grabbing his stomach melodramatically and groaning while my mother and I had laughed and teased him for being such a Greedy Guts.

He used to say he loved to watch me work – would come into the bakery sometimes just to sit and chat with me while I measured and mixed and beat eggs to within an inch of their lives. I could, if I closed my eyes, see his smile now and hear his gentle words of encouragement. I could almost hear him whisper that he was proud of me – and that I was never to settle for anything less than happiness.

Instinctively I started to weigh and measure my ingredients. And I started to mix them together – moving around the kitchen as if it were my own, taking immense pleasure in the smoothness of the batter – the sweet smell of the cake mix. Enjoying the blast of heat from the oven when I opened the door and the warm, sweet aroma as the cakes baked. I opened the doors to the garden and walked outside, a glass of cool water in my hand and I looked at the sky. The air was thick and muggy – a threat of rain, and perhaps thunder hung around me. My daddy always said you could smell the rain in the air and despite the heat I knew it was almost time for the storm to break.

I was reminded of his words as the first fat drops of rain started to fall. The storm would pass – the sun would shine. I stood there for a moment, revelling in the feel of the warm rain on my skin. The storm would pass. The storm was, I was sure, passing right then – for all of us.

The buzz of the timer on the cooker distracted me from my reverie and I walked back into the kitchen, soaked by the shower, and lifted the cakes from the oven, and left them on the cooling rack before going and standing under a hot shower, changing into some comfortable clothes and setting about decorating the cakes in time for Sam's return home from work.

* * *

"I may have gone overboard," I said, as he walked back in to find thirty-six cupcakes baked, cooled and decorated, waiting in his kitchen. "But you have what you wanted – vanilla, chocolate and red velvet. The chocolate ones have a sticky chocolate filling as well. I'm not saying they will give you diabetes from one bite, but you might find them on the rich side."

"My lovely cousin, you are spoiling me!" Sam grinned, lifting one of the aforementioned chocolate cupcakes and taking a bite, his face contorting with pleasure. "You should never, ever stop baking," he said when he had composed himself. "Oh my God, Annabel, these are divine. Can I take some into the shop tomorrow? Package them up, give them to my customers?"

I nodded. I didn't see us getting through them somehow.

"These are amazing."

I couldn't help but grin, delighted to see him enjoying them – proud for the first time in a long time of something I had done.

"Right, missy," he said, when he had washed the last crumbs of the cupcake down with a glass of milk. "I have a surprise for you. Wait you there!"

He disappeared out to his car as I cleared away the remaining dishes into his dishwasher. He returned with a number of bags, each bearing the distinctive Second Hand Rose logo.

"Now, it's only an idea," he said, reaching into the first of the bags. "And you don't have to say yes just because I think it is the most beautiful dress in the world ever – but if you would like to I really think this Dior dress could be the perfect thing for you to wear. Now it's not the one that I showed you before, but one I ordered a few weeks ago and it arrived today. And as happy coincidence would have it, it is from the 1950s. Not 1959, unfortunately – that would be too perfect – but near enough. What do you think? I think I could trust you to return it to me in one piece?" He raised his eyebrow and pulled the dress from the bag fully, unwrapping it from its covering of tissue paper.

It was, simply, stunning. A soft pink, it had a graceful elegance. It had a skirt which I imagined would fall to just below the knee and a wrapover at the bust. At the (tiny, I panicked) waist, several fabric flowers added the only detailing to it. I could, if I wanted, imagine my mother wearing such a garment in her heyday if only money had been no object. It looked like it had arrived straight from a movie set – and just as Sam's face had contorted with pleasure on eating my cupcakes, I'm pretty sure my own face contorted just a little with pleasure at the sight of this beautiful dress in front of me.

"Annabel," he said, with a flourish, "you shall go to the ball!"

I nodded, blinking back tears. I could barely believe this man, who I had met just over a week ago, was being so kind to me. I crossed the room to hug him, throwing myself at him like a woman demented who hadn't been hugged in ever such a long time.

"I make a good Fairy Godmother, don't I?" he whispered in my ear.

"The very best."

Chapter 33

Stella felt nervous – completely unsure of herself. Dolores had almost had to drag her out of the house that morning. It had been forty-eight years since they had last lived under the one roof but Dolores still had the power to get her sister to do just what she wanted.

"Sam is waiting for us, and your daughter too and sure it would do us both a bit of good to get pampered. Especially if we have a big night ahead of us! Can you imagine – how long has it been? Too long!" Dolores pulled a brush through her hair. "And to be honest, Stella dear, I don't know what you are worried about. At least you still have the figure you had all those years ago. I only wish I did." She rubbed her hand over her rotund stomach. "I suppose six kids will do that to you – that and a lifetime of turnovers and other treats from the bakery! Tell me this – how did you manage to stay so trim with your daughter running a bakery of her own? I'd have ended up the size of two houses – not just the one I am now!"

Stella smiled weakly. She appreciated Dolores' banter but her nerves were jangling. It was starting to feel real. Even though she had been here a week, even though she had shared the intricacies and intimacies of her relationship with Annabel, and even though Dolores had assured her time and time again that she was among friends and would be most welcome at the reunion, her heart still felt a little heavy.

"I'll be with you soon," she said, shooing Dolores out of the room they had shared when they were younger. "Just give me a few moments."

When Dolores left, Stella sat on the bed and took a deep breath, trying to settle herself. She had been surprised at Annabel's reaction. She had expected the earlier outbursts of emotion – fully expected her daughter to feel a loyalty to Bob. She hadn't quite expected her daughter to come round – and to set about trying to give her a make-over for the big event. A part of her, she realised, had hoped that Annabel would dig her heels clean in and tell her she was a disgrace to want to go to the reunion. Then, although she dearly wanted some form of closure, she would have a legitimate reason for walking away. She didn't want to, of course, not really, but as the moment drew closer she felt herself falter. She had come this far – but she wasn't sure she could go any further.

She remembered all too well the walk back to the bus station that day – how with each step her legs felt heavier and her heart felt as though it was crumbling. It was all her own fault, of course, she told herself. She should have been honest with him – but it had seemed so much like an all or nothing situation. She knew now, looking back, she had been lost in a haze of grief and she had felt she had no choice. Just because she had pined for him every day, she could not have expected him to pine for her back. She had stopped beside the bus depot and called into a small diner where she had ordered a cup of coffee, which she stared at, the hard lump in her throat stopping her from swallowing.

"You look like you have the weight of the world on your shoulders," the waitress had said.

Stella had shrugged her shoulders. "Something like that," she said. "How do you pick yourself back up when you've lost everything and start all over again?"

"You just do, doll," the waitress had drawled. "And let me let you into a little secret. Even when you think everything is lost, you always have something. You might not see it today, but you will."

Stella had nodded tearfully, thanked the waitress, left a large tip, climbed back onto the bus and travelled back into the city.

With the benefit of years of hindsight, she realised the waitress was right. She still had her job, her family back home and a visa to work in America. She would stay there until she met Bob and they would have many happy years together. She smiled as she thought of him now – how he would tell her to stop being silly and to get on with life.

"I've had a good run," he told her on one of the few occasions they had talked about his mortality. "I couldn't have asked for more in my life – you, a woman who loved me, and our daughter. I'm leaving this world happy with what I have, even if I wish I could have it for a bit longer. But we don't get to make those choices, do we, love?"

Stella had lain down beside him in their bed and put her head on his chest.

"You know, we are lucky," he said. "We get to say our goodbyes. People don't always get that chance. And I know it's hard – and I'd rather we didn't have to – but you know we can part ways knowing we've said it all. Stella Hegarty," he said, smiling at his use of her maiden name, "I thank God every night that I met you and that we have had a life together. I know when you came here it wasn't with the intention of living the life you have – but I'm glad life brought you to me."

She had nodded through her tears. "Me too. I could not have asked for better. Please don't ever think I spent a life longing for someone else. He was my first love, but you are my love forever."

Bob had stroked her hair and kissed her head and they had lain together until the sun rose the following morning.

It was only after he died that she found the letter from him – in amongst a file of paperwork he had said she would need to look through once he was gone. All his arrangements were made, he said. He was leaving her nothing to worry about. One of the other benefits of being able to say goodbye, he said, was that he could be organised – he could dull the pain of leaving her by taking care of the practicalities. She found it hard to tell him the pain was far from dull. Still, the morning of the funeral as she went over his paperwork – making sure everything was just as he wanted for the service and the wake – she found a letter from him. It spoke of love, of friendship, of shared experiences and it gave her strength to get through the day that lay ahead. But as she read she saw that he had left her a little challenge.

I know I'm an old stick in the mud, Stella. How you put up with me all these years, I'll never know. I know I tried to be good to you but I know I frustrated the life out of you at times. I know you have said I made you happy – but would you have travelled more, lived more if it had not been for me holding you back?

I should have gone back to Ireland with you. It was, believe it or not, my plan to take you home sometime in the coming year, before this illness got in the blasted way. But I want you to go now – without me. When you are ready – the money is there. Of course, more than that is there. I've taken out a few extra insurance policies over the years. You know me, sensible to the last. You and Annabel will be well looked after, I promise. But I have one condition, please, if you would indulge me, for your return trip home. Please take her with you. She's not happy. I know that. And I know this won't be easy on her – she always was a daddy's girl. Didn't you always say it? Like two peas in a pod. Get her to live a little – don't let her get stuck into the same ruts I have fallen into. I'm not saying I've been unhappy, Stella. You and she have made me the happiest and proudest man on earth – but I know a rut when I see one. Only when you run out of chances do you realise all the chances you would have liked to take but never quite got the chance to.

Force her if you have to – use every trick in your armoury – but get her to see even a little of the world.

And my darling – I know you loved me. I have never and will never doubt it. Not even when I am long gone. But be happy. Forgive yourself for things which happened in the past – things which you had little control over and things which brought you to me. Find him, Stella. Find him and explain, and if that brings you peace, or happiness, find that and grab onto it.

She read over that letter again now in Dolores' bedroom and closed her eyes and tried to think of everything and everyone who had brought her to this point. She thought of her mother, urging her to follow her heart, her father's quiet approval of Ray, Bob's smile, Annabel's determination and there, in the bedroom where she had grown up she took a deep breath.

"Time to put on my big girl pants and get on with the day," she whispered, slipping her feet in her shoes and going downstairs to where Dolores, already with her coat on, was waiting.

* * *

Sam's shop was, simply, delightful. Stella was entranced as soon as she walked with Dolores through the doors into the little treasure trove that greeted them. It was hard to think that such shops existed in Derry – but then again she had to remind herself this was a city transformed and this, the Cathedral Quarter, was a hive of boutiques and craft shops showcasing the quirky side of the city. It was all so close to where she had grown up that she could, if she closed her eyes, almost picture the streets as she remembered them – and picture walking along them arm in arm with her friends. She could almost smell the smoke curl from the chimneys – the smog that hung in the air – and yet here she was walking into her nephew's shop, packed with designer clothes and vintage pieces that made her feel young again.

As she walked through the door she noticed Annabel in deep conversation with a customer just outside the changing room, her head thrown back with laughter. Her daughter looked at her and smiled, acknowledging her presence, before turning her attention back to her customer. The customer was smiling, twirling around in a soft cream knitted dress she must have been interested in buying.

"You should treat yourself, Anne," Annabel said. "It's beautiful on you. Very elegant. Just the thing to wear to the theatre. I've always wanted to go to a Broadway show, or the West End."

"Then you should," the woman, who Stella placed in her late fifties or early sixties, smiled. "Life is too short not to be happy. I've learned that over the years. All that matters is family and happiness."

"Very true, Anne. You know, maybe I should treat my mother as well. We've had a tough few months."

"Life has a way of testing us all," Stella heard Anne say, "but as long as you remember what is really important, then you won't go far wrong. I have four children myself – they've kept me right. And in return, well, I'd do anything for them."

"You're very lucky," Annabel said, lifting a soft lilac scarf and handing it to Anne to accessorise her dress with.

"You make the most of what life gives you," she replied and Stella stood there for a moment listening to the wisdom of the woman she had never met telling her what she knew in her heart.

And she stood there watching her daughter smile – in her element – and she knew that Bob had been right all along and that Annabel had needed to find something that made her happy again.

Stella's reverie was broken by an exclamation of excitement from Dolores who had located a glittery multicoloured dress and was swishing it around in front of her, a smile broad on her face, as if she had found the answer to all her prayers.

"Oh, isn't this lovely?" she asked. "Sam, Sam, what do you think of this one?"

Sam pulled a face and Stella had to stifle her giggles. "Mum, that's not quite 50s vintage. It's from our 80s collection – and it's not a dress – more a top – and don't take this the wrong way but if you wore it would have more than a touch of drag queen about it."

Dolores looked indignant but Stella couldn't help but laugh.

"Don't worry," Sam added. "We will find you, both of you, something that makes you look stunning."

"I have to say," Stella said, "this shop is a real treat. I can see why you love it so, Sam."

"It's fab, isn't it?" Annabel interjected. "And the people who come in here – the stories we hear, it's just humbling."

"Have you had the poor girl working here her entire holiday?" Dolores asked.

"She has demanded it," Sam said, with a smile. "So yes, and I've even had her baking cupcakes for the customers. Tonight, she bakes muffins. I'm a slave driver and don't you forget it."

Annabel laughed. "Pay no heed. I've loved every moment. And baking a few muffins is the very least I can do."

"I have to say, it's nice to see you smile again," Stella said, her heart warmed.

"I'll smile even more when we get you kitted out for this reunion of yours," Annabel said.

Chapter 34

"He's on the list," Niamh said, as the five of us sat in a council of war at Sam's house. "I went out to the Beech Hill today and got the list from the organisers. Said I was doing a bit of research into family history, that kind of thing. Anyway – he's on the list. Or at least an R Cooper who served at NAVCOM Derry in 1959-60 is going to be there so I guess that narrows it down more than a little! And, get this," she was almost beside herself with glee, "there is no 'plus one' listed with him. See!" She thrust the letter at us.

A list of names of officers and marines and their guests. R Cooper was on his own. I didn't know whether to faint or cheer. Did I want my mother to come face to face with the man whose heart she had broken and the partner who had helped him heal it, or did I essentially want them to meet on even terms?

I steadied myself. If I was feeling this nervous, I could only imagine how my mother was feeling. I looked at her and sure enough she had gone a funny shade of white – although Niamh, who had thrown herself into our family drama with gusto, seemed undeterred.

"Things like this don't really happen, do they?" she said. "You know, these big happy endings?"

I watched my mother get up and walk out to the kitchen.

But Niamh still continued. "Can you imagine? How romantic!"

I looked out the door, to where my mother was, and to Sam who was looking at me and Dolores who seemed to be enraptured with what Niamh was saying. I nodded my head at Sam who nodded back. We didn't need to speak. We knew it was code for my going after my mother and him shutting Niamh up and reminding her that this was real life and a delicate situation.

I walked to the kitchen where my mother was standing, her hands clasped around a cup of tea, her face still white.

"He might tell me to go to hell, right there in front of everyone. He would be well within his rights to do so."

"He won't," I soothed.

"You don't know that," she said softly and of course she was right.

I didn't know, so I shook my head. "Look, Mom. You may be right. I may not know that, but I do know if he does I will be there to pick you up. And Dolores will too. And Sam. Even Niamh with her misguided notions of romance. We all will be."

My mother smiled, a weak smile but a smile nonetheless. "Tell me this," she said. "Who is that Niamh one anyway? She seems a bit . . . well . . . crazy?"

"Her heart is in the right place," I said. "Even if she does come across as a bit full on and in your face from time to time."

"Dolores has her eye set on her for Sam," my mother said. "I think I might need to have a word with her about how she treats him – how she assumes he'll change his mind someday and start looking for a woman. He's too long in the tooth to be hiding his true self."

"Aren't we all?" I answered.

"Whatever we may say of this time away," my mother said, draining her cup, the colour slowly returning to her face, "it has been an adventure."

"I'm glad we did it. Even if I thought you were clean mad."

"Part of me still thinks I'm clean mad," she laughed.

"You know, Mom, maybe I am running away from everything but here I feel I've been able to breathe out for the first time in years. Does that make sense? I think I was just so caught up in trying to make everything work for so long that I forgot who I was. I forgot to have fun. Strange, isn't it? Daddy dying has made me realise that I need to live."

My mother nodded. "Grief makes you do strange things. It teaches you strange lessons – who would have thought I would find myself here again? Who would have thought back then my life would have taken the path it did? But the fact is, I'm better for it. Stronger for it and you will be too."

"I don't want to go back," I said, voicing what had been growing in my mind the last few days. "Not yet anyway. Not now. Maybe I need to be somewhere else for a while and I will be ready to go back someday – but not now. Am I running away, do you think?"

"No, pet, I don't think you are running away at all. You are running in exactly the right direction – towards what makes you happy. That's all I ever wanted for you. All your father and I ever wanted for you."

"And he wanted *you* to be happy too," I said and she simply nodded.

She had known that all along.

Chapter 35

Derry, July 2010

Ray Cooper stood in front of the mirror in his hotel room, putting on his tie. He could barely believe he was back in Derry. He had arrived the day before and had tried to retrace his steps – places he had visited, streets he had walked. Tillies was gone now – an empty hole in the landscape where it once stood so majestically. The quay, transformed – now filled with families out walking, or cycling or stopping to chat or drink coffee from one of the riverside cafés. The smell of smoke was gone, the air was clear. There was an air of optimism, a sense that the city had changed, and yet to him a part of it would always feel like home.

He had walked past the old Hegarty home, almost tempted to knock on the door just on the off-chance she would be there. He wondered, as he had done over the years, what had become of Stella. Who had she married? Had she stayed all her days in Derry – close to her family? Had she really only been using him? Even now, all these years later, he could not quite bring himself to believe it. He knew how she kissed him – how she held on to him so tight, as if she never wanted to let go – that what they shared had been love. The letter had come as a bolt out of the blue – and he had gone on a bender which had almost ended in a court martial.

Thankfully his commanding officer had enough faith in his good character to take him aside and give him a stern talking-to instead – telling him not to lose his head over a woman.

"Marines are made of sterner stuff," he told him.

And although he didn't feel that way at the time he decided to act as if he was. So he closed himself off and made it through each day as best he could, trying not to let the daily realisation that she wasn't coming wind him.

When he left the Marines and returned home, his mother took him in and assured him it would be okay. He would settle and move on. He took up a job in the family business, married the girl next door – who would be a good friend to him. They rubbed along together nicely but, in the back of his mind, he knew she was never the one. That theirs had been a marriage born out of convenience and expectation rather than any grand love affair. When she had left him, after thirty-five years of marriage, to be with someone who truly did love her, he couldn't even bring himself to be angry. Jealous, yes, because she had what he wanted so badly – but not angry. They remained friends and it had been Marilyn who had persuaded him to come back to Derry for the reunion.

"You never know," she said. "She might be there."

It was a long shot, he knew. If her letter had been genuine she would hardly want to have anything to do with the returning marines. And yet, he still felt a nervous flutter in his stomach. There was a feeling there that he would see her again. Perhaps it was just foolish hope – the dreams of a silly old man. But he hoped that he would see her and ask her to her face if she had meant all those things she had written. If she had – if he heard it from her – then he would deal with it . . . but how he longed to see her face just one more time! He straightened his tie and ran his fingers through his hair.

"You are an old fool, Ray Cooper," he said aloud. "A silly old fool."

* * *

I pinned one last curl into my mother's hair. She had been transformed – she stood before me in an elegant cream dress, her

293

skin soft and dewy, her white hair pinned and curled. There was a softness to her features that had been missing in the last few months – she credited it to good home cooking, Derry style – I credited it to finally being free of the stress and grief of nursing my father. You know when people use that expression that someone looked as though a weight had been lifted off their shoulders? She truly did. She carried herself differently even if she said she wasn't sure about the height of her heels or the soft string of pearls around her neck.

"Is it not too much?" she asked me as she looked at herself in the mirror.

"No, Mom," I replied softly. "I don't think it's too much at all. I think it's just perfect. You look beautiful."

She brushed down her dress and stood tall. "Should I take the brooch off? Is that too much?"

"Nothing is too much, Mom. Please don't worry."

It seemed fitting she wore the brooch. Dolores had told her that it would be one sure-fire way to make sure Ray would know who she was, but I knew that he would know her as soon as he saw her. The years may have passed, but her eyes were still as bright, her smile still as warm. If they had been as in love as it seemed they were, he would have no doubts when he saw her.

"Oh God, are we really doing this?" she asked, nervously giggling.

Dolores had offered her a glass of champagne as we got ready but she said she very much wanted to keep her wits about her. I was glad she had said no – she was giddy enough, her nerves clearly getting to her.

"We are," I said, stepping back. "And it's the right thing to do."

"You look stunning too, Annabel, really," she smiled.

I glanced at myself in the mirror and had to agree. I didn't think I knew I could ever look this elegant and yet here I was, wearing a beautiful gown, my hair behaving itself, my make-up tastefully applied – more than the usual stroke of a blusher brush

and slick of mascara. I had cheekbones! I looked feminine and
dainty. There wasn't a pair of Converse anywhere near me and I
didn't mind one bit. I stood, cheek to cheek with my mother, and
smiled into the mirror.

"We clean up pretty well, Mom," I said.

She kissed my cheek and looked back at our reflection. I
could see it then, how we looked similar. I'd always considered
myself a daddy's girl but there in the mirror I could see how I
and my mother were so intrinsically linked.

"I'll be right there beside you," I whispered. "I'll be there for
you."

She nodded. "You always have been, Annabel. I know that.
And I hope you know, tonight aside, I'll be there for you too.
Trust in yourself, girl. Follow your heart. Take chances – but not
chances such as these, years after you should have . . ."

"You took your chances then too, Mom," I said. "Life just
got in the way."

"A good life got in the way."

We stood enjoying each other's company in silence for a while
until a knock on the bedroom door interrupted us.

Opening the door, I saw Sam there, dapper in his black suit
and sharp white shirt which showed off his naturally swarthy
skin. He smiled and I couldn't help but smile back.

"Ladies, you look magnificent and it is high time we were
making our way. The taxi awaits."

"I'm nervous," my mother said.

Sam tutted. "Now, now, Auntie Stella, nothing to be nervous
of – except showing up every other woman in the place! This
will be brilliant. I feel it in my water and tomorrow we will have
yet another amazing story to tell. Just think about it!"

He linked his arm in my mother's and guided her down the
stairs to where Auntie Dolores and Uncle Hugh were already
waiting.

I looked at them, standing there in the living room where so
much of my family's life had played out, and I felt a lovely warm

glow, which I was sure hadn't come from the glass of champagne I had sipped from.

When Niamh arrived at the house just then I could sense Auntie Dolores almost explode with excitement. This vision – in her usual bright colours, bright make-up and brighter smile – walked in as if she were gliding.

"I am so unbelievably excited about this," she said, and it wasn't clear whether she was focusing on the party ahead or the emotional significance of what might or might not happen. But then we were all trying to hide our true feelings at that stage, trying to keep whatever stiff upper lip we had as stiff as possible.

This was a night out, with friends, with family. I had to stay as calm as I could to stop my mother from melting down completely. So we focused on the pretty dresses and the smart suits even though Uncle Hugh looked as if his suit might choke him at any moment.

"He normally only wears suits to funerals," Dolores confided. "How Sam here got his sense of style growing up with your man as his influence is beyond me!"

She looked at Sam then, and at Niamh and she took a deep breath. She watched as Niamh fussed over Sam's jacket and straightened the lapels and as Sam admired the jewel-like colours of her satin gown. I watched her and was sure I saw a twitch of something there. Something I couldn't quite put my finger on.

"They would make a lovely couple, don't you think?" she said.

"Sam's a good man," I said. "He really is."

Dolores sniffed and turned to leave the small room. My mother looked at me and I shrugged back at her. All the while Sam and Niamh were lost in some excited conversation while Uncle Hugh was pulling at the collar of his shirt as if it were a hangman's noose and he had just been let drop.

My mother followed Dolores into the kitchen and I went after her. Dolores was already at the cupboard, taking out a bottle of brandy and pouring herself a shot.

She turned to look at us. "Medicinal," she said abruptly.

"Anyone else need one?"

To my surprise my mother nodded as I shook my head and she lifted the poured glass from Dolores and downed it in one while Dolores followed suit.

Both of them laughed, silly laughs born of nerves or excitement or both, but when the laughter subsided Dolores took yet another deep breath as if to steady herself.

"I know he's gay, you know," she said. "I know you think I'm in some sort of denial. But I'm not. Then again, maybe I am. I just . . . he's my baby and I want his life to be easy. I don't want him to be picked on or pointed at."

I looked at my aunt, her sometimes harsh features softened by her make-up and feathered haircut. "He's a grown man, Auntie. And a great man – with lots of friends and a successful business. He's mostly very happy, except that he wants you to be happy for him to be the person he really is."

"You have to be careful not to push him away," my mother interjected. "Even if you have the best of intentions. If you push him away you may not get him back – and that is not the best place to be. Believe me."

Dolores looked at the brandy bottle and for a moment I thought she would lift it to her mouth and guzzle back another few shots. But instead, slowly, she screwed the lid back on and put the bottle in the cupboard.

"I never wanted to make him unhappy."

"Then just love him," my mother said. "For who he is – be proud because you made that! You raised him to be a great boy – a great man. He's compassionate and caring. He loves you and his family. He's successful. No mother could want more."

"You're right," Dolores said, softly. "You're right. I know."

She walked across to my mother and I watched her hug her, the pair of them locked together in a sisterly embrace and a part of me was instantly and totally grateful for my mother, my father, my trip to Ireland and where life had taken me, even if it the journey had been the toughest of my life.

In the days following my father's death I had felt alone, and now I felt part of something much bigger – and that something much bigger would give me the strength to get through whatever would come over the weeks and months to follow. Wherever I would go and whatever I would do – whether I went back to my Bake My Day or moved on – it would be fine. It would be better than fine.

* * *

Stella knew him as soon as she saw him. She did not have to ask. She did not have to squint at the name badge he wore. She did not have to ask was it him, was it really him? She knew. Almost as soon as she walked into the bar in the elegant settings of the Beech Hill she saw him, standing at the bar, a glass of whiskey in his hand.

He was talking to some men – men she imagined he had served with – and she knew that he didn't see her and she revelled in that moment. All the noise in the room faded away as she watched him. That wonderful moment of seeing his smile, the crinkle on his brow as he laughed, knowing that she was so close to him without him realising it. Being able to drink him in for those few moments. This was still so unreal – still with the possibility of a happy ending. These moments when she could hear his laugh and nothing else brought her back to all those days she had known and loved. They brought her back to the Bollies, to the flat, to the cinema, to the City Hotel, to Christmas dinner at the Hegarty household with her daddy there holding court. The years simply slipped away and she took a deep breath, closing her eyes and allowed herself to slowly breathe out again. How she had longed for this moment, in those early years! How she had dreamed of this moment – almost every night when she closed her eyes!

She opened her eyes and the noise of the room rushed back in again, Dolores asking had she seen him yet, Hugh asking would she like a drink from the bar, Niamh declaring everything to be gorgeous, and elegant and wonderful. She felt a touch on her elbow which jerked her back to reality fully and she turned to see Annabel looking at her, asking if she was okay. It seemed too much. So many emotions ran through her. He was there and she didn't know whether to run to him or run away and keep running.

She closed her eyes and thought of Bob, willing her to be happy. She thought of Annabel, assuring her that she was with her. She thought of how she had missed him – how she had always felt connected to him.

"He's there," she said, her voice catching in her throat.

How do you do this? How do you swipe away all those years of love and longing, of missing and moving on, of wanting to say sorry, of wanting to explain? How do you tell someone you travelled to the other side of the world to find them? That you had never stopped thinking about them?

"Where?" Annabel asked just as Stella felt her nerve fail.

She turned and walked out through the lobby, through the covered porch and into the gardens where she tried to find the courage that had deserted her.

Her heart was thumping so fast she wasn't sure it wouldn't just stop – just give up with the exertion of it all. She was a foolish woman – a silly foolish woman, there in her fancy dress, with her brooch and her hair pinned up like she wasn't a widow still grieving the loss of her husband.

Stella could hear the chatter from the hotel drift across on the evening breeze. She tried to focus on it – and not to let the sound of her heart, thumping against the inside of her chest drown out the other noises.

She closed her eyes and took a deep breath then exhaled before repeating the process, steadying herself and forcing her breathing to settle. As she breathed in she caught the familiar smells of her home town on the air. The cut grass. The cool dampness, despite the summer months. She wrapped her arms around her, aware of how her waist had thickened over the years despite her best attempts to keep her eating healthy.

She tried not think of how much older she was since the last night she had danced with the Yanks in a fancy hotel – how much of life had slipped past in the years. She tried not to think of the man she had just seen inside. The man she had recognised instantly – who she would know anywhere.

For a second she longed to be twenty again. To have her daddy telling her he loved her – her mammy to reassure her that she wasn't being foolish just to be here.

Would she have done it differently? It was a question she had asked herself over and over again.

Once she met Bob of course, it had been different. She'd had fewer regrets. She was happy. But a part of the jigsaw was missing. A part of her was missing. It had been from the moment she had kissed Ray goodbye and left their flat not knowing that she would never see him again.

Images floated past her. People she knew, people she loved. The places she had lived and the people who had formed her life. Her breath caught in her throat when she heard a familiar voice speak.

"Stella? Stella Hegarty?"

She turned, brushing a tear hastily from her cheek, to find a woman standing opposite her – a woman old like herself but who she would always recognise.

"Molly Davidson!" she exclaimed as her old friend crossed the courtyard and embraced her in a hug.

"Well, I never thought I'd see the day!" Molly said.

"I don't think I did either," Stella said as she pulled back and looked at her friend, taking her hands in hers and holding them. "I don't know how we ever lost touch."

"Things happen," Molly said, shrugging her shoulders. "I just can't believe I'm seeing you after all these years. Tell me you were happy, my friend?"

"I was. I was and I am," Stella stuttered. "I had a good

husband. We have had a good life. And I'm here now and . . ."

She stood, Ray's name catching in her throat. She could not mention him. Even though he was so close that if she wanted she could speak to him within seconds. "And you?" she asked, diverting her thoughts from her very reason for being here.

"It all worked out in the end," Molly said. "I married a lovely local man. I have six children, would you believe? And ten grandchildren now. I've been blessed."

Stella smiled, pleased beyond measure that the friend who had returned from America broken had been pieced back together and had found love.

"Were we young and foolish?" she asked.

Molly shook her head. "We were young, yes. But we weren't foolish. We just thought we knew it all. They were different times. It's hard to think how much has changed – how much our wee town has come on. We just, we just went with our hearts. For better or worse. But we did okay? Didn't we?"

Stella nodded. "We did. But, oh Molly . . . he's here," she muttered. "My Ray, he's here."

Molly nodded. "I know," she said. "I spoke with him. He seems fine. Happy."

A sob left Stella's mouth – relief that he was happy, that he had been okay. After all that had happened.

"Talk to him," Molly said. "I'm sure he'd be happy to see you."

"He would," she heard her daughter's voice say behind her. "I have someone here who does want to see you."

Stella turned to find Ray facing her.

Time froze. Stella hadn't really understood how that could happen before, but in that instant it made sense. Time could freeze. The world and everything around you could drift away to insignificance. For that moment she was lost in his eyes – in the gaze that had once looked at her with such love.

"I knew she was your daughter," he said, his voice shaking. "As soon as I saw her, it was like being back in time. I knew she had to belong to you. I just asked her and she said yes and she called me Ray. Can you imagine that – she knew my name? So I knew, Stella, I knew you were here and I knew you still remembered me . . .".

His voice trailed off as Stella stood shaking. She wasn't sure if she would be able to stay standing. Her legs went weak below her, and her head started to spin. This moment – the moment she wanted so much all those years ago – was here. She was with him again, breathing the same air. She felt her hands fly to her chest, as if to quiet the beating of her heart. She saw his eyes fall to the brooch on her dress and instinctively she moved her hand to it. Would he think her silly for holding on to it? When she had told him so coldly how she had never loved him, when the truth was she had loved him with all her heart?

"I had to c-come," she stuttered.

"I know what you mean. I had to be here too."

"I never meant to hurt you," Stella said, longing to take the few steps to where he was – to touch him, to hold him. Yes, he was older but he was still her Ray.

He shook his head. She watched his eyes cloud. She saw that he was filled with emotion too and that had to mean he felt something. Did that make her feel better or worse for hurting him? She didn't know. So many emotions were swirling through her at that moment that she couldn't think straight.

"I'm sorry, Ray," she blurted, aware of Annabel and Molly stepping away from the scene unfolding in front of them. "I tried to write again. I tried to explain. I wrote so many times! To tell you I did love you!" She heard a sob, echoing her own, from her beloved Ray. "I just couldn't leave. My daddy . . . my daddy died and they needed me and I didn't want to hurt you more."

"I would have come back," he said, his voice cracking.

"And I couldn't ask you to do that. To come back here where we had nothing? And you, with all the prospects in the world laid out in front of you?"

She watched him shake his head and she reached out to hold

his hand, to feel his skin on hers again. The warmth of that touch that she had missed so much.

He held her hand tightly and shook his head. "I never got any letters. None. I only ever received one letter. That letter. The one where you told me you had been using me."

She released her hand and fished in her bag, pulling a letter out and handing it to him, their hands brushing.

He looked at the scrawly handwriting and let out a small gasp. "My mother," he muttered.

The tragedy of what had happened hit her like a body blow. "I assumed the handwriting was your wife's – your mother told me you were married," she said. "I came to find you. To America. I came and you were married and I had to let you be happy. I came to your house, I spoke to your mother . . ." The sight of this marine, this man who she had loved, crying before her was breaking her heart.

He shook his head. "She never said. She never told me."

"I'm sure she was protecting you. I'm a mother, Ray. I would do the same for my child. She thought I had used you."

"It could have been different," he whispered. "Oh Stella, it could have been so different! We could have been so different."

At this, she couldn't resist any longer and she rushed to his arms, feeling a peace settle in her very bones as he hugged her back.

Crying, she whispered into his ear, "I'm so, so sorry I broke your heart, Ray. I loved you with every fibre of mine."

She felt him kiss the top of her head, felt him hold her close. She allowed herself to sink into his embrace, to feel the warmth of his arms around her.

"Oh my Stella," he whispered. "I always knew. I always knew you loved me. And I always knew, someday, some way, you would find me again."

"*When Life says give up*," she whispered her mother's wise words, "*Hope whispers, 'Try one more time'.*"

The End.

Acknowledgements

I have worked as a journalist for the last fifteen years and the great thing about the job is that you never know where it will take you. Every day has been a school day as I have learned new stories and been invited into people's lives.

Two summers ago I was tasked to cover the story of a Derry woman returning to the town she loved so well after almost fifty years, with the man she had fallen in love with in the late 50s.

Avril and Bob, who later married, inspired me with their personal happy ending. While this story is not theirs, with their permission and help it certainly borrows from their shared experience. I could not have written it without them both sharing their belief that love never gives up hope or that you can find happiness at any age. I also could not have written it without Avril sharing so beautifully and openly many of the details of her youth in Derry in the 1950s – from the beautiful dresses, the factory experiences, the make-up, hair and the stolen kisses.

Any historical errors are my own. And some dates have been played with to suit the chronology of the story of Stella, Ray, and her family.

Thanks must go to all the GI brides who offered their help or shared their experiences, and to family and friends who filled in details of life in Derry in the 50s and 60s.

This book was also hugely inspired by the people of Derry and their spirit and hardworking ethos. It was inspired by my grandparents who worked hard to raise their families in difficult circumstances.

The cameo character of "Anne" is based on Derry woman Anne O'Kane, whose daughter Denise paid for her cameo role in support of local charity Circle of Support (COS) who offer support to families of children with Autism. COS carry out amazing work in the Derry area and I have been happy to support them in whatever way I can. I hope Anne enjoys her 15 minutes of fame.

In addition I need to thank all those who encouraged me throughout the writing process. As always thanks to my husband and children for allowing me to disappear into a different world for hours at a time – and to my mammy and daddy for supplying a kitchen table with no distractions for the crucial final push and for believing in my ability to do it.

Thanks to my brother and sisters, and to my nieces and nephew for providing cuddles and support when I have needed them. And to Blue the dog for keeping me company during the mammoth writing sessions at that kitchen table.

This book was written with the unending support of my friends – who read, or encouraged, or planned launches, or listened to me tell the story over and over again. In particular Julie-Anne, Marie-Louise, Carla, Joanne, Edel, Auntie Raine, Nuala, Fionnuala Kearney, (Auntie) Kaela and the "rascals" for getting excited on my behalf.

Thank you to the media and the booksellers who have shown their support over the years and to my writing friends and Twitter followers who have been there for me over the last year.

To my colleagues at the *Derry Journal* – thanks once more for your support – and to my editor Martin McGinley who sent me out on that fateful day to meet Avril and Bob.

My agent Ger Nichol has once again been my biggest cheerleader while I have been writing this book and I cannot thank her enough for her faith in a story which marked a change in direction for me. This was a book I had to write and she encouraged that every step of the way.

And to the team at Poolbeg Press, including Gaye Shortland who once again has been a pleasure to work with. Every book has been better because of Gaye's input.

Special thanks to Paula Campbell – who has stood firmly behind this book and this story and who has championed me over the last seven years. Thank you from the bottom of my heart.

And to you, lovely readers, you make this happen. Thank you. xxx

Now that you're hooked why not try
What Becomes of the Broken Hearted?
also published by Poolbeg
Here's a sneak preview of chapter one:

What Becomes *of the* Broken Hearted?

Claire Allan

Chapter 1

Kitty

The bomb dropped at 4.17 p.m. on a Thursday. It had been a fairly ordinary kind of day before then – maybe even a good kind of a day. The shop had been busy and I had made two mammies and two bridesmaids cry with joy. Two brides-to-be had left feeling like the most beautiful girls in the world.

I had been planning on making celebratory lasagne to mark the general loveliness of the day and had developed a craving for a very nice bottle of Merlot that I knew they sold at the off-licence two doors down from Mark's office. I had tried to call him to ask him to pop in and get it but, rather unusually for a man whose Blackberry even went to the toilet with him, he hadn't answered.

So I did something I never, ever do because I didn't ever want to seem like one of those needy wife types who calls her husband at work. He didn't have a direct line, you see, and I would have to go through the gatekeeper, aka the harridan of a receptionist, who worked at his building. I chewed on one of my false nails, balking at the slightly plastic taste while I contemplated just picking up a bottle of wine from the supermarket. But no, even though it was only a Thursday, I decided we should treat ourselves. A bottle of wine. A nice feed of lasagne. Maybe an early night? I smiled as I dialled his office number and asked for him.

It was then, in the second between me asking "Hi, can I speak to Mark Shanahan, please?" and the receptionist answering, that something shifted forever in my world.

That's all it took – the time it took her to breathe in and start to speak – for things to shatter. I kind of wish I'd known. I can't help, when I look back at it now, but feel like a bit of a stupid bitch for smiling so brightly as I spoke to her. If I had known, my voice would have been more sombre, doom-laden . . . I might even have sobbed.

"Mr Shanahan doesn't work here any more," she cheeped. "Can anyone else help you?"

It was the strangest thing. I heard what she said and it did register – and a weird floating feeling came over me – but I felt kind of calm and maybe even a bit giddy.

"No, no, it's fine," I said.

"Okay then. Can I ask who's calling?" she cheeped back.

I suppose a part of me wanted to just hang up, but another part of me was thinking of the lasagne which probably wasn't going to get eaten and the bottle of wine that I had really been looking forward to and I knew things had changed – and changed utterly.

"Kitty Shanahan," I replied. "His wife."

There was a pause, and I could hear her sharp intake of breath. I could almost hear her brain ticking over and as she spoke, softly and slowly, all hints of the cheerful but very guarded gate-keeperness gone, I almost felt sorry for her. She must have felt in an utterly awful position, to be honest.

"I'm sorry," she said. "Mr Shanahan left last week. I'm sorry."

I thought of Mark, doe-eyed and smiling as he fixed his tie that morning and turned to kiss me as I left to open the shop. He had looked at his watch and declared he was running late and wouldn't be long leaving after me and had rushed downstairs and into the kitchen. He had shouted to me if I knew where his keys were and I had replied that, yes, they were on the worktop.

It had been ordinary, absolutely ordinary, and now it really wasn't. I put the phone down, resting the old-fashioned cream Bakelite receiver on the hook and I sighed.

Her sense for scandal piqued, my stepmother Rose peeked at me over the rim of her glasses and raised one eyebrow. "Everything okay?"

"*Hmmm*," I replied, not quite sure what was going on. I didn't want to say my husband had been going out to a fictitious job for the last week and I had known nothing about it, so I sat back on the cream-covered stool behind my desk and looked at my hands.

"*Hmmm* good, or *hmmm* bad?" Rose asked, putting down the delicate lace she had been hand-stitching in her armchair in the corner of our workroom and looking at me again.

I couldn't lie to Rose, especially not when she was giving me her full and unadulterated attention.

"Mark's not at work," I mumbled, lifting my mobile phone and walking absentmindedly down the spiral staircase to our dressing room and on through the French doors to the garden. I knew Rose would follow me, and I would let her, but now I had to try Mark again even though I knew he already had at least four missed calls from me logged on his phone and that if he wanted to call me then he would have done. I supposed, then, if he had wanted me to know he had – for whatever reason – left his job a week before, he would have told me.

His phone started to ring and I tried to keep my breathing calm even though there was a distinct increase in the volume of adrenalin coursing through my veins.

It went to answer-phone and I listened to his voice jauntily telling me he couldn't take my call right now but would get back to me if I just left my number. As the message beeped to a halt, heralding my turn to start talking, I heard a strangled squeak spring forth from my lips.

"It's Kitty! Your wife! Call me!" And for effect I added the number of the shop, even though he knew it or at least had it in his phone and would easily be able to find it. I hung up and turned, nodded to Rose who looked utterly confused – but not as confused as I felt – and dialled his number again. He would answer this time. I felt it in my water. It would be fine. There would be two Mark Shanahans working in his office and the other one would have left – or the gatekeeper had just been feeling extra-vicious and gate-keeper-y and had decided to tell me a big fat lie. No. Everything was fine.

My waters were wrong, as it turned out. He didn't answer. He didn't even answer when I rang back a third time and shouted "*Answer the shagging phone!*" at the handset in my hand. Rose walked towards me and very calmly said, "I think maybe we should close the shop early."

She had a point. No bride-to-be would want to walk in on this. This was not what anyone needed when they were contemplating their Big Day – a rather pale and shaking wedding-dress salesperson screaming into her iPhone for her husband to talk to her.

I nodded and watched as Rose left the garden to go and lock the door while I stared at my phone and willed it to burst into life. There was still time for this to be okay.

"A cup of tea will do the trick," Rose said, bustling back through towards me. "I'll just go upstairs and put the kettle on."

A cup of tea sounded nice. It sounded soothing, even, so I followed Rose up the stairs and through the office into our kitchen – clutching my phone to me as I went and I sat down and watched as Rose boiled a kettle and put two mugs out, making her tea.

Rose was like that – an oasis of calm. Nothing phased her. She was the kind of person who, if she developed a slight case of spontaneous combustion, would simply douse herself with some cold water and mutter "Ah well, never mind" before getting on with her day.

"Mark wasn't at work," I said, as she mixed milk into the china mug and stirred it gently.

"Yes," she nodded. "Custard cream?" She reached for our biscuit jar and offered it to me.

"He hasn't been at work in a week," I said, raising an eyebrow and challenging her to look surprised. "And he hasn't told me. He hasn't mentioned it to me at all."

She looked at me and bit on a custard cream before taking a sip from her mug.

"The receptionist had to tell me," I said, willing her to agree with me that it was a Very Big Deal Indeed.

She nodded, and polished off her biscuit.

"And he's not answering his phone. I've tried, seven or eight times. He left a week ago but he's been getting dressed every morning and heading out as usual and coming home his usual grumpy self."

She nodded again.

I fought the urge to snatch the biscuit from her mouth and give her a good shake. "When I say 'left' I don't mean just, you know, left. I mean he doesn't work there any more. I phoned and the receptionist said, very clearly, that Mark Shanahan doesn't work there any more."

Rose sipped from her tea before setting her mug, slowly and carefully, back on the worktop.

"I'm not sure I like the sound of that," she said. Which was bad. Rose saying she didn't like the sound of something was akin to us mere mortals running around screaming hysterically that we were all doomed, doomed, I tells ya.